MW01134060

OCCUPIED EARTH (ASCENSION WARS BOOK 2)

(1st Edition)

by Jasper T. Scott

JasperTscott.com
@JasperTscott

Cover Art by Tom Edwards
TomEdwardsDesign.com

CONTENT RATING: PG-13

Swearing: Some brief instances of strong language
Sex: Mild references
Violence: Moderate

Author's Guarantee: If you find anything you consider inappropriate for this rating, please e-mail me at JasperTscott@gmail.com and I will either remove the content or change the rating accordingly.

ACKNOWLEDGMENTS

Writers write alone, but they publish with a whole village of people to help out. A big thanks to everyone in my village—to my editor, Aaron Sikes, to my proofreaders, Ian Jedlica and Bornraj, to Tom Edwards for a great cover, as usual, and to all of my many advance readers: Harry Huyler, Howard Cohen, Gary Matthews, Raymond Burt, Paul Burch, William Dellaway, Bruce Thobois, Lara Gray, Dave Topan, Dara McLain, Barbara Boller, Victor Biedrycki, Davis Shellabarger, George Geodecke, Mary Kastle, Rose Getch, Lisa Garber, Jeff Belshaw, Daniel Eloff, Bic, Ambralyn Brook, Jackie Gartside, Jim Meinen, Jim Kolter, and Wade Whitaker. The village wouldn't be the same without you! And of course, many thanks to the Muse.

To those who dare,
And to those who dream.
To everyone who's stronger
than they seem.
—Jasper Scott

*"Believe in me / I know you've waited
for so long / Believe in me / Sometimes
the weak become the strong."*
—STAIND, Believe

PREVIOUSLY IN THIS SERIES

WARNING the following synopsis contains spoilers from the previous book in this series, *First Encounter (Ascension Wars Book 1).* If you would prefer to read that book first, you can get it on Amazon: https://www.amazon.com/dp/B07Z6SPM72

Synopsis of First Encounter

The Forerunners left Earth to colonize nearby star systems and to search for intelligent life. *Forerunner One* left in 2060 AD under the command of Captain Clayton Cross, bound for Trappist-1. After a ninety-year journey to reach it, his ship arrived and made landfall on Trappist-1E. There, the crew discovered a world teeming with life. They encountered the Trappans, an arboreal species of primitive natives with ten legs and hairless brown skin. The initial encounter resulted in a brief conflict, and the ground team was forced to retreat to their shuttle.

Soon after that, they discovered that Dr. Grouse, one of their first contact specialists, was missing. With the shuttle surrounded by

Trappans, the crew was forced to venture out. Coming to an understanding with the natives, the crew went looking for Dr. Grouse. They found him via his locator beacon in an underground laboratory. Several of the native Trappans were lying unconscious on metal tables with tubes and wires trailing from their bodies. The same was true for Dr. Grouse, and like the Trappans, he was unconscious.

The crew disconnected Dr. Grouse and fled, but before they could leave, an avian alien intervened and tried to stop them. There was a brief conflict in which the alien killed the ship's XO, before being killed itself. The remaining crew members fled the laboratory, and Captain Cross received word from *Forerunner One* that multiple unidentified contacts had just appeared on an intercept course with *Forerunner One.* They were accelerating at over 10Gs, a speed that the *Forerunner* couldn't hope to match.

Captain Cross and his ground team beat a hasty retreat back to their shuttle. In the airlock, Dr. David Grouse's vitals crashed. His colleague, Dr. Lori Reed, was able to resuscitate him with help from the ship's chief medical officer, Dr. Stevens, and Dr. Grouse woke up with a warning: "They know where Earth is."

Back on *Forerunner One,* Captain Cross set an outbound course and readied the ship for a fight. The pursuing alien vessels did not attempt to contact them, but continued closing range at an almost impossible rate.

While retreating, both Dr. Grouse and his colleague, Lori Reed, were placed under quarantine. Lori was cleared, but Dr. Grouse was found to be infected with a mutating alien virus that was systematically altering his DNA. Dr. Grouse was changing before their eyes, turning into something not entirely human. Doctor Stevens gave the order to place him in cryo to halt the progress of the virus.

Just as *Forerunner One* reached the boundary of interstellar space, the alien ships broke off pursuit. To Captain Cross, the message was clear: *leave our territory, or else.*

Right before the crew was set to enter cryo for the journey home, Dr. Lori Reed discovered that she was pregnant. Her birth control implant had failed, and Richard Morgan, the ship's ambassador, was the father. The child was later born during regular crew rotations with features resembling those of the Avari that they had encountered in the underground lab on Trappist-1E. Somehow, Lori's brief contact with Dr. Grouse *had* infected her with the alien virus, but it hadn't infected *her* directly, it had infected her unborn child and turned it into something alien. Lori named her Keera after the ship's XO, who had been killed on Trappist--1E. Richard Morgan refused to acknowledge Keera as his daughter, despite DNA tests revealing that she was in fact related to him.

After just six months, Keera reached a level of development comparable with that of a six-year-old human girl, and she looked more alien than ever. She was talking, walking, and developing vicious claws and teeth. She'd unintentionally injured both of her parents on several occasions, and she was becoming increasingly aggressive. One night she couldn't sleep because she imagined that she'd brutally killed the two officers on the bridge. A little while later, her parents discovered that those two officers were dead, and they found Keera there, covered in their blood.

The Captain and his section woke up and discovered the carnage. The security logs had been erased, and Keera was the only suspect. The child insisted that she hadn't done it, but no one believed her.

Keera fled into a maintenance tunnel before she could be captured. The crew split up to search for her, and in the process, several crewmen were killed, but no one got a good look at their killer. Finally, Keera was captured and placed in cryo, and then everyone went to bed, thinking the crisis over.

In the middle of the night, Captain Cross awoke to find one of the alien Avari standing over him and some kind of device on his head. He managed to remove the device, and the alien vanished into thin air, having cloaked itself.

The aliens were on board, and they probably had been this entire time. Maybe Keera really hadn't killed the officers on the bridge. The crew woke up and began hunting for the cloaked alien. Several more crewmen died in the process. The Avari abducted both Lori and Keera, taking them to a cloaked alien shuttle that was docked to one of the *Forerunner's* external airlocks. On board the shuttle, Lori encountered Dr. Grouse, who now looked just like an adult version of Keera. He admitted to killing both of the officers on the bridge and to erasing the security logs. Lori concluded that he must have been brainwashed by the Avari.

Captain Cross and his chief of security, Lieutenant "Delta" Sanders, jumped in a pair of Scimitar starfighters to give chase. During a brief conflict, Delta was killed, and Captain Cross was forced to break off pursuit when the alien shuttle cloaked and disappeared.

Captain Cross returned to the *Forerunner*. He set a course for Proxima Centauri, not Earth, and went back into cryo with his crew for the long journey home.

Upon arrival at Proxima Centauri, almost seventy years later, the *Forerunner* was greeted by Keera, now all grown up, and an Admiral leading an Avari fleet of warships. She told Captain Cross that her people were actually known as the *Kyra,* and she welcomed him to the Kyron Federation. The Kyra had beat them to Earth, having traveled there with FTL drives. They invaded and occupied the planet, annexing it.

Keera demanded permission to come aboard, and Captain Cross met her with his crew at one of the *Forerunner's* airlocks. Keera's mother, Lori Reed, was also there, still alive after all these years, thanks to Kyron longevity treatments. Keera saw her father again, but it was an awkward reunion at best.

And there was another surprise waiting for Captain Cross. He was reunited with his long-dead wife, Samara. Prior to her death on Earth, he'd had the contents of her mind saved to digital records. Keera had wanted to repay his kindness and impartiality toward her, so she convinced her people to clone and resurrect his wife from her memories.

This happy reunion blinded Captain Cross to what had really happened during the invasion. After a short journey aboard Keera's ship to reach Earth, he discovered that his home-world had been almost entirely destroyed. The devastation was everywhere, cities ruined, and billions had died. Only a few city centers remained, all of them walled off to keep out failed human-Kyra hybrids known as *Dregs*.

During the trip down to what was left of Houston, Captain Cross witnessed one of the Chimeras kill two colonists from the *Forerun-*

ner just because they took too long to get out of their seats.

On this ominous note, Captain Cross vowed to oppose the alien occupation in any way that he could. The invasion might be over, but the rebellion had just begun.

OCCUPIED EARTH

CHAPTER 1

2238 AD
—88 Years Since The Invasion—

Clayton's heart hammered in his chest as he sat on the foot of the bed with his wife, Samara, waiting for the test results to materialize before their eyes.

"Maybe you're just late," Clayton suggested.

"Six *days* late?" Samara countered with eyebrows raised. Her deep blue eyes looked black in the shadowy bedroom. Her blonde hair was just a golden outline, aglow with the lights of New Houston shining through the windows beside them.

Clayton focused on his breathing while he waited: deep, slow breaths. He was hoping for a miracle—or rather, the absence of one. "How long is this supposed to take?"

Samara just looked at him. "You're asking me? It's not like the test came with instructions. It was just a pill in a box."

"I know, I just thought maybe you were seeing some kind of status bar on your ARCs." Augmented Reality Contacts. Most humans still had them, but few Chimeras and none of the Kyra did. They preferred regular displays to miniature ones they could wear directly over their sensitive eyes.

"No status bars yet," Samara replied.

They'd requested the pregnancy test from a Kyron dispensary less than fifteen minutes ago. It had been provided to them immediately, free of charge, like most basic necessities. The nano-technology behind the smart pill was from the Kyra, and just as mysterious as they were.

Clayton was about to get up and start pacing the floor when the result appeared on his contacts, a glowing green block of text, accompanied by an upbeat female voice:

"Congratulations, Samara and Clayton Cross! You are pregnant. It is a girl. Please proceed to the ascension center at 10 AM for your first prenatal checkup."

A girl, Clayton thought. Another womb for the Kyra to use to breed slaves and soldiers. Or worse—a new Chimera for their army if they could brainwash their little girl into ascending.

"What are we going to do?" Samara whispered, staring at her hands.

Clayton blew out a breath and shook his head. This was the insidious plot behind the Kyra's invasion and occupation of Earth. *First,*

*they make birth control illegal and then indoctrin-
ate our children in Chimeran-run schools until
they're all tripping over each other to ascend and
join the Guard.*

Clayton reached over to cup his wife's
cheek and turned her face to look at him. He
smiled tightly at her, but the smile was too
heavy to hold on his face for more than a few
seconds. "We'll raise her right, Sam."

Tears welled in Samara's eyes, making
them gleam in the glow of New Houston's
lights. "What if that isn't enough?"

"It will be."

"How can you be sure?"

"Because she's ours."

"But if she..."

"She won't," Clayton insisted. "She can become a breeder like us. There's no shame in
supporting the war like that." *And if our daughter chooses to stay on Earth, then she can join
the resistance like me,* he thought but didn't say.
He was tempted to tell Samara what he *really*
did in his job, but he couldn't risk it. This was
the Kyra's city. They'd supervised reconstruc-
tion after the invasion, and there were rumors
about listening devices wired into the walls
of every single building on the planet. Besides,
even if Samara did know about his ties to
the resistance, he knew she wouldn't approve.
She'd told him on multiple occasions that she
thought resisting the occupation was point-

less.

Instead of filling the space between them with words, Clayton leaned in and kissed Samara on the lips. Her tears moistened his cheeks. He withdrew and wiped them from her face.

She sniffed and flashed a wry, broken smile at him. "I guess we don't have to worry about getting pregnant anymore."

Clayton returned her smile. "There's a bright side to everything."

Samara's expression turned serious. "What's the bright side of the invasion?"

"You," he replied and pulled her in for another kiss. Clayton still couldn't believe that Samara was alive. She'd died almost two centuries ago, but the Kyra had resurrected her in the body of a clone just in time for his return to Earth. Everyone else should be so lucky. She was a rare exception to Kyron superstitions, and now to recently-passed laws which had made cloning illegal and an anathema to the Federation.

Samara withdrew, shaking her head. "You always were the romantic one," she said, wiping her cheeks on the sleeves of her white lab coat.

"The garbage man and the nurse," Clayton said. "It's a real modern-day fairytale. I bet you make all of the other princesses jealous."

Samara gave him a sobering look. "You'll

always be *Captain* Cross to me."

Clayton smiled. "Thanks. You'd better get going, or you're going to be late for your shift."

"Yeah." Samara was back to staring at her hands again,

"Don't worry. We'll make this work. It's a blessing, not a curse."

"Then why does it feel like we've opened Pandora's box?"

"Maybe we have," Clayton agreed, reaching for her hand and giving it a reassuring squeeze. "But who says the curse has to be on *us?*"

Samara looked around quickly with big eyes, as if afraid that he'd strayed too close to treason with that suggestion. Maybe he had. She nodded silently and rose from the bed, her fingers slipping through his. "See you in the morning, Clay. Be careful out there tonight."

"I will. I love you," he replied.

"Me, too," she said without turning as she hurried out of the bedroom.

Clayton listened to her sneakers receding down the hall, squeaking on the polished concrete floors of the apartment; then he heard the front door slide open and shut.

He lay back on the bed and rubbed his eyes and face in an attempt to massage away an encroaching headache. *A baby. What the hell were we thinking?*

He raised his now-antique smartwatch to his face. It was the same one he'd had when he'd left Earth in 2060. Now it was almost two hundred years later. The time glowed to life: 22:16. His shift wouldn't start until 24:00, so he still had plenty of time to kill. Samara's smiling face greeted him behind the glowing numbers on the digital face of the watch. His wife's mind map was still encrypted in its quantum crystal matrix.

When he had returned from Trappist-1 with his ship and crew, he'd discovered that he was too late to warn Earth about the aliens they'd encountered. The Kyra had used their FTL drives to beat Clayton and his crew home by almost ninety years. When Clayton had finally arrived, he'd been greeted by his first contact specialist, Lori Reed, and her Chimeran daughter, Keera—now *Admiral* Keera Reed of the occupying fleet. Keera had been just a child when the Kyra had abducted her and her mother from his ship, but apparently, she hadn't forgotten her time aboard the *Forerunner*. To thank Clayton for his unbiased treatment of her, she'd convinced the Kyra to resurrect his wife from a copy of her memories in a cloned body.

It had all seemed too good to be true, and in a way, it was. Since then, Clayton had witnessed dozens of summary executions. The human-Kyra Chimeras that policed the Earth in the name of the Federation were judge, jury, and executioner. Offer the slightest resistance to them, and you'd be killed. On top of that, the human race was being farmed for its children.

That might not have been so bad if it weren't for the fact that ascension changed them. They were physically altered with the Chimeran virus, and the ones who failed to respond properly to it became mindless Dregs.

Clayton got up and walked over to the windows beside the bed. He deactivated the privacy setting with a wave of his hand, and the windows went from blurry to clear. New Houston swirled into focus—a towering wall of lights from at least a hundred different skyscrapers. He had a bird's eye view from the 92nd floor of his apartment building, the Grand Sheridan. The city lights ended abruptly at the walls just ten blocks away. Beyond that was nothing but darkness. New Houston had been reduced to a bright speck of civilization adrift in a sea of shadows.

Like most places, only the city center had been rebuilt after the invasion. Densely-populated areas were easier to wall off against the Dregs. They roamed the *Wastes* like animals, feeding off the booming populations of wildlife, steaming piles of garbage from the cities, and even each other. The Dregs' population was self-limiting, but they were fantastic stalkers, and dangerous as all hell to unwary travelers.

And I'm the crazy fool who goes out there every night to feed the bastards with fresh loads of garbage.

A flicker of movement on the horizon drew Clayton's eyes up to a dark teardrop-shaped vessel sailing slowly in front of a blue wisp of moonlit clouds. That distant specter didn't even light up the sky with the comforting glow of viewports. It hovered like some kind of futuristic blimp. A Kyra destroyer teeming with Chimeras and held up by anti-grav tech that humanity could only dream about. That ship was the blade of a guillotine poised over the collective necks of everyone in New Houston. Dare to defy the Kyra, and they could rain fire on the city and wipe it all out in the blink of an eye. There were ships just like it drifting over every major city in the world, a constant reminder of who was in charge.

Clayton snorted and waved to polarize the windows once more, blurring the view of the city and the enemy starship.

He turned away and went to the closet to get dressed in his work uniform: thick gray pants with reflective neon yellow piping, a matching long-sleeved shirt, and a neon yellow vest with the letters SWMD stamped in black on the right side—*Solid Waste Management Department.*

Clayton tried not to wrinkle his nose as he pulled on the shirt and vest. Even freshly

20

cleaned, the uniform still smelled like rotten eggs and putrefied vomit. Garbage collection wasn't the most glamorous job, and nowhere near the safest, but there was a good reason that he'd chosen it. Samara thought it was because he didn't have a lot of options, which was partly true, but the real reason was that a garbage truck was the perfect way to smuggle supplies to resistance camps in the Wastes.

Long live the Union, Clayton thought, straightening his neon vest with a grim smile.

CHAPTER 2

Lori Reed touched the nearest bulkhead, and it became transparent, revealing the gleaming circle of light below that was New Houston. She could still remember when those lights had sprawled out in all directions as far as the eye could see. Now, the city was just a speck. All of Earth's biggest metropolises were the same, just a few square kilometers of fortified apartments and office buildings surrounded by farms and ranches, all of it patrolled day and night by Chimeras from the Kyron Guard. And destroyers like this one.

"You should rest, Mother. It's been a long day."

Lori turned to see her daughter, Admiral Keera Reed, the very first human Chimera, heading for the door to the quarters they shared aboard her flagship, the *Sovath*. Like all of the human Chimeras, Keera was as tall as any human. She was bald, but four cranial stalks tipped with cone-shaped auditory canals rose from the back of her head. She had a gaunt, bony face, bright red eyes, and a chalk-white skin with faint fish-scale patterns of black veins running underneath. Sharp black claws tipped her fingers and toes, but they were clipped short so that her feet would fit into boots and her hands into gloves.

"Where are you going?" Lori asked.

"I need to oversee the interrogation of our prisoner," Keera said as she waved the door open.

"That resistance leader?" Lori asked.

"Yes."

"I'd like to join you."

Keera turned from the door, her red eyes narrowing as she considered the request. "It will not be pleasant."

"I don't care," Lori insisted. *After witnessing almost ninety years of atrocities, what's one more?* she thought. It was hard to believe that she was over a hundred years old. One of the few positive sides to the invasion: Kyra biotech. They'd created an ageless population of breed stock to raise soldiers for their war with the *Chrona.*

Keera inclined her head to Lori. "Very well. Come."

Lori left the bulkhead to join her daughter by the door. They strode out together and down the corridor. As they went, Lori caught sight of the Federation emblem emblazoned on the upper right sleeve of Keera's sleek black Admiral's uniform. The emblem was made of a textured, shiny white metal. It consisted of a 2D depiction of a Kyra with its wings spread out behind it in a fan-like shape, surrounded by a glittering circumference of white stars. Keera's rank insignia was less visible, a simple series of eight blue and red bars over her right breast.

Lori looked away, her eyes back on where she was going. The walls of the corridor were slanted at the top and bottom, forming a hexagonal shape. Exposed conduits lined the ceiling, and removable metal grates lined the floors, concealing a shallow trench full of maintenance hatches and air ducts. Dim blue light strips lined both sides of the corridor. The poor lighting was hard on Lori's eyes, but after all this time, she was used to it. The Chimeras and Kyra both shared the same sensitivity to light. The Kyra's homeworld, Kyros, was tidally locked to its star, and the Kyra had evolved on the dark side. Their only light came from their world's phosphorescent flora —in shades of blue, red, and violet.

Lori and Keera walked past a handful of Chimeran officers coming from the ship's transport tubes. They stopped and stood at attention as Keera walked by. "Carry on," she said.

Rounding a bend at the end of the corridor, the glowing red outlines of the transport tubes came into view. Keera opened the nearest one with a wave of her hand, and a Chimeran Lieutenant stepped aside to let her in before he came out.

"Admiral," he said.

Keera nodded back as they entered the tube. She activated the controls remotely, via a verbal command, and the door slid shut. The tube went screaming down with only the slightest tug of acceleration.

Lori was told that the customs, ranks, gestures, and mannerisms of actual Kyra were all much more alien, but she'd rarely had the chance to see it; here, supervising Earth among other Chimeras who had all once been human themselves, it was simply easier to default to human equivalents.

Even so, Lori felt badly out of place. She was the only actual human on board—except for the prisoner in the brig, but he wouldn't be around for long. Lori's status among the Kyra made her unique. She'd carried Keera to term, giving birth to the very first human Chimera. That was supposed to be impossible. The virus should have turned her into either a Dreg or a Chimera before that could happen, and then she would have miscarried.

But she was naturally immune to the Chimeran virus, a fact which had made her a subject of constant study for the past eighty-eight years. Even after all that time, the Kyra still hadn't learned what made her different from every other human they had encountered. These days, she was mostly left alone, but she wasn't allowed to travel to the other planets and sectors of the Kyron Federation like the Chimeras were, and she wasn't allowed to go anywhere on Earth without an escort. The re-sistance would want to study her immunity even more than the Kyra.

If she weren't Keera's mother, the Kyra probably would have executed her long ago.

The transport tube arrived at the brig, and the door slid open to reveal another hexagonal corridor. This one ended in a security door. Keera led the way to that door and opened it by standing under the scanner and speaking her name: "Admiral Keera Reed," she said in her deep, husky voice.

The door slid aside, and they walked up to the guard station. A bored-looking Chimera rose to his feet and saluted. "Admiral."

"At ease, Corporal," Keera said. "We've come to attend the interrogation."

"Of course. This way, ma'am."

They turned and walked past the guard station, their footsteps ringing on the grated floor as they followed the Kyron Guardsman to another security door, located behind his station. "Corporal Markus Haney," he said. The door slid open and agonized screams boiled out.

Keera hissed and fixed the corporal with a

sharp look. "What is happening?"

"Overseer Damos came, and—"

"He was supposed to wait for me," Keera growled.

"Yes, Admiral. I told him that. He was impatient. And he is the overseer, so..."

"Never mind." Keera turned and hurried down the corridor, this one lined with prison cells. Lori and the corporal struggled to keep up.

The last door on the right was already open. Keera stepped in, and the cries of pain stopped.

Lori reached the opening with the guardsman and gasped. The floor was covered in red, human blood, and a man was lying there, his chest heaving deeply, his face beaded and glistening with sweat. His thigh was shredded. It looked like a shark had been gnawing on it. A diminutive Kyra stood over him, its claws and mouth dripping with blood. Overseer Damos. Keera stared intently at the Kyra, saying nothing for several seconds. Lori wondered if she was reading his mind. Keera was special, a telepath. The Kyra called people like her *K'sara,* and they believed that telepaths were chosen by the gods to rule, but Keera had kept her ability a closely-guarded secret. The higher her standing among the Kyra, the more that others would challenge her for it.

Keera growled something in *Kyro* at the

Overseer, and he hissed in return. Lori didn't catch what was said. She was busy wondering how this Kyra was able to breathe the same air as them. Then it wiped its mouth on the black sleeve of its uniform and grabbed a breathing mask that was clipped to the center of its chest. It put the mask on and sucked in a deep, rasping breath.

Keera pointed to the man on the floor and said something else. This time Lori heard and translated for herself.

"How are we supposed to get him to talk now? He thinks you're going to kill him whether he speaks or not."

"Maybe I will," the overseer replied. *"He deserves to die."*

"I told you that I would get him to speak."

The Overseer hissed and flexed bloody claws, as if itching to tear Keera apart.

Lori stepped in, hoping to defuse the situation. "I have a better idea," she said, speaking in English.

Both Keera and the overseer turned to look at her. Keera's eyes widened, and the overseer's narrowed. Twin sets of demonic red eyes. Lori heard footsteps retreating quickly behind her as the corporal withdrew.

"Mother, stay out of this," Keera said. "You're here to watch. Not interfere."

"She shouldn't be here at all," the overseer said, switching to English as well. "But, I am curious." The alien cocked its bony head to one side, and all four of its cranial stalks wavered and twitched on top of its head. "Perhaps she will have better luck getting answers from one of her own. *Dakka gra Dakka.*" *Sewer rats understand sewer rats.*

Lori took another step into the cell and stopped at the feet of the prisoner. Blood bubbled steadily from his leg, and he was moaning softly.

"He's not going to be conscious for much longer," Lori said.

"Then speak quickly," the overseer suggested.

Lori dropped to her haunches beside the man. His face was pinched in pain, his eyes squinting shut. Lori grabbed his hand. It was cold and clammy. *Forget staying conscious, this man won't be alive much longer if I don't stop the bleeding,* she thought.

"What do you need to know?" Lori asked, glancing up at the Kyra.

It hissed through its mask. "We need the encryption code for the implant we found in his brain." The Kyra produced a bloody quantum crystal and held it up to the light. It was a semi-transparent wafer no bigger than the tip of her pinky finger with thin, hair-like neural wires trailing from it.

Lori nodded and turned back to the man in front of her. She squeezed his hand to get his attention. Green eyes cracked open, bright through a thin layer of tears. Those eyes widened suddenly at the sight of her.

"You're human," he croaked.

"Yes," Lori replied.

"They captured you, too?" He coughed up a dark clot of blood and smiled bitterly. "Lucky us."

"I'm not a prisoner," Lori said.

The man's eyes hardened. "How?"

"I'm an exception," Lori said. "I'm immune. I gave birth to a Chimera." Lori turned and nodded to Keera, who was looking on with a frown.

"Hurry up," the overseer growled.

Lori looked back to the resistance leader. "I can get them to spare you, but you need to give me the code for your implant."

The man laughed but quickly broke off, coughing up more blood. Lori frowned, looking for another injury that she'd missed. She probed his chest, and it gave way with a sickening grinding sensation. The man cried out, and Lori recoiled from him and turned to glare at the Kyra. "You crushed his chest!"

"It was an accident," the overseer said, but he sounded amused, not sorry.

"I am already dead," the man on the floor said through a gasp.

"They can still save you," Lori insisted.

"They can, but they won't. And I don't care.

I'm not helping them."

"Then let's end this charade," the Kyra said. "Get out of the way!" Lori felt claws digging into her shoulders, pulling her back.

"Wait!" Lori cried. "What do you need the code for?"

Keera replied, "They planted a bomb in one of the ascension centers. We don't know which one, and we already tried scanning his brain. He doesn't know where the bomb is, but he is a ranking member of their leadership. We suspect the resistance is using implants to store critical information and somehow keeping their biological memories clean."

Lori looked to the man in horror. "Is that true?" Do you know where the bomb is?"

Another bloody laugh bubbled from his lips. "No. The location is in that data crystal, and I don't even know the encryption key. You'll have to shut down all of the centers if you want to avoid a massacre."

"There are women and children in the ascension centers!" Lori cried.

"Women who give birth to children who become Chimeras. No one is innocent anymore." The man's eyes hardened and drifted to the overseer. "Kill me. I'm not talking."

"As you wish."

"No!" Lori cried.

But the Kyra flayed him open with two sweeping strikes of its claws. The man's throat vanished in a crimson wave of blood, and his stomach burst open.

Lori recoiled, screaming as gore spattered her face and uniform.

She scuttled away as the overseer removed his breathing mask and ducked his head to feast on the corpse.

Lori was still screaming.

"Come," a low voice intoned, and she felt strong hands lifting her up and turning her away. It was Keera. Lori sobbed as her daughter carried her away like a baby. She cried herself hoarse all the way back to the transport tubes.

Keera set her down once they were inside. The tube whisked them back up through the ship. "I warned you that it would not be pleasant," Keera said.

"What was the point of capturing one of the resistance leaders if the overseer was just going to kill him?" Lori demanded.

"An example," Keera whispered. "The interrogation will be broadcast to Earth as a warning to others."

"And then the resistance will detonate their bomb and kill hundreds or thousands of innocent women and children. Where does it all end?"

"It ends when they realize that their struggle is pointless," Keera replied. Her chalk-white face was flushed dark gray from the exertion of carrying Lori. "Or it ends when the Kyra find a way to engineer human Chimeras that can breed with each other."

"And then what?" Lori asked. "Humans go extinct, and we all become like them, vicious and bloodthirsty."

"It would bring peace," Keera whispered. "And we are not all like that. I am not."

Lori scowled. "It's been almost ninety years, and they still can't figure out how I gave birth to a live Chimera. I'm pretty sure that means they never will."

"Then things will stay the way they are," Keera replied. "It's not perfect, but the bloodshed is limited, and your people get to go on living."

"Under the Kyra's thumb," Lori sneered. "And only because the sons of bitches need us to breed more soldiers for them."

"Careful," Keera replied, glancing around the transport tube nervously. "You are lucky that they have kept you alive all this time."

The transport tube stopped, and the door opened. Lori glared at her daughter. "Maybe you think they should have killed me."

"That's not true," Keera whispered. She glanced out of the open door, then back, as if checking to make sure no one was there to hear her. Then she stepped in close and whispered in Lori's ear. "You know that I share your views. I wish they would leave your world and set your people free."

Lori smiled bitterly as her daughter withdrew. "Wishing doesn't make it so, Keera."

CHAPTER 3

Clayton's garbage truck bumped and thundered over a broken section of the old I45 highway. His shift partner, Alan Reese, cursed and shook his head. The greasy black ponytail leaking from his baseball cap flipped over his shoulders.

"You'd think with all their high technology, the Kyra would do something about the roads between the cities. It's a miracle we can even get out this far."

Clayton nodded his agreement while steering around an old, broken-down mech with a shattered cockpit and a skeleton dangling over the dash. A remnant from the invasion, the pilot long dead.

It still seemed to Clayton like there had to be better places in the galaxy for the Kyra to invade. But then again, maybe not. After all, they weren't interested in Earth's natural resources or even in looking for a new planet to colonize: they were after its people. Slaves and soldiers for the war with *their* enemy—*whoever the hell that is.*

Clayton wondered why they didn't just build robot armies instead. It seemed much easier than invading alien worlds and using a virus to turn native populations into hybrid Chimeras. Making their strategy even more dubious, the failure rate of that virus was spectacularly high—hence the *Dregs*. Of course, the Kyra had a different story to tell to the indoctrinated masses of kids going through their school system. Couldn't have volunteers thinking there was a high likelihood that they'd turn into brainless monsters.

"We should just dump here, Clay. This is far enough," Alan said. He was peering out the windows with wide eyes, both his knees bouncing anxiously, rattling the Kyron laser rifle balanced in his lap. "We'll just say we got mobbed by Dregs and had to run for it."

Clayton glanced at him. The drop site was still 10 kilometers away. Plenty of haulers spooked and dumped their garbage early to avoid encounters with Dregs at the designated landfill. They wouldn't get in trouble if they did the same thing.

But the landfill was also the supply drop for *Phoenix,* New Houston's resistance cell, and dumping early would compromise the delivery of vital supplies. Clayton couldn't tell Alan that, though. Instead, he said, "You want the Dregs to have a reason to get closer to our farms? We have enough problems with them raiding us as it is."

Alan sighed. "Well... shit. You wanna know what I wonder? Why don't they just automate these trucks? No reason they need to have drivers. They used to be fully-automated before the Kyra showed up, so what changed?"

Clayton arched an eyebrow at him. "I wonder the same thing every night. On the bright side, we wouldn't have jobs if they did that."

"Sure we would. We'd sign up for the agri-corps and go tend crops or drive cattle with the ranchers. Hell, we could even go work in the lunar factories, churning out spaceship parts."

"Speak for yourself. I don't want to live on the Moon."

"I dunno. Might be nice. No Dregs up there, for one thing."

"So why don't you go?" Clayton asked.

"Maybe I will," Alan said, nodding sagely to himself.

With that, their conversation lapsed, and Clayton focused on his driving. Mist swirled under the headlights, casting wraith-like shadows between the piles of rubble and burned out cars, mechs, and tanks that formed high berms on either side of the buckled road. Those wrecks could be hiding hundreds of hungry Dregs. To them, garbage haulers like this one were food delivery vehicles. Garbage was one of their staples.

Alan was back to looking around furtively, his pudgy hands tightening on the grip of his rifle.

"Almost there, Al," Clayton reassured him. "Relax, buddy."

"Easy for you to say. If we break down out here, who do you think they're going to go for first?" Alan spared a hand from his rifle to grab a fistful of belly fat and jiggle it for emphasis. "I'm a big juicy target, and you're all bones."

Clayton smiled wryly. "And even with that incentive to go on a diet, you're still the first one to grab a donut with your morning coffee."

"When you've been alive as long as I have, you learn to stop giving a shit."

Clayton snorted at that. Alan barely looked thirty years old, but he was actually well over a hundred. He was one of the survivors of the invasion, and he'd been first in line to get the Kyra's longevity treatments. Like everything else, though, it came with a catch: if you never die and you can't use birth control, you just keep having kids forever. The perfect breeding stock.

"You should go to the dispensary and get a nanite-injection to melt away the fat," Clayton said.

Alan snorted. "I tried that! They just cut my rations. The Kyra think it's inefficient to burn fat with nanites. Why do you think I'm always grabbing the donuts? Because they've already got me on a fucking diet, and I hate the hell out of it."

Clayton began chuckling.

"It's not funny. Life's shitty enough without them taking away one of the few pleasures I have left in life."

"Look on the bright side, you'll get more dates after you shed the weight," Clay said.

"Yeah, and then what? Raise another brood of kids for them? No, thank you. I'm celibate and proud of it."

"Better not say that too loud," Clayton whispered. He'd heard rumors about cullings, about the Kyra rounding up people who hadn't had kids in a few decades and forcibly exposing them to the virus.

"Screw it," Alan said. "I'm a hundred and twenty-six years old. I've given the bastards ten kids already. I deserve a break. They want more outta me they're just gonna have to wait a few more years until I'm good and ready."

Clayton wondered about that. To listen to him, Alan sounded like he had resistance leanings, but the one time Clayton had come close to telling him about his own ties to Phoenix, Alan's face had scrunched up like a plump raisin, and he'd said: "Please tell me you haven't thrown in with those goddamn terrorists."

And so Clayton hadn't told him. Alan was an enigma. Not happy with the occupation, but unsupportive of the human resistance to it. Clayton suspected that he just liked to complain. One of those people who was never happy, no matter how good they had it. It didn't help that Alan used to be a wealthy man before the occupation. Now he was a garbage truck driver. Maybe that gave him a good reason to be bitter.

They rode the rest of the way in silence. The lights in the cab glowed and blinked. With two steering wheels, several joysticks to control the robotic loading arms of the truck, multiple displays for guidance, and buttons everywhere, Clayton felt more like the pilot of a lumbering spaceship than a garbage truck driver.

After about twenty minutes, the spotlights from the landfill glowed on the horizon. A few minutes later, Clayton picked out shadows crawling around under those lights: Dregs hunting through the mounds of garbage for food.

"Shit," Alan muttered. He grew suddenly still, his knuckles turning white on the grip and handguard of his rifle.

Clayton glanced at him. "We do this every night, Al. Dump and run."

"Remind me why they make us do this at *night*?" Alan said.

"Because Dregs are more active at night, and the trucks lure them away from the cities and the farms."

"So we're the bait," Alan said.

"The garbage is, yeah."

"A petty distinction when we're sitting right next to it. Fresh meat versus rotten. What do *you* suppose is more enticing?"

Clayton snorted but didn't reply.

It would have made sense for the Kyra to exterminate the Dregs, just as it would have made sense not to augment their numbers by exiling petty criminals and all of the latest failures from the ascension centers. Clayton figured they must be using the Dregs to keep Union resistance cells in check, and to justify keeping people contained in isolated pockets that were easy enough for the Kyra to police. *The best way to keep people happy in a prison is to show them that life outside of it is worse.*

He drove past a pair of flickering spotlights that marked the entrance of the landfill.

"Dump it," Alan said, his eyes darting over the crumbled remains of old buildings and the scattered mountains of trash in between.

"Not yet. We don't want to block the road."

Alan let out a frustrated breath.

Dregs were everywhere, crawling on all fours over the garbage, screaming, growling, and chattering to each other, fighting over scraps like dogs. A few of them looked up as the truck drove by, red eyes squinting against the combined glare of the truck's headlights and the flickering spotlights at the entrance of the landfill. Dregs all looked just like human Chimeras, but for the dull, feral look in their crimson eyes. They were beasts, not people.

The resistance drop site was coming up, marked by old, sagging traffic lights hanging over the street.

Before they reached it, a Dreg jumped in front of their truck, clothed in rags and covered in oozing sores. It screamed, and Clayton swerved, narrowly missing it.

"Come on, man!" Alan cried. "Just dump and let's go!"

"All right!" *Close enough,* Clayton thought. He found a reasonably empty spot to back into between two ruined buildings, and then flipped the switch to raise the tail gate at the back of the truck and activated the pusher plate to squeeze out all of the garbage.

Clayton heard Dregs shrieking over the steady groaning of pneumatics.

"Hurry up, Clay! You're getting them all excited."

"You want me to get out and push?" Clayton quipped.

But Alan didn't have a chance to reply. The high-pitched report of a laser rifle discharging interrupted them.

"What was that?" Alan asked, his brown eyes wide with terror.

"Another driver. Has to be," Clayton said. He used his ARCs to activate the emergency radio. "This is SW27, is there anyone out there in need of assistance?"

Static answered. Followed by another discharging laser bolt. This time Clayton spotted a bright emerald flash of light lancing out from a side street a few blocks away. He pointed to it, "Over there."

Clayton put the truck into drive and hit the gas, leaving the back of the truck open and spewing garbage all over the street.

"What are you doing?!" Alan asked.

"What if that was us out there?"

"It *is* us out there, goddammit!"

Clayton ignored his partner's protests and gunned the engine. The truck squawked to let him know that it had dumped everything, and he shut the tailgate to avoid picking up stowaways.

Dregs ran along beside their truck in streaking shadows, drawn by the smell of fresh garbage and human meat.

"Let's go! They're swarming us already," Alan insisted.

"Just one more block," Clayton said.

They reached the next intersection and found another hauler stopped halfway down the left side of the intersecting street. The street around it was bathed in red brake lights and flashing yellow hazards that flickered intermittently over the mob of Dregs that surrounded the truck. One of the drivers was standing on top of the cab and firing a laser rifle at the Dregs who were climbing up. Both the windshield and the passenger's side window were broken and blood-spattered, and a large group of Dregs were screaming and clawing at each other, playing tug of war with a bloody human corpse in a neon yellow vest.

"Shit. They got him," Alan said.

"Only one of them," Clayton replied. "The other is alive. Pass me your rifle and grab your wheel. Drive by as slow and close as you can."

Alan looked at him like he'd just grown a cranial stalk. "Are you insane? What are you going to do?"

"I'm going to get up on the roof and help the other driver jump over. We'll ride up there and keep the Dregs off of us while you drive us out of here."

"No."

"Alan. You don't want that man's death on your conscience. Come on! We're running out of time." Clayton was still driving, and the other truck was coming up fast.

Alan relented with an angry sneer. "Damn you, Clay!" He passed the rifle over and grabbed his steering wheel.

Clayton lowered his window, and the pungent smell of garbage swirled in. He gagged and coughed, but pushed through the urge to vomit and began climbing out. A Dreg running along beside their truck spotted him and lunged. Clayton whipped the rifle around in a one-handed grip and flicked the safety off with his thumb. A bright green laser beam stabbed out and burned a hole in the monster's chest. It dropped and rolled with its momentum, arms and legs flopping around limply and kicking up a tiny cyclone of dust. Clayton pulled himself up onto the roof just as Alan brought their truck alongside the other one. The shrieks and snarls of the Dregs swarming the other vehicle were deafening. Clayton caught the besieged driver's eye and gestured quickly. "Jump over!"

The other man didn't need to be asked twice. He took a few steps back to give himself a running start and then ran and launched himself off the roof of his truck, flying over the three-foot gap between the two vehicles. He landed on Clayton's truck with a *bang*, and Alan gunned the engine a split second later. Clayton grabbed the other driver to steady him before he could fall off, and then both of them were crouching on the roof and firing backward at the scrambling mob of Dregs chasing after them.

Alan reached the next intersection and pulled through a screeching left turn to circle the block. They bumped and thundered through potholes and broken sections of the road with the truck bucking like a bronco. Clayton and the other driver grabbed whatever handholds they could and flattened themselves to the roof.

"Take it easy, Al!" Clayton shouted, but Alan wasn't listening. The next pothole knocked Clayton's grip loose and sent him flying over the side. There came a sickening moment of weightlessness as he fell. He hit feet first and rolled with the landing and his momentum, but he hit his head a few times anyway. The impacts left him dazed and with ringing ears.

He lifted his head on a sharply aching neck and saw the tail lights of his truck speeding away with no signs of stopping.

The ringing in Clayton's ears retreated a step, and a new sound crowded in: a rising roar of growls and snarls, accompanied by the hoof-beating thunder of countless bare, calloused feet striking broken asphalt.

Clayton pushed himself up on one elbow. He spotted the moonlit gleam of his laser rifle lying well out of reach, at least fifteen feet away—and an onrushing horde of Dregs beyond that. They were all racing each other to reach him, driven mad by the smell of fresh meat. Clayton scrambled to reach his weapon, his mind ablaze with just one thought: *this can't be how I die!*

CHAPTER 4

Samara dragged her medicine cart into the surgical recovery wing and rolled past the curtain into one of the cubicles there. The patient, Mrs. Hill, was a fifty-year-old woman that looked twenty-five. She'd come into the ER with her husband a few hours ago with bruises on her face, a dislocated shoulder, and a broken arm from 'falling down the stairs' but the hand-shaped bruise on her upper arm had told a different story.

As if we don't have enough violence, Samara thought. And with the Chimeran Guard in charge of meting out justice, there was nothing Mrs. Hill could do about her husband beating her. Chimeras didn't care about misdemeanor crimes, particularly not between couples with children. They didn't believe in divorce or separation, so if they did respond, their only response would be to exercise their fists on her husband's face. Then he'd be the one lying in this bed instead of her. *Still a better outcome,* Samara thought. She rolled her cart over to Mrs. Hill's IV bag. The woman was still asleep from

47

the anesthesia they'd administered during surgery to repair her broken arm and pop her shoulder back into place.

Samara looked away and bent to unlock the drawer in her cart that was assigned to Mrs. Hill's tracking ID. She ran her fingers lightly over the vials of *nanobiotics* and painkillers in the drawer, checking the type and potency of each. She took half of the nanobiotics—two vials—but left the painkillers alone. Mrs. Hill was going to be in a lot of pain once the anesthesia wore off.

A sharp pang of guilt shot through Samara as she pocketed the stolen vials in her nurse's uniform. She had to pick carefully which patients to steal meds from, and how much to steal. The resistance needed the nanobiotics even more than most of her patients did, but she couldn't let her patients die because of that need. As it was, she'd already had a few close calls where additional meds had to be ordered to combat an infection that should have been prevented by the ones she'd stolen. It was a balance, and Samara always felt dangerously close to the edge. She wished she could talk to Clayton about it, but it was just too risky to talk about such things inside the city walls. Besides, it would be unfair to him. Telling him about her ties to the resistance would make him an accomplice. They'd both be executed in the arena if she were ever discovered.

Samara laid out the remaining vials of nanobiotics with shaking hands and extracted the contents with a syringe.

The curtain swished open behind her, and she jumped, almost dropping one of the vials.

"Sam?"

She turned to see Dr. Galen Rath standing in the opening, leaning against the wall. A puzzled look flickered across his face. Galen was a tall, trim, dark-haired man with a perpetual aura of charisma drifting around him. He could have had any nurse begging for his attention—with the possible exception of Carla, the charge nurse, who wasn't into men—but for some reason, Galen had fixated on her, despite Samara's constant reminders that she was happily married.

"You're jumpy," Galen said. "Maybe lay off the coffee, huh?" He grinned as he pushed off the wall and crossed the cubicle. "How's Mrs. Hill doing?" he asked, stopping beside her bed.

"Fine," Samara said as she went back to her job, injecting the first dose of nanobiotics into Mrs. Hill's IV bag.

"I need your help with another patient," Galen said.

"You should let Carla assign my patients."

"She did. I'm just the messenger."

Samara frowned, doubting that story. Galen had probably convinced Carla to assign her another one of his patients. He was looking for every excuse he could to spend more time with her. Samara injected another vial into Mrs. Hill's IV bag. "Fine, I'll bite. Who's the patient?"

"Funny you should say *bite*," Galen said.

Samara stared at him in horror. "What is a bite victim doing here? They could infect the whole hospital! We need to quarantine anyone who has come into contact with the patient, and call in the Guard to get them out of here immediately!"

Galen started chuckling. "Relax. It's a transfer from the ascension center, Harold Neem. He's a farmer who checked himself in, thinking he'd been bitten by a Dreg in his sleep. Turns out, he just got shit-faced and slept with a Chimera. She bit him a few times during the uh..." Galen mimed awkwardly with his hands. "And then took off before he woke up. The farmer saw the bites when he came to, but couldn't remember the encounter... not until later, anyway."

Samara blinked. "You're joking."

"Dead serious."

"Was it consensual?"

"He says it was."

"A human and a Chimera..." Samara trailed off, shaking her head in disbelief. They wouldn't be the first inter-species couple that she'd heard of, but the Chimeras frowned on such liaisons, and most humans found Chimeras to be unattractive at best. Her nose wrinkled with the thought. "Ick."

"Takes all kinds. At least he doesn't have to worry about making her pregnant. You all done there?"

Samara scooped the empty vials and used syringes into the garbage bin beside her cart. "Now I am."

"Great. Time to go give Harold his rabies shots," Galen said, chuckling again.

CHAPTER 5

Clayton's hand closed around the butt of the rifle just as the first Dreg reached for him with outstretched claws. Bloody spittle flew from the creature's cracked lips. Red eyes flared wide in eager anticipation of the kill.

A high-pitched shriek sounded, and then a bright green flash tore through the Dreg's chest, lighting up its entire torso from within and revealing a spider's web of black veins.

"Come on!" someone said. That wasn't Al's voice. Clayton felt strong hands pulling him up. He scrambled to his feet and dragged his rifle into line with the next wave of Dregs. He held the trigger down, raking a solid green laser beam over the next two Dregs to reach him. They crumpled in a heap on top of the first, but there were dozens more still coming, staggered in waves of three and four. "Let's go!" the man behind Clayton said.

Clayton turned and ran, seeing at once that it was the other driver who'd come to his aid. He must have seen when Clayton fell off the truck and jumped down to help.

They ran side-by-side, a flat sprint, casting frantic glances behind them to the surging horde of Dregs. "Where are we going?" Clayton asked between gasps for air. He scanned the ruined buildings and mounds of garbage to either side of the buckled street, but found no sign of a refuge that they could barricade. All the doors were either missing or hanging off their hinges. The windows and glass doors of ancient storefronts all smashed.

They hit an old intersection, and the other driver veered left. Clayton followed, almost tripping over a jutting piece of rubble. Here the street was only one lane wide, the other side completely piled with stinking piles of garbage from New Houston. Flies buzzed in noisy clouds, and the stench made Clayton's head spin. He wondered desperately if the Dregs would be able to find them if they burrowed into those stinking mounds of trash, but there wasn't any time for digging. He could hear the thundering footfalls of the horde chasing them. Their ragged cries and snarls blurred together in his ears.

Clayton's lungs burned, and his legs grew heavy. He began to stumble and trip over the scattered chunks of debris and garbage. Twice he almost fell. And twice the other driver caught him by the arm and yanked him back up.

"Almost there!"

"Almost where?" Clayton asked. They neared the end of the side street, and he saw the one they'd come in on—the main road leading into the designated landfill. For a moment, Clayton thought that Alan might be waiting for them near the entrance, but they emerged onto the main street to find it empty. No signs of a garbage truck or even the crimson glow of its taillights. Red eyes turned their way instead, glinting hungrily in the darkness. Those Dregs only hesitated for the briefest instant, and then they charged, leaping and skidding down their collapsing mountains of garbage with shrieks and roars of delight.

"This way!" The other driver sprinted down the street, aiming for a jutting piece of asphalt.

Clayton's heart began to pound from more than just the exertion. They were running *toward* more Dregs, and the ones behind them weren't getting any farther away.

"Where are you going!?" Clayton cried.

"Trust me!"

And then he saw it. The jutting chunk of debris in the middle of the road wasn't asphalt —it was an open manhole cover. Someone was holding it open from underneath, waving frantically to them from the opening.

Even before they reached the open manhole, Clayton could tell they weren't going to make it in time. The Dregs in front of them were converging, mere seconds from reaching them. There would be no time to scramble down a ladder. Clayton brought his rifle up, struggling to take aim and run at the same time, but the barrel swayed violently with each lunging stride.

And then a tinny thunk sounded, and Clayton spotted something like a can of soup rolling out of the manhole toward the onrushing Dregs. The other driver yelled, "Shut your eyes!"

Clayton slammed his eyes closed just as the rolling can exploded with a deafening *bang* and a starburst of light that blazed through his eyelids, blinding him anyway.

He blinked his eyes open to see the world wrapped in fuzzy black cotton. The same cotton that stuffed his ears. He felt himself trip, then fall, pavement scraping through his thick pants and shirt. Hands seized him and dragged him forward. For a second, he thought it must be the Dregs, but then he felt himself falling. A light snapped on, and he was rolled aside like a giant sack of flour. Shadows moved around him. Darkness receded steadily, and details snapped into focus.

The other driver appeared, nodding quickly as someone in gray and white camo fatigues crouched in front of him, checking him over with an old angle head flashlight. The one in fatigues was probably looking for signs of bites or scratches. Unlike Chimeras, who were only contagious while they were changing, the Dregs were always contagious.

Clayton noticed that the other driver had a craggy face, pale blue eyes, and razor-short black hair glistening with sweat. He looked familiar, but Clayton didn't know his name. Most of the drivers knew each other, at least by sight, but Clayton stuck to himself, and he was relatively new to the job.

The other man shook his head and cupped a hand to his ear, indicating that he couldn't hear whatever the one in fatigues was saying. Then he made an okay sign with his thumb and forefinger and pointed to Clayton.

The man in camo fatigues turned to look at Clayton just as he struggled to his feet. Dark skin peeked out around a breather mask and night-vision goggles. The man pulled the mask down and put the goggles up on top of his head to reveal dark eyes and a shiny patch of scar tissue from an old burn on one side of his face. An old-fashioned Velcro name tape read *Sgt. Sutton*. He had a machete dangling from one side of his belt and a bulky black sidearm in a holster on the other.

The sergeant checked Clayton for bite and claw marks, his eyes lingering where the pavement had scraped through Clayton's clothes to bloody his knees and elbows. Clayton made an okay sign like the other driver had, but the sergeant ignored him and went on with the visual examination.

When he was finished, the sergeant withdrew and said something that Clayton could barely hear through his cotton-stuffed ears. What he'd thought was a soup can had actually been an old flash-bang grenade. Clayton wondered where Sutton had even found such a thing, but the resistance was known for using outdated weapons and ordnance. They'd probably found an old cache of weapons somewhere.

The unidentified driver with the craggy face sank to the ground beside the ladder leading down from the manhole. Clayton sat down on the opposite side of the tunnel and leaned back against the curving concrete wall.

Their rescuer cast the beam of his angle head flashlight up to the manhole. Rivers of dust trickled steadily down. The Dregs were trying to dig through with their claws.

Sergeant Sutton brought the light back down, flicked the beam over each of them, and then said something that neither of them could hear.

Apparently realizing that, he gave them a hand signal instead—an upraised fist. Clayton understood it perfectly. *Hold position.*

The sergeant turned and started down the tunnel, dragging a thick train of shadows over them as his flashlight swept away. Clayton's pulse ratcheted up a notch. He watched the sergeant disappear around a bend in the tunnel, hoping he'd be back soon.

It took another five minutes of sitting in silence and darkness before Clayton began to hear something through the cotton in his ears. The sound grew quickly louder, resolving into the muted thunder of countless claws scraping furiously over the manhole cover. Pinhole shafts of light filtered down from above, revealing a steady trickle of dust pouring through the manhole. But determined as they might be, they couldn't claw through a half-inch of steel.

Clayton jerked his head to the shadowy silhouette of the other driver and worked some moisture through the grit in his mouth. "You're with the resistance," he tried.

"So are you," the other man said.

"How do you know that?"

"Lucky guess. That, and you were at the drop site. Not a lot of haulers bother to go this far out into the Wastes."

Clayton nodded. "Thanks for coming back for me."

"You saved me. I'd have to be a real piece of shit to leave you behind after that."

"Fair enough. What's your name?" Clayton asked.

"Bruce Paige. You?"

"Clayton Cross." He looked up to the manhole cover as it shuddered with a particularly loud *thump* and *scraaape* of a Dreg's claws. Suddenly worried that they might find some way to get it open, Clayton cast about for his laser rifle. It was too dark to see, but he'd probably lost it when that flash-bang had sent him sprawling. Bruce still had his rifle, though, a shadowy metal gleam in his lap. Better than nothing.

"So, what now?" Clayton asked.

Bruce shrugged. "We'll have to wait down here until morning. Should be safe enough to make it back to my truck and call for a pickup after that."

Clayton nodded and eased his head back against the side of the tunnel. With their chalk-white skin and sensitive eyes, the Dregs shunned daylight and slept during the day. *Safe* was a relative term, but so long as they were quiet, they'd be okay. He just hoped they'd be able to get back to the city before Clayton's shift was supposed to end. He didn't want Samara worrying and wondering what had happened to him out here.

That thought prompted another. He raised his head and nodded to Bruce. "What happened to you up there?"

"I must have driven through some particularly tasty shit. Dregs smelled it on my tires and slashed straight through them thinking they were food."

Clayton grimaced. "Perils of the job."

"One of many," Bruce agreed.

An approaching echo of footsteps drew their attention to a bobbing cone of light coming around the corner of the tunnel. A few seconds after that, Sergeant Sutton appeared. He stopped in front of them and tossed a canteen of water to each of them before dropping a single bedroll at their feet. Then he reached around to his pack and unhooked a Kyron lantern. He flicked it on with a pale wash of blue light that cast everything in monochromatic tones, and set it on the ground beside the bedroll.

"It was the best that I could do on short notice," Sutton explained in a thick southern drawl that Clayton could finally hear.

"Thank you," Clayton said as he unscrewed the cap of the canteen and threw his head back to gulp greedily. Cool rivulets of water leaked down his chin and soaked through his shirt.

He wiped his mouth on his sleeve and noticed Sergeant Sutton peering warily up at the ceiling with his angle head flashlight. Trickles of dust filtered down in time to each scraping *thump* of a Dreg's hand or foot.

"They can smell us down here," Bruce whispered. "Probably hear us, too."

"Is there any way in?" Clayton asked.

"That we know of?" Sutton asked. He shook his head, eyes still on the cracked and crumbling ceiling.

Fear gathered sickly in the pit of Clayton's stomach. He looked down to the other end of the tunnel, but it ended in a wall of rubble not far from where they sat.

The sergeant brought his eyes down to their level with a tight smile that was probably meant to be reassuring. "We've been using this tunnel to access the drop site for months, and we haven't run into any problems yet, but one of you should keep watch just in case."

Clayton grimaced. "I guess it's too much to ask that you take us back to your base for the night."

The sergeant's burn-scarred cheek twitched. "No can do, sir. The fewer people who know where we are, the safer it is for everyone."

Clayton sighed. "Fair enough."

"Phoenix appreciates your service, though." Sutton looked to Bruce and nodded, then dragged his eyes back. "Without supply drops like yours, we'd be in a bad way."

Clayton smiled. "Where would the desert be without a few drops of rain?"

"It's a helluva lot more than that. Don't lose faith, sir. One day we'll find a way to really hit 'em where it hurts. And we're making progress on a vaccine."

Clayton snorted. "I've been hearing that since I joined the resistance a year ago."

A conspiratorial look crept into Sutton's eyes, and he looked from Clayton to Bruce and back again. "You two want to strike a real blow?"

Bruce's eyebrows elevated slowly, and Clayton pulled himself up an inch. "I'm listening."

"We have a special package for pickup. A defector who needs to get out of New Houston."

"A defector?" Clayton asked. "A Chimera?" That would be a first.

"No," Sutton replied. "She's human."

"Human..." Clayton repeated slowly, as if the word itself were a riddle. Human collaborators weren't common. Most people with any real power or wealth were Chimeras, so what was the point of the resistance securing a *human* defector?

"We need to smuggle her out as soon as possible."

Clayton considered it. Smuggling supplies out was hard enough. Even with reinforced supply boxes packed in with actual garbage, the trash compactors in the trucks often cracked them wide open. A live passenger would be killed instantly.

"Well? How about it, gentlemen?" Sutton asked.

"We'll have to ride together," Bruce said. "We can't have an unsympathetic shift partner figuring out what we're doing and reporting us."

"I see two drivers here," Sutton said. "And you're both with the resistance."

"I already have a shift partner assigned," Clayton said.

"You could request a transfer," Sutton said.

"He's right," Bruce added. "My partner is dead, and yours just left you for dead. You have a good excuse to ask for someone else, and we have some history together after tonight, so you could ask for me and get the request approved."

"Even if we do, we'll have to turn off the compactor or she'll be crushed," Clayton said. "That means we won't be able to finish our route, and that means someone could get suspicious."

"She could climb in at the last stop," Bruce said. "We'd have a full load, and she'd just be the cherry on top—so to speak."

"Yeah... maybe," Clayton agreed.

"Just tell us where she needs to be waiting, and we'll make it happen," Sergeant Sutton replied. "But the pickup has to be tomorrow night."

"We'll do it," Bruce answered for both of them.

Clayton frowned, but didn't contradict him. "What's so important about this defector?"

"I'm afraid that's classified," Sutton replied. "Just know that securing her will be a hell of a lot more than a few drops of rain. This will be a damned monsoon."

Clayton let out a shaky breath. "You know where the old stadium was?"

Sutton nodded. "You mean the Kyron Arena?"

Clayton grimaced. Rather than sporting events, it was used for public executions and challenges between Chimeras. Ironic that an advanced race of aliens had brought back an old, barbaric tradition from the Roman Empire. "Have her waiting around back in the dumpsters. That's the end of my route tomorrow night," Clayton said.

"She'll be there."

"How are we supposed to drop her here without the Dregs tearing her apart?" Bruce asked.

"Drive up to the manhole, get out and knock three times as loud as you can. I'll be waiting."

Clayton winced. "You'd better be. We won't have more than a few seconds to make the drop. Longer than that, and Dregs will be swarming us."

Sutton smiled. "We know how to deal with Dregs." The sergeant reached out and patted Clayton's shoulder. "Sleep tight, boys." With that, he rose and headed back down the tunnel.

"Lucky he was waiting here," Clayton remarked as the sergeant disappeared around the corner once more.

"Not luck," Bruce replied. "I called for help." He tapped his ear to indicate a comms unit.

Clayton arched an eyebrow at him. "You have comms contact with them? You must be pretty special." He'd been making supply runs for a year already, and he still didn't have any direct point of contact.

"I've paid my dues, so to speak," Bruce replied.

Clayton was about to press for details, but the other man broke eye contact and nodded to the bedroll. "You should get some sleep. I'll take first watch."

Clayton snorted. "We work nights. I just woke up a few hours ago."

Bruce shrugged. "I guess it's going to be a long night then."

A skittering, scratching sound punctuated that sentiment, drawing their eyes to the abbreviated end of the tunnel behind the ladder where the sewer had collapsed. Something was digging on the other side of that wall of debris. The scratching went on, and a pebble broke loose and tumbled down on their side. Clayton cast about for his rifle once more, but there was no sign of it.

Even if he were tired, there was no way he'd

be able to nod off with a horde of Dregs digging just a few feet away from where he slept. "A long night indeed..." he muttered.

CHAPTER 6

"**G**et ready to run for it," Bruce whispered from the top of the ladder.

"If we're quiet, we won't need to run," Clayton replied.

Bruce shrugged. "So we'll run quietly. Best of both."

The Dregs had given up digging through to reach them just after dawn. Hopefully, that meant they'd all gone to bed now.

Bruce eased the manhole cover open a few inches. Clayton's hands tightened on the lower rungs of the ladder, his whole body tensing to launch him up to the surface.

"All clear," Bruce whispered after looking around for a few seconds. "Follow me." He pushed the manhole the rest of the way open, drawing a rusty screech from the hinges. They both froze. Bruce twisted around in a quick circle, sweeping for targets with his rifle.

After a few seconds of that, Bruce climbed out and waved to Clayton from the top. He was already on his way up, rising into the fetid embrace of rotting garbage warming in the sun. He crawled out beside Bruce and looked around quickly for Dregs. The clouds were still blushing pink with the sunrise, but there was no sign of any activity in the dump.

Bruce eased the manhole cover back down, letting it drop the last quarter of an inch as he pulled his fingertips out. The sound of it *thunking* against the street was like a bomb going off in the deadly silence of the Wastes. Bruce straightened and crept away with his rifle up and sweeping. He waved over his shoulder.

But Clayton lingered, searching for his own weapon, the one he'd lost last night. It lay a few feet away from the manhole, covered in a fine coating of dust.

Clayton crept over to it and checked the charge. Still full.

A sudden *crunch* of gravel sent adrenaline boiling through his veins. He jammed the rifle's stock to his shoulder and swept through a quick circle, searching for targets.

Bruce caught his eye with an apologetic smile and pointed to his chest.

Quiet, Clayton mouthed as he walked over to join the other driver. As soon as he reached Bruce's side, they both began jogging quietly down the street.

Clayton kept pace with him, scanning the ruins of two and three-story buildings as they went. Old storefronts glared back at him darkly with empty window frames for eyes.

Shadowy piles of rubble inside could be hiding any number of Dregs.

Clayton grimaced and looked away. The intersection he'd turned down with Alan the night before was coming up. They ran into the middle of it and stopped to catch their breath. Bruce pointed to his truck with his rifle.

"Almost there," he whispered.

Clayton nodded and looked around quickly, checking to make sure no Dregs were creeping up on them.

Nothing.

Bruce ran for his truck. The brake lights were still glowing and the hazards still flashing. Clayton hesitated just a second before hurrying after him.

They reached the side doors and pulled them open simultaneously. Beads of blood-stained safety glass spilled out as Clayton pulled the left side door open. He climbed in and eased the door shut. Bruce jumped in on the other side and pulled his door shut, too. He let out a sigh and spared a hand from the rifle in his lap to work the radio.

"SW26 calling central, my truck broke down in the dump north of New Houston, requesting emergency pick-up, over."

Static buzzed while they waited for a reply.

Clayton looked around anxiously and used the blood-spattered screens inside the truck to check the external cameras for Dregs. He wished Bruce had whispered into the radio.

Static hissed on ominously.

"Nothing?" Clayton asked.

Bruce shook his head. "We're pretty far out. I'm going to have to boost the signal and try again."

"Quietly, please," Clayton whispered.

"Relax. They're all fast asleep with their bellies in the air."

"You hope."

Bruce repeated his message. "This is SW26 calling central, my truck broke down in the Northern Wastes, requesting emergency pick-up, over."

Clayton was still checking the cameras when he heard it—a shrill cry. It was soon echoed and taken up by a dozen others.

"Shit," Clayton muttered. He caught a flicker of movement in the corner of his eye and turned to see pale, dusty creatures crawling out of the ruins. "We've got incoming! I count five Dregs."

"Six over here," Bruce whispered, already leaning out his broken window and taking aim with his rifle.

Clayton grabbed his arm before he could fire. "If you shoot that, you'll draw every Dreg within two klicks to our location."

Just then, the radio crackled with a noisy reply. "SW26, this is central, it's good to hear your voice. A tow truck is already on the way.

You can ride back with them."

"Copy," Clayton whispered sharply before reaching over to kill the volume.

Another shrill cry sounded, followed by a hungry growl. Three more Dregs appeared, crawling out of ruined buildings farther down the street.

"It's not going to matter if we attract more of them at this rate," Bruce said, his rugged features tensing in a grim expression. "There's already too many. We need to thin the herd while we've still got some distance between us."

"How did that work out for you last night? Clayton countered.

"So, what's your suggestion?" Bruce asked.

Clayton jerked a thumb over his shoulder. "We climb in the back."

"Someone needs to stay up here to operate the switch," Bruce said. "Unless you're planning to sit back there with the hatch open."

He was right. Remote operation of the haulers had been disabled ever since the resistance used it to hack and steal a pair of vehicles last year.

More growls and shrieks interrupted them. The Dregs were getting closer.

"We're running out of time, Clay. What's it gonna be?"

His mind raced for an answer as he watched the Dregs approaching. They were walking slower than usual—probably still tired from a long night of picking through garbage.

"What if I stay here and flip the switch once you're in?" Clayton suggested. "I can scramble back there before the hatch shuts."

"You'll only have about five seconds before that happens."

"I'm fast."

Bruce grinned. "Maybe, but I'm faster."

Clayton was about to object, but Bruce stopped him with a shake of his head. "My truck, my choice, and there's no time to argue. You need to get back there now. I'm opening the hatch."

Clayton gave in with a reluctant nod and climbed out his window onto the roof of the cab. The Dregs spotted him almost instantly and went into a frenzy, shrieking and growling. They went from a lazy, shambling walk to a flat sprint.

The hatch was already open, so Clayton jumped down into the back of the truck and called out to Bruce. "I'm in!" His voice boomed ominously in the hollow metal chamber. He spotted the other driver climbing up onto the roof of the cab just as the hatch began swinging shut.

But the timing was all wrong. The hatch didn't take five seconds to close. More like three. He had just enough time to catch a lopsided salute from Bruce before he turned and pressed the stock of his rifle to his shoulder, taking aim on the first Dreg.

The bright flash of light dazzled Clayton's eyes, and then the hatch sealed him into darkness with a resounding *boom.* Realizing he'd been tricked, he began banging on the sides of the truck. "Bruce! Let me out, damn it!"

But the only reply he got was the periodic high-pitched reports of his laser rifle firing over and over again. Dregs cried out, shrieking as they fell, but soon their claws were scraping the sheer metal sides of the truck and setting Clayton's teeth on edge like chalk on a chalkboard.

Eventually, those sounds shifted to the roof with hollow metallic thunder as multiple sets of feet landed on the back of the truck and scrabbled for purchase on the smooth metal surface.

Laser blasts sounded repeatedly; then came Bruce's screams, followed by wet crunching sounds, and the angry growls of the Dregs as they fought over their kill. Clayton sank to the floor of the truck, feeling dizzy and sick. The sounds of feeding faded into a long, bitter silence. Clayton raised his watch, filling the darkness in the back of the truck with a pale blue light. 7:05.

By 7:25, he heard the tow truck arrive, followed by the muffled, gravelly voices of Chimeras and the heavy, crunching footfalls of their armored boots. Central had called in the

Guard for this recovery. They'd been expecting trouble. Clayton had made the wrong call. If he and Bruce had made their stand together, they might have both lasted long enough for the Chimeras to arrive and chase off the remaining Dregs. Bruce might have lived if they'd done that.

Swallowing past a painful knot in his throat, Clayton climbed wearily to his feet and banged on the sides of the truck, yelling until he was hoarse to let the Chimeras know he was in there.

Seconds later, the hatch swung open, letting in a blinding swath of sunlight. An armored Chimera appeared crouching on the blood-smeared roof where Bruce had been torn apart. "Take my hand," the Chimera growled, reaching down. Its eyes and features were hidden by a glossy black visor and helmet that helped to shield its sensitive eyes from daylight. Matching body armor shielded its pale skin. Clayton grabbed the hand and climbed out. The Chimera jumped to the ground, landing heavily, the impact buffered by the exoskeleton inside its armor.

Clayton climbed down more carefully, and one of the Chimeras grabbed him by the arm. "This way," it said and dragged him roughly toward an armored transport as if he were their prisoner. He walked in a daze between two Chimeras. A sheep among wolves. If they knew that he was with the resistance, they'd have executed him on the spot.

The resistance—damn it! Clayton's blood iced over as he remembered the job he'd agreed to do for them tonight. Transporting the defector. Without Bruce to help him, he was going to have to smuggle that person out of the city with the added risk of getting caught and reported by an unsympathetic shift partner. And then the Chimeras really would execute him.

Clayton thought about that as they pushed him into the back of their transport. Tiny windows lined the inside of the walls—nothing big enough for a Dreg to break and reach through.

Clayton sat on a bench seat lining one of those walls and stared blankly out the nearest window, considering his options. He saw the Chimeras loading the garbage hauler up on the flatbed of a massive tow truck, four of them standing watch the entire time, scanning the ruins with the sensors inside their faceless black helmets.

But there was no sign of Dregs. *Probably because they can't smell the Chimeras through their armor,* he realized.

Clayton pushed that thought aside to rather focus on the problem at hand. He had no line of communication with the resistance, so he couldn't tell them what had happened. Bruce was the one who'd had contact with them. *And then the idiot went and got himself killed.*

As Clayton saw it, he had only two options: abandon the op and leave the defector waiting in that dumpster behind the arena, or try to pull it off anyway, but at great risk to both himself and the defector.

Maybe Alan won't see anything, he thought. *It'll be dark around the arena.*

But even if there were no problems with the pickup, he still had to get out at the drop site and knock on that manhole cover to make the transfer. There'd be no hiding that.

He had to abandon the op. It was the only way. Sergeant Sutton would have to find someone else.

Eventually, the Chimeras came crowding in with Clayton, and the transport jerked into motion, rumbling and bumping along the broken highway back to the city. Clayton spent the trip thinking about his wife and their unborn daughter, and about how maybe Samara was right: resisting the occupation was futile. *You don't fight an interstellar empire by harassing them on one planet out of hundreds,* he thought. Even if they could somehow defeat the Kyra here—what would that accomplish?

Nothing. They'd be back.

Clayton eased his conscience with the realization that it didn't matter how important that defector was to the resistance; they were fighting a war that couldn't be won. It was time for him to cut his losses and get out before it was too late.

* * *

Samara pulled the curtain aside and stepped into the recovery room with a tight smile.

"Did you need something, Kent?" She went to check the half-empty IV bag hanging from a stand near the fifteen-year-old boy's head. He didn't move a muscle, but his eyes tracked to her. His lip was split, so he didn't return her smile. Besides the split lip, he had a broken nose, a knife wound in his abdomen, and two cracked ribs. He'd just come out of surgery to fix both his nose and the internal bleeding from the knife. He'd been asleep until five minutes ago.

"Kent?"

The boy took a few seconds to work some moisture into his mouth before speaking. "Can I get something to drink?"

"Let me just check with Doctor Rath, and I'll let you know."

"Okay," he croaked.

"Is everything else fine?" Samara insisted. "Are you in any pain?"

Kent's eyes slid shut, and he rocked his head slowly from side to side. "No."

"Good. The meds are working, then. I'll be back with Doctor Rath in a few minutes."

"Okay."

Samara slipped out of the cubicle and left the recovery room to join the bustling chaos of the ER in the New Houston Medical Center. She used her ARCs to mentally communicate Kent's request to Doctor Galen Rath. His answering system replied with an automated message saying he'd get back to her just as soon as possible, which meant he was probably in surgery. Samara left it at that and went to deal with her other patients. Galen might be a jerk who couldn't take no for an answer, but he was an excellent surgeon.

There were at least a dozen others like Kent, most of them victims of internal conflicts. Usually, it was the more indoctrinated kids beating on the ones who'd expressed negative sentiments toward the Kyra. Or worse, it was the Chimeras themselves, letting out some of their innate aggression to teach dissidents a lesson.

Kyra DNA made Chimeras more aggressive and violent than humans, just as it did with the Dregs.

"Samara!" She turned to see Dr. Rath approaching. "I got your message about Kent." He stopped a few feet away and fixed her with a charming grin.

Samara evaded his gaze before he could interpret eye contact as an invitation.

"Let's go see him together." Galen wrapped

an arm around her shoulders and turned her in the direction of Kent's cubicle.

Samara shrugged out from under his arm and sidestepped away from him.

He looked to her with eyebrows innocently raised. "Something wrong, Sam?"

"Yes. I have a husband. Hands to yourself."

Galen grinned mischievously and held up both his hands in surrender. "Yes, ma'am."

This was yet another part of civilization that had disappeared with the occupation. Before that, a doctor touching her in *any* way would have been grounds to press charges for harassment, but now no one cared. The Guard wouldn't bother about anything short of rape, and sometimes not even that. People had to look out for themselves. Women especially.

Galen waved open the doors to the surgical wing as they approached. They strode down the corridor to Kent's recovery room together. The boy's eyes cracked open as they pulled his curtain aside.

"How are you feeling, Kent?" Doctor Rath asked, stepping over to his bed.

"Thirsty."

"Yes, I can imagine. Samara, would you get the boy a drink, please?"

She withdrew with a nod and came back a minute later with a cup full of water. She passed it to Kent and held it to his lips while he drank.

"Easy," Samara chided. "All right, that's enough. You shouldn't have too much yet."

Kent looked like he wanted to argue, but fatigue won out, and he relaxed against the pillow.

Galen spent a few minutes asking Kent questions and checking the boy's vitals. "You're already well on your way to recovery," Galen declared. "You should be able to leave in the morning."

"Does my dad know yet?" Kent asked.

Galen hesitated, looking busy as glowing displays flickered across his ARCs. "We tried to contact him..." the doctor replied absently. The screens cleared from his eyes, and he fixed the boy with a reassuring smile. "He was out of comms range at the time, but we'll try again soon."

"He's probably out dumping garbage in the Wastes," Kent said.

"Most likely. We'll let you know as soon as he answers—or maybe you'll let *us* know if he contacts you first. Until then, you should rest. Let your body recover. If you need anything, just buzz, and one of the nurses will be here in a flash."

Samara smiled and nodded her agreement.

"Thank you," Kent whispered in a raspy voice.

"Of course. Sleep well, Mr. Paige."

Samara and Dr. Rath left the cubicle together. Once they were back in the ER, he blew out a breath and shook his head. "Poor kid."

Samara stopped and stared at him. "What?"

"His dad's dead."

Samara gaped at him. "How do you know that?"

"Because when we couldn't contact him directly, we called his work. He works with the SWMD. They told us that his tracking ID registered his death about an hour ago, somewhere out in the Northern Wastes."

Samara felt the world start to spin around her. She groped for support, and Galen caught her by the arm. "Whoa there, Sam, are you okay?" he asked, his light brown eyes searching hers as he held her up.

"Yes. It's just... my husband works that route."

Galen frowned, his eyes darkening with concern. "That's right... he drives a garbage truck, doesn't he? Is he okay? Have you tried to contact him?"

Samara shook her head. "This is the first I've heard of there being any trouble."

"You should call."

"If he's not in the city, he'll be out of comms and tracking range."

"Out of range for civilians, but not the Guard. They use the satnet. Call at his work. They should have access to it."

JASPER T. SCOTT

"That's true. You're right. Give me a second." She stood up straight, and Galen released her. He crossed his arms and watched while she fished a comm unit out of the front pocket of her uniform. She reached into the wrong one by mistake and rattled the stolen vials of nanobiotics that she'd placed there earlier.

The blood drained from Samara's face. Her eyes darted to Galen, but he hadn't noticed anything. He was checking out the charge nurse's ass as she breezed through the doors to the surgical wing beside them.

Samara reached into her other pocket and retrieved the comm unit. She fitted it into her ear and placed the call to the SWMD with her ARCs. Two long rings trilled in her ear, and then
—

"Solid Waste Management Department, this is Desiree, how may I help you?" a bored voice answered.

Samara explained the situation and gave Clayton's name and ID number. She waited while the woman looked him up in their system.

"Looks like he's on his way back now. He's riding with the tow truck and their escort. They're ten minutes out from the gates. Don't worry, ma'am, I'm reading that his vitals are strong and steady, so it's unlikely that he's been bitten."

Samara's heart rate sped up. "What do you

mean, *it's unlikely that he's been bitten?* You had to send a tow truck out to get him? What *happened?*"

Desiree explained that his shift partner had come back without him after a failed attempt to rescue another driver.

"And you don't know if he's been bitten," Samara repeated.

"No, ma'am."

"Can't you ask them?"

"I could try, but the Guard isn't likely to give us an answer. If he's bit, they'll take him straight to the ascension center for isolation and processing. If not, he'll be brought back here to file an incident report. You could come down to the station and see for yourself if you like."

Samara swallowed thickly and said, "I'll be right there." She ended the call and looked to Galen. "I have to go. Can you get someone to cover for me?"

"Of course. Is your husband okay?"

"I don't know. He's on his way back. I have to go."

Galen nodded. "Get out of here. I'll talk to Bree about covering your shift."

"Thanks." Samara flashed a fading smile before turning and running down the corridor. She whipped past the examination rooms and on to the exit.

Cool early morning air enveloped her as

she stepped through the sliding doors and onto the street in front of the ER. Rather than call for one of the automated *Rydes* that circulated the city day and night, she sprinted straight up the sidewalk, holding the stolen vials of nano-biotics to stop them from clinking together in her smock. As she went, she set SWMD Central as the destination on her ARCs. It was only four blocks away. It would take just as long to wait for a Ryde as it would to get there on foot.

CHAPTER 7

Clayton sat with his hands in his lap, staring at dirty palms while Paul Vanderson, the director of the SWMD, started going through his questions again.

"One more time, Clay. From the beginning. Where were you all night?"

Clay? Since when does the director call me by my first name? Clayton looked up into Paul's squinting black eyes. He had dark skin to match, and a thick midsection that pressed firmly into the edge of his desk whenever he pushed his chair in to reach his computer. Right now, his hands were folded over his belly, and he was leaning back in his chair.

"I told you," Clay began, "I hid in the ruins with the other driver. At dawn, we made a run for his truck, and I took cover in the back while he held off the Dregs."

The director arched a thin eyebrow at him. "So, after trying to rescue Bruce, you decided: the hell with it, I'm just going to save my own skin?"

Clayton frowned. "No. We were supposed

to get in the back together, but there wasn't enough time. Maybe if you authorized remote activation of the haulers, Bruce would still be alive right now."

Paul smiled thinly and spread his hands. "You know that isn't my call to make. The Guard ordered me to remove ARC control after that incident in the Wastes last year. I can't restore the functionality without their permission. I answer to the Chimeras just like everyone else."

Clayton blew out a breath and looked away, out the third-floor window of the director's office. The ascension center was visible from here, a stark black edifice with no windows that covered four city blocks. It was rounded and dome-shaped at the bottom, and rose to a height of fifteen stories at the zenith. Four elevator shafts, leaning in at fifteen degree angles, shot up from each of the corners to support a broad, flat landing platform thirty floors above the top of the dome. The sun shone golden between those pillars, steadily rising in the pale blue sky.

"Are we done here?" Clayton asked, sensing a lull in the interrogation. He dragged his eyes back to the director to see the man watching him with squinty-eyed interest.

"Almost," Paul said. "I have to make sure I get everything straight for my report to the Guard. You know how they are. Sticklers for details."

"Yes," Clayton said, a muscle jerking in his cheek. "I do know."

"While you were with Bruce Paige, did you have a chance to speak with the man?"

"Not really, no."

"You were with him all night, and you didn't talk at all? About anything?"

Clayton slowly shook his head. "We took turns keeping watch. Why?"

Paul held Clayton's gaze for several seconds without blinking or even moving. Something seemed to click behind his eyes, and he heaved his massive shoulders. "Because Bruce Paige has been under surveillance by the Guard for the past month. He was a suspected member of the resistance, and we've been tracking him to find their hideout."

Clayton widened his eyes and dropped his jaw by half an inch. "I had no idea. Did you learn anything from him?"

Paul smiled thinly. "Not much. That's why I'm asking if he might have said anything to you... or if you saw anything while you were with him."

Clayton shook his head again. "No, sir. He wasn't much of a talker. And like I said, we hid in the ruins, so there wasn't much to see."

"Yes. Amazing that you managed to find a place that was safe enough to hide from the Dregs. You must have barricaded yourselves in very well."

"Well, that's the other reason we didn't talk. As you know, the Dregs have excellent hearing."

"That they do," Paul agreed. "Thank you, Mr. Cross. That will be all."

So now I'm Mr. Cross again, Clayton thought as he rose from his chair and headed for the door.

* * *

"Clay!" Samara cried as she ran down the aisle between cubicles on the administrative level. Her hand was still in her pocket, muffling the sound of nanobiotic vial clinking together. Clayton's eyes widened at the sight of her. They collided and she wrapped her arms around him in a fierce hug. "I was so worried! Why didn't you send me a message when you reached the city?"

Clayton withdrew with a grimace. "I didn't want to worry you. How did you find out there was trouble?"

"We had a patient who was the son of a driver who died in the Wastes this morning. I got worried, so I called here, and they told me what happened."

Clayton's face paled. "The son of... what was his name?"

"Kent Paige."

"Shit. Does he know about his father?"

Samara shook her head. "No. Not yet."

Clayton let out a slow breath and ran his hands through wavy, sweat-matted black hair.

"What about you?" Samara asked, her eyes flicking up and down, scanning him from head to toe.

"I'm fine."

Samara felt heat rising in her cheeks, and her eyes began to sting. She bit her lower lip to keep the tears from falling. "You can't keep risking your life like this."

A few people looked up from their desks, peering over the tops of their cubicles to listen in.

Clayton appeared to notice the scrutiny of a freckle-faced woman with fiery red hair sitting in the cubicle beside them. "Eyes on your own business, Mrs. Dempsey!"

The woman started at the sound of his voice, and her head snapped back to the front, her ARCs already glowing with the light of administrative data that only she could see.

Clayton grabbed Samara's hand and pulled her briskly down the aisle, back toward the elevators she'd come up a moment ago.

Once they were inside, she tried again, more softly now: "We're about to have a child, Clay. You need to be there for her. Paige's son will have to grow up without his father. Do you want that for our daughter?"

"Obviously not," he replied as the elevator began dropping down to the ground floor. "But it's good pay, Sam. How are we supposed to raise a kid on less?"

"We can get by on less. All of the basics are already provided for us. What else do we need?" she asked, her eyes searching his.

"Maybe I want more than just the basics for Pandora."

"Pandora?" Samara asked, giving her head a slight shake. Then a smile broke through the swirling cloud of worry that seemed to be suffocating her. "You've been thinking about names."

"I guess I have," Clayton admitted.

"I love it. We could call her Panda for short."

Clayton's lips twitched into a brief smile just as the elevator dinged open. "Come on." He tugged on her arm, pulling her out with him. "We're going to be late for your first appointment."

CHAPTER 8

"**S**hould we get a Ryde?" Samara asked as they reached the front steps of SWMD Central.

Clayton took a moment to respond. He was still thinking about what Samara had said. Driving haulers *was* dangerous. Maybe it wasn't enough for him to quit working with the resistance. Maybe he needed to find a new job as well.

"Clay? A Ryde?" Samara prompted.

"No, let's walk. I could use the fresh air."

They descended the stairs together and started down the sidewalk. The ascension center towered over the mid-rise apartments and converted office buildings that rose like walls on either side of the street. New Houston was primarily devoted to residences, and the actual jobs in the city were more make-work than anything really useful. The SWMD was a great example of that. The entire city employed barely twenty drivers, but the admin levels at the central office employed over forty people in the business of warming chairs.

Consumerism was dead and gone. Capitalism, likewise. The occupation had brought back communism in a big way. All of the basic necessities were given out freely from dispensaries around the city: food, medication, clothes... and no one had to pay for rent or utilities. Wages were modest and went toward recreation and luxuries. The system wasn't really any more successful than it had been in the past, but the threat of summary execution for slacking off did help motivate people to do their jobs. The Kyra didn't care how well Earth's economy was doing. *The slower the better, probably,* Clayton thought. *All they want is our kids. And I've just given them another one.* He glanced at Samara's belly—still flat as a board.

Samara noticed his scrutiny and grabbed his hand to put it over her abdomen. "It's going to be okay."

"You don't know that," he said.

A group of young men in black uniforms with silver piping walked by, coming up from behind them. A few of them eyed Clayton briefly, taking in his SWMD vest before nodding to him and looking away. They were headed in the same direction, on their way to the training academy in the lower levels of the ascension center. The silver trim on their uniforms identified them as being in what used to be Grade 10, or year two of cadet training. It was a kind of boot camp to weed out the weaker kids before exposing them to the virus.

No sense producing more Dregs than they had to. The dropouts became seat warmers and breeders. *Like us,* Clayton thought.

They came to Restoration Park. It was full of dark, leafy trees and bright green grass. Toddlers squealed and laughed as their stay-at-home parents chased them around a playground. Clayton slowed to watch the bustle of activity. A smile crept onto his face as the sun crested over a nearby skyscraper, making him squint.

"It's not all doom and gloom, is it?" Samara said. "We're still alive and free."

Clayton shot her a skeptical look. "Alive yes. Free, not so much."

Before Samara could reply, a man in jeans and a denim jacket ran into him and almost knocked him over.

"Hey!" Clayton snapped, his eyes flashing as the man stepped back. He had long, stringy hair and a dirty, gaunt face with sunken, haunted brown eyes. "Watch where you're going..." Clay added, his voice losing some of its volume as he noticed the man's appearance. No one in the city was technically homeless, so why did this man look like he was?

"Sorry," the man mumbled, and then side-stepped Clayton, brushing shoulders with him as he left. "Left pocket. Put it in," he whispered.

Clayton checked the left pocket of his vest and found a comms piece inside. He frowned and dug a hand into his pants pocket where he remembered putting his personal comms. Suddenly he had two.

"What is it?" Samara asked.

"I don't know," Clayton replied, and then he stuck the new unit in his left ear.

A gruff voice spoke to him just as he did so: "Walk into the park."

Clayton hesitated, glancing at his wife. "Who is it?" she asked.

"Ah..."

"Don't worry; she's with us," the voice added.

That sent Clayton rocking back on his heels. Us *who?* The resistance? That would mean that Samara was working for them, too. He'd been trying to keep her safe by keeping her out of it, but maybe she'd been doing the same thing with him.

Samara's eyebrows drifted up, her blue eyes widening. "Is everything okay?"

He slowly shook his head. "Everything is fine. Let's go for a walk in the park." He grabbed her hand, and tugged her off the sidewalk, up onto the grass.

"What about the appointment?"

"It can wait. We've still got half an hour," Clayton replied, noting that the clock in the top left of his ARCs said it was 9:28 AM.

"Barely," Samara replied.

"Keep walking straight down the path," the

voice in his ear interrupted.

Clayton did as he was told, walking on for five minutes. They passed the playground, then a dense stand of trees, followed by rolling stretches of grass, and then more trees.

"Now what?" Clayton asked.

"Benches by the pond on your left."

Clayton spotted the benches, half-hidden by the trees along the edge of a small pond. There was a man with short blond hair wearing a blue suit sitting on one of the benches. He was breaking off pieces of bread from a loaf in a brown paper bag and tossing the bits to the ducks in the pond.

Samara's grip on Clayton's hand tightened as he left the path and angled for those benches. "Clay, who are you talking to?" she asked in a hushed voice.

"A mutual friend, apparently," he replied.

They rounded the trees and approached the benches. The man turned his head and looked up at them with a smile widening above his chiseled jaw. His piercing blue eyes danced with amusement, and Clayton almost fell over backward.

"It's good to see you again, Captain Cross," the man on the bench said as he reached up and removed the comms piece from his ear.

"Likewise, Richard," Clayton managed, still unable to believe his eyes.

"What are you doing here?" Samara demanded, still speaking in a hushed voice.

Clayton's eyes snapped to her. "You two know each other?"

"Barely," Samara replied.

"Don't be so modest," Richard said. "You're one of my most valuable operatives."

All this time, Samara had been an operative for the resistance. And apparently, Ambassador Richard Morgan was her handler. Clayton had lost track of Richard in the year since they'd returned to Earth together. He'd half suspected that Admiral Reed might have had him executed. There'd never been much love lost between Richard and his Chimeran daughter, but maybe he'd been wrong about that.

The former ambassador gestured to the bench beside his. "Have a seat, Clayton. We need to talk about tonight."

CHAPTER 9

"**H**ere," Richard passed his brown paper bag to Clayton. "Take a look inside."

Clayton peered into the bag, past the small chunk of bread near the opening. At the bottom were several small devices. Clayton reached in and pulled the first one out. It was a vial of clear liquid with a gray lid.

"What is it?"

"Nanites. Programmable," Richard explained. "Once swallowed they'll make their way to your brain. There they'll interact with your ARCs and your neural implant, allowing you to erase biological memories and copy them to digital storage. It keeps our secrets safe in case you're ever captured."

"This isn't our tech..." Clayton said slowly.

"No. It's Kyron."

"How did you get...?"

"The less you know about it the better," Richard said. "Check the bag again."

Clayton did, and this time he pulled out a black circle no bigger than the tip of his thumb. "What is it?"

"A signal blocker and spoofer. It attaches to the skin above your ID implant. Soon as you apply it, you'll vanish from their tracking system."

Clayton rolled up his sleeve and turned over his arm to find the blinking green light of his ID implant shining through the skin on the underside of his wrist. ID implants had been common throughout the Union before the occupation, but these were the Kyra version: they didn't just keep track of people and their money. They could also be used to remotely kill a person with deadly toxins.

"If I vanish, they'll see it and suspect that I tampered with my implant," Clayton pointed out.

"Put it over your implant and then twist off the top of the device. It comes apart in the middle."

The disk felt sticky and rough to the touch —self-adhering with microscopic hooks. Clayton placed it over the skin on the underside of his wrist and then twisted. The top came off easily, and the bottom vanished against his skin. Kyra cloaking tech.

Samara gasped, and Clayton shook his head.

"Where did you get this..." Clayton whispered.

"Again, the less you know, the better," Richard replied.

Clayton studied the top half of the signal blocker in his palm. It was blinking green, just like an ID implant.

"That is now broadcasting your tracking signal and a fake version of your vitals," Richard said. "It won't move around on its own, though, so its best to use it while you're supposed to be asleep. Remember to put the two halves back together before you remove the signal blocker, or else you'll suddenly be broadcasting two tracking signals. Finally, the last item is the one you're already wearing. A secure comm line to me, your handler."

"Why are you giving me all of this?" Clayton asked. Suddenly he was afraid that his plan to leave the resistance was about to make a sharp 180-degree turn.

"Because Bruce Paige and his partner are both dead. That means you're getting a promotion. And you're going to need that equipment for the op we're pulling tonight."

"I can't do it without Paige," Clayton replied. "My co-driver will report me if he sees anything suspicious."

"Not if he's unconscious," Morgan replied, reaching into one of the front pockets of his suit and fishing out another stoppered vial of clear liquid, this one with a blue lid.

Clayton frowned.

"Wait for your last stop, then get him a coffee and pour it in. He'll sleep through the rest of your shift."

"What are they getting you to do?" Samara asked.

Clayton glanced at her, then shook his head and nodded to Richard. "Fine. I'll do it."

"You'd better. We're counting on you. Long live the Union," Richard added in a whisper as he rose from the bench and left him and Samara alone.

"All this time you've been working for them?" Samara whispered. "Why didn't you say something?"

"The same reason you didn't," he replied, pocketing the two vials and the dime-sized signal blocker and spoofer before rising to his feet. He held out a hand to Samara. She took it and stood up from the bench. "We'd better go back to our apartment before we go to your appointment."

"There isn't enough time," Samara objected.

"I can't take these things in there. The scanners will pick them up. I'll go drop them off and then catch up to you at the center."

Samara's face jerked into a sudden grimace, as if she'd just remembered something important. Reaching into her doctor's coat, she withdrew a pair of long, skinny vials with a clear fluid in them. "Take these, too," she said, folding his hand over them.

"What are they?"

"Meds for our friends."

Clayton snorted. "Be careful. You know I don't like you walking around on your own."

"It's just two more blocks. I'll be fine," Samara said.

He nodded and dropped a quick kiss on her lips before turning and running back the way they'd come.

"Don't miss the appointment!" Samara called after him.

CHAPTER 10

Before Samara even reached the ascension center, she realized something was wrong. Chimeras in glossy black armor stood in a line barring the walkway to the entrance of the facility. Their faces were all hidden by matching helmets, and a crowd of at least a hundred human civilians had gathered there—most of them teenagers wearing black cadet uniforms with varying colors of trim. The ones who'd walked by her and Clayton were there as well, all of them here to continue their training.

"What's going on?" one of the kids asked.

"The center is closed for today," one of the Chimeras replied in a deep, husky voice.

Samara pushed through to the front of the crowd. "Excuse me," she said, waving a hand around above her head to get the guards' attention. "I have an appointment. A prenatal check-up. I'm actually five minutes late. Is it just the training academy that's closed?"

Several faceless black helmets and glossy visors shifted to her, and the nearest Chimera flexed a hand restlessly on the grip of a repeating laser rifle. "The center is closed. Come back tomorrow."

Samara frowned. "May I ask why?"

The entrance slid open, and a group of eight Chimeran soldiers came striding out. The ones barring the walkway parted to let them pass, and then the crowd parted, too. The Chimera who'd spoken turned to face one of the newcomers. A growling, hissing language passed between the Chimeras. They were speaking in Kyro. Samara didn't understand a word of it, but some of the cadets began whispering, and Samara overheard snatches of what they said.

"...sweeping for a bomb," a boy beside her muttered.

"Planted by the resistance?" another asked.

"Who else?" the first one replied.

The Chimeras grew suddenly silent and then turned to look at the crowd. Samara could imagine their crimson eyes narrowing inside their helmets.

"Disperse and go home!" one of the Chimeras said. "This is your last warning."

The crowd began flowing away to all sides, muttering and whispering amongst themselves. Samara retreated with them. As she did so, she fitted her comms piece to her ear and used her ARCs to call Clayton.

"Sam?" he asked, sounding out of breath. "Is everything all right?"

"The center is closed," she replied. "I'm on

my way home."

"Closed?" Clayton echoed. "It's never closed. Did the Chimeras say why?"

"No, but I overheard some of the cadets talking about a bomb."

"A bomb at the center?" A rush of static came over the comms as he exhaled. "The resistance is going too far. The centers are full of kids and pregnant women. They may as well bomb an apartment building!"

"At least no one got hurt," Samara replied.

"What about your appointment?"

"They told me to come back tomorrow."

"Will it be safe by tomorrow?" Clayton asked.

"I guess they won't open the center if it's not."

"You mean you *hope* they won't," Clayton replied.

"It's probably just a false alarm," Samara added. "Anyway, I'm heading back. I'll be home soon."

"Call a Ryde this time. I don't want you walking," Clayton said.

"I will."

"Good. See you soon, Sam."

She ended the call and then used her ARCs to summon a Ryde. A street map appeared in the top right corner of her contacts, indicating the nearest pickup point with a flashing red dot. It was about twenty feet away. A group of cadets already stood there waiting, their uniforms decorated with silver, gold, and red trim. The pickup point looked a lot like an old bus stop, with concrete benches under a roof and metal pillars rising between the benches. Samara went to stand with the kids and wait.

The cadets were all chatting loudly about the implications of a bomb in the ascension center.

"How did the resistance smuggle explosives past the scanners?" one of them asked loudly.

"And where did they even get the explosives?" another asked.

"We were there! If the Chimeras hadn't found it, we could be dead right now!" a girl added.

"Fucking terrorists," another boy said.

Moments later, their Ryde came whistling around the corner and down the street, floating a few feet above the ground on a soundless cushion of grav engines. It was a large, armored transport with sloping black sides, small windows, and a gun turret on the top. It looked more like some futuristic tank than a public transport, but it had obviously been re-purposed after the invasion. Maybe this was an older model that the Kyra didn't need for their war.

A narrow door in the middle of the transport slid open, and the Ryde dropped down closer to the ground. The cadets surged forward, flowing into the cramped confines of the vehicle. Samara pushed and elbowed her way on board with them, finding a seat along one side of the transport. The cadets kept coming until they ran out of room and had to stand. By the time the door slid shut and the transport glided off, there were at least twenty kids on board. Sweat and sharply-scented soap mingled together in the close confines of the transport, making Samara's nose itch.

The kids' conversations were even louder inside the Ryde than they had been at the pickup point. Raucous laughter and shouted conversations flew back and forth, making her ears ring. These kids were behaving as if they were going on a field trip. Not at all what Samara would have expected from the survivors of a bomb scare, but maybe that's all this was —a bluff to scare people away from the centers and disrupt Kyron recruitment. Surely the resistance wouldn't target children and pregnant mothers with an actual bomb.

All of a minute later, the Ryde stopped to let off the first group of kids. The ones in the aisle had to squeeze over into the laps of those who were seated to let the others out. A chubby boy with curly black hair and the unmarked black uniform of a 1st-year cadet fell into her lap with a grin. Samara grimaced as her legs immediately began to ache under his weight. She gave a strained smile and looked away, out the small window beside her. She eyed the street map on her ARCs. Her stop was marked by a flashing red dot with the number five in the center of it. Four numbered blue dots marked the rest of the stops. Hers was dead last.

The transport glided off again, but the boy in her lap took a few extra seconds to return to his place in the aisle. Samara glared briefly at him, then dragged her eyes back to the fore and began massaging her temples to keep a sudden, stabbing headache at bay. She was exhausted. She'd been up all night working, and that scare with Clayton had sapped all of her remaining strength. Now all she wanted to do was get home, eat, shower, and crawl into bed before she had to do it all over again for her next shift.

It was the same thing every day, over and over, without variance or reprieve. There weren't a lot of options for entertainment: no holovids or holostreams to watch. No more social media. Sometimes Samara envied the people who'd been born after the invasion. She had been brought back as a clone, so she still remembered how everything had been before the Kyra. Clayton did, too.

Sometimes Samara wondered if the Chimeras had it any better. There were plenty of rumors that they enjoyed luxuries that humans didn't have access to: better pay scales, for one, and access to Kyron culture and entertainment—as well as the ability to travel beyond Earth. But Samara wondered what a violent, sadistic race like the Kyra would have to offer in terms of culture and tourism. Maybe not much.

No, things were still better down here. Trading her humanity for second-class citizenship in a war-driven society was not a step up. Besides, there were no guarantees that anyone would become a Chimera. The screening tests were far from accurate, and according to the resistance, the centers produced just as many Dregs as they did Chimeras.

Samara glanced around the inside of the transport as it stopped again to let off more cadets. They were still joking and laughing with each other, all of them eager to finish their training so that they could ascend. Samara shuddered to think that fully half of them would turn into violent, mindless beasts. She was tempted to warn them, to tell them what she knew. But saying something like that out loud would only get her killed. And they wouldn't believe her anyway.

The Kyra were nothing if not smart. They took over the schools and set up the cadet training programs for the older kids, focusing all of their efforts on indoctrinating children to fight for them. Rather than force people to ascend, they waited for the kids to volunteer.

Better a willing soldier than a reluctant conscript. Parents were rarely able to dissuade their children from pledging their lives to the Guard.

Samara winced, and she noticed that her hands were clutching her abdomen. *How are we going to stop you from going down that road?* she wondered. Even if they did manage to convince her not to join her peers, Pandora was a girl, so she would only bear more soldiers for the Kyron Federation.

One way or another, we all serve them, Samara realized. *Whether we like it or not.*

CHAPTER 11

Clayton's eyes cracked open to stare up at a ceiling, still fuzzy with darkness. His neural implant had just released a burst of cortisol to wake him. He lay there for a moment, trying to coax himself out of bed. His head felt thick, his body heavy and aching in a dozen different places from the narrow escape and the failed rescue of the night before.

Bedroom lights to 25%, he thought, and the bedroom lights swelled to a pale golden hue.

A groan sounded beside him, and Samara dragged a pillow over her eyes. "It can't be time to get up already," she said.

"No point fighting it," he replied. Her implant would have released the same burst of cortisol as his.

Clayton pulled the pillow away and began kissing her lips, then her neck... trailing his hands down.

"Mmmmm, what's the occasion?" she mumbled through a sigh.

Clayton stopped and looked up with a wry smile. "Well, you're already pregnant, so..."

Samara snorted and pushed him away. "We don't have time for fun and games."

"We never do," Clayton replied, but there wasn't any hint of an accusation in his tone. He looked away, to the door. "We'd better get dressed. We have a long night ahead of us." He glanced back at Samara to see her blue eyes wide and glassy with fear. Silence lingered between them as they both remembered what he was supposed to do for the resistance tonight. Samara didn't know the details, because it was too risky for them to talk about it, but she knew it would be dangerous.

She reached up and pulled him back down. Her lips closing over his and her hands trailing lightly down his back.

They both gave into the moment this time, and soon Samara's nails were digging into his back.

They showered together, running the soap over each other's bodies and kissing each other as hot water poured over them.

Clayton had lost her a lifetime ago only to get her back just last year, and now he'd learned that she was risking her life on a daily basis. It was enough to drive anyone mad. She felt so tenuous and fragile in his hands, like a ghost or a dream. He couldn't lose her again.

He withdrew from Samara's lips and leaned in close to her ear, trusting the sound of the running water to conceal a whisper: "I'm done after tonight, Sam, and so are you. Promise me. We have to think about Pandora now."

They stared into each other's eyes. Steam swirled between them, and droplets of water beaded on Sam's eyelashes, clinging briefly before they fell into deep, sapphire pools. "And you'll find a safer job?"

He nodded. "This is my last run."

"Then I promise."

Clayton kissed her again, tasting the salt of tears in the water running off her cheeks. But to him, they were happy tears. Relief spread through him like a wave, and a world of tension left his body. Ever since coming home to find Earth decimated and occupied by a hostile alien force that *he* had led there—however indirectly—he'd been carrying that guilt like a noose around his neck. He'd felt obligated to fight them, to resist in any way he could. But now he'd finally come to realize what most people already knew: resistance was pointless.

The clincher was what Sam had told him this morning: that bomb scare at the center. He wouldn't risk losing Sam again for a cause as bankrupt as that. Anyone who would target women and children in a war wasn't on the right side of it. Scare tactic or not, Clayton was done. He withdrew from Samara and placed his hand on her stomach.

Samara smiled, adding her hand there and lacing her fingers through his. A rare sparkle entered her eyes, and he smiled back.

* * *

Clayton opened the driver's side of the hauler and climbed up into an old, cracked leather seat.

On the other side, his partner, Alan, grunted as he used the handrails to pull himself up. He settled into the co-driver's seat and straightened his old, ratty baseball cap. "Hey man, about last night..." Alan began.

"Forget about it." Clayton shook his head as he put the hauler into reverse. Keeping an eye on the rear and side-view screens hanging above the dash, he began backing out of the garage at SWMD Central.

Before long, they were rolling down the streets of New Houston, stopping in all of the alleys to empty the dumpsters between buildings. Silence filled the cab of the hauler, thick as a wall between him and Al. *I guess the bastard feels guilty for leaving me behind,* Clayton thought. *Good.*

Flickering streetlights shone orange through the windows as they rolled by, and Clayton marveled for the umpteenth time since returning to Earth at how familiar everything still was after the occupation. "You know if it weren't for the Wastes and the walls around the city, I could almost imagine that I'm back in the 21st century," Clayton said.

Al snorted. "Yeah, well I was born in

the 22nd century, and this sure as shit isn't what I remember." He gestured vaguely to the blank black sky through the windshield of the hauler. "See that?"

Clayton shook his head. "No, what?"

"Exactly. The sky used to be choked with traffic! Glowing lines of it racing between towers, some of them ten times as high as the pitiful buildings you see here. We had just as many cars in the air as we had on the ground." Al dropped his chubby hand and pointed to the deserted sidewalks and empty streets. "We had people and bots walking around, all hours of the night. And that's another thing, every family had at least one bot. You see any bots walking around these days?"

Clayton slowly shook his head. He hadn't been on Earth when that paradigm shift had come.

"Damn straight. Not a one," Al replied. "The Kyra came and wiped them out faster than they did us. To this day, I haven't seen them using anything near the level of automation that you'd expect from a race as advanced as theirs. They've got those self-driving transports we call *Rydes*, but that's about it. Hell, even when they landed their mega-factories and armies of alien Chimeras to help us rebuild, they didn't use bots for any of it.

"We were nowhere near their level of advancement when they arrived, but we had as many bots as we did people, and I'll tell you what, it was paradise! People didn't even have to work anymore. Just claim their UBI and call it a day, go back into the metaverse and their digital worlds. Now look at where we are! We all have to work in shit jobs, there's no real entertainment, and we're all basically making the same pittance. Your wife's a nurse, right?"

Clayton nodded.

"And she makes, what? Five hundred credits a month?"

"About that, yeah."

"And we make six hundred. But what's a doctor make? Seven-fifty? Eight hundred at best." Al just shook his head. "They fixed the rich-poor gap by making everyone dirt poor."

"I don't think they care about us having luxuries," Clayton replied.

Alan took a moment to operate the robotic arm on his side of the truck and empty another dumpster. "Which brings me back to my point: life is shit since the Kyra came."

"So, what's the alternative?" Clayton asked, deciding to pull at that thread as he drove on to the next dumpster.

"There is no fucking alternative! That's the problem. The resistance is a joke. The occupation isn't going away, no matter how many farms and supply trucks they raid."

"You could always ascend."

Al's head slowly turned, his expression

frozen in disbelief. "And get myself shot to hell in a war? No thanks. I haven't lived for over a century just to become cannon fodder now."

"They might make you a worker instead of a soldier. You could wind up working off your term of enlistment in one of their factories."

"Have you ever heard of a Chimera working off all eight years in a factory?" Al challenged.

Clayton shrugged. "No, but I'm sure there's plenty of them. The Kyra need laborers to build their ships just as much as they need soldiers to fill them."

"You want to know what I think? I don't think there is a *term* of enlistment. I think the term is life, and when your eight years are almost up, they send you to the front lines to make sure you see it through."

Clayton secretly suspected the same thing. Why go to all of the trouble to occupy alien worlds and breed soldiers and workers from their people if the Kyra were just going to let them go after eight short years? It seemed more likely that that was another lie, just another part of the propaganda that they fed to cadets at the ascension centers.

Clayton sighed. "You want my advice?"

"No, but something tells me you're gonna give it to me anyway."

"Settle down and make a life with someone. Find joy in the little things."

Alan's expression turned contemplative,

his brow furrowing in thought. He raised his baseball cap and scratched at the greasy hair underneath, pulling dark strands of it from the ponytail behind his head.

"Well, shit... I never thought of that..." he put the cap back on. "In all this time, after five wives and ten kids, I never considered that maybe what I should do is go settle down with wife number six and have me another couple of stupid brats!" Alan nodded to himself.

Clayton focused on driving to the next dumpster. He wondered if that was how he would feel when he reached Al's age: full of bitterness and impotent rage. He'd already come to the conclusion that the resistance wasn't worth it. So what was left? Have ten kids like Al and watch them all sign up to become Chimeras, with fully half of them turning into Dregs along the way? He shuddered to think of Pandora turning into one of those mindless monsters.

They ran the rest of their route in silence, and Clayton sank further into his thoughts. Immortality used to be a dream, but that was back when people had led rich and fulfilling lives. Now all of that was gone and they were just marking time between raising conscripts and serving as workers for the Kyra.

"Time to head back out," Al said, and Clayton noticed that the truck's sensors were reading a full load.

JASPER T. SCOTT

Al reached around behind him to pull the laser rifle off the rack above his headrest. "You ready, hotshot?"

"We can fit in one more stop," Clayton replied.

"Are you crazy? We won't be able to close the hatch if we do that, and we don't need any Dregs smelling that shit and jumping in the back."

"The arena. It's on the way," Clayton insisted. "The dumpsters are going to be empty, anyway. There haven't been any challenges or executions since the weekend."

"Fine, but I'm gonna say I told you so when that hatch gets jammed halfway open."

"Sure, you do that." Clayton drove on down the street, passing a hovering black Ryde with dim blue headlights that somehow reached farther than the bright white ones of his hauler.

Down at the end of the street, about four blocks away, the thick concrete walls of the city rose to impressive heights. Chimeras stood on top, keeping watch, and dim blue floodlights shone down. The northern gates weren't far from here.

Feeling suddenly cold with anticipation of what was to come, Clayton glanced at Al. He still had to drug the man before he could pick up that defector for the resistance.

He scanned both sides of the street, looking for a place to stop and grab a coffee. He had the vial with the sedative in his pants pocket along with the signal blocker and spoofer that Richard had given him.

Driving straight through a four-way stop, Clayton spotted the telltale glow of a blue sign that read: *Kyron Dispensary. Open 24 Hours.* A pair of Chimeras stood guard outside the doors, armored, but not wearing their helmets, their cranial stalks twitching restlessly as they listened to sounds that only they could hear.

Clayton pressed on the brakes, easing to a stop in front of the dispensary.

"You want something? I'm going to get a coffee."

Al shook his head. "Nah. I've lost my appetite."

"How about a donut? They've got you on a diet, right? My treat."

Alan grinned. "Twist my arm. All right, fine!"

"And a coffee?" Clayton asked. "Got to have something to wash it down with."

Al snorted. "Yeah, why not."

Clayton popped his door open and jumped down to the sidewalk. He strode up to the doors of the dispensary, nodding to the Chimeras as the doors slid open for him.

Squinting red eyes tracked him as he went in, but neither guard spoke.

The aisles inside the dispensary were crowded with cans and packets of food, just like the aisles of supermarkets that he remembered from the 21st century. What was different was that when he looked at the products with his ARCs he only got the most basic information: Bread. Beans. Rice. Sugar. Flour. He couldn't delve deeper to get the marketing spiels from companies that produced the products, or the nutritional information. And there wasn't even close to the same variety as there used to be.

Clayton stalked down the aisles to the cafeteria at the end. A human woman with dark skin and heavy-lidded eyes stood there, blinking slowly at him.

"Can I help you?" she asked after a moment.

Her name flashed up on Clayton's ARCs: *Louise Harmon.*

"Two coffees and two of those donuts over there," Clayton said, pointing over her shoulder to pastries and breads lying under warming lamps in paper-lined steel baskets.

Louise glanced behind her, then back. "You paying with rations or credits?"

Clayton took a second to think about it. Rations and credits were basically interchangeable, but rations were worth twice as much when they were spent on basic necessities like food and clothing. "Rations," Clayton decided.

"That'll be four and a half, plus another two for the cups."

Clayton nodded his agreement. He hadn't brought coffee cups from home or the station because if he had, Al might have noticed that he'd been planning this stop.

Louise picked up a small handheld scanner that looked like a miniature hair trimmer with a bar of blue light shining where the blades should have been.

Clayton held out his right arm, turning it over to reveal the blinking green light of the ID implant in his wrist.

Louise pressed a button on the scanner, and the light brightened, illuminating his wrist in a wash of blue light as she scanned the implant. Numbers flashed up on her ARCs, clouding her dark eyes with brightly-glowing displays. A reciprocal display appeared before Clayton's eyes, listing the items he'd purchased and the total he'd been charged. He was down to a hundred and ninety-five and a half rations now.

The glowing screens vanished from Clayton's and Louise's eyes at the same time, and she turned away to dispense a pair of plain, black coffees into reusable white cups. She slid them across the counter and then went for the donuts—the plain sugar-crusted variety. Louise handed them over next in a brown paper bag. Yet another familiar artifact from his world.

"Thank you," he said.

Much of it was mimicry. The Kyra had put people in interrogation rooms to learn about human society, and then they'd duplicated as much of it as they'd seen fit. *Enough to keep us comfortable, but not enough to empower us,* Clayton thought.

He grabbed the bag and pinned it under his arm, then nodded to the coffees on the counter.

"Can I get some sugar for those?" he asked.

Louise fixed him with a look of strained patience. "You asked for two coffees. That's how they come. You want sugar and milk, that's going to be another half a ration."

"Never mind." Some dispensaries were more generous than others. This obviously wasn't one of them.

He grabbed the cups and spun away, heading for the doors. On his way out, he lingered in one of the aisles, pretending to check out some of the fresh produce—ears of corn and green apples. While he was there, he set the coffees down on a shelf beside packets of sliced bread and quickly fished the vial of sedative from his pocket. Making sure it was the one with the blue lid, he pulled out the stopper and emptied the contents into one of the coffees.

Slipping the vial back into his pocket, he picked up both coffees, making sure to remember which was which, and made his way back

122

outside. The air was cool, sticky and humid, and perfumed with the stench of garbage emanating from the hauler parked out front.

Shifting both coffees awkwardly to one hand and clenching the bag of donuts between his teeth, Clayton pulled open the driver's side door and climbed back up. "Here you go," he said as he handed the drugged coffee to Al. He pulled the door shut behind him and then passed over the bag of donuts.

Al almost tore it open in his hurry to get at the contents. He stuck his nose inside and inhaled. "Mmmmm. Maybe you're right."

Clayton arched an eyebrow at him. "About?"

"Finding joy in the little things." Al dug a donut out of the bag and took a giant bite before swilling it down with a steaming gulp of coffee.

Clayton set his coffee in the drink holder beside him and stuck the hauler back into drive, rolling on down the street. He turned down the first side street before reaching the city walls to drive on to the arena.

"Oh, yeah... so gooood," Al mumbled between bites of his donut.

Clayton smiled faintly at his partner's contented munching sounds. More coffee washed down several more bites, and soon Al's eyes were sinking shut.

"Did you get me decaf or something?"

"You know, I didn't specify. Maybe the woman just figured since it's so late at night..."

"Goddammit." Al kept shaking himself awake and muttering about not sleeping well enough last night, only to sink back into a slumber once more. Soon his double chin was resting on his chest, and he was snoring softly with his faded red baseball cap shading his eyes from the strobing blue light of passing streetlights.

"Sweet dreams, Al," Clayton whispered as he stopped behind the arena and jumped out of the hauler beside the dumpsters. Walking quickly over to the nearest one, he glanced around to make sure that no one was watching before grabbing the edge of the dumpster and pulling himself up for a look inside. It was only half full. There was the usual collection of garbage bags and junk, but no sign of a defector.

"Hello?" Clayton whispered.

No reply.

Looking away, he peered down the street to the next dumpster in line. There were six of them behind the arena. Cursing under his breath, Clayton ran back to his hauler and jumped in. He drove on to the next one, and then jumped out again to repeat the process. Peering in once more, he found it almost entirely empty. There wasn't any point in calling out to see if someone was hiding between the two solitary bags of garbage inside.

He jumped down and turned back to his hauler, grinding broken wedges of glass under his boots.

But just as he was reaching for the handle to his door, he heard a voice. A *familiar* voice.

"Captain Cross?"

He spun around to see someone stepping out of the shadows behind the dumpster. It was a tall woman with long brown hair that shone like cobalt in the glow of the street-lights. As she stepped into the light, the shadows fell away from her face, and Clayton's jaw dropped.

"Dr. Reed?" It was Dr. Lori Reed, Admiral Keera Reed's mother, and one of his two first contact specialists from the *Forerunner.*

Clayton took a quick step toward her. "You're the defector?" he whispered sharply.

She nodded.

"I thought you were on their side." Ever since she and Keera had been abducted from his ship by the Kyra, Lori been in captivity with her daughter. She'd spent almost a century living amongst the enemy, an apparent exception to their rule that only Chimeras could leave Earth.

"I was," she confirmed. "Not anymore."

Clayton looked about quickly, wondering if this was some kind of trap. "Why change sides now?"

"I used to think we could co-exist. Not so

long ago, we used to treat people differently just because of the color of their skin. I thought maybe there would be a peaceful path to emancipation and equality." Lori swallowed thickly. "But I was wrong. It's been almost ninety years since they arrived, and things are only getting worse. I need to do something before it's too late."

"Do something? Like what?"

A resounding metallic *bang* sounded from somewhere deeper in the alley. Lori flinched and fled back into the shadows. A moment later, Clayton saw a small, four-legged creature jumping down from one of the dumpsters.

"It was just a stray cat," he whispered, waving her back over.

Lori came creeping into the light again, her eyes wide and darting. He led her around to the open hatch of the hauler and helped her climb up on the robotic arm and into the back.

"Don't make any noise back here," Clayton warned as she burrowed between the garbage bags to conceal herself. "We still have to get past the gates."

"Don't worry," she replied. "I know what's at stake."

Clayton considered that with a knitted brow as he climbed back into the driver's seat. Sergeant Sutton had claimed that she was critically important to the resistance, but why?

Intel? he wondered. After spending so much

time amongst the enemy, she had to have plenty of information about them.

CHAPTER 12

Clayton drove to the city gates with Al still fast asleep in the co-driver's seat. He poked Al in the ribs as a pair of Chimeras walked over to their vehicle. "Wake up!" Clayton whispered.

"Wha...?"

"Wake up! We're at the gates!"

"Oh. Right. Sorry. Yeah, I'm awake." He rubbed his eyes and sat up a few inches straighter in his seat.

Clayton lowered his window and nodded to the Chimeran Sergeant who came up to his side of the vehicle. Red eyes tracked up to his.

"First run of the night?" the Chimera asked in a gruff voice, his nostrils flaring and cranial stalks twitching. The auditory cones at the end of those stalks widened, then narrowed as they honed in on Clayton.

"Yes, sir," Clayton replied.

"What's wrong with your partner?" The Chimera pointed to him.

Clayton glanced back over to see that Al was asleep again.

"He had a rough night," Clayton said through a grimace.

"You should call it in. There's a reason they send you out in pairs. You need a gunner out there."

Clayton smiled. "I don't want to get him into trouble. They might dock his pay, and he needs the credits."

"Your funeral," the Chimera snorted. He produced a scanner from his belt and held it out as he began walking down the length of the hauler.

Clayton's heart hammered in his chest, watching in his side-view mirror as the Chimera scanned the back of his truck with a flickering blue fan of light. He wondered what those scanners could detect, and if they could pick out Lori hiding in the back of the truck among the bags of garbage.

A few tense seconds later, the sergeant came walking back over. He nodded to Clayton and gestured to the guards standing on top of the gatehouse. "You're clear. Safe travels." At that, the heavy metal gates began sliding open, parting in the middle to let the hauler through.

Clayton drove slowly between them with his hands sweating on the wheel. He took a few deep breaths to calm his nerves.

Minutes later, he was cruising down the cracked and broken highway that used to be the I45. The Kyra had patched it up just enough to make it possible for haulers to get out to the dump.

Clayton came to the same old broken-down mech from last night, the pilot's skeleton dangling out; dry, hundred-year-old bones silver with the moon. It stood there like an ancient harbinger to warn travelers away from the Wastes. He swerved wide around it and kept a steady foot on the accelerator. Like before, ruined commercial buildings rose in crumbling, jagged walls, their floors collapsed and piled high with rubble. Old cars and tanks lined the sides of the highway. Darting shadows scurried behind them, fleeing from the light and noise of the hauler's approach.

Those Dregs wouldn't attack unless he stopped or slowed down. They were simple beasts, more aggressive than most, but still just animals. To them, a giant hauler bumping and clanking along was like an elephant to a hungry lion—too much work to attack it unless the opportunity presented itself.

Without Al to make conversation, the drive to the dump was long and eerily quiet. A crescent moon and a bright wash of stars domed the craggy shadows of the Wastes. Before long, scattered clumps of trees began to break through the ruins. After almost ninety years, Mother Nature was well on her way to claiming back the planet.

The crumbling asphalt undulated slowly

under the hauler. Piles of garbage began to crowd the sides of the highway like giant snowdrifts. Here and there, the long, arcing lanes of old highway exits appeared, all of them lined with garbage like everything else.

Yet another mystery: with all of their advanced technology, the Kyra had decided to rebuild Earth's wasteful, throwaway culture instead of building a more sustainable one. It wasn't as bad as it had been, since most of the packaging was biodegradable and would vanish within a decade of lying around. But the cities still produced garbage faster than it could decompose.

A distant cacophony of shrieks and growls interrupted Clayton's thoughts, and a jolt of adrenaline shot through him, reminding him to stay alert. His eyes darted between the screens attached to the truck's various external cameras, checking for signs of Dregs. The night-vision screens were all colored green. Dregs and other hot-blooded creatures would show up as bright white, but for the moment, everything around the hauler was black and green.

"Where are you..." Clayton wondered aloud as he reached into his door-holster for a SWMD-issue plasma pistol. He needed at least one hand free to steer the truck so he couldn't use one of the more powerful automatic laser rifles.

Clayton glanced at Al. His co-driver's rifle was sitting on the floor, pointed up at the roof and rattling against his knees with every bump in the road.

Another shrill cry split the night, much closer now. It was coming from somewhere up ahead.

Clayton lifted his foot off the accelerator just as the hauler came over a gentle rise in the highway. On the other side of it was a herd of at least twenty Dregs. They were all shrieking and growling at each other as they played tug-o-war in the middle of the highway with the bloody carcass of a cow.

Clayton stomped on the brakes and ground to a halt about forty feet from the herd. A few of the monsters looked up with entrails dangling from blood-smeared jaws.

Clayton stared at them, and they squinted back, their red eyes gleaming in the hauler's headlights. Jaws chewed restlessly, and cranial stalks twitched. *Don't do it,* he thought. *Come on, you've got a meal right in front of you...*

A few more of them looked up, and the tug-o-war stopped. Then the remainder of the herd lost interest in the meal at hand and raised their heads with nostrils flaring to sniff at the cloud of putrid air swirling around the hauler.

One of the creatures shrieked, and then fully half of the herd broke away from the cow and charged the hauler.

"Shit!" Clayton threw the vehicle into reverse and hit the accelerator. "Al, wake up, damn it!"

CHAPTER 13

Clayton kept an eye on the rearview screen as he gunned it down the highway. But haulers were slow as hell in reverse, and the Dregs were gaining fast.

A booming knocking sound erupted behind Clayton, and he flinched. The knocking continued, and he realized that it was coming from the back. Lori. What was she doing back there?

Maybe she'd realized they were in trouble. Clayton shot a quick glance at Al, the laser rifle knocking against his knees. Fast asleep. Dregs were bounding after the hauler. Twenty feet away. He estimated thirty seconds or less before they were slashing through his tires with their teeth and claws.

Coming to a snap decision, Clayton stabbed the button to open the back hatch, and then another to lower Al's window. He flicked a switch to disengage the hauler's internal surveillance system. The feeds weren't actively monitored, but he couldn't have someone going back over the footage later to see

Lori sitting inside the cab.

Almost as soon as he'd disengaged the system, the vehicle's comms began trilling with a call from SWMD Central. Clayton cursed under his breath and ignored it. Disengaging the surveillance system must have triggered an alert on their end. He'd have to tamper with it later to make it look like a routine malfunction. First things first: he had to make it out of this alive.

Thunder sounded on the roof as Lori clambered over. A split-second later, she swung down and in through Al's window, landing in his lap. The big man grunted and stirred, but still didn't wake up. *What the hell was in that sedative?* Clayton wondered.

"Need some help?" Lori asked, nodding to the approaching herd of Dregs. She squirmed in Al's lap and snatched his rifle off the floor.

Clayton nodded quickly, his eyes fixed on the screens relaying views from external cameras. He veered sharply around the larger holes and debris in the road, trying not to wreck them against mountains of derelict cars and garbage in the process.

Lori leaned out the side window with Al's rifle. A moment later, he heard the high-pitched whine of the weapon discharging. A bright green laser beam snapped out, and one of the dozen Dregs chasing them fell in midstride. It went limp and rolled, somersaulting several times with its legs and arms flopping lifelessly around it.

The next bolt lanced out, and a second Dreg fell. The others reacted by shrieking angrily and pouring on a burst of speed. They were within reach of the cab now. One of them came alongside the wheel on Clayton's side. He veered suddenly and knocked the Dreg sideways. It screamed as one of its arms got caught under the wheel and snapped like a twig. The creature rolled away, kicking up a sparkling cloud of concrete dust, and lay in a thrashing heap. Lori fired again, and again, taking out two more.

The next Dreg came alongside Clayton's door and reached up to rake its claws through the metal. A piercing screech set Clayton's teeth on edge, and he saw the creature's head appear on the other side of his window, at eye-level with him. It had used its claws like a climber's pick. The creature's chalk-white skin, prominent facial bones, and snaking black veins contrasted sharply with its sunken red eyes. A horror of sharply-pointed, blood-smeared teeth appeared. The Dreg head-butted the window, and it shattered into a million tiny beads of safety glass. Snapping jaws lunged for his throat.

Clayton released the wheel and grabbed the creature's neck to hold it back. One bite and he'd be infected, just like them. "Grab the wheel!" he cried.

Lori grabbed the wheel on Al's side and pulled her rifle back in to aim it one-handed at the Dreg he was struggling with.

"I can't get a clear shot!" she said as she divided her attention between steering around obstacles behind them and aiming at the Dreg.

Clayton gritted his teeth as the monster squirmed in his grasp, trying to reach his arms now instead of his throat. Fortunately, Dregs had relatively flat faces like their human relatives, so there was no snout to bring those snapping teeth any closer.

"Just shoot!" Clayton cried. The Dreg got one of its feet into the broken window frame and pushed, giving itself extra leverage. Rancid breath piled hotly on Clayton's face. His arms shook, the muscles aching as they gave way.

A high-pitched shriek accompanied a burst of emerald light that blinded Clayton. He felt a searing heat on his right hand, and arm, and then the pressing weight of the Dreg vanished, and he was free. He sat blinking furiously to recover his eyesight.

"You're welcome," Lori said.

Another pair of shots sounded with subsequent flashes of light. Clayton's vision returned, and he saw the last two Dregs scattering into the ruins to either side of the highway. Lori dragged the rifle back in and raised her window. She passed the weapon over and said, "I'll drive the rest of the way. You keep us covered out that broken window of yours."

He nodded absently.

Lori was seated awkwardly on the edge of the seat between Al's legs, using his torso as a backrest. She was lucky she had a small frame.

"Where did you learn to shoot like that?" he asked as he cleared broken glass from his window. He noticed as he did so that his right hand and forearm were bright red from the near-miss that had saved his life.

Lori brought the hauler to a gradual stop and then threw it back into drive and hit the accelerator again. "When you've lived as long as I have, you develop a few extra skills along the way."

That's an understatement, Clayton thought. Back when they'd served on the *Forerunner* together, Lori had been a civilian with almost zero experience handling weapons. Now she could fire a Kyron rifle one-handed with better accuracy than he could manage with both his hands free.

"What about the other Dregs?" he asked. "There were at least twenty in the road. They were fighting over a dead cow. Some of them are probably still there."

"If they are, we'll gun it and make them scatter," Lori said. "Your mistake was stopping."

Clayton frowned. She was right. He should

have just pushed through the herd. "You sure you haven't been moonlighting as a hauler driver?" Clayton asked as he propped the rifle's barrel on the side-view mirror to give his aching shoulders a break.

Lori chuckled darkly. "No, I've been too busy playing guinea pig for the Kyra."

Clayton arched an eyebrow at her, but before he could ask about it, the comms began squawking again. Lori's eyes darted from the road to the flashing light on the comms panel. "That'll be central calling," Clayton said. "Don't say a word."

"Wasn't planning to," Lori replied.

Clayton flicked a switch on the panel to accept the transmission, and speakers crackled to life inside the hauler.

"SW27, this is central, we've detected multiple anomalies from your hauler. Your dash cam is offline, and you appear to have reversed course recently. Do you need assistance?"

"Negative, central. The system must be malfunctioning. As for the course-changes, we ran into some Dregs in the road, but we've settled it now."

"I see... very well. Keep us in the loop 27."

"Copy that."

"Central out."

Clayton killed the comms and then looked to Lori. "You've been a guinea pig for the Kyra?"

"I guess you might as well know." She

paused and seemed to take a moment to collect her thoughts. "I'm immune, Clay. It's the only reason they've kept me alive all this time."

"You're immune? Are you sure?"

"How else could I give birth to a Chimera and not become infected myself? Normally, that would cause a miscarriage as I turned into either a Dreg or a Chimera. Instead, the virus infected my unborn child, and I stayed a human."

Clayton marveled at that. "Okay... but what do they want with an immune?"

"An immune who can breed Chimeras, you mean?" Lori asked. She smirked and slowly shook her head. "Right now they have to wall our cities and keep whole divisions of Chimeras down here to guard them from the Dregs. Imagine if we could expand into the Wastes without fear of infection? No more quarantine measures to protect their breed stock, no more ascension centers and schools to indoctrinate our kids. It would mean a whole lot less hassle for them—but not only that: they'd get a 100% conversion rate. Every child born would be a Chimera. And then there's the fact that Keera matured much faster than a human child. The Kyra could quadruple their enlistment rates overnight if they could figure out how to make humans have Chimeran babies."

Clayton sat blinking in shock. "I never thought about that." Up ahead, the highway swept up into a familiar, shallow hill. "Watch out," he said. "We're coming up on that carcass."

"Copy that," Lori replied. Rather than slow down, she gunned the engine. There came a loud, electric *whir* of the engine turning faster, and a clanking rumble from the heavy machine as it bumped and skipped over ancient potholes at forty miles per hour. Lori veered wildly around the worst of them, and jumped through the others. They came over the rise and saw the bloody smear in the middle of the highway where the dead cow and the herd of Dregs had been. But now just a few bloody bones remained, with no sign of either the carcass or the Dregs.

Lori eased off the pedal. "Stay sharp," she warned as they raced toward the blood-soaked patch of asphalt. Clayton divided his attention between the screens of external cameras and the night-vision scope of the laser rifle. He swept the rifle in a narrow arc, tracking it over the shadowy blur of ruins, trees, old cars, and garbage. They rumbled through the blood-soaked patch in the road without incident, and Clayton let out a slow breath, hoping that meant the danger had passed. He rolled his shoulders to work some of the tension out of his muscles.

JASPER T. SCOTT

Al groaned and stirred under Lori's weight. She glanced over her shoulder at him and then eased off his belly to lean over the wheel instead.

Clayton's mind wandered back to the topic they'd been discussing a moment ago. "So the resistance wants you to help them develop a vaccine," he guessed.

Lori nodded.

"That means they want the same thing as the Kyra. What makes them think they'll succeed where the Kyra have failed?"

"They didn't fail. The Kyra already developed a cure that does exactly what the resistance wants it to, but it doesn't give the Kyra what they want."

"Why would they develop that?"

"It was an accident."

Clayton took a break from peering through the rifle's scope to study Lori. She looked smug. "Let me guess: you stole the cure and defected?"

"No, the Kyra destroyed it," she replied. "All I have to offer is myself. But the secret is in my blood. The Resistance can use me to duplicate the Kyra's discovery. And I know enough about what the Kyra were doing to help them figure it out."

"And then what?" Clayton asked.

"Then we'll finally have a way to fight back. We'll inoculate everyone we can. Immunize the world, and the Kyra will have no more use for us."

"Is that a good thing? If we're no longer any use to them, they might just kill us all."

Lori appeared to consider that. "I don't think so. It's too much work. They'll probably just leave and find another species to harvest."

Clayton snorted. "You don't *think* so. That's reassuring."

Lori shook her head. "Keera is in charge of the human occupation. She doesn't believe in pointless bloodshed. She's not like them."

"Well, I hope you're right about that," Clayton replied. "Regardless, how the hell are you going to spread a cure all the way around the globe?"

"We'll find a way. Phoenix has sister cells all over the planet, and we have sympathizers on our side with access to Kyron technology."

Clayton thought of the technology that Richard Morgan had given him in the park: a cloaking signal blocker and spoofer for his ID implant, nanites to wipe his memories in case he was captured—and the sedative that had knocked Al out.

Maybe they could pull it off. The Kyra's reaction to a vaccine might still be a problem, but either way, it was a promising development in the fight against the occupation.

Maybe I shouldn't walk away just yet, Clayton thought.

CHAPTER 14

"**R**eady?" Lori whispered as she drove alongside the manhole cover where Clayton had taken cover the night before.

He scanned the piles of garbage between the ruins. The stench wafting through his broken window was like a physical thing, reaching out and choking him. He pushed down the urge to vomit. Mind over matter. So far there was no sign of Dregs. The smell of all the older garbage was masking the fresh load in their truck, but that wouldn't last long after they dumped the hauler's contents.

Clayton spent an extra second sweeping the ruins with his rifle before pulling his eyes away from the scope. He nodded and twisted around to reach behind his headrest and grab a second laser rifle from the mounting brackets. He passed it over to Lori, then held up a hand for her to wait while he removed the thumb-sized signal blocker and spoofer from his pants pocket. He stuck the self-adhering device over the blinking green light of his subdermal ID implant. The light vanished under the black disk. Then he twisted off the top half that was the spoofer, and the blinking green light of his tracking ID returned, now emanating from the device. He set the tiny device on the dash of the hauler and then nodded to Lori.

"Ready," he whispered.

They both eased their doors open and clambered down.

Clayton rounded the front of the hauler and joined Lori by the manhole cover. She bent down and knocked loudly on it, three times, just as Sergeant Sutton had told Clayton to do. Apparently she also knew the drill.

The sound was loud in the silence of the dump. Clayton stood behind Lori, shielding her back with his body and scanning the shadowy ruins. No signs of movement yet.

He connected his ARCs to the night-vision scope of the rifle, and his view dropped a few feet to just below his chest where he held the weapon. He raised it to his shoulder and swept around, looking for targets. It was strange to be holding the rifle and not to see either the weapon or his arms in his field of view—just the floating crosshairs. It was no different than peering down the scope, except he didn't have to squint one eye shut.

A sudden crunch of gravel grinding against asphalt sent an electric jolt coursing through Clayton's system. He disconnected his ARCs from the scope and turned to Lori. She was busy sweeping for targets with her rifle, too. *Was that you?* he mouthed to her, pointing to her chest for emphasis. Lori turned to him with big eyes and slowly shook her head.

Clayton pressed his right eye to the scope and swept the rifle around quickly, checking everything within sight on this side of the hauler. Nothing but dark, hazy green debris and garbage piles. Not even a stray rat lit up his scopes with a glowing white splash of life. That meant whatever they'd heard, it was creeping up on them from the other side of the hauler, using the bulk of the vehicle to cover its approach. The Dregs were getting smarter by the day.

Clayton pointed to Lori and then down to the back end of the hauler, indicating she should get a look around the back. She nodded and began creeping down that way. Clayton turned and went to the front of the vehicle. He arrived first and reconnected his ARCs to the scope before aiming his rifle around the corner of the cab. He half expected to see a horde of Dregs creeping up on them.

But there was nothing there.

Disconnecting from his scope again, he glanced at Lori. She was doing exactly the same thing that he had done, aiming her rifle around the back end of the hauler, her eyes aglow with the green light of the night-vision scope.

A moment later, she looked over at him and shook her head.

Clayton's skin prickled with dread. If they'd been followed from the city, there could be Chimera in cloaking armor out there. They needed to move fast.

He made a circle in the air and pointed to the manhole cover, suggesting they regroup there. Lori nodded and crept back over to the manhole. It was still sealed. No sign of the resistance. So much for *knock three times, and we'll open up.* Clayton blew out a frustrated breath and went down on his haunches beside the manhole. He knocked again. Three times more, as loud as he could.

Lori stood watch while he waited for a reply. This time he heard something going on below them: a soft clanging of boots on the metal rungs of the ladder. The manhole swung open, and Sergeant Sutton's head popped out. He gestured hurriedly to Lori, and Clayton stepped back while she started down the ladder.

Then Clayton heard it again, louder and closer this time. Another crunch of gravel, followed by a *click.*

"What was that?" Lori hissed, freezing on the rungs of the ladder.

"Just keep moving!" Sutton warned from below.

With his pulse thundering in his ears, Clayton spun through a wide arc, sweeping for targets with his own eyes. But again, there was nothing. He was just about to connect to his scope to check with night-vision when a high-pitched shriek split the air, and a dazzling emerald flash connected to Lori's chest. She dropped the rest of the way down the ladder, and Clayton heard a muffled cry from Sergeant Sutton.

Clayton hit the ground just as a second laser tore through the space where he'd been standing. He rolled over, aiming in the direction that the shots had come from—

But there was nothing there.

Another bolt tore into the asphalt beside him with an explosion of superheated pebbles that bit into the exposed skin on his arms. Clayton scrambled away from it, dragging himself into the open manhole and falling head-first down the ladder. He cried out as he fell, arms flailing. With a desperate cry, he hooked an arm through the rungs of the ladder. His shoulder wrenched hard, leaving him gasping in pain.

"Shut the manhole!" Sergeant Sutton cried.

Clayton glanced up and saw an open circle of stars framed in shadows. He scrambled back up the ladder, gritting his teeth against the pain of his wounded shoulder. Hesitating only briefly, he stuck an arm out and reached for a handle on the underside of the manhole cover.

A bright green laser beam splashed into the manhole, right beside hand, making the metal glow molten orange. The handle scalded Clayton's hand, but he yanked the cover shut. It fell with a resounding *boom,* and he let go, his palm stinging furiously from the heat.

"Did you lock it?" Sutton demanded.

Clayton noticed that the handle had a simple locking bolt built into it. He grimaced and reached for it with his other hand, sliding it across as fast as he could. He released the scalding metal and hurried down the ladder.

At the bottom, Sergeant Sutton crouched over Lori, cursing under his breath. She wasn't moving, and there was a ragged black patch over her left breast where the laser had burned through her simple black uniform.

"Is she..."

Sutton straightened from checking her pulse and kicked the side of the sewer tunnel. "Goddammit!" he cried.

Clayton stared at Lori's body in shock. "You can still use her to make the cure, right?"

Sutton's eyes narrowed swiftly, and he took a quick step toward Clayton. "What do you know about it?"

"She told me that—"

"That she's the only one who knows how the Kyra did it?" The sergeant scowled. "How the fuck is she going to tell us anything now?

Before he could even venture a reply, the

sergeant spun away and recovered Clayton's laser rifle. He shoved it into his chest. "You're going to have to cover us while we run."

"Run?" Clayton asked, glancing back up at the manhole cover. "Run where?"

"You were followed. That was a Chimera shooting at you." Sutton bent down and scooped Lori up to drape her over his shoulders. "They took out Lori, which means they ID'd you, too." Sutton looked to him, his dark eyes grim. "You're an exile now, Captain. Welcome to the Wastes."

CHAPTER 15

"**E**xcuse me. Sorry. Excuse me," Samara said as she squeezed past the people standing in the narrow aisle of the Ryde. She got off at her stop with the rising sun just now peeking between two adjacent buildings to reveal diamond-sparkles of quartz and silica in the road and sidewalk.

It was another half a block from the stop to her apartment building. She walked quickly with her head down and eyes darting, her hands stuffed in the pockets of her doctor's coat. But she needn't have worried; a pair of armored Chimeras were walking up ahead, about a block away, and between them and her was a long line of people waiting outside a cafe on the ground floor of her apartment building. There were too many witnesses around for her to run into trouble.

Dead eyes tracked listlessly to hers as she walked by the people outside the cafe. The smells of fresh bread and coffee wafted out, stirring hunger pains to life in Samara's stomach; but that line was too long, and she had

an appointment at the center to get to. Samara nodded and offered a tired smile as she
walked by; no one nodded or smiled back.
Most of them wore plain, civilian clothes: t-
shirts and jeans, blouses and skirts, a few
flowery summer dresses—but gone were the
uniforms stamped with franchise logos that
Samara remembered from her other life. These
were service workers from local, Chimera-
owned shops, salons, restaurants, and dispensaries, with a handful of higher-paid white-col-
lar office jobs thrown in. It was so familiar and
alien at the same time. Like she'd died and
woken up in a parallel universe ruled by aliens.

And that was almost exactly what had happened.

A sweaty surge of panic began clawing in
Samara's chest, making her scalp itch. Gasping for air, she pushed through the glass doors
of her apartment building. Bold signage above
the doors read: *The Grand Sheridan.* Darkness
crowded around the edges of her vision, narrowing her view of the gleaming, faux-marble
tiles that covered the walls and floor. *Not now,
please,* she thought as she groped and lunged for
the elevators at the back of the lobby.

Her knees grew weak, and she collapsed on
a gray couch bleeding yellow stuffing. Feelings
of desperation and despair rolled over her in
waves. A soundless scream built inside of her
chest, and an overwhelming feeling of *wrong-*

ness overcame her. *It's not real; it's not real. This is a dream!* She glanced about quickly, her eyes wide and darting. Nausea rolled in her gut, and her head swam, floating somewhere above her shoulders.

"Are you feeling all right, darling?"

A beautiful woman with bouncy blond curls, bright green eyes, and an infectious smile appeared in front of her. She waved a hand in front of Samara's face. "Hey there. Are you okay? Do you need me to call..." The woman's eyes flicked down, taking in Samara's attire. "Another doctor?" she suggested.

"I'm a nurse," Samara whispered.

"What was that, honey?"

"Mom! I'm gonna be late for school!" another voice interjected.

"Just a minute, Liam!"

"It's Harrison, Mom."

"Of course, dear." Green eyes pinched to slits. "Honey?"

Samara's vision expanded once more, and the panic attack faded, leaving her feeling shaken and weak. "I'm okay," she said. "Thank you."

"Here. Let me help you." The other woman grabbed her arm in a firm grip and pulled Samara to her feet.

"Thank you," Samara said again.

"Of course." Another flash of that infectious smile, and the woman's green eyes sparkled anew. Samara frowned and shook her head, not recognizing the woman as one of her neighbors. It was a big building, but she felt like she would have remembered that face. "You live in the Grand?"

"Mom! School!"

Samara followed that voice to a pair of identical boys by the doors of the building. They couldn't have been more than eight years old. Both had their mother's blond hair, buzzed to a razor-short length, and her green eyes. They also had round, baby faces that made them look somehow younger than their height would imply. Both wore their school uniforms: plain gray jumpsuits in the same cut and styling as the black ones that the Guard and cadets wore.

"Just a minute, Harrison!" their mother said.

"I'm Liam!" he cried.

Samara couldn't help but smile. Not even their mother could tell them apart.

"Sorry." The other woman smiled back. "We were just moved here from New San Antonio. Population redistribution."

Samara nodded along. She knew what that was about. The Kyra weren't interested in expanding the cities. Instead, they moved people around to accommodate for fluctuations in birth rates.

"Welcome to the building. I'm Samara," she

said, sticking out a cold, clammy hand.

The other woman took it and said, "Marcy Mayfield. Those two scoundrels over there are Liam and Harrison."

"I gathered as much," Samara replied, while absently holding a hand over her flat stomach.

Marcy's eyebrows fluttered up. "Are you...?"

Samara nodded.

"Congratulations!"

"Mom!" one of the twins shouted from the doors of the apartment. He dropped a heavy pack at his feet and crossed his arms over his chest. His face had turned bright red with frustration.

Marcy glanced over her shoulder at them. "I'd better go," she said. "It's their first day at a new school. They're eager to go."

Another piece of this new world that didn't seem to fit: kids, eager to go to school. The Kyra didn't believe in distractions from work and study, so entertainment was strictly limited, and kids actually enjoyed school.

"It was nice to meet you," Samara said as the other woman turned to leave.

"Likewise," Marcy replied, waving over her shoulder as she walked out the doors with her kids.

Samara turned and continued to the elevators, summoning them with her ARCs before she arrived. The nearest one dinged open, and she stepped in, riding all the way up to the 92nd floor.

She was still thinking about that young mother and her twins when she waved the door to her apartment open. She kicked off her shoes beside the door and went straight to the bedroom, calling, "Clay! Are you here?"

She stopped in the open doorway to their bedroom. The bed wasn't made yet. Clayton always made it when he got home. Samara's ears rang with the silence in their apartment. The overwhelming sense of panic was back. Where was he? His shift ended an hour before hers. He should have been back already. She'd been so busy at the hospital that she hadn't thought to check in with him.

Feeling weak in the knees again, Samara sat on the foot of the bed and reached with a shaking hand for the comms piece in the front pocket of her smock. "Call Clayton Cross," she said aloud rather than mentally. She needed to hear something other than the maddening silence.

"Calling Clayton Cross," the comms piece replied in a calm female voice.

It rang and rang...

And rang...

A beep sounded, followed by an automated message from the service provider: "I'm sorry. Clayton Cross is out of comms range. Would you like to leave a message?"

Samara gritted her teeth in frustration. Even in the 21st century, they'd had a global wireless network, but now, somehow, comms coverage began and ended within just a few kilometers of the city centers. The Chimeras and the Kyra had no such restrictions, however. Yet another way that the Kyra kept them all contained and under control.

"No," Samara all but shouted. "Call SWMD Central."

"Calling, SWMD Central," the comms unit replied.

It rang just twice, and then—

"Solid Waste Management Department, this is Desiree, how may I help you?"

"I'm calling for information about one of your drivers, Clayton Cross."

"One moment please, ma'am..."

The silence on the other end stretched to eternity and back before the operator's voice returned.

"I'm sorry, Mr. Cross did not return from his run last night."

"What do you mean he didn't return? What about his partner, Alan Reese?"

"No, ma'am. Neither of them made it back."

"What?" Samara cried. "What happened?"

Desiree paused. "I assume they ran into trouble."

"You *assume?* What about their tracking

signals? Where are they?"

"I am very sorry, ma'am. The Guard reported them both dead just a few hours ago."

Samara ended the call with a stifled cry, and she fell back against the bed, blinking tears. This was supposed to have been his last run.

Samara clutched her stomach in both hands and curled into a fetal position in the messy bed covers. Violent sobs wracked her body over and over. Time stretched into an endless moment of horror. The suffocating panic was back. Suddenly she wanted nothing more than to open the bedroom window and jump. Before she even realized what she was doing, she was standing up and walking to the windows.

And just as she reached them, she heard the comms piece in her ear trilling with an incoming call. She flinched, her whole body jumping with adrenaline. Maybe it was Clayton!

"Hello?" she answered, her eyes too blurry with tears to see the caller ID on her ARCs.

The gruff, rasping voice of a Chimera replied: "Mrs. Cross, this is Doctor Orison from the Ascension Center. I have a prenatal appointment with you this morning. You're fifteen minutes late. Can I assume that you are on your way?"

"I can't go. I'm not—" Samara broke off, holding a shaking hand to her mouth.

"I'm sorry for whatever distress you might be feeling, Mrs. Cross, but as you surely know, these appointments are not optional...." The unspoken threat was there, lingering in the brittle silence. And then he clarified it for her: "Do I need to call the Guard?"

"No," Samara replied. "I'll be there soon."

"Good. I will be waiting."

Samara ended the call. Her whole body felt cold and numb. She stared out over the city from the 92nd floor. The panic was gone and along with it went the brief impulse to jump to her death. She had Pandora to think about.

"It's going to be okay," she whispered, rubbing her belly. "We're going to be okay."

THE WASTES

CHAPTER 16

Clayton stirred and woke up to a familiar, groaning roar of machinery in his ears. Daylight sliced down from an ever-widening opening in the ceiling, revealing that he was lying in the back of a hauler for the second night in a row. Clayton frowned, his mind racing to fill in the blanks. How had he ended up back here?

"Captain Cross," a deep, familiar voice called, echoing down to him. He placed the voice a second later. Sergeant Sutton went on, "Time to get up. You've slept long enough."

Clayton eased off the sticky metal hull and clambered to his feet, stumbling toward the light. He winced as a spreading wave of pins and needles raced down his right leg. His head felt thick. His thoughts muddled.

He reached the hatch and saw Sergeant Sutton standing there, balanced on the robotic arm they used to pick up dumpsters and bins. Sutton reached down with a hand, and Clayton took it, letting the sergeant pull him out into the light. An instant, throbbing headache began pulsing behind his eyes as he crouched on the roof of the cab. He winced and spent a moment shading his brow from the sun and looking around to get his bearings. He was in a section of the Wastes that he didn't recognize. Maybe even beyond the Wastes, in the Wilds. The hauler was parked between high trees on a patch of tall brown grass. Sutton jumped down, and Clayton climbed down more carefully to join him beside the vehicle. As he did so, he noticed that the hauler was draped in a thick, glossy black blanket that adhered to the hull almost perfectly. It bubbled up in a few places where extra fabric bunched, but otherwise, it seemed to have been made for the hauler.

Clayton remembered the pair of stolen haulers from a year ago, and he began nodding slowly. "So this is where they went..."

"One of them," Sutton agreed, nodding once and patting the side of the hauler.

"What's with the blanket?" Clayton asked. He was still struggling to pry the memory of how he'd come to be here from his throbbing head.

A faint smile twitched onto Sutton's lips, and his eyes glowed briefly with light from his ARCs; then the air around the hauler shimmered, and it vanished.

Clayton felt his eyes widen in shock. Only the bottoms of the wheels and the open hatch remained visible.

That demonstration of Kyron cloaking tech triggered a memory. He turned his right arm over and looked at the underside of his wrist. The blinking green light of his ID implant wasn't there. He ran his fingertips lightly over the space where it should have been and felt a rigid disc of metal. The signal blocker.

And then the memories came flooding back, but the last thing he remembered was running through the sewers with Sergeant Sutton carrying Lori's body out.

Clayton spun around. "How did I get here?" he demanded. "Why can't I remember anything?"

"We had to erase your memories and sedate you. For our safety and yours. You haven't formally joined us yet. Until then, the less you know about our operations the better."

Clayton cast about once more. This time he spotted tire tracks leading up a grassy trail behind the hauler. Snatches of bright blue sky peeked between trees and bushes at the top of that gentle rise. Clayton broke into a run.

"Captain! Wait!" Sutton said.

But he wasn't listening. He ran twenty meters to the end of the trail and came to a thicket of naked bushes that had been dragged across the entrance to hide the tire tracks. Fighting through them and scratching his arms and face in the process, he staggered out onto a broken road with clumps of grass and the occasional sapling growing between the chunks of asphalt. Here the ruins weren't piled with garbage, they were completely overgrown with grass, trees, and wildflowers. In the distance, cresting above it all, Clayton could just pick out the tips of the tallest towers of New Houston.

We're not that far away, he thought. Relief crashed through him with a sweaty surge of desperation right on its heels: how was he going to get back into the city? Whoever had ambushed them and shot Lori would have marked him for elimination. The minute he removed his signal blocker, they'd either home in on his tracking signal and send a shuttle to pick him up, or else they'd just remotely trigger the release of toxins in his implant, executing him from a distance.

"You can't go back," Sutton said quietly from behind him.

Clayton whirled around, his eyes flashing. "This is your fault!"

Sutton stood looking down on him from an upturned chunk of concrete, cracked and blackened from some ages-old explosion. "You knew the risks when you agreed to help us."

Clayton glared, considering his options. "I have a wife."

Sutton inclined his head to that. "I know, and I'm sorry about that."

"What the hell am I supposed to do? Let her

think that I'm dead?"

"That's up to you," Sutton replied. "We can get a message to her, if you think it would be easier for her to know that you're still alive. But I wouldn't use your comms if I were you. They'll track the signal back to you in a heartbeat."

Clayton felt for his comms piece in his left pocket and flicked the power button to turn it off, just in case. It couldn't be traced if it wasn't transmitting—unlike the ID implant still buried in his wrist, but Clayton also had the comms piece the resistance had given him via Richard Morgan. Maybe Sutton didn't know about that one. It was supposed to be a secure, direct line of contact with Richard. Maybe it could be used to call other people, too? If so, he could use it to call Samara and let her know that he was okay.

The question was, should he? Would it be easier for her to know that he was still alive, or to assume that he was dead?

"Where is everyone else?" Clayton asked, changing the topic. He leaned around the sergeant to get a look back down the trail where the hauler was parked. "Is this where the resistance is hiding?" Clayton started past the sergeant, heading for the brambles and bushes that blocked the entrance of the grassy path.

Sergeant Sutton stepped down off his perch on the rubble. "Yes and no. The others are out hunting."

"Hunting *what?*"

"Deer, if we're lucky," Sutton replied.

Before Clayton could reply to that, a distant clap of thunder sounded behind them. He turned toward the sound and found himself staring at New Houston. Moments later, a dark column of smoke appeared, rising far above the tips of the tallest buildings.

"They did it," Sergeant Sutton whispered.

"Who did *what?*" For a second, Clayton was confused, but then he remembered the bomb scare at the Ascension Center yesterday morning.

He rounded on Sutton in horror. "The bomb in the center was real?"

The sergeant's eyebrows drifted up. "Of course. If it was a bluff, the Kyra wouldn't take our next threat seriously."

Clayton flew across the short span of feet between them and grabbed fistfuls of the sergeant's old camo-colored army fatigues. "You miserable bastard! There are women and children in the center!" Clayton's mind reeled, remembering that Samara's appointment had been rescheduled for today. He released the sergeant, and his eyes snapped back to the rising column of smoke. He sank to the ground on shaking legs. Terror clutched Clayton's heart in a bloodless fist, making it hard to breathe, let alone speak.

"This is war, Captain," Sutton said after a long, aching silence. "There are bound to be innocent casualties."

A hand landed on Clayton's shoulder. He flinched and ducked out from under it, scrambling away on his hands and knees and cutting his palms on jagged debris in the process. "Don't you fucking touch me! My wife was there!"

Sutton's expression became stricken, and his dark eyes pinched to slits. "What would she be doing—"

"She's pregnant," Clayton said.

Sutton winced. "I am truly sorry. If we had known—"

"What? You would have waited?" Clayton barked a laugh. "What about all the other pregnant mothers? What about the cadets? For God's sake, they're just kids!"

Sutton slowly shook his head. "They're Chimeran soldiers in training, and those pregnant mothers are waiting to give birth more of the same. It's a shame about the mothers, but there are only so many ways that we can fight the occupation. This is one of the few lines of attack we have that actually hits them where it hurts."

Clayton wiped a trickling tear from one cheek and smirked. "Well, congratulations, Sergeant. You've just done the Kyra's job for them."

"How so?"

"They've been telling our kids for years that they're really the good guys, and now they actually *are*. What do you think is going to happen when all of the sympathizers in the city stop tossing supply boxes in their trash?"

A muscle jerked in Sutton's cheek. "This wasn't my call to make."

"No? Then whose call was it?"

"I can't say," Sutton replied.

"Fine. Keep your secrets. I don't care. I'm done. Whatever the hell is going on, count me out of it. I'd rather get eaten by Dregs than join terrorists." With that, he stood up and began stalking away.

"Captain, wait!"

"Fuck off!"

Sutton ran up behind him, his boots crunching in the rubble of the broken road. Clayton rounded on him, about to punch him in the face.

But Sutton ducked out of the strap of his laser rifle and thrust it into Clayton's chest.

"You can't go wandering around the Wastes unarmed. Take it."

Clayton accepted the weapon with a shallow nod. He couldn't bring himself to say thank you.

Sutton removed his equipment belt and passed it over. "Spare charge packs for the rifle, and clips for the M99."

Clayton eyed the holstered sidearm before ducking through the rifle's shoulder strap and clipping on the belt. The M99 was an old projectile-based weapon from the Union. Ancient tech, but much more serviceable than Kyron weapons.

"Good luck out there, Captain," Sutton said as Clayton turned to leave once more. "And don't forget to cut out your implant before that signal blocker runs out of juice. It can still kill you."

Clayton didn't reply. He'd figure that out later. Right now he needed to get away as fast as he could. His throat and chest ached, his boots crunching steadily as he walked back toward New Houston for lack of any other direction to choose. It looked to be four or five kilometers to the walls. He could make it there in about an hour. For whatever reason, the resistance hadn't gone very far. Maybe they'd needed to stay close to detonate their bomb.

Clayton's eyes burned with the threat of tears, but a warm dry breeze blew across the Wastes, rustling leaves and grass, and sucking the moisture from his eyes before his tears could fall.

His heart pounded erratically in his chest. Samara might not have been caught in that explosion. She would have waited for him to come home first. When he didn't, would she have gone anyway? Even if she had, she might have lived through the blast.

Somehow, he had to find out.

He thought about turning back, of pretending to have a change of heart and using the resistance's communications channels to find out what had happened to her. But once he knew their secrets, he had a feeling they wouldn't let him go again so easily, and he couldn't be a part of what they were doing. Not anymore.

There was another way. If he could get close enough to the city, he could try calling Samara with one of his two comms units. Or the hospital where she worked. If she had been injured, that was where she'd be.

Clayton wiped his cheeks on the backs of his hands. His life was over, but Samara's might not be. Finding out if she was still alive had just become his only reason to live.

CHAPTER 17

Admiral Keera Reed sat in the command chair on the bridge of her ship, the *Sovath,* as it cruised low over the Wastes.

She was gazing *through* the deck and bulkheads, which were currently relaying views from outside the hull to give her a better view. The effect made it look and feel as though she and her bridge crew were floating across the dead landscape in hovering chairs.

Scraggly trees, jutting ruins, and mountains of trash seemed to reach for the massive, six hundred meter-long destroyer as it scraped by with just a few meters of clearance. Dregs ran shrieking from their hiding places, roused from sleep by the whistling roar of the grav engines keeping the ship aloft.

The Chimeran officer manning the gravidar reported, "There's no sign of Miss Reed or her remains."

Keera glared at the man, and all four of his cranial stalks flattened before he broke eye contact and looked back to his screens.

"I am sorry for your loss, Admiral," Commander Treya said from the seat beside her.

Keera looked up from the ruins scrolling by below, and glanced at her executive officer. Commander Treya had a narrower jaw and longer face than the average Chimera, with hollow, sunken cheeks, and deeply-shadowed red eyes. "What about the mercenary? Leeto Voth. Do we have any idea whose orders he was acting on?"

"No, ma'am. He claims to have been acting on his own initiative. He met your mother in the ward room last night and thought she was acting suspiciously. Voth decided to keep an eye on her tracking beacon after that. He says he saw her sneaking aboard a shuttle and hiding in one of the cargo crates, but her tracking beacon continued transmitting from her quarters."

Keera hissed with displeasure. She had been away on a surface mission last night, and her mother had taken full advantage of her absence to sneak away from the *Sovath*. By itself, that wouldn't have been a serious offense, but she had apparently also made arrangements to sneak out of New Houston and defect to the resistance.

"Did Voth explain why he didn't simply report my mother's absence?" Keera asked.

"He wanted to be the one to bring her back, and he wanted to do so quietly. I'm sure he expected there would be some type of reward for doing so."

"Then why didn't he capture my mother instead of *shooting* her?" Keera screamed.

A stunned silence rang in the echoing chambers of the bridge. "Didn't he know how valuable she is?" Keera asked in a deadly whisper.

Treya hesitated. "Voth claims he didn't have a chance to capture Miss Reed. And he knew how valuable she would also be to the resistance. Apparently, the Overseer has already authorized a substantial payment to Voth for proof of his kill."

Keera's whole body grew cold, but she couldn't afford to show her feelings. "I see. And Voth is sure that he killed her?"

"Sensor data from the scope of his rifle confirms that Miss Reed's life signs began fading almost instantly. That is also consistent with where she was hit. The laser went straight through her heart. Without drastic medical intervention, she would have died in a matter of seconds," Commander Treya explained.

"It doesn't make sense."

"What do you mean, ma'am?" Treya asked.

"Voth took out a key asset to the Federation. He had to know he would get paid more to bring her back alive. Unless..." Maybe the overseer already knew about Lori's plan to defect, and he had given Voth an explicit contract to kill her. Damos and the other Kyra had never been happy about allowing a human to mix with Chimeras aboard the *Sovath*. Maybe Damos had finally decided that Lori had out-lived her usefulness to them.

But he hadn't anticipated the ripple effects that killing Lori would have. He'd made an enemy of Keera—both he and Leeto Voth, along with anyone who'd had anything to do with the plot to help her mother defect.

Keera considered that for a moment. "Commander, who was driving the hauler that smuggled Lori Reed out of the city?"

Imagery flickered in the air in front of Commander Treya. "Alan Reese and Clayton Cross."

Keera's skin prickled. "Did you say Clayton Cross?"

"Yes, ma'am. Why? Do you know him?"

Keera shook her head. "No," she lied. Wrong associations could be dangerous, even for her. "I know *of* him," she explained. "He was the captain of a Union ship that returned to Earth a year ago."

"Ah. I see," Treya replied.

"What happened to the drivers? Have we interrogated them yet?" Keera asked.

"Cross was last seen escaping into the sewers with your mother, right before she was shot. And Reese died during an interrogation at the Ascension Center early this morning."

"Fools." Keera scowled. "I want all of the drivers' tracking data pulled up and correlated to find anyone they met with over the last week."

"Yes, ma'am..." Treya said slowly. "What are you hoping to find?"

"Anyone else who was involved," Keera explained. "Helm, bring us about. Take us back to the city."

"Aye, Admiral."

Keera watched the ruins sweep around beneath them until the gleaming spires of New Houston soared into view. A dark column of smoke was busy rising from what was left of the Ascension Center. That sight provided a welcome distraction from the boiling rage and the hollow, soul-sucking grief now ripping through Keera's entire being.

"Admiral—" her comms officer began.

Keera looked to the woman. "Yes, Lieutenant?"

"We're getting a transmission from the *Gothora*. It's Overseer Damos."

Keera's hands balled into fists, her claws digging into her palms until she felt blood leaking hotly between her fingers. Damos was the last person she wanted to speak with right now. "Very well, put him through."

"Sorry, Admiral. I should have clarified. The message isn't specifically for us. It appears to be repeating from the satnet. It's being broadcast system-wide on an open channel."

"I see." Keera opened her fists, and fat drops

of black blood splatted to the deck. "Let's hear what he has to say."

* * *

Clayton crouched on the crumbling remains of the second floor of an old concrete building. He peered out an empty window frame at the lumbering, teardrop-shaped destroyer cruising low over the Wastes. Windowless, with a matte black hull, it hovered impossibly like some kind of gravity-defying asteroid.

The destroyer slowly banked around and lit its thrusters with a bright, fiery blue flare of plasma escaping from six massive exhaust cones.

As Clayton sat there on his haunches, watching the ship leave, he felt a subtle vibration in his pocket. It was the comms piece that the resistance had given him. Clayton's heart soared: had Sam found some way to contact him? He should have been out of comms range, but maybe the resistance had access to better tech. He fished the earpiece out of his pocket and stuck it in his ear. The caller ID flashed up on his ARCs: *Overseer Damos.*

Clayton froze. Was the Overseer calling him personally? If so, he was a dead man.

Then he thought to check the details of the transmission. It was being relayed globally via the satnet on an open channel. Curious what it was about, he accepted the transmission.

A deep voice rumbled through his ear-piece: "Citizens of Earth, this is Overseer Damos. At eleven thirty-nine local time this morning, a bomb went off at the ascension center in New Houston. Initial reports suggest that the human casualties alone are over a thousand. This cowardly act by the resistance will not go unanswered. Rest assured, we will find those responsible.

"We have been too lenient. From now on, anyone found living outside of designated settlements will be executed. Exile is no longer an option for dissenters or criminals. I am authorizing a bounty of one thousand credits per head. Any Chimera who would like to join the hunt is welcome to report to the nearest ascension center. Access to transport and weapons will be provided if you do not already have such access. Together, we will eliminate this threat to Federation sovereignty."

The message ended there, leaving a hiss of static in Clayton's ear. He pulled out the comms piece and turned it off before putting it back in his pocket. As if it wasn't bad enough to have to hide from the Dregs, now he had to worry about credit-hungry Chimeras hunting him as well.

Clayton turned his arm over, checking the signal blocker on the underside of his wrist. No sign of the blinking green light of his implant. Sutton had warned him to cut it out before the signal blocker ran out of juice, but how long did he have?

There was no way of knowing, but he couldn't afford to wait any longer. Not with all the Chimeras in New Houston getting ready to sally out and hunt exiles like him.

Clayton ducked out of the strap of his laser rifle and set it aside. Finding a chunk of concrete to sit on, he drew the hunting knife from the utility belt that Sergeant Sutton had given him. Shrugging out of his neon yellow SWMD vest, he used the knife to cut a strip of cloth for a tourniquet. He was sorry to see the vest go —it would provide welcome warmth at night —but he couldn't afford to wear something so conspicuous anyway.

Clayton tied the strip of neon yellow cloth around his forearm and then bit down on the padded shoulder strap of the rifle. Grabbing the knife in his left hand, he placed the tip at the edge of the signal blocker and pressed it in until he saw a bead of blood appear. *That wasn't so bad,* he thought. Then he began tracing the blade around the signal blocker in a shallow circle. The pain lit his whole arm on fire, making his head swim and his hand shake. He bit so hard on the strap that his jaw ached.

When he was done, he peeled away the top layer of skin to reveal the tiny silver capsule that was his ID implant. The blinking green light was still off, indicating that it couldn't make contact with the satnet. A welling pool of blood quickly hid the implant from sight, but Clayton felt for it with his fingers and dug it out with the tip of the knife. He removed it, along with the invisible, disc-shaped signal blocker, wincing as he tore away the layer of skin between them.

Pinching the bloody implant and signal blocker together between his thumb and forefinger, he set them both down and raised his foot.

He hesitated, his foot poised to grind them both to dust. He might need the signal blocker again, but he couldn't risk separating it from the implant. The tracking beacon would reconnect and broadcast his location instantly. Instead, he pressed the blade of the hunting knife into the implant and pushed down with all of his weight until the tiny capsule gave way and broke in half. That done, he removed the invisible disc of the signal blocker. It reappeared as a blood-smeared black wafer. He stuck it into his pants pocket with the comms piece from the resistance and then untied the tourniquet around his forearm. Casting about for some way to bandage his throbbing, stinging wrist, he found nothing clean at hand, and decided to leave the wound for now. It would dry and scab over. He could still easily get an infection from it, but without any medical supplies at hand, there was nothing he could do. Hopefully he would be able to scavenge something before too long.

Clayton spat out the rifle strap and slung the weapon over his shoulder once more. He wiped off the hunting knife on the remains of his vest and then slipped the blade back into its sheath.

Jumping down from the second floor of the building, he landed on a pile of rubble just a few feet below. From there he rejoined the broken, grassy road that led back to the highway and New Houston. He still had a few kilometers to go.

A hot breeze blew across the Wastes, rustling the leaves of trees growing along the street. A pair of crows took flight from a nearby tree. Clayton placed a hand to his forehead and watched as they spread their wings and flitted briefly across the sun with a grating *caw-caw, caw-caw.*

Clayton dropped his eyes back to the horizon with a scowl. *Lucky bastards,* he thought. Animals were immune to the Chimeran virus. Birds especially were in an enviable position: they were too fast for the Dregs to catch. To them, life went on much the same as it always had, with the difference that now they had a lot more of the world to themselves.

A forlorn howl interrupted Clayton's thoughts. He froze and spun toward the sound. It was coming from the ruins along the left side of the road. He worried that it might be a Dreg.

Then it came again, and he identified it: a deep, throaty *aahrooooo.*

A dog. Clayton blinked in shock. How long had it been since he'd seen a dog? Since before he'd left Earth. The Kyra didn't believe in letting their human pets keep pets of their own, so this animal would have to be a descendant of wild dogs that had survived the invasion.

That piteous howl came again, and Clayton started in the direction of the sound, aiming for a shadowy alley between two shattered buildings. His hands flexed on the grip and handguard of his rifle, eyes tracking the shadows inside the ruins as he began walking down the alley. He picked out other sounds as he went—the crunching footsteps and hushed, hissing growls of Dregs.

Clayton slowed his pace and flicked the selector on his rifle to *kill.* He emerged from the alley on another overgrown street. To his left, two Dregs wearing nothing but bloody scraps of clothing were down on all fours, their pale backs and rippling muscles standing out sharply in the midday sun. They were facing away from him, crouched low in the tall grass and slinking slowly toward the source of the howls—a three-story building on the far side of the street.

Clayton jammed the stock of the rifle to his shoulder and peered through the scope at the first Dreg—thirty-two feet away according to the range finder. He held his breath to steady his aim and then pulled the trigger. A bright green laser beam shot out and struck the Dreg between its shoulder blades. It went down with a shriek and began thrashing loudly in the grass. The second creature recoiled from its companion and spun around to face the threat. Slavering jaws with black, rotting teeth swept into line under Clayton's sights. He pulled the trigger a second time and shot a hole straight through the back of the creature's throat. It fell and lay still. The first one was still thrashing in the grass. Clayton snapped off another shot, and it stopped.

Releasing a slow breath, Clayton hurried in the direction that he'd heard the howls coming from. The dog was quiet now, as if it had just realized how much attention it was attracting to itself. Checking the rifle's charge via his ARCs, a circular charge meter appeared at the bottom right of his field of view. Tiny blue segments ran around the circumference of the display. Three of them were grayed out, and the number 27 sat in the middle, indicating how many shots he had left. Keeping his eyes and aim on his surroundings, Clayton spared a hand from the rifle to check how many spare charge packs he had on the utility belt. Three. And two clips for the M99 pistol. That wasn't going to last long in the Wastes. He needed to come up with another way of dealing with Dregs when there were only a few of them. He needed to save his ammo for the hordes.

Clayton pushed through a wall of dry brown grass where he'd felled the Dregs just in time to hear another howl. It was coming from the third floor of the building he'd seen. A big black and brown mutt was sitting up there, peering down with floppy ears draping the sides of its head.

Clayton frowned, searching the ground floor for a stairwell that might lead up there. As he approached the building, the dog barked loudly at him. The sound echoed resoundingly, scaring up a group of birds from the grass.

Another bark followed the first, followed by an endless series of them. Clayton glanced over his shoulder, checking for signs of more Dregs. Nothing yet, but that wouldn't last long with that dog barking and drawing them in.

Clayton stepped through a broken window into the lower floor of the building. Shadows fell over him, and debris crunched underfoot. He moved quickly, searching for stairs. Seconds later, he found a naked concrete staircase, crumbling on one side, and followed it up to the second floor. The stairs ended there. Clayton searched the second floor for another way up. That dog had to have gotten up there somehow. As he searched, the mutt bounded around playfully, barking at him through holes in the floor above, its butt in the air, tail wagging. It had short black fur with brown patches, and a big square jaw and face. Clayton doubted it was anything close to a purebred, but to him, it looked like a Rottweiler. Clayton scowled grumpily as he turned over every inch of the second floor with that dog barking at him the whole time.

"Shut up, would you? You're going to get us both killed!"

A groan answered him, and the dog shut up, its head snapping toward the sound.

Clayton froze. Someone was up there. Injured. *Bitten?* he wondered. Moments later, something came crashing down through a hole in the floor above. It was a ladder made of saplings and tree branches, and tied together with old strips of clothing.

Clayton picked it up and leaned it against the edge of the third floor. He tested his weight on the first rung, found it held, and then started up. As he came to eye level with the third floor, the mutt reappeared, growling and baring its teeth.

A strained female voice snapped at it. "Friend, Rosie! Friend!"

The dog flattened its floppy ears and slunk away, pacing in restless circles in front of its master. Clayton froze at the sight of her leaning against a wall on the third floor. She was resting under the eaves of a ramshackle roof made from corrugated metal sheets. Her skin was translucent and glistening with sweat. Black veins stood out sharply underneath, and stringy tufts of long, dark hair clung to her balding scalp. Four lumps protruded from the back of her skull where her cranial stalks were growing, getting ready to burst free, and her eyes were so bloodshot that they might as well be red already.

Clayton pulled himself the rest of the way up the ladder. The woman cracked a broken smile and nodded to the mutt pacing around in front of her.

"Take her. Please. Just get her away from here before I finish... changing. She's all I've got. I can't..." The woman broke off in a fit of coughing that speckled her lips with black blood. She subsided with a ragged sigh and rocked her head back and forth against the wall. Bloodshot eyes flicked up to his. "Better yet... just shoot me."

Clayton swallowed thickly, then nodded. He cast about, his gaze passing over a scattering of belongings: clothes, a few old pots, a bow, and arrows. A hatchet. A coil of rope and what might be a collar for the dog. His eyes roved on, looking for a way to get the dog down that didn't involve carrying it down the ladder.

The woman seemed to understand what he was looking for. "Rosie can use the ladder, but she won't go down as long as I'm here."

Clever girl, he thought. Looking back to the woman, he drew his pistol and started toward her. Rosie darted between them, snarling and baring her teeth at him. "You'll have to do it," he said, taking a step back. "She might attack if she sees me shoot you."

The woman nodded slowly, her eyes wincing shut.

Clayton set the pistol down gently at his feet, and waited until Rosie began pacing again before he kicked the M99 over to the woman.

She groped blindly before closing a translucent hand around the grip of the weapon and lifting it to her head.

"Wait. What's your name?" Clayton asked.

The woman's eyes cracked open, leaking blood from the corners. "Who cares?" she croaked.

And then she pulled the trigger, and Rosie darted away whimpering, with her tail between her legs.

CHAPTER 18

Rosie slunk back over to her dead master a few seconds after the woman blew her brains out. The dog sniffed gingerly around the exit wound in her master's head. Black blood pooled on the dusty concrete floor, dribbling out like molasses. Rosie recoiled from the smell of the infected blood with a snort and retreated with a high-pitched whimper. The dog curled into the farthest corner she could find, dark eyes watching Clayton from the shadows.

He grimaced and looked away, his gaze skipping over the woman's belongings, then to the pistol he'd given her to put herself out of her misery. He crept back over and used a clean shirt from the woman's belongings to pry the gun from her hand. He wiped down the grip to be extra sure he couldn't later catch the virus from the weapon. The Chimeran virus was highly active during the changing phase, but it wasn't airborne, and catching it from surfaces was rare. It took a proper exchange of body fluids to actually get infected. Thank God for that, or by now everyone on the planet would have turned into either a Dreg or a Chimera.

Holstering the M99 pistol, Clayton went to check out Rosie's rope leash and collar. The latter turned out to have been adapted from a Chimera's utility belt. Seeing that, Clayton conducted a more thorough search of the area. He soon found a small, long-barreled Kyron laser pistol with a quarter charge and one spare charge pack. He used another clean shirt from the woman's pile of old clothes and stuffed the weapon into a pack from the Guard that she'd apparently also stolen. Grabbing the pack in one hand, Clayton went picking through the remainder of the woman's belongings. He recovered an empty canteen, a Kyron solar lamp with a full charge, a few old pots, a metal hatchet, a jacket, a blanket, and a Chimeran first aid kit.

Inside the kit, he found a half-empty tube of *sterigel*, one vial of nanobiotics and a needle, a roll of compression bandages, and several large patches of *synthskin* for wounds. He used the sterigel and one of the bandages to disinfect his wrist and make a proper barrier against infection. After that, he stuffed everything but the sterigel into the pack. He zipped it up and squeezed some of the gel onto his hands to wash them. Then he squeezed some more onto the grip of his sidearm and rubbed it around for good measure. Rare or not, he didn't want to catch the virus from anything this woman had touched. He'd have to sterilize everything else in the pack later. The virus was nanite-based—part organic, part synthetic—but boiling water would kill the organic part, making it inert.

When he was done, Clayton walked over to Rosie with the leash. She backed away, deeper into her corner.

"Come on, girl," he coaxed. "You can't stay here." He took another step toward her, and Rosie bared her teeth in a snarl.

Clayton gave up with a sigh and sat down on the dusty floor, glaring at the dog. He didn't have time for this. He needed to get back to New Houston and find out what had happened to his wife. Once he was close enough to the walls, he could use the comms piece the resistance had given him to call her. Turning the device on and beaming a signal from outside the walls was a risk, but maybe if he kept the time short, he could avoid detection.

The sun beamed down on the back of Clayton's neck, prickling his skin with sweat and the beginnings of a bad sunburn. His throat was parched, his stomach empty and rumbling. It was still at least three kilometers from here to the walls. In this heat, it would be better if he could at least find water before trekking the rest of the distance. The canteen he'd found would work to carry water—after he boiled it the pot—but he still needed to find a river or a stream to fill it.

Clayton glanced at the dead woman. Bloodshot eyes stared blankly back. She lay in the shade of a roof that she'd fashioned from old, rusted metal sheets. She'd made her home up here. That meant it had to be close to water, maybe also close to good hunting grounds.

He looked over his shoulder, to the ladder he'd climbed up. He could leave Rosie here to grieve while he went looking for water. Probably a good idea.

He nodded to Rosie, and said, "Hang on, girl, I'll be back soon." Clayton eased off the floor and started toward the ladder. As he did so, Rosie raised her head, her eyes tracking him intently.

"It's okay," he said again. "I'll be back soon."

Rosie sat up, and her tongue lolled out of her mouth. She began panting loudly. Clayton hesitated. It was shaping up to be a hot day. How long had it been since the dog had something to drink? He looked at her master's corpse. Based on how far along she was, she'd been bitten at least twelve hours ago. Had they been up here the whole time since then? If so, then Rosie had to be badly dehydrated.

Clayton held up the leash and shook it at the dog. "You want to come?"

Her tongue popped back into her mouth, and she cocked her head at him, staring for a long second; then she eased off her haunches and came padding over. Rosie nosed his hand and the leash with her snout and gave his fingers a quick lick. Her nose was dry, tongue likewise.

"Good girl, Rosie," he whispered as he bent down and clipped the collar around her neck. "Let's go find something to drink."

Clayton held her on a short lead as he went to the ladder. Rosie waited at the top, peering down. She looked to him, then back at the ladder.

"You need some help?" he asked, noting how steep the ladder was. He couldn't imagine her being able to climb down that by herself. Grabbing the top of it, which protruded a few feet above the edge of the floor, he adjusted the angle to make it more like a ramp. As soon as he did that, Rosie began stepping down the rickety rungs as if they were stairs. She took her time, carefully testing her footing on each rung. Clayton braced his feet and let out the rope leash gradually as she went, making sure he could save her from a fall if she slipped.

As soon as Rosie reached the bottom, she stopped and looked back up at him with those sad brown eyes and floppy ears. Her tail flicked up and wagged once.

Your turn, she seemed to say. Clayton smiled and started down the ladder after her.

* * *

It didn't take long to find the stream that

Rosie's master had been using as her water supply. The banks were lined with tall grass, bulrushes, and oak and birch trees creaking and rustling in the hot summer breeze. Frogs chirped steadily in the rushes as Clayton bent to fill both his canteen and the cooking pot with water. Rosie trotted up beside him and lapped greedily from the stream.

Clayton eyed her enviously. She was lucky she could drink the water like that. He couldn't afford to risk it. For all he knew, a Dreg had died or defecated somewhere upstream.

Rosie finished drinking, and Clayton straightened up with both the pot and canteen now full of water. He walked carefully up the bank of the river with his rifle swinging from the strap, and the contents of his pack dragging him down. Rosie's lead was wrapped around his wrist to make sure she didn't run off, but she stayed glued to his side, never even getting far enough away to let the leash pull taut.

Clayton headed for a grassy knoll with a big oak tree growing on it. If he was going to be tied down to one place, waiting for a fire to sterilize a pot full of water, he needed to have good sightlines on the surrounding terrain.

He reached the top of the hill, set the pot down beside the tree in the rooty ground, and leaned against the tree trunk to catch his breath. He was out of shape. Living in the Wastes was sure to fix that—assuming he lived long enough to improve his physical condition.

Clayton placed a hand to his brow and scanned his surroundings for signs of trouble. Nothing moved in the long, brown grass growing around the hill. Dregs hated the heat and light of the day, so they wouldn't be out yet —not unless they were desperately hungry, or they heard something that woke them up.

The riverbank was relatively clear of ruins. Mostly overgrown with trees and grass. It might have been a city park at one time. From here, about two hundred meters east, Clayton could still see the three-story building where he'd found Rosie and her master. It peeked out above the other ruins. A handful of other crumbling structures soared up around it, and beyond that, he glimpsed snatches of the road that he'd followed from where he'd parted ways with Sergeant Sutton. Due south, the tips of the skyscrapers in New Houston were a hazy, smoke-clouded blur against the horizon.

Panic gripped Clayton as he remembered the bomb. He needed to sterilize the water and make his way to the walls. As soon as he came within comms range of the city, he could try calling Samara.

Clayton looped Rosie's leash around the trunk of the tree. "Stay here, girl," he whispered and patted her once on the head. Then he drew his hunting knife and went about cutting big bundles of dry grass. Soon he had a big pile at the base of the tree. He studied it with a speculative frown and wiped the sweat from his brow. That grass would burn fast. Too fast to boil water. He needed something slower burning. Unslinging his pack, he pulled out the metal hatchet he'd taken from Rosie's owner, and went farther down the hill, cutting down saplings as he went. They were green, so they'd smoke like hell, but hopefully no one was around to see it.

After about fifteen minutes, he'd piled up a good amount of wood and grass beneath the oak tree, and he had a ring of rocks and concrete debris around it to make sure the fire didn't spread out of control. But after all that work, he was soaked through with sweat. He must have lost at least a cup of water. How many cups did that canteen hold? Maybe three? How long before the boiled water was cool enough to drink? Clayton stood beside the tree, his chest heaving from the exertion, blinking stinging rivers of sweat from his eyes. He couldn't do this every time he needed a drink.

Rosie lay in the grass watching him. Her tongue popped out, and she began panting. Like she was laughing at him.

"It's not funny," he said.

Rosie looked away, out to the horizon, and sniffed at the air, her nose twitching with some smell that only she could detect.

Clayton turned his attention back to the pile of sticks and grass, trying to figure out how to balance the pot full of water above the fire once he lit it.

He looked at the pot, still working the problem in his head. Loops of metal wire were twisted around the handles. He hooked his fingers through them and tried lifting it. The pot didn't suddenly tip to either side. This must be how Rosie's owner had used the pot to cook. She'd probably mounted it on a stick or a piece of rebar and rested it on chunks of rubble to either side.

Clayton cast about for more rocks or debris that he could stack to create such a stand for the pot, but it had taken him fully half an hour just to find the ones he'd used to make a firebreak. Seeing a low-hanging branch of the oak tree beside him, another idea occurred to him.

He looked to Rosie's rope leash, tied around the trunk of the tree, and smiled. Clayton untied the rope from the tree and removed the collar from Rosie's neck. As he did so, he pointed a finger in Rosie's face. "Don't you go anywhere."

She licked his finger. A dog's version of a pinkie promise. Clayton smiled. He carried the pot and rope over to the branch and slung Rosie's leash over it. He clipped the collar around the top of the rope and then fed the loose end through the loops on the pot. Hoisting it carefully up, he tied the rope around itself and left the pot to dangle freely about two feet above the ground. It swung gently back and forth, spilling precious water over the sides. Clayton watched it for a second, then rebuild his fire under the pot. When he was done, he stepped back from his handiwork, freshly drenched in sweat, his back aching from the work.

Dialing the intensity setting on his laser rifle down to the minimum, he took aim at the bunches of grass beneath the saplings and pulled the trigger. A bright green laser beam cracked out, and the grass ignited. He watched it burn, thinking how much trouble he could have saved himself by using the rifle on its lowest setting to boil the water instead of building that fire.

But grass and saplings were free, abundant fuel. His rifle's charge was a limited resource.

Soon the fire was smoking violently and stinging Clayton's eyes and throat. He waved to clear the smoke in front of him and backed away steadily, moving up-wind of the fire. Rosie backed away with him, sneezing and shaking her head. They watched the fire burn from a safe distance, flames licking the already-blackened bottom of the pot. Smoke churned ever-higher into the sky, veiling the sun and cloaking the hilltop and the oak tree in a dusty orange light.

"Damn it," Clayton muttered. He hadn't been thinking straight when he'd built this fire on a hill. The elevation would only make it even more visible. Growing nervous and impatient, he stepped over to the pot and pulled the rope to bring it closer. The water wasn't boiling yet. He stuck a finger in—

And bit back a cry as he burned his skin. The water had to be close to boiling. He waited another twenty seconds, until bubbles began scurrying to the surface, then reached up and unclipped the rope. Using it to hold the pot, he carried it away from the fire and set it down. The wind shifted, and his eyes began streaming with tears from the smoke. He had to put that fire out and fast, before some Chimera standing on New Houston's walls spotted smoke curling above the horizon.

Clayton used his hands and the back of the hatchet to dig through the grass around the base of the tree, getting enough dust to smother the fire. It didn't work. If anything, the fire grew bigger and smokier than before. Growing desperate, he poured the water out over the fire, canteen and all. The flames died quickly down, and he shoveled on some more dirt for good measure. The combination killed it, and he stamped out the final flaming bits of branches and grass. The canteen sat in the middle of it all, covered in dirt and soot. Clayton scowled as he picked it up, scalding his hands in the process. He clipped it to his belt, leaving the cap unscrewed. If the fire hadn't sterilized it, he didn't know what would.

He'd have to clean it off in the river, though.

Clayton shook his head, peering up at the murky curls of smoke still drifting through the oak tree's branches. Hopefully he'd put out the fire in time. He looked away, down south to New Houston. They had their own clouds of smoke to worry about. Maybe the blast at the ascension center had them distracted, all eyes turned inward.

He stared at the horizon for a minute or two, wanting to make sure that nothing was coming. The city garrison had Lancer fighters, assault shuttles, and hoverbikes, all of which could reach him in a matter of minutes. If they came to investigate, he wouldn't have time to get away.

But nothing was moving above the city. Not even a solitary black speck—just the massive bulk of that Kyron Destroyer. It was probably the *Sovath*. Admiral Keera's flagship spent most of its days hovering over New Houston, poised like a giant boot, ready to crush the human ants below.

Clayton tore his eyes away with a sigh. "Come on, Rosie. I still need something to drink."

He led her back down to the river's edge and washed out the canteen before filling it with water and gulping greedily from the spout.

Rosie took the opportunity to lap up some more water for herself as well.

"You'd better hope I don't get sick," Clayton said as he refilled the canteen and screwed on the cap. He clipped it to his utility belt and climbed back up the hill to get his things. Putting the hatchet and the pot back into his pack, he slung it over his shoulders and then put Rosie's leash back on and wrapped it around his wrist. "Ready?" he asked Rosie.

She just looked at him, then back to the horizon. Her floppy ears were perkier than usual, her whole body tense and rigid. She'd seen something. Clayton followed her gaze. He saw it a split second later. A black, wing-shaped wedge with a humanoid shape hunching over it. A Kyron hoverbike. It was flying slowly over the ruins, searching.

Clayton dropped to the ground, flattening himself in the long grass. Rosie stayed standing. He reached over and pressed firmly between her shoulder blades.

"Get down, Rosie," he whispered.

She resisted at first, then yielded and lay down beside him, but her head stayed up, eyes tracking the hoverbike's approach.

Clayton dragged the rifle out from under

him and dialed the intensity back up to the max.

Connecting his ARCs to the scope and setting the field of view to wide-angle, he tracked the hoverbike at 10x zoom. A pilot wearing a full suit of urban gray armor sat hunched over the controls. The Guard wore black armor, so this wasn't a Federation soldier. *A Kyra?* he wondered. *No, too big. Kyra are small.* It wasn't human, either. No human would have access to a hoverbike. This had to be a Chimeran mercenary.

The bike flew slowly over the three-floor structure where Rosie's owner had built a shanty roof to keep out the sun and rain. Then the bike looped back around and dropped behind a crumbling wall, landing on the third floor.

Clayton's heart beat hard and slow in his chest, his mind racing. Had he left behind any clues that he'd been there? The pilot would find the dead woman in the throes of changing. He'd also find fewer belongings than he should, thanks to Clayton's scavenging. And he'd see the hole in the woman's head from a gun that was no longer in her hand.

Rosie let out a low growl. Clayton spared a hand from his rifle to slowly stroke her back. "It's okay, girl. He hasn't seen us—"

Yet, he added to himself.

CHAPTER 19

Leeto Voth prided himself on having good instincts. It was how he'd known to follow Admiral Reed's mother last night, and it was how he knew that something was wrong with the way this exile had died. She'd been shot in the side of the head, which was an odd angle for starters, because she was lying in the corner of the building, surrounded by walls on both sides. That meant she must have shot herself. The weapon used was also strange—no laser or plasma burns. A *bullet* had punched through her skull, which meant the weapon was from the Union, pre-invasion. But there was no sign of that weapon now. Someone else had been here, and since the pool of blood under the woman's head was still fresh, they couldn't have gone far.

Leeto looked away from the body, out the nearest of several crumbling windows, to where he'd seen smoke rising from the Wastes. He spied a snaking blue river peeking between a pair of trees in a broad, grassy field. There was a hilltop with an even larger tree growing on it, but the smoke was gone now, having dissipated in the wind.

Leeto walked over to the nearest window and crouched behind the opening, using the optics in his helmet to scan the grassy field between him and the river for signs of a camp. Almost immediately, his scan identified the remains of a fire built on top of that hill, right beneath the tree.

But where were the exiles who'd built it? He turned his head back and forth, scanning the slopes of the hill, the field...

A bright green flash of light and the high-pitched whine of a rifle firing caused his helmet to polarize and his personal shield to flare brightly around him. A second laser bolt immediately followed the first, and his shield overloaded with a loud *pop.* Leeto recoiled from the window and planted his back to the nearest wall. A greasy curl of smoke wafted from his chest plate, a molten orange circle fading where the second laser had hit.

Leeto glanced at his shield's power level, but it was completely overloaded, and the power supply spent. He'd have to be more careful from here on. He still had the advantage. Armor. Scanners. A bike. A slow smile curved Leeto's lips as his eyes tracked over to his hoverbike. It was floating a couple feet above the dusty floor, humming softly as its grav engines idled.

That exile should have run while he had the chance. Now, like a wounded *gronta,* Leeto would be twice as deadly.

* * *

Clayton stood with his back to the tree, breathing hard and cursing under his breath. He'd managed to land two clean shots, but it hadn't been enough. That Chimera was wearing armor *and* a personal shield. It wasn't a standard shield from the Guard, because then the first shot would have overloaded it and the second would have killed the wearer.

Rosie's hackles were up, and she was tugging on his arm, trying to tear the leash out of his hand.

"Come on, girl, don't do this to me," he whispered.

Rosie looked at him with wild, terrified eyes. She'd recognized the sound of his rifle going off, and it had scared the hell out of her.

Clayton risked peeking around the trunk of the tree. He was just in time to see the pilot and his hoverbike lifting off and jetting away, back toward the city. He frowned, watching as the pilot zigzagged in the air to avoid making himself an easy target. Then he dropped down to the road on the other side of the buildings, and the whistling roar of the bike's engines faded into the distance.

Clayton couldn't believe his luck. The tension left him and a sigh escaped his lips. The

Chimera probably didn't want to risk his life in a firefight. Without a personal shield to rely on, he'd be almost as vulnerable as Clayton.

Rosie tugged on her leash again, but more gently this time. She looked up at Clayton with a stupid grin.

"Come on, girl. Let's get out of here before he comes back."

He led Rosie down the river-facing side of the hill and walked along the grassy embankment at the river's edge. Hopefully that would keep them out of sight of any other hunters who might still be coming to investigate the smoke from his fire. Clayton followed the riverbank for at least a kilometer to where it met with more ruins and the crumbling remains of a bridge. Here the river flowed up and over ancient chunks of that bridge, creating a noisy patch of rapids.

Clayton stood staring at them for half a second, taking a short break for a sip of water from his canteen. "Looks like we're going to have to hop across. You up for that?"

He looked to Rosie and noticed her standing at attention. She glanced back the way they'd come, as if she'd just heard something.

Clayton's skin prickled with anticipation. He dropped to the grassy riverbank just as a laser tore through the air where he'd been standing.

Twisting around, he grabbed his rifle and

sighted down the scope to a blurry black speck, approaching fast. He popped off a shot of his own, but missed, hitting the water beside the hoverbike with a fountain of steam. The bike veered off sharply in response, flying up the embankment and out of sight.

Rosie barked once and lunged after it. Her leash, still wrapped around his left hand, pulled taut, jerking his hand away from the rifle. He spared precious seconds to untie it, and then Rosie took off, racing up the hill in a black and brown blur.

He wanted to call after her, but he couldn't afford to make himself any more conspicuous than he already was. Clayton rose to a crouch, his eyes tracking the grassy slope beside him and ears straining to follow the fading whistle of the bike's engines. For a second it was flying away from him—

But only for a second. Then it was racing back, the noise rising swiftly in pitch and volume with its approach.

Clayton snapped his rifle up and aimed for the sound. The bike came screaming over the top of the riverbank, dropping a shadow over his head. He fired and knocked off a piece of its landing skids.

He was just about to fire again, when he noticed what was wrong: the bike was riderless.

Clayton threw himself sideways, and the heat of a passing laser beam scalded his right arm. It hit the dry brown grass beside him and ignited it instantly in a burst of orange flames. Clayton withdrew sharply from the heat and smoke and whirled around, searching for the source of the attack. Something caught and reflected a glimmer of sunlight, and Clayton spotted a tiny gray speck peeking out of the grass just above his current position.

Time slowed to a crawl. He dragged his rifle up, his legs already churning to make himself a moving target.

And then a giant shadow leapt onto the enemy's back, and the Chimera's shot went wide, igniting another patch of grass.

The sounds of Rosie's snarling and growling filled the air. Clayton ran up the hill, aiming hastily from the hip with his rifle.

The Chimera was struggling to throw Rosie off, all the while that her jaws were snapping and crunching on his armored hands. She was aiming for the soft seam of fabric that covered his throat, but her teeth were obviously getting through the Chimera's gloves, because Clayton could hear muffled cries escaping the helmet.

He reached point-blank range and aimed his rifle at the Chimera's head. The alien stiffened, and that helmet turned fractionally to look at him. Clayton's finger tensed on the trigger.

"Clayton Cross," a gruff male voice said,

amplified by speakers in the chin of the helmet. "We meet again." The Chimera knew who he was, but he sounded surprised that it was him.

"*Again?*" Clayton echoed. "Who are you? How do you know me?"

Rosie was still trying gamely to reach the alien's throat.

"Call off your mutt, and I'll tell you," the Chimera said, his voice strained from the task of keeping her jaws at bay.

Rosie lunged, her jaws reaching a few inches closer to the Chimera's throat.

Clayton shook his head. "You're not in a position to negotiate. Answer the question first."

"Last night. Lori Reed. You escaped," the Chimera spoke in clipped tones through gritted teeth from the strain of holding Rosie off.

Understanding dawned, and Clayton's knuckles whitened on his rifle. "That was *you*."

"If you kill me, my implant will broadcast my death, and the Guard will be swarming all over this location within minutes." Rosie lunged again, and this time she grazed the Chimera's jugular. "Call off your mutt!"

Remembering what the dog's previous owner had said to stop Rosie from attacking him, he glanced at the dog, and said, "Rosie, friend!"

Her jaws stopped snapping and she backed

away from the Chimera, looking confused.

"Smart move," the alien hybrid said as he propped himself up on his elbows.

"Thanks for the bike," Clayton replied.

Then he pulled the trigger, and the Chimera dropped back down with a smoking hole in his visor. That was when he noticed that the alien's hand was gripping a sidearm holstered to his hip.

"Too slow," Clayton muttered.

Rosie's tongue lolled out, and a giant grin sprang to her face.

CHAPTER 20

Clayton glanced down the embankment to the river. The hoverbike had sailed straight over the rapids to the other side. He mentally calculated a path across the jutting tips of debris from the bridge. He might make it. Or he might slip.

Either way, he needed to act fast. The bounty hunter hadn't been lying about his implant calling in the Guard when he died. By his calculations, Clayton had three minutes at best before a dozen more Chimeras on hoverbikes descended on his location.

Clayton bent down to steal charge packs from the Chimera's belt and stuff them in his pack. He took the sidearm, too, but passed on the rifle. Equipment like that was precious, but he couldn't afford to weigh himself down right now. The spare charge packs would have to do—he slipped those into the pack.

"Stay," he said to Rosie, hoping she understood.

And then he ran down the embankment, aiming for the nearest jutting piece of rubble in the rapids. Rosie ran after him, bouncing and barking excitedly as if it were a game.

"I said *st*—shut up, Rosie!" he snapped, then felt instantly guilty as his tone killed her playful mood. She'd just saved his life, but there was no time to thank her. And besides, she was going to call a horde of Dregs down on them if she kept barking like that.

He stopped running as soon as he reached the river. Rosie looked up at him, as if to say, *Now what?*

Conscious of the weight of the rifle dangling from its strap, and the much heavier burden of his pack, he shrugged out of both and laid them on the shore of the river.

"Here goes," he said to Rosie as he stepped across the gap from the grassy shore to the first piece of rubble. He almost slipped and fell in, but managed to steady himself by stepping to the next piece of rubble in line. The water running over the debris made each step treacherous.

By the time he was halfway across, Rosie started barking again. Clayton risked glancing back and saw her pacing the shoreline. He felt too exposed out here, standing in the middle of the river. Making matters worse, he'd left his guns behind. Clayton hurried on. Just five more steps and he'd reach the other side and the hoverbike.

On his next, he slipped, and he went down

fast. Cold water enveloped him, and Rosie's frantic barking was replaced by the muffled roar of water in his ears.

He felt himself tumbling. His head knocked into something solid, and a cry escaped his lips in a stream of bubbles, taking precious air with it. Then he was free, drifting downstream on a swift current. He fought through to the surface to find Rosie just a few feet away, fighting the current to reach him.

A smile touched his lips. "This way!" he called, and began swimming with the current to reach the opposite shore.

They emerged from the river together. Clayton dragged himself out and rolled over to stare up at the blazing blue sky. Rosie shook herself repeatedly, spraying him with fur and water. He lay gasping on a small, pebbly beach with his whole body aching and exhaustion setting in. The sun beamed down, warming him through his sodden clothes. The steady rhythm of rushing water lulled him. Pushing his growing exhaustion aside, he struggled to his feet. A fresh spurt of adrenaline set his heart pounding, and he scrambled over to the bike. His eyes skipped quickly over the equipment and displays around the control bars—

There. He spotted the blinking red light of the comms panel. Feeling around for his sidearm, he found the holster empty. "Shit." He must have lost it in the river. His hunting knife was still there, but good luck stabbing the comms to death. He bent down and grabbed a fist-sized rock instead. Clayton hammered the comms unit over and over until it began to break free of its mounting. Soon it was dangling by a single, twisted metal bracket. He ripped the unit out with his bare hands and threw it in the river. No one would be able to track the bike now.

Clayton hopped on the seat and took a second to familiarize himself with the controls. Like almost everything else the Chimeras built, the bike was based on old Union tech, and the controls were almost identical to those of an old ground cycle. He planted his feet on the footrests and crouched low over the seat, lying almost prone against the vehicle and sheltering down behind the windshield. He shot a glance at Rosie and nodded.

"I'll be back." Then he turned the handlebars and twisted the throttle on the right grip to jet across the river. Using the brakes under his right foot to slow down on the other side, he leaned over to pick up his rifle and the pack. A second later, he had them both balanced under his chest as he turned around and raced back across the river. Rosie barked once at his approach, and he winced at the noise. He was starting to see how her master had gotten bitten by Dregs.

Jumping off the bike, he cast about quickly

for a way to balance Rosie on the back. The back end of the vehicle contained a decent trunk for cargo. Clayton opened it and peered in. It was half-full of equipment, but there was still about a foot of room for Rosie on top. As long as he didn't make any sudden moves, she should be able to balance in there just fine. Clayton bent down and scooped her up, grunting with the effort, and then dropped her in the trunk. She sat inside, watching him with a goofy grin. "Stay," he warned her.

Her ears perked up, and she glanced back across the river. It was the same thing she'd done before that hunter had come screaming toward them.

"Hang on," Clayton said as he leapt on the bike and twisted the throttle. They raced up the riverbank and out across a field of tall brown grass. Jagged ruins and thick clumps of trees peppered the horizon in front of them. Clayton flew low and close to the ground, hoping that would be enough to hide them from any approaching Chimeras. Grass swished loudly with the wind of their passing.

Clayton checked the bike's scanners, dead center of the dash, right below the windshield. He saw a 3D hologram of the landscape around him. Jagged ruins, the river, the field, the hill with the tree, but not a single blip from incoming hoverbikes. Glancing up to the sky, Clayton looked for signs of aerial pursuit. Again, he saw nothing. Still not convinced, he checked his side-view mirrors.

But all he saw was Rosie lying down in the trunk: her tongue out and snout up, a huge grin on her face, and brown eyes wild with delight.

They reached the line of ruins beyond the field, and he slowed down to follow a cluttered street choked full of the old, rusting shells of parked air and ground cars.

Clayton released a shallow sigh, allowing himself to relax. But then he heard it: a sky-shattering boom, followed by two more. Twisting around in his seat, he spotted the source. Three Lancer fighters wreathed in cone-shaped shock waves were racing toward him from the *Sovath*.

Clayton's heart raced in his chest as he guided them through the ruins, searching for a place to hide. He didn't have long to deliberate, so he took the first place he could see: a long, rectangular building set back from the street with its own parking lot. At least half of it was still standing, the other half collapsed. But the intact portion stood four stories high. A wide entrance gaped darkly at him as he jetted toward it; both doors were missing.

What were the odds that such a big structure this close to the city would be abandoned? Clayton spared a hand from the control bars to reach for his rifle.

He was running from one certain death to

another that could be far worse. If Chimeras found him, they'd just shoot him, but Dregs would eat him alive.

CHAPTER 21

Keera landed her Lancer Fighter beside the blinking red X that marked the spot where Leeto Voth had died. Her two wingmates landed their fighters to either side of hers, the grav engines whistling as they powered down. She pulled a red lever set into the right side of her cockpit, and the canopy slid open, revealing the world in all of its glaring brightness. Her eyes weren't quite as sensitive as a Kyra's, but the glare of full daylight was still too much for her to handle. Reaching around behind her headrest, she grabbed the helmet mounted there, and slipped it over her head. The visor gave a much dimmer and cooler, blue-tinted version of her surroundings.

Keera climbed out and jumped down from the cockpit. She landed on the edge of a grassy slope leading down to a river below. A guttering flame was dying in a patch of blackened grass. Another blackened patch not far from that one had already burned out.

Her eyes tracked away, following the small map in the top right of her helmet visor to the red X that marked Leeto's final resting place. She strode over to him and kicked him with the toe of her boot just to be sure he was dead.

Footsteps followed her, long grass rustling. "Shot in the head. Point blank," Commander Treya said as she appeared beside the corpse. Keera glanced at her. Treya also wore a helmet, her face inscrutable behind the glossy black visor. "Time of death was only five minutes and twelve seconds ago," Treya said. "Whoever killed him has to be close by." Her head turned, looking to the patches of burned grass. "There was a firefight. Maybe more than one assailant? Had to be to get the better of a hunter like Voth. They wouldn't be armored or shielded. He was."

"We're not here to hunt down his killers," Keera whispered.

"Then why are we here, Admiral?"

A good question. Keera stared into the dead man's helmet for a moment, then dropped to her haunches and pulled it off. A ruined face stared back at her, a big hole punched between his eyes, puckered and glaring just above the bridge of the man's nose.

"We're here to make sure he's dead." Tracking beacons and ID implants didn't lie about such things, but they could always be hacked. It was a long shot, but she'd been hoping that Voth was somehow a part of her mother's plan to defect to the resistance. Her mother might have planned to fake her own death. In which case, Voth might have faked his own soon afterward.

But now, seeing the hole in Voth's head, and using her helmet's scanners to match his face to the digital records of his identity, Keera realized that there could be no doubt about what had really happened. Voth had killed her mother, claimed his bounty from the Overseer, and moved on to his next target: random exiles in the Wastes. But one of them had proved too much for him. A sneer lifted Keera's upper lip.

"Let's go," she said, straightening and turning toward her Lancer Fighter once more. The vehicle sat hunching on the ground like a giant black spearhead. It was streamlined and sharply-pointed to give the smallest possible cross-section to enemy gunners during a head-on attack.

"Shall I make Voth's tracking data public again?" Commander Treya asked as she headed back to her own fighter.

"Why? Whoever killed him will be long gone by the time the nearest squad can get here."

"I respectfully disagree. If we're not going to follow up on this, at least someone else should. Whoever killed him can't have gone far on foot."

Keera stopped and stared hard at her

executive officer. "Who says they're on foot? Voth would have used a bike to get here. Do you see it anywhere?"

"Then we have an exile with a stolen vehicle. That is even more reason to hunt them down."

Keera took a shallow breath. "Voth killed my mother, Commander. Leave it be."

Treya hesitated, saying nothing for several seconds. When she spoke, her voice was faint, but cold and sharp as a knife: "She was a traitor, Admiral." An amplification of that statement rippled through Keera's thoughts—*she was also a disgusting human. Good riddance.*

Keera's ire rose, filling her whole body with a blazing heat that made it hard to think straight. Telepathy was an ability that few Kyra had, let alone Chimeras. It supposedly meant that Keera was of royal blood and born to rule. If she hadn't had a *human* mother, and if she had been a Kyra and not a Chimera, she would have become an Overseer by now.

Keera smiled thinly at her XO. She imagined ripping Treya's throat out with her teeth and popping her eyeballs with her claws. Instead, she took a deep breath and spoke as calmly as she could: "Are you challenging my orders, Commander?" If Treya said yes, then Keera might actually have the chance to rip the other woman's throat out.

Instead, Treya hesitated, saying nothing.

Her cowardice had squelched her ambitions to steal Keera's command more than once in the past. And with good reason. Keera was undefeated in combat. Being able to read her opponents' thoughts in the arenas had won her every challenge she'd ever fought.

Keera and Treya stared at one another, their glaring eyes hidden behind their helmets. Before the silence between them grew too long, Treya gave in and bowed her head. "No, Admiral. I submit."

"As you should," Keera replied, then turned and stalked the rest of the way to her fighter.

CHAPTER 22

Clayton cruised through the broken doors of the building where he'd chosen to hide. The shadows enveloped him, and Rosie let out a low growl. He tapped the brake under his right foot and drifted to a stop inside the entrance in front of a pile of concrete rubble with twisted rebar poking out. Dust danced in the jagged rays of sunlight slanting through cracks in the ceiling. Clayton blinked furiously to get his eyes to adjust to the gloomy light, then he swung his leg over the bike and hopped down with his rifle and his pack. He spent a moment digging through the pack until he found the Kyron solar lamp he'd taken from Rosie's dead master. He dragged it out and activated it. A dim blue wash of light peeled back a broad swath of shadows. He turned to Rosie, and found her lying flat in the back of the bike, head on her paws, watching him. Her eyes flicked up, regarding him skeptically.

"I know it's not much better, but it's all I've got," he whispered. Not for the first time, he questioned the wisdom of the SWMD sending hauler drivers out at night with rifles but no tactical lights to go with them.

The logic was that the night-vision scopes were better and would attract less attention from the Dregs with their sensitive eyes. That was true enough, but the tunnel vision afforded by the scope could be deadly in close quarters like these, and Dregs would hear and smell him long before they saw him.

"Come on, girl," Clayton whispered, and snapped his fingers lightly beside the bike.

She got up and peered over the edge, inspecting the floor before looking back to him expectantly.

"Lazy mutt," he mumbled, shouldering his rifle and setting the lamp down. He scooped her up and plopped her on the floor, grabbed her leash, and wrapped it around his left hand.

"No more running off," he said, scratching her behind one ear. "We need to do this together, okay?"

Rosie's only response was to start panting. *I'll take that as a yes.*

Clayton grabbed the lamp with his left hand and held his rifle out with his right, keeping the stock clamped under his arm for added stability. At least laser weapons had zero recoil. Taking a moment to get his bearings, Clayton shone the lamp down a long corridor to the left full of deepening shadows. He swept the lamp to the right and saw broken scraps of sunlight gilding the dusty, rubble-strewn floor.

Left it is, he thought. It seemed counter-intuitive since Dregs would also prefer hiding in darker warrens, but he'd rather surprise them while they were asleep than the other way around.

The corridor grew progressively darker as they went. Clayton walked as slowly and carefully as he could, but no matter how careful he was, his boots still crunched in the bits of concrete and other debris that littered the floor. Old, rusting metal doors with flaking blue paint lined the corridor on both sides. Broken rectangular windows gaped at the top of each door, letting in dusty bars of sunlight.

Clayton stopped and peered through the nearest window to see a familiar room setting: a *holoboard* with a metal tray for markers, turned gray with dust. The twisted metal skeletons of desks and chairs were scattered around the room, their wooden seats and surfaces long-since rotted away.

This was a school, Clayton realized. He looked to Rosie, and she looked up at him. She wasn't panting anymore, and her eyes were big and round in the dim blue light radiating from the lamp. She looked terrified. Or maybe that was boredom. He was probably projecting his own fears onto her.

Turning away from the classroom, he gave Rosie's leash a tug and continued on, chasing the shadows ever deeper into the school.

He reached the end of the hall and turned right down another one. It was lined with more rusting metal doors with flaking blue paint, but halfway down the length of it was a stretch of matching blue lockers.

He didn't bother checking rooms to his left; they were all flooded with natural light coming in from banks of windows on the ground floor. Dregs would never hide in such brightly-lit rooms. Not during the day, anyway. The doors to his right were another story. There were fewer of them, and he found several that were windowless. Nothing but solid metal. He tried the handles, sparing two fingers from the lantern rather than the hand that held his rifle. The first two doors were locked, but the third one wasn't.

"Get ready, girl," he whispered, his finger tightening on the trigger of his rifle. The door was shut, but Dregs weren't entirely dumb, and they had hands just like humans did. Opening a door was no problem for them.

Pushing gently, he began easing the door open...

A loud screech issued from rusty hinges. Clayton winced at the noise and froze, waiting for a reaction from something on the other side.

His scalp prickled with sweat, his heart skipping in his chest.

Nothing.

He pushed the door open the rest of the way—

And the dim blue light of the lantern flickered over metal racks and shelves full of cleaning supplies. He passed his lantern back and forth, probing the depths of the space. It wasn't a bad place for him to hunker down. Only one entrance to watch. He checked the other side of the door for a lock. It had a simple push knob built into the handle, but the mechanism was rusted to bits. The knob went in, but the handle didn't lock. Probably just as well. He was just as likely to wind up locking himself in as the mechanism got stuck. He could drag a shelving unit in front of the door instead.

Clayton's stomach growled, reminding him of another imperative. Food. The school wouldn't have any—it looked like it hadn't been inhabited since the invasion, and after almost a century, not even canned food would be edible. The cans would be rusted or their contents putrefied.

His mind worked the problem for a moment. He couldn't risk going out to hunt, or for that matter, making another fire to cook whatever he might catch. But maybe the hoverbike had some kind of emergency rations in that cargo compartment? He hadn't checked the contents thoroughly yet.

He looked to Rosie, then back to the storage room. He'd be better off scouting the rest of this place without her—if she heard or saw something, she would just bark and summon every Dreg for miles. This was as good a place as any to leave her for now.

He led her inside, tied her leash to the metal post of a shelving unit, and then went down on his haunches to scratch her behind the ears. "I'm going to be right back," he whispered. "Wait here and don't make any noise, okay Rose?"

Her tongue popped out, panting in the hot, stuffy room. Casting about quickly, he found an old plastic bin. He tipped out a pile of black, moldering papers and then poured the remainder of the water from his canteen into the container and carried it over to Rosie. Her head dipped inside the bin, and she lapped noisily from it.

"Good girl."

He left her like that and eased the door shut behind him. Darkness enveloped the storage room, and he winced, wishing he could have left her the lantern. He waited for a minute, listening for howls or barks, but she didn't make a sound. Taking that for encouragement, he hurried back the way he'd come. Upon reaching the bike, he noticed that it was standing in plain view of the entrance. He dragged it toward the hall; it was almost too wide to fit, so he didn't take it in too far. Besides, he needed to be ready for a quick getaway. Once he was satisfied that the bike couldn't be seen from outside, he powered it off to save its charge. The bike slowly sank down to the dusty floor.

Clayton heard a muffled *boom* and roar of engines. He ran to the entrance of the school to see those three Lancer fighters that had sent him into hiding in the school now flying back to the *Sovath*. His racing heart slowed somewhat, relief coursing through him. Going back to his hoverbike, he quickly searched the contents of the storage compartment. He pulled out a high-powered laser rifle, the kind that a sniper might use, a spare charge pack for the same, followed by a tightly wrapped solar sheet and pegs to stake it to the ground. There were adapters and cables for both the bike and various types of charge packs. Clayton grinned at the find. He would be able to recharge his weapons with this.

Below the solar sheet, he found a length of stun cord, a bandoleer of grenades, a medkit, and a repair kit for the bike. Finally, right at the bottom, was a metal case stamped with the silver, spread-winged Kyra and ring of stars that were the emblem of the Kyron Federation.

He opened the case to find it packed full of blood-red bars and squares. They were all coated in a shiny film of edible plastic. Knowing the Kyra, they'd taste just like a rare steak.

Not Clayton's favorite flavor, especially when they also looked about as dry as a protein bar, but food was food, and he was starving.

Clayton packed the rest of the contents back into the storage compartment, and then unslung his pack to stuff the rations in.

When he was done, he hurried back down the hall. Time to barricade himself in with Rosie. When night fell, they could come back out. It would be bad timing to avoid Dregs, but they'd be much less likely to run into bounty hunters and soldiers from the Guard. Better to deal with primitive beasts than intelligent ones armed and armored with the latest technology.

As Clayton walked down the corridor to the storage room, he was surprised to note that Rosie hadn't made a peep in all this time. She was sitting in the dark, all alone, and yet rather than howl about it like any other dog Clayton had ever known, she was keeping her snout shut. Maybe she was smarter than he thought.

Clayton came to the door of the storage room—

And found it ajar, a gap of about an inch revealing the darkness beyond. He froze, his heart hammering in his chest. Had he left it open? Could a breeze have done it?

He reached for the door and pushed it aside. A rusty screech sounded, and the lantern flooded the storage room with dim blue light.

Clayton's mind captured the scene in an instant: Rosie, crouching low, her hackles up and teeth bared in a quiet snarl; the skeletal form of a hunching humanoid with skin so pale that it seemed to fluoresce in the azure glow of the lantern. The creature turned with a hiss and a phlegmy cry. Red eyes that looked purple in the blue light squinted against the glare.

Clayton aimed for its chest, but hesitated. The sound of the rifle discharging might draw in more of them. He stepped through the open door, intending to shut it behind him to muffle the sound.

But just as he advanced, the Dreg threw its head back, and a high-pitched screech escaped its dry, cracking black lips. Clayton pulled the trigger, and a dazzling flash of green light burned a glowing orange hole straight through the Dreg's chest. It collapsed with a guttering tongue of flame dancing briefly around the entry-wound.

Rosie got up and barked, tugging at her leash to get at the fallen creature.

Clayton winced at all the noise and quickly shut the door of the storage room with another rusty scream of protest from the hinges. He leaned back, planting his weight and his ear against the door, listening...

But that Dreg's cry wasn't echoed by any others. He sagged with relief and looked to

Rosie. She'd abandoned her attempts to get at the fallen Dreg. Now she was looking at the door, her ears more erect than usual. She began panting and whimpering and tugging to get at the door. Clayton planted his ear against it once more, shut his eyes, and held his breath.

All he heard was the muted drumbeat of his own heart.

But then—

A distant, fading screech. Followed by a cacophony of at least a dozen more.

Clayton eyes flew open, and he cast about quickly, looking for something he could use to block the door handle or barricade the door.

That was when he noticed the narrow slice of light spilling in on the side with the hinges. Only one of two hinges still held the door to the frame. The bottom one was missing, leaving a jagged, rusty gap in the frame. Clayton went for a closer look, scanning the upper hinge with the lantern. It was loose, hanging on by a thread. He grabbed the door handle and tugged it a few times, and the door rattled noisily in its frame.

It wouldn't hold against a swift kick, let alone a horde of hungry Dregs.

Another cacophony of screeching sounded, closer this time, and Clayton began backing away from the door toward Rosie. He checked the charge of his rifle via the segmented circular display in the bottom left of his ARCs.

Twenty-three shots left. Hopefully enough, but he had a bigger problem: the rifle would overheat if he fired it too fast, and Dregs weren't going to hold back and wait for a coolant flush.

Grimacing, he dropped to one knee beside Rosie and sighted down the scope to the door. A cackling cry shattered the silence, and then came the muted thunder of bare feet slapping concrete.

Rosie heard it, too, and she began to growl.

"Easy, girl," he whispered, sparing a hand from the rifle to stroke her back. "Easy..."

CHAPTER 23

The stampede raged past the storage room, and Clayton let out a shuddery sigh. The sound of receding footsteps quieted as the horde ran around the corner to the front entrance of the school.

But then he heard something else: a snorting sound. A shadow passed over the faded bar of light below the door, followed by another snort. A Dreg was sniffing around the door. Rosie growled, and Clayton grabbed a fistful of fur and skin at the back of her neck. *Don't,* he thought at her.

The snorting sound stopped and the shadow retreated. Rosie got up from where she lay beside him and cocked her head—first one way, then the other, her eyes locked on the gap of light between the entrance of the storage room and the dusty floor. When the shadow didn't return, Clayton rolled his shoulders to let out some of the tension. He pried his fist away from the scruff of Rosie's neck.

And then she barked.

Clayton froze, his heart racing loudly in

the trough of silence that followed.

The shadow came back, snorting and scrabbling at the bottom of the door. Then came the teeth-aching shriek of claws on metal as the Dreg tried to dig straight through the barrier.

Rosie barked again and again, and the Dreg outside screamed like some prehistoric monster, driven mad with the promise of fresh meat. That cry was answered almost immediately by dozens more.

"Good job, Rose," he muttered.

She never took her eyes away from the door.

The shadow disappeared again, and a rattling sound drew Clayton's eyes up to the door handle. It began to slowly turn.

Rosie sat down and cocked her head at the door, waiting patiently.

Clayton acted without thinking and shot the door handle. The laser beam fused the metal handle, and the door around it glowed brightly as it dissipated the heat. The Dreg holding the handle on the other side shrieked as it burned its hand.

Try turning that, you bastard, he thought.

The shrieking of claws returned as the Dreg tried digging through again. The door began to shudder against the frame, rattling violently on its single hinge. Rosie got back up and began barking incessantly, as if goading the creature.

Stampeding footfalls reached Clayton's ears through the racket, followed by a clamoring roar of shrieks and snorts. The rest of the horde had arrived.

The sound of scraping claws doubled, and the door began shuddering more violently as at least one other Dreg joined the first.

Clayton's hands flexed restlessly on the handguard and grip of his rifle, his palms slick with sweat. *Not long now...* he thought.

Something snapped with a *ping,* and the door fell inward with a *boom*. Dusty light flooded in. Clayton took aim, sighting down the scope to a crowd of gaunt, bony Dregs standing on two legs. Their red eyes were wide and feverish in sunken sockets; cheeks sucked in, with gaping hollows beneath their sternums, and scraps of old clothing clinging to their dirty bodies.

The two Dregs behind the door dropped to all fours and lunged through at the same time. Their shoulders got stuck in the door frame, and Clayton took the opportunity to shoot them both in the head. They collapsed on top of each other in the door, and the next pair came surging blindly through, their eyes squinting to slits and flowing with tears. The glare of the laser beams had momentarily blinded them, buying him precious seconds.

The Dregs stumbled through on two legs, bounding and leaping over the fallen pair.

Their jaws snapped restlessly as they went. Clayton shot them both in the chest with another two quick trigger pulls. They collapsed a few feet away from him, but one of them was still alive and struggling to drag itself toward him and Rosie. She lunged and tore the back of its neck open with a spray of dark black arterial blood.

The rest of the horde hesitated for the briefest instant, and then surged forward as one. Clayton pulled the trigger over and over, dropping five more Dregs before the rifle gave a sullen *click*. The barrel glowed white-hot, and steam leaked from vents in the sides. Jumping to his feet, Clayton flushed the coolant with a button just above his thumb. A sharp hiss of thick white steam escaped the rifle's vents, and he groped with his left hand for the M99 holstered to his hip—

But his hand swiped through empty space. He'd left the bounty hunter's pistol in his pack instead of holstering it to replace the one he'd lost in the river. Big mistake.

The next Dreg in line came lunging for him with gaping jaws. Another two fell on Rosie. She wriggled free with a sharp yelp as claws tore open her side.

Clayton backpedaled fast and flipped up the stock of his rifle, slamming it into the jaws of the Dreg in front of him.

Bones gave way with a *crunch,* and the creature screamed, stumbling away with the momentum he'd imparted.

A subtle vibration thrummed through the rifle, indicating that it was ready to fire again. He flipped it back around and raked the room with dazzling pulses of green light. The Dregs shrieked and threw up their hands to shield their sensitive eyes as a blinding emerald fire filled the confined space. Clayton dropped eight more of them with ten shots before the rifle *clicked*, overheating again. He hit the coolant flush button, and scanned the room for more targets. Nothing but a tangled field of bodies. Good thing, too, because he only had one shot left.

He ejected the charge pack and replaced it with a fresh one from his utility belt. The charge meter showed thirty shots again, and the rifle thrummed in his hands, signaling it was ready to fire. He swept the barrel around, checking to make sure that all of the Dregs were really dead.

Clayton's eyes tracked back and forth through the room, seeing nothing but the bony, chalk-white bodies of the Dregs. Rosie was missing. Her rope leash ended in an empty collar. She'd managed to pull her head out in her hurry to get away.

"Rosie!" he cried.

Silence.

Maybe she'd run out the door.

He started that way, stepping on and over the cooling corpses of Dregs as he went. "Rose!"

Just as he reached the door, he heard the telltale, whistling cry of a dog in pain. His head snapped around and he followed the sound around the back of the shelving unit where he'd taken his stand. There, backed into a corner, Rosie lay in a pool of black blood, pinned under a Dreg with its throat ripped out.

He rushed to her side and rolled the dead monster off her, heedless of the infected blood that slicked his hands.

Rosie's side was flayed open. A big flap of fur and skin was hanging down, exposing deep, bloody red muscle and the glistening white of her ribs.

Clayton's heart slammed in his chest, and his stomach flipped queasily. Rosie whined again and lifted her head and shoulders weakly, as if trying to get up. A fresh pool of dark red blood welled over her ribs.

"Shhh. It's okay, Rose. I'll get you fixed up." He placed a hand above the injury, on her shoulder, to push her down. She snapped at him from the pain that caused and subsided with a sigh, her breath coming in short, ragged gasps.

Her exposed ribs were moving strangely with each inhalation. Two of them were broken. He winced. She had to be in a hell of a lot of pain. But worse yet, if a claw had punctured one of her lungs, he wouldn't be able to do anything for her.

Tears stung Clayton's eyes as Rosie's breathing slowed and her eyes began sinking shut.

"Hey!" he snapped, his voice booming through the storage room. "Don't you even think about it! You hear me?"

Rosie's eyes flared wide open once more, and Clayton unslung his pack, digging through it for the medical supplies he'd scavenged from her master. He needed to act fast before Rosie lost too much blood or went into shock.

CHAPTER 24

Clayton wasn't a medical expert, but he'd picked up a few things from Sam. He ran for the medkit in the back of the hoverbike and added its supplies to the ones he'd taken from Rosie's former master. He found several hypos and vials full of potent painkillers and injected one just above the site of Rosie's injury. Soon after that, her whining became less frequent, and her eyelids grew heavy with sleep. This time Clayton let her relax, hoping that she would wake up when he was done.

Working fast, Clayton injected the nanobiotics and sprayed the open wound with a can of Regenex to speed healing. Then he pasted the loose flap of skin to Rosie's side and sprayed the ragged edges where claws had torn through with synthskin and more Regenex. Finally, he applied four of the biggest synthskin patches he could find and wrapped it all with an entire roll of compression bandages. When he was done, Clayton was about to shake her awake, but he noticed that her chest was rising slow and steady with shallow breaths, so he decided to let her sleep.

Clayton packed the remaining medical supplies into the kit from the bounty hunter's bike and then zipped it into his pack. Getting up, he stretched out his aching lower back and looked around. The storage room was crowded with dead Dregs. He could drag them out, but their blood would be contagious for a while still, and it was congealing all over the floor. Better to find another place to wait for nightfall.

Bending back down, Clayton scooped Rosie up. She stirred and whimpered in her sleep, one eye cracking open. "Shhh," he soothed, and her eye sank shut once more.

Clayton walked out and carried Rosie deeper into the school. As he went, he glanced into every alcove and open door, hoping that there weren't any more Dregs about. With Rosie in his arms, he wouldn't be able to shoot.

Up ahead, near the end of the hall, the shadows were parted by a patch of sunlight shining on the dusty floor. He hurried over there and found a stairwell crowded with chunks of concrete and other less recognizable debris. If there were classrooms on the second floor, one of them might be safe. The windows would all be broken, but at least he wouldn't have to worry about Dregs coming in. They didn't have wings like Kyra.

Starting up the stairs, Clayton grunted and

adjusted his grip on Rosie as his hands began to slip. His arms were weakening. By the time he reached the first landing, he was breathing hard with exertion, and Rosie was squirming in his arms.

"Easy, girl. Almost there."

He managed to get her to the top of the stairs before he had to set her down and take a break.

Rosie lay there looking at him with sad brown eyes. Her breathing was still shallow, but she looked more alert now. The painkillers and healing sprays must be doing their job. "Ready?" he asked, and then scooped Rosie up again.

Shuffling down a hallway on the second floor, he walked past more lockers and classrooms. Peering through the broken windows in the doors, he soon found one with a sturdy door and two working hinges. It was on the right side of the hall, and the windows were facing away from New Houston. Hopefully that would be enough to keep them hidden from hunters.

Clayton opened the door with a rusty squeal from the hinges and shut it behind them. This time there were two locks—a twist knob built into the handle and a deadbolt. Clayton spared a few fingers from holding Rosie and tried the deadbolt. It took a lot of force to get the ancient mechanism to turn, but he managed to get it halfway locked. He set Rosie down in a corner beside the rotting remains of a teacher's desk. Walking back to the door, he used both hands to turn the deadbolt the rest of the way and then tested the door, turning the handle and throwing his weight against it. The deadbolt held, and the door barely moved in its frame.

He blew out a relieved sigh and turned to a wall full of broken windows on the far side of the classroom. A few of them still had jagged chunks of glass clinging to the frames, sparkling in the deep golden light of the sun. It was busy sinking below overgrown ruins, dry brown grass, and scattered clumps of trees. Clayton frowned. Had that much time passed already? A quick glance at his smartwatch confirmed it: 19:11. Just half an hour before nightfall.

Walking over to the windows, he gazed down, trying to gauge the distance to the ground. At least sixteen feet. He scanned along the length of the room, checking the piles of debris shored up against the base of the building. The highest of them reached maybe five or six feet up the wall. *Good,* he thought, nodding to himself. No Dregs would be climbing in through these windows.

Noticing that his hands were covered in blood, both black and red, he took out his tube of sterigel and used it to wash his hands thoroughly. He wiped them off on a clean shirt he'd taken from Rosie's master. Looking back to Rosie, he saw that she was awake and watching him with her head on her paws. He smiled tightly at her. She was definitely doing better now, but still in no condition to go anywhere. Besides, she'd already proved to be a liability when it came to the Dregs. How much more so when they got close to the city and she saw a garbage hauler or a squad of Chimeras out on patrol?

No, he needed to do this on his own. Looking back to the windows, Clayton searched for a way that he could get up and down. He couldn't unlock the door and go out the way he'd come in without leaving Rosie exposed to Dregs. That ladder her master had built would have been great to have right now. His gaze tracked back to the highest pile of debris, sitting below a window near the far corner of the room. Walking over, he estimated the drop to be around nine feet. He could lower himself from the window sill and decrease it to around two feet. Nodding to himself, he went back over to Rosie and dropped to his haunches beside her. He rested a hand on her head. Her eyes flicked up, as if to ask what was wrong.

"I need to leave you here for a while," he explained. Rosie didn't react to the news, so he went on, "I'm going to leave you with food. We're all out of water, but I'll bring some back for you later, okay?"

He stood up and unslung his pack, fishing through it for the rations. He opened the ration pack and pulled out a handful of red bars, scattering them around in front of Rosie's nose, which began twitching immediately. She lifted her head and turned it to grab the nearest one. The blood-red ration bar vanished in two quick chews.

Rosie perked up and began struggling to her feet to get the next one. Clayton stopped her with a hand on her back and moved the bars into range so she wouldn't have to move. He stroked her back and patted her head while she ate. "Good girl."

When she was done, she subsided with a sigh and lay on her side, panting in the still, stuffy heat of the classroom. Soon the heat would get sucked out with the night. He wished he had some more water for her, but he didn't have time to get any now. He needed to get back to New Houston and contact Sam.

"I'll be back soon, Rose," he said again, and then turned and picked his way between the rusting frames of overturned chairs and desks to the window with the pile of debris below it. Being careful to mind the shards of glass still embedded in the frame, he stepped out the window to the ledge and grabbed the window frame to steady himself as he lowered himself down. Soon he was dangling by his hands from the ledge. He let go and landed with a *crunch* and a sharp jolt of pain from the arch of his right foot. He winced and tested his weight on it, but the pain was already fading. Nothing serious.

Clayton picked his way down the pile of concrete boulders and ran around the base of the building to the front doors. The sun was now vanishing between the tips of towering oak trees. Golden petals of sunlight danced between those scraggly shadows as a breeze rolled across the Wastes.

Clayton kept one eye on the grassy, over-grown fields that appeared between the crumbling metal stands of old football fields. He kept a hand close to his rifle as he ran, worried about early-risers, but there was no sign of any Dregs yet.

By the time he reached the front door and powered up the hoverbike, night had fully fallen, but a three-quarter moon was up and shining bright with the stars. Clayton flew out of the school, through the grassy field that used to be a parking lot, and down the street beyond. Moonlight colored everything silver. Pale, red-eyed monsters snarled and growled at him from the shadowy recesses of crumbling buildings as he raced by. He was going too fast for them to catch up.

Clayton used the holographic map in the center of the console to guide himself, following old streets back to New Houston, all the while twisting and pulling back on the handlebars to maneuver around and over the larger chunks of debris. The rusting skeletons of old ground and air cars were the worst, forcing him to pull up suddenly. Soon he was clear of the ruins and back to the river where he'd fought the bounty hunter.

He turned and flew over the river, heading straight for the ruins on the other side. But then he had a better idea and rather flew down the river itself. It was the perfect road—no debris to dodge and no Dregs to worry about. Here and there, he saw them picking their way down to the river's edge to drink. A few snarled at him as he went whirring by.

Clayton followed the winding curves of the river, sticking to the middle of it. At first he was flying parallel to the distant, gleaming spires of New Houston, but then the river snaked back and he was headed straight for the walls. Realizing that put him directly in view of any Chimeras on the walls, he left the river and began dodging and weaving through the ruins again.

A few Dregs were out, walking on the streets between crumbling buildings. They made an attempt to catch him—swiping with deadly, infected claws as he screamed by—but the shape of the bike protected him, with two swooping wings sloping down to either side of the seat. One Dreg managed to rake its claws over the wing on the right side—

Only to scream in agony as the bike yanked its arm off.

The hordes grew progressively thicker the closer he got to the city, and soon fresh air was replaced by the festering stench of garbage. Towering piles of it covered the rusting hulks of cars to either side of the roads. Dregs combed those mounds, picking and nosing through them for edible scraps.

Using his knowledge of the SWMD's current routes, Clayton stayed clear of any path that might take him close to haulers. Instead, he headed down the east side of the city where the farms were.

Soon the ruins faded to rolling moonlit fields of wheat and corn, and Clayton slowed his approach, dropping down into the tall grass and sticking to the shadows between soaring trees. The sheer walls of the city rose steadily over the horizon with a line of faint blue spotlights shining down from the top to illuminate cone-shaped patches of the wall.

Beyond that, the tallest spires of the city soared into view, blotting out the stars with the glittering white lights of human-inhabited apartments and the dim, fuzzy blue glow of Chimeran buildings. In the foreground, automated sprinkler machines rolled slowly across fields of crops with harsh white spotlights shining down along their length and misty streams of water gushing out. Chimeran patrols were out and strolling along the inner perimeter of a glowing red *razorbeam* fence that ran around the farm. Four parallel laser beams ran between emitter posts, forming a deadly barrier that Dregs could neither cross nor climb.

Clayton guided his bike into the shadowy recesses of a shattered building with just two crumbling walls still standing. Those walls met in a corner that faced the city, and he parked the bike there. He glanced at the scanners to check for the nearby life signs of Dregs or Chimeras—not a blip, and yet he'd clearly seen the Chimeras walking along the fence below. Finding a dial on the scanner's display, he turned it and increased the range. A handful of purple blips appeared that corresponded to the Chimeras patrolling the wall. Still no sign of Dregs.

Encouraged, Clayton hopped off the bike and went over to a shattered window. He crouched behind it and peered down at the farm below, his eyes tracking up from there to the city walls. He had to be within comms range by now.

Fishing through his pocket for the comm piece that Richard Morgan had given him last night, he fitted it to his ear and connected it to his ARCs. Then he tried searching for *Samara*

Cross.

The unit should have found her number instantly, but instead it spat out an error: *Illegal Connection.*

What the hell does that mean? he wondered. He decided to try the hospital where she worked. Someone there should know if she was okay.

But he got the same error.

Frowning, Clayton checked the contacts list—nothing. Then he tried the call log.

There was only one entry, listed as *Unknown Number.* That had to be his contact with the resistance. He thought about calling and asking them to check up on Samara for him. It was either that, or turn on his personal comms and call her directly himself. But his comms were traceable and unencrypted. The signal would pinpoint his location instantly and bring every Chimera in the city down on him. Not to mention the ones patrolling that razorbeam fence.

No, the resistance was his only option. It was a bitter irony that he had to rely on the very group that might have killed Samara just to find out if she was still alive.

Clayton called the contact in the comms log and waited while the device trilled in his ear... He stalked back over to check the bike's scanners while he waited. Still no sign of Dregs.

But the comms just rang and rang...

CHAPTER 25

Keera stood in front of a solid gunmetal gray door, scowling up at the door scanner and jabbing the buzzer repeatedly. After a few seconds of that, she heard footsteps approaching.

The door slid open, and her father's face appeared. Richard Morgan's thick blond eyebrows darted up. "What are you doing here?" He leaned to one side, trying to peer around her, as if expecting a squad from the Guard to be standing behind her.

Keera smiled thinly at him. "Relax. I came alone." She pushed through the entrance, deliberately shoving him aside as she went.

Richard's apartment was brightly lit, but her eyes were shielded by auto-polarizing contacts—not the augmented reality version that humans preferred, just simple membranes to protect her eyes from excessive glare.

The door slid shut behind her, and Keera heard Richard's footsteps following her into the apartment.

"What have I done to deserve a house call from the Admiral herself?" he asked.

Keera stopped in front of the living room windows at the far end of the open-concept space and stood silently gazing over the city below.

"Let's drop the act, Father," Keera said through a quiet hiss. She turned to find him sitting on the couch, his arms spread wide across the back of it, a faint smile on his face that suggested he knew exactly why she was here. "I know you're working with the resistance," she added.

Richard Morgan's eyebrows scrunched together in a frown. "What are you talking about?"

"Relax. We can speak freely. I'm wearing an acoustic dampener. All anyone monitoring your residence will hear is white noise."

Richard set his jaw. "An unnecessary precaution. I am not guilty of anything."

"Really? Because I traced the tracking data of the driver who smuggled my mother out of the city. Do you want to know what I found?"

A flicker of surprise crossed Richard's face, but he said nothing.

"Two things," Keera said, holding up a pair of pale fingers ending in razor-sharp black claws. "One, that the driver is a mutual acquaintance of ours—none other than Captain Clayton Cross; and two, that you met with him less than twelve hours before he smuggled my mother out of the city."

"I did?" Richard appeared to be searching his memories, then he trailed off shaking his head. "When was this?"

"Yesterday morning, at Restoration Park. On the benches by the pond."

"I was feeding the ducks," Richard said. "I don't recall meeting anyone there."

"So it's just a coincidence? Fine. Stick to that story, but you and I both know better."

Again, Richard said nothing.

"She's dead, you know," Keera said.

Richard's eyes hardened. "Who is?"

"My mother."

A flicker of surprise stole across his face, and she realized that he hadn't heard yet. "I'm sorry to hear that, Keera," he said in a quiet voice, his blue eyes drifting out of focus.

"Because you needed her," Keera supplied.

Rather than confirm or deny it, he left the silence to stretch between them. "Why are you here?" he finally asked.

"To warn you. You need to be more careful. I've already lost one parent. I don't need to lose another."

Surprise furrowed Richard's brow, and Keera smirked. They'd never had any kind of relationship, but that didn't stop her from wishing that they did.

Keera went on, "I altered your tracking logs, but if you make another mistake like that, I won't be able to help you."

Richard nodded once. "Thank you."

Just then, something began vibrating in his pocket. A comms piece. He reached for it. "Excuse me."

Keera stalked over to him and snatched it out of his hand before he could put it in his ear. "Hello?" she hissed. "This is Admiral Keera Reed. Who am I speaking with?"

A static-filled silence answered, followed by a *click* as the caller hung up. Keera dropped the comms piece on the floor and ground it under her heel.

Richard watched her with a bemused frown. "What did you do that for? Those things are expensive."

"Now the resistance knows that you're compromised, so you have a good excuse to stay out of it."

"How do you know who it was?"

"Because no one else would dare to hang up on me." Keera turned to leave, her whole body shivering with rage from that brief contact with Richard's contact. It was the resistance's fault that her mother had died! She should have taken the unit back to the Sovath and tried to trace the call.

"Wait," Richard said, his footsteps chasing her to the door. She turned and crossed her arms over her chest. She wasn't wearing her uniform, but rather a gray, nondescript jumpsuit.

"Yesss?" she hissed.

"We could use your help."

Keera's eyes widened, and she felt a vein start to throb in her forehead. "My help? With what? Bombing ascension centers?"

"That was a mistake," Richard replied.

"Clearly." Keera shook her head. "You can't win. No matter what you do, Earth is just one world out of thousands of occupied planets in the Federation, and there are a thousand worlds besides those, all of them teeming with Kyra and Chimeras of every sub-species that you can imagine."

"What about the Chrona?" Richard asked quietly. "We could join them."

Keera smirked and shook her head. "You're assuming that the Chrona are any better. Trust me, Father, if your cause had any hope, you wouldn't have to *ask* me to join you. I would already be on your side."

"But there is hope. Your mother—"

"Is dead! Thanks to you!" Keera thundered. She pushed him up against the nearest wall and bared her teeth in his face, hissing and glaring at him. Richard paled but didn't flinch.

"She was going to help us to find a cure."

Keera released her father with a shove. "That won't solve anything."

"It will. If we can inoculate everyone, the Kyra won't have any reason to stay here. We'll be useless to them."

"Assuming that were possible, they would just sterilize the planet out of spite."

"We could evacuate the cities. Flee to the Wastes. There would be enough survivors to start over. It wouldn't be worth the Kyra's time to hunt us all down."

Keera snorted. "I guess you should have taken better care of your defector then. It's too late now."

"But it isn't," he said quietly. Reaching into his pocket again, he fished out a small black box. "Here."

"What is it?" Keera asked, accepting the device with a frown.

"Your mother's genome. You can use it to clone her."

Keera stared at the box in her hand and slowly shook her head. "I can't do that."

"Can't, or won't?" Richard countered. "You did it once before. For Captain Cross's wife."

Keera looked up quickly. "That was before Primark Thaedra took over the Federation and declared cloning a heresy."

"Surely someone with your resources could still find a way."

"Cloning her won't bring her back."

"You mean in all the time that Lori was in captivity the Kyra never interrogated her? Never once mapped her mind?" Richard frowned. "I find that hard to believe."

Keera thought back over the years. Her

mother had been a subject of constant suspicion, and she'd been subjected to mind scans on multiple occasions. Assuming that data was still kept somewhere, there was a chance it could be used to do what Richard was suggesting.

He smiled and slowly nodded. "That's what I thought. I'll leave it up to you."

"Even if I could do it," Keera began, "she's too recognizable. The Overseer knows her; my entire fleet knows her... everyone would know what I did."

"Not if you delivered her to us. No one outside of the resistance even saw her die. If she were ever found in the Wastes, people would just assume that she miraculously survived."

"And then you could use her to develop your cure," Keera replied, her eyes narrowing swiftly.

"Win, win," Richard said. "Besides, we didn't abduct her. This is what your mother wanted. It's what she would still want if we could ask her now."

"I need to leave," Keera said.

"Of course." Richard waved the door to his apartment open, and she stalked out and down the corridor to the elevators. As she rode down to the street level, she stared at the black box in her hand, her mind turning endlessly over the possibility of actually resurrecting her mother.

Maybe it could be done, but if anyone learned of it, she would be executed in the arena as a heretic. And no one would be bringing either her *or* her mother back after that.

CHAPTER 26

Clayton stomped on his comms unit just as soon as he heard the admiral's voice on the other end. Richard Morgan must have been captured. The Chimeras were probably going crazy searching for whoever had bombed the ascension center.

Despair clawed inside of Clayton's chest. He'd come all this way for nothing. Glancing around, he checked to make sure no Dregs were sneaking up on him. He was still clear. He could retreat to that school, hunker down with Rosie for the night, and then go make a life for himself with her—somewhere far enough from the nearest occupied city that they would be safe.

His eyes strayed back to the crumbling window where he stood, to the fields of corn and wheat beyond that razorbeam fence. An old farmhouse stood about a mile from the fence, surrounded by sheds and barns, and a cluster of giant, cylindrical grain silos. A new idea began to filter through his churning thoughts. It was a long shot, and dangerous as hell, but it might work. There would be humans in that farmhouse running the farm, not Chimeras. Chimeras were the property owners, but they were only ever trained for one thing: war and killing. Everything else was left to regular humans.

The farmhouse itself would be vulnerable, and if Clayton could just find some way past the fence, he could sneak in and borrow a comms piece or a computer terminal while the occupants slept. Using a borrowed comms unit to contact Sam wouldn't raise any red flags in the system, and there weren't likely to be any patrols at the house. Humans and Chimeras preferred to keep their distance from one another.

Clayton's gaze tracked down the length of the glowing red lasers that made up the fence. There wasn't enough space between the beams for him to slip through, and any part of him that accidentally touched those beams would be sliced clean off.

He could fly over the fence with the hoverbike, but it was far too conspicuous. He'd be spotted by patrols instantly. Digging under might work, but it would take too long, and the patrols would find him before he could finish.

Scanning the fence, he saw just one possibility. There was a clump of trees growing close to the fence, and one of them had thick branches that actually reached over to the cornfields on the other side.

Clayton judged the distance to those trees. It was at least a few hundred meters. He'd have to skulk through the ruins to get closer, and then make a run for the back of them to avoid being seen by passing patrols. It would be risky, but he could do it.

Clayton grabbed his rifle in both hands, his eyes darting among the ruins and tall, waving clumps of grass behind him. He walked over to the hoverbike and checked the scanners one last time to make sure no Dregs were nearby. Again, he only saw the purple blips of Chimeras down by the fence. Reassured by that, he powered the vehicle down and left it in the corner of the building. He'd be far less conspicuous on foot.

Clayton connected one of his ARCs to the night-vision scope of his rifle, and confined that view to a picture-in-picture window. Holding the rifle stock to his shoulder, he moved as quickly and quietly as he could through the ruins, sweeping the barrel back and forth to look for the telltale white heat signatures of Dregs in the monochromatic green and black display. The bike's scanners wouldn't have detected anything through the walls of ruined buildings, so if Dregs were hiding nearby, they would hear him now and come crawling out of their dens.

That might not have been a problem, but

he couldn't risk firing a weapon this close to the walls and those patrols. Clayton spared a hand from his rifle and drew the hunting knife from his belt. Six inches of steel against the two and three-foot reach of a Dreg's arm and their razor-sharp claws. He cast about the crumbling street where he stood, checking the debris for something he could use to extend his reach. What he needed was a long stick and something to affix his knife to the end. The compression bandages from the medkit might work.

Clayton shouldered his rifle and hurried down the street, checking the ground. Nothing but grass, chunks of concrete, and old rusty sheets of metal. He checked the saplings growing between chunks of asphalt in the road, but they were all too green. They'd bend like spaghetti with a good thrust.

Continuing down the road, he turned left into an alley, his eyes still on the ground. What he wouldn't give for a good sturdy length of rebar.

A rock thumped down in front of him, and Clayton froze. His head snapped up, scanning the buildings to see where it had come from.

A hunching white creature stood watching him from a window on the second floor of the building to his left. Their eyes met, and it bared sharp teeth at him, black with rot. A low snarl escaped its lips. Clayton grabbed his rifle

JASPER T. SCOTT

and took aim, hesitating. He couldn't risk it, and the sound would only draw in more Dregs.

He kept his aim and eyes on the creature and began backing slowly away. It watched him silently, its cranial stalks twitching and auditory cones tracking him as he went.

It made no move to leap through that window. Maybe it wasn't hungry.

But then it snarled again and bent down. Its arm blurred, and a rock came sailing after him. It hit him in the shoulder this time. A burst of pain sent white-hot sparks shooting down to his fingertips. He bit back a cry and smiled coldly up at the creature. *Thanks for the idea, shit head.* Sheathing his knife, he bent to retrieve the rock and tested the weight of it in his hand. Maybe three pounds and a little larger than his fist. He reared back and took aim, hoping he still remembered something from all those little league games with his father. If he'd only known back then that he was practicing to kill alien mutants, he might have taken the practices more seriously.

His arm snapped straight, his torso pivoting to add force to the throw. The chunk of concrete flew from his hand, straight up and through the window...

And smacked the Dreg in the head.

He expected it to drop where it stood. Instead, it shook itself and stumbled sideways. A trickle of thick black blood streamed from the side of its bald head. Red eyes narrowed swiftly as they found him once more. The Dreg's arms spread from its sides, and hands and claws came up. Then it's head snapped forward, jaws yawning wide, and every muscle in the monster's body flexed at once. Thick black veins popped out everywhere, and a horrendous shriek erupted from its lungs.

Shit. Clayton turned and ran, sprinting down the alley, his footsteps crunching loudly in the debris. He skidded on a piece of rubble at the end and ran left down the street, now moving parallel to the farm and heading in the general direction of the trees.

Glinting eyes pricked through the shadows of the broken windows and missing doors of buildings to either side of the street. Hisses and shrieks followed. Galloping footsteps ratcheted into hearing behind him. Clayton shot a look over his shoulder to see the wounded Dreg racing after him on all fours, gaining fast.

Clayton's eyes darted to either side of the street, looking for a place that he could barricade himself into, but the ruins were overrun with Dregs. Every building had at least one or two sets of eyes peering out.

How the hell are there so many of them? he wondered. It didn't seem possible for the Wastes to support such a large population of Dregs. There wasn't enough food to go around.

Unless they're eating each other, he thought. Fresh supplies of Dregs were constantly being expelled from the ascension centers in the cities.

The Dreg chasing him grew close enough that Clayton could hear its ragged breathing. He threw another quick look behind him and saw two more Dregs climbing out of windows to join the chase on two legs. They held back, content to let the one snapping at his heels do all the work.

Clayton reached the end of the ruins and burst out into a field of tall brown grass, silvered with moonlight. His lungs were burning, his legs shaking. He couldn't keep this up. Reaching for his knife once more, he drew the blade, stopped, and spun to face the incoming monster. It came bounding toward him with jaws wide and slavering, red eyes wild with bloodlust.

Come on! Clayton thought.

He waited until the last possible second. Saw the Dreg leaping into the air like a lion—

And dove to the side, lashing out with the knife as the Dreg sailed by. The blade found its mark, and the creature screamed.

It landed and rose up on two feet with black blood streaming from a gash in its side. The Dreg came walking toward him this time, with hands flexed and claws gleaming darkly.

Clayton tossed a look back the way he'd

come. The other two Dregs were walking now, too, approaching warily.

Focusing on the one in front of him, Clayton backed away, trying to keep out of range of its claws. His mind raced for a way to land another blow without getting torn to pieces in the process. One slash of those claws and he'd be infected. On the bright side, he wouldn't have to worry about turning into one of them. They'd eat him alive long before that could happen.

The Dreg in front of Clayton approached steadily, and he backed up just as fast, all the while getting closer to the other two. He angled the other way to keep all three in front of him.

His right foot rolled over something, and he almost fell. He glanced down to see a twisted length of rebar with a chunk of concrete clinging to the end. Clayton's eyes widened. He shouldered his rifle and sheathed the knife, bending down to pick up the rebar. It was at least three feet long, and the piece of concrete at the end was heavy enough to make a good club.

Clayton grabbed it in both hands and stopped backing away. "Now it's a fair fight," he whispered.

The Dreg stepped into range, and he swung. It ducked and ran at him. He sidestepped and swung again. *Thunk.* The concrete connected with the back of the Dreg's skull. This time it went down and lay still in the long grass.

Spinning back to face the other two, Clayton saw them both hesitating. "Come on," he muttered. "I don't have all night."

And as if they'd understood him, they both came surging forward. One went left, the other right, trying to outflank him. *And people say Dregs are brainless,* he thought.

Clayton backed away again, angling sideways to keep them both ahead of him. The first one snarled as it came within six short feet. Clayton spat at it and bared his teeth, hoping to goad the creature into a premature attack. The other one shrieked at it, as if to warn it away. Impatience won. The nearest Dreg lunged, and Clayton swung hard.

The chunk of concrete shattered against its skull, and it went down in a heap.

The last one roared and went down on all fours, bounding toward him. Clayton grabbed the twisted length of metal in both hands and braced his feet, waiting. The last Dreg did just as the first one had, leaping up to cover the last few feet, jaws gaping wide and aiming for Clayton's throat.

Rather than evade the attack, he stood his ground and held the rebar out like a spear. The Dreg fell on it with its full weight and impaled itself. It landed thrashing and screaming in the grass with blood gushing from its stomach. It was making such a terrible noise that even the Chimeras at the farm had to be able to hear.

Careful to mind the claws, Clayton stepped around it, drew his knife, and slammed the blade through the side of its head. The Dreg's cries and struggles immediately ceased. He pulled the knife out and wiped it on the grass, careful not to dirty his hands with infected blood.

A quick look around confirmed that no other Dregs were coming. His eyes tracked back down the field to the distant stand of trees growing beside the razorbeam fence. He couldn't see the fence from here, so hopefully none of the Chimeran patrols had seen him either.

Just in case, he ducked ran the rest of the way as a hunchback, hiding in the long grass.

Five minutes later, he reached the trees; his legs were shuddering violently from the strain of crouching for so long, and he was gasping for air. He straightened and leaned against the trunk of a maple tree. Three whistling black specks of hoverbikes descended on the ruins where he'd been a few minutes ago. They were searching the area. Clayton ducked down again and backed deeper into the shadows between the trees. If those Chimeras were smart, they'd realize that the Dregs hadn't killed each other, and then they'd realize that they were dealing with an exile. They'd probably find his stolen hoverbike. Clayton cursed under his breath, wishing he'd had the sense to hide it better.

He turned and ran through the trees, heedless of dry leaves and branches crunching and snapping underfoot. He needed to hurry. The cornfield was tall enough that he could hide in it, and those Chimeras wouldn't be looking for him *inside* of the fence. Sneaking into the farm was now his only chance of survival.

CHAPTER 27

Clayton clung to the trunk of the oak tree, looking down on the deadly razorbeam fence below. He'd knocked a handful of leaves free as he'd tested his weight on that overhanging branch, and now he watched as the laser beams sliced them into confetti.

If the branch broke as he shuffled down its length, he would turn into confetti too.

Wincing at the image that provoked, Clayton scanned down the length of the fence, checking to make sure there weren't any patrols nearby.

He was lucky. The commotion with the Dregs had served as the perfect distraction. Only two Chimeras had stayed by the fence, and even they were staring up at the ruins, their attention focused outward.

Seeing his chance, Clayton stepped out onto the branch. Holding the trunk of the tree for support while he found his balance, Clayton concentrated on the tightrope ahead of him. It would have been easier if the branch weren't balanced above deadly laser beams.

Sparing a glance for the two Chimeras standing down the fence to his right, Clayton braced himself and let go of the tree trunk. He walked quickly, thinking that would make it harder to fall. But as he neared the end of the branch, it began to shake and bend under his weight. The fence wasn't below him anymore, but if the branch broke, it would disrupt the beams and set off an alarm.

Hearing the first warning crack from the tree, Clayton leapt free, aiming for the stalks of corn below. He managed to cushion his fall with them, but still landed hard on the packed dirt. A starburst of pain exploded in his left ankle, and he bit back a cry, rolling onto his back and gasping with blinding agony. A quick check revealed that his ankle wasn't broken, but it was probably sprained. He could spray Regenex on it and hope for the best, but it would still take a good night's rest to recover, and right now he didn't have time to go digging through his pack.

He heard Chimeras shouting in the distance. Thinking they must have seen him jumping down, he began crawling as quickly as he could through the field. He did his best not to disturb the cornstalks as he went, knowing that their tips could be seen waving if he did.

Crawling was slow going, and his ankle was throbbing like hell.

The Chimeras had stopped shouting, but he

didn't take that for a good sign. If they were hunting him, they'd rely on stealth. And if any of them were officers, they'd be wearing the more expensive cloaking armor. He could run right into one of them and never see them standing there.

All he could do was hope and pray that they didn't find him. Time passed like molasses dripping through a funnel. Sweat drenched Clayton's body from head to toe. He kept glancing back, expecting to see a Chimera creeping up behind him.

But seconds dragged into minutes and still nothing happened. After a while, he risked taking a break to spray Regenex on his ankle. It was already swollen. He injected a painkiller from his medkit and let out a slow breath as the throbbing ache immediately receded. Soon it was numb enough that he could risk putting his weight on it. The leg held, so he got up to a crouch and began moving as quickly as he dared through the cornfield. He shuddered to think how bad that ankle was going to hurt when the painkillers wore off.

Clayton hurried on for at least fifteen minutes. It was impossible to see clearly through the field, so he had no way of knowing if he was headed in the right direction. He just hoped that he wasn't circling back around to the fence and those Chimeran patrols.

At last the cornfield parted, and the farmhouse appeared. Clayton crouched at the edge of the field, scanning darkened windows for signs of life—and the exterior of the house for any patrols.

It was clear. Glancing back the way he'd come, he judged that the Chimeras at the fence wouldn't be able to see him over the tops of the cornstalks. All the same, he kept his head down as he ran across the grassy stretch between the cornfield and the house. He reached the building and walked quickly down the side of it and around the back. New Houston's walls soared up in front of him, maybe five hundred meters distant: big and shining a dark gray-blue in the light of their spotlights. He didn't see any Chimeras up there gazing down, but he wasn't going to linger long enough for one to show up. Walking quickly along the back of the house, he quietly tested the sliding windows, looking for one he could jimmy open.

Then he found one that was already open, a screen with a thumb-sized hole in it the only barrier to keep him out. He peeked over the window sill and shaded his eyes with his hands, trying to see inside.

Hazy outlines appeared: a bed with two people asleep on it, one of them snoring softly. Two nightstands and two lamps. A wardrobe. A door.

Too risky. Walking down further, he came to the back porch. It was made of old, sagging beams and shaded by a roof of the same. The door beyond was open, nothing but a flimsy screen door between him and the inside of the house. Clayton smirked and shook his head. Whoever lived here had been lulled into a false sense of security by their fences.

Clayton crept up a flight of two wooden stairs and stepped lightly over the sagging porch. Just as he reached the screen door, one of the beams groaned noisily under his weight. He froze, sweaty hands twitching on the grip of his rifle...

But no reciprocal sounds of people waking issued from the house. Reaching for the door with a shaking hand, he pulled it open easily. The pneumatic arm of the door was broken, so it didn't resist or try to shut itself. He stepped into a darkened hall and crept gingerly across buckling and bulging wooden floors.

Just as he reached the kitchen, another beam creaked under his foot, and again he froze with his heart hammering in his chest. Straining his ears for the sound of someone getting out of bed, Clayton heard nothing but the crickets outside and the soft, steady rhythm of that man snoring. Encouraged by that, he started forward again, his eyes darting around the darkened interior of the house. No sign of technology. Comms pieces would probably be close at hand, inside or on top of nightstands. But surely there was a computer terminal around here somewhere. Clayton crept down a hall toward the bedrooms, his eyes scanning the doors, trying to guess which one might actually be an office. At least the sound of that man's snoring told him which door to avoid. Growing impatient, he tried the door right after that one. It creaked loudly as it opened, making Clayton wince. His entire body shook with adrenaline. This was worse than sneaking through Dreg-infested ruins. He peered through a gap in the door, spotted a sink, a toilet, and a shower curtain. Not an office. Turning away, he headed for the door at the far end of the hall.

"Who are you?" a small voice whispered. And then a light snapped on, and he heard a sharp intake of breath.

Clayton stopped cold and slowly turned to see a little girl standing in the hall. She was wearing plain white pajamas. Long blonde hair flowed to her shoulders, and big dark eyes squinted up at him. She couldn't be more than seven years old.

"Shhh," he said, smiling and holding a finger to his lips. "I'm a friend of your father's."

"What are you doing here in the middle of the night?" she asked, her voice rising from a whisper.

He took a quick step toward her, not knowing what else to do, but knowing that he had to keep her quiet. She took two steps back. "Come any closer and I'll scream."

He stopped. Tried another smile. "I'm here to leave a surprise for his birthday." It was the only excuse he could think of.

"His birthday was last month."

"Oh, I know, I know," Clayton said, thinking fast. "But better late than—"

And then she screamed.

CHAPTER 28

Clayton cringed at the sheer volume of the little girl's cry. Whoever was asleep in the other room reacted immediately. A loud thump sounded, followed by hushed mutterings. Clayton's eyes tracked over to the door, and his rifle snapped up.

"Dad, be careful!" the girl cried.

The door cracked open, and the barrel of a repeating plasma shotgun popped out, aimed straight at Clayton's chest. "Hands in the air!" a gruff voice said, using the door as a shield.

"You first," Clayton replied, keeping his aim steady. His laser rifle would burn a hole straight through the door and whoever was on the other side, but at this close range that shotgun would cut him in half. It all came down to whoever shot first.

Clayton's finger tensed on the trigger.

"Haley, get back in your room and lock the door!"

The little girl's eyes darted to Clayton, then to her father's room, and she withdrew with a stifled scream and slammed her door.

Clayton heard her muffled sobs retreating behind that door, and something inside of him clicked. This man was a father. Maybe he had a wife. It wasn't worth it.

He eased his finger off the trigger and slowly raised his hands in the air, aiming his rifle at the roof. "Okay, I give up," he said. The door swung wide, and a big man with red hair and tanned, leathery skin stepped out wearing a black bath robe. He had a quarter-inch of beard growing all over his face and looked to be in his mid-forties—the same age as Clayton himself. That was odd, because the Kyra usually administered longevity treatments to people in their twenties or thirties to keep them in prime reproductive health.

"Gun on the ground! Now! Slowly..."

Clayton bent to place the rifle at his feet.

"That it?"

Clayton nodded, even though he had two pistols in his pack. He couldn't get them, though.

"Who are you, and what are you doing in my home?" A flicker of light passed over the farmer's eyes as he answered that question for himself via facial recognition. His whole body stiffened as the result appeared on his ARCs. "You're an exile, wanted in connection with the resistance. Well, you picked the wrong house to raid numb nuts. Any last words?"

A shadowy form appeared behind the man,

scurrying around inside the bedroom and periodically stooping to pick up articles of clothing.

"I can explain. I'm not with them."

"Says here that you are."

"I was, but I left after they bombed the ascension center."

The farmer grunted. "Doesn't matter. You've still got blood on your hands."

"Maybe I do," Clayton agreed. "But I'm not here to add any more. My wife was supposed to be at the ascension center when the bomb went off. I came here looking for a comms unit that I could use to contact her. I..." Clayton trailed off, shaking his head. "I just need to know if she's okay."

The farmer's aim wavered slightly. "So what's the rifle for?" He nodded to the weapon at Clayton's feet.

"The Wastes are teeming with Dregs."

"Fair enough. How'd you get past my fence?"

"There's an oak tree growing over it. I climbed that and jumped down."

"Hmmm. Say I lend you my comms, and you contact your wife, what then?"

"If you let me leave, I promise you'll never see me again."

The shadow behind the man stepped into the light of the hall. A ghostly white face appeared with vaguely feminine features, red eyes, and sharp, jutting facial bones. Cranial stalks twitched above her bald head.

"Let me kill him," she growled, flashing sharp teeth in a predatory grin.

"Easy, Mona. No one's doing any killing yet."

"His head is worth a thousand credits," she purred.

The farmer dropped his aim with a frown and half turned to the Chimera behind him. "That don't make it right to cut it off."

"He's an exile. A criminal."

The farmer looked back to him and jerked his chin. "You ever killed anyone?"

Clayton hesitated, but decided to stick with the truth. "A few Kyra."

The barrel of the shotgun dropped the rest of the way to the floor, astonishment flashing across his face.

"Bullshit."

"I was captain of the ship that first encountered them."

"One of the Forerunners?"

Clayton nodded. "*Forerunner One.*"

"Well, goddamn, Captain! You didn't just kill a few Kyra. You killed nine out of ten people on the whole fucking planet! You led them here." He began shaking a finger at Clayton and nodding his head. "Give me one good reason why I shouldn't shoot you and then deliver your head to the Kyra for my reward."

Clayton grimaced. "Because the Union sent us out there looking for intelligent life. It was part of our mandate. We took every precaution not to lead them here, but there was nothing we could have done. They found Earth by mind-scanning one of my crew. It wasn't because they followed us."

"He's right," the Chimera standing behind the farmer said.

"I only got back with my crew a year ago," Clayton added.

"Mona, get my comms, please, sweetheart."

She hissed and bared her teeth again, but the farmer glanced at her, and she withdrew.

Clayton frowned at the exchange. A human giving orders to a Chimera? And what were they doing together in the first place? The pieces clicked belatedly into place, and Clayton's jaw dropped.

"She's your wife?"

"Not legally. Chimeras and Humans aren't allowed to get married."

"Your lover then."

The farmer conceded that with a nod and a shrug. "She doesn't find Chimeras attractive. Can't blame her for that, I suppose."

Mona returned, her red eyes flashing at him. The farmer cracked a crooked smile and winked. "Except for you, sweetheart. You're sexy as hell."

She grinned and snapped her teeth at him,

as if to take a bite. Then she handed over the comms unit and the farmer held it out to Clayton, keeping one hand on his shotgun. "Go on. Take it."

Clayton took a cautious step toward the man. "Thank you," he said as he accepted the device and fitted it to his ear.

"Don't thank me yet. You don't know if your wife's alive."

"Assuming he was telling the truth," Mona added.

"We'll see soon enough," the farmer replied.

Clayton said nothing to that as he connected his ARCs to the device. A moment later, he searched for Samara Cross and called her number. It was the middle of the night, so she should be on her shift at the hospital.

He held his breath, listening to the comms unit trilling over and over in his ear.

"Hello?" a familiar voice said.

A dam of emotion burst inside of him. Tears stung his eyes, and a shaky smile sprang to his lips.

The farmer nodded once and dropped his aim once more. "That's the reaction I was looking for."

"Hello?" Samara asked again. "Who is this?" A pause. "Harold Neem? How did you get my number?"

Clayton was about to reply and identify

himself, but the words caught in his throat.

"Why isn't he saying anything?" Mona whispered darkly. "I told you he was lying!"

Harold held up a hand for her to be quiet.

It was tearing Clayton apart, but he knew what he had to do. He ended the call without a word and handed the comms piece back to Harold. "Thank you," he whispered, his voice full of gravel.

"That doesn't prove anything," Mona said.

Harold fitted the comms piece to his ear and the bright glow of screens flickering across his ARCs, clouding his blue eyes. "No, but the comms log does. He just called Samara Cross. Facial recognition identified him as Clayton Cross." The light vanished from Harold's eyes. "Story checks out."

"Thank you," Clayton said.

"Now what?" Mona prompted. "You can't just let him go."

"No? And why not?" Harold replied.

"Because if anyone finds out, you'll be executed!"

"Hmmm. Well, she has a point there."

"I won't be seen. And if I am, I won't tell anyone that you helped me."

"You won't have a choice. They'll pull it out of your head with a scan," Mona said.

Clayton gave in with a sigh. "Do what you have to do. But I need you to promise something."

Harold raised bushy red eyebrows at him.

"I have a dog. She's locked in on the second floor of an old school about five miles northeast of here. If you kill me, at least go and get her."

Harold looked to Mona with a furrowed brow. "Now we definitely can't kill him. The man's got a dog to take care of."

Mona hissed, but said nothing.

"Look, I'm gonna be honest. Letting you go is a big risk for me, but maybe we can help each other out and make it worth my while. You said you used to be with the resistance."

Clayton nodded slowly, confusion etching his brow.

A file share request popped up on Clayton's ARCs. He accepted it, and a picture of an attractive woman with long red-blonde hair and bright green eyes appeared. She looked to be at least thirty years old.

"Who is she?" Clayton asked. "Your wife?"

"My other daughter. Veronica Neem. I'm older than I look, but nowadays who isn't? I was alive during the invasion, if you can believe that."

Clayton nodded slowly.

"You know where the resistance is hiding?" Harold asked.

Clayton hesitated. "Maybe. I could find them, though."

"Good. You do that, you find my daughter,

and you tell her that her daddy sends his love. Then you come back here and let me know how she's doing. Think you can do that for me?"

"And how is he supposed to do that?" Mona demanded. "He's lucky he made it this far the first time. The patrols will catch him if he comes back."

"Good point," Harold replied. "We'll meet at that school you mentioned. Fair enough?"

Clayton nodded.

"Good. It's settled then."

"This is a bad idea," Mona said. "If someone catches you..."

"Overseer Damos made it open season on exiles. I'll just say I'm out hunting them."

"How do you know he'll keep his end of the deal?" Mona asked, jerking her chin to Clayton.

"Because if he does, then I'll do the same for him with his wife."

"You'd do that?" Clayton asked.

Harold nodded. "Count on it. What do you say?"

"Not a lot of downsides for me," Clayton said.

"Guess not," Harold agreed.

"It's a deal."

Harold smiled and then looked to his Chimeran partner. "Let's get him out of here. Would you retrieve the man's rifle, please?"

Mona hissed and shook her head, but then

stepped by him and retrieved the weapon. She jabbed the barrel in Clayton's stomach. "Move," she growled.

"Thank you," he added, his eyes on Harold.

A door clicked open, and blue eyes peeked out. Harold glanced at her. "Haley..."

"Is he bad?" she asked.

"No, honey. Go back to bed."

"Get moving," Mona ordered, and jerked her head down the hall, in the direction he'd come from earlier. Clayton nodded and started forward. Mona's aim shifted to his back as he marched back the way he'd come.

"I'll find her," Clayton said as he walked past the farmer.

"Good luck," Harold replied, watching as he left.

Once he was back outside, Clayton ran with Mona to the cornfields, hurrying back to the point where he'd come in. When they drew near, he felt a hand pulling him back, Mona's claws digging in above his shoulder.

"Wait," she whispered.

Footsteps went rustling by, then stopped. Mona stepped in front of him just as the dim blue beams of two Kyron flashlights swept their way. "It's just me!" she called.

"Sergeant?" another voice replied.

"Yess," she hissed.

"What are you doing in the cornfields?" the voice replied.

"None of your business. Now move along, private!"

"Yes, ma'am."

A pair of footsteps receded into the distance, blue flashlights sweeping away as they went. Clayton sagged with relief. He heard a muffled muttering among the two Chimeras as they continued on, and one of them laughed a little too loudly.

Mona came crunching back over to him, her boots crushing old cornstalks as she went. "Come on," she whispered, waving him on toward the fence. They reached the edge of the cornfield together, and Mona stepped deliberately toward it. As soon as she came within a few feet of the glowing red laser beams, they snapped off, and she waved to him again.

Clayton hurried out of cover, trading cornstalks for the tall grass on the other side of the fence. Mona handed his rifle back to him and nodded once. "I still think this is a bad idea. Prove me wrong," she whispered.

"I will," Clayton promised, shouldering the rifle and melting away into the field. He followed it up to the ruins where he'd left his hoverbike, hoping the Chimeras hadn't found it.

To his surprise, the bike was still there. Powering it on, he checked scanners and found the area clear of both Dregs and Chimeras. *At least for now,* Clayton thought.

Purple blips were walking in pairs along

the razorbeam fence around the farm, but none were close enough to see or hear him. Clayton hopped on the back of the bike and quietly reversed out of the ruined building.

Soon he was racing back over crumbling, moonlit streets. He reached the river and followed it back to the school where he'd left Rosie, stopping once to refill his canteen. He drank deeply, draining it twice, and then filled it again for Rosie. He went to her old home, retrieved the ladder, and balanced it awkwardly across his lap as he flew the rest of the way to the school.

It was time to get some sleep. Tomorrow he could go looking for Harold's daughter.

Clayton flew back across the river, racing through a pocket of cold air as he headed for the school. He was barely a block away when he heard the screams. Not Dregs—*human* screams.

He eased off the thrusters, drifting down the broken street that ran by the front of the school. Those screams were getting louder, not coming from the school, but from somewhere farther down the street.

He should just fly off the street now, hide his bike in the school, and climb back up to Rosie. Hiding would be the smart move.

Another scream split the air. A woman. Then came the high-pitched whine of a laser rifle discharging, followed by more screaming.

Clayton gritted his teeth and slowed to a crawl in front of the school. He dropped the ladder there, and then gunned the engine, racing toward the sound of that woman's cries.

CHAPTER 29

It didn't take long for Keera to find her mother's most recent mind scan. It was just five months old. *Good enough,* she thought as she patted the front pocket of her flight suit, feeling through the fabric for the black box that her father had given her and the matching one with her mother's mind scan data on it.

Keera's boots rang on the vented floor panels of the *Sovath*. Officers nodded to her as she strode by. None commented on the metal case she carried or the flight suit she wore, and none of them dared to ask where she was going.

She made it to the hangar without incident, and waved a hand to open the glossy black canopy of her Lancer fighter. The cockpit slid open, revealing a relatively cramped interior with two seats, one directly behind the other, but she wouldn't be taking a co-pilot on this flight. Climbing a short ladder, Keera stowed the metal case back there and then clambered into the pilot's seat. She hurriedly buckled her flight restraints and pulled the red lever beside her right arm to close the cockpit canopy. It slid over her, revealing a high-resolution display on the inside of the armored alloy canopy. It was clearer than glass, to the point that the canopy actually looked invisible. Keera diverted her eyes from it and ran through a quick preflight check. That done, she keyed the comms: "Helios One, to *Sovath* Flight Control, requesting clearance for launch."

"One moment, Helios One," a male Chimeran voice answered. Lieutenant Drake.

Another familiar voice replaced his just a second later. "Admiral, what do I tell Overseer Damos when he asks where you are?" It was her XO, Commander Treya. Her prying for details wasn't as subtle as she probably thought. Treya was looking for any excuse to get her into trouble.

Keera's eyes narrowed. "You tell him that I left to handle a personal matter, and that I will be back within a day."

A hesitant pause answered. "Are you sure you wouldn't rather share your flight plan with me? Secrecy begets questions."

Keera clamped down on a frustrated hiss. "I will answer them when I return. That will be all, Commander."

"Yes, ma'am."

Lieutenant Drake's voice returned. "You are cleared for launch, Admiral. Thaedra's blessings for your flight."

Keera gave no reply as she fired up the grav engines and hovered off the deck, turning on the spot to face the open side of the hangar. The fuzzy white glow of its atmospheric shields blurred her view of the towering spires of New Houston below. Inching the throttle up, she roared out of the hangar bay and pulled up hard, burning for the stars. The amorphous glow of the city fell away below her, and shadowy clouds enveloped her cockpit.

Keera set course for the jump gate at Lagrange point one, and entered the queue of vessels waiting to use the gate. Pulling up a holographic star chart from the nav, she selected the Aldrian System, or Kapteyn's Star, as Humans knew it. Sending that destination to the jump gate, Keera left the fighter's autopilot to handle things from there.

She set the ship's alert system to warn her if any threats were detected, and then reclined her seat and crossed her arms over her chest, allowing her weariness to finally trickle through and drag her thoughts into a hazy wash of daydreams. Her uneasy rivalry with Treya brought back old, painful memories from her youth. Normally, Keera would shut them down, but this time she allowed her mind to go there, to remember...

She saw herself standing in a blood-soaked arena on Mars, red sand turned grainy and black where blood had recently soaked through. Thousands of Chimeras and Kyra were standing around the arena, hissing and shrieking for her to finish the fight. Keera's hand shook as she held a blurry black *sikath* to her best friend, Asha's throat. The edge of the blade was nano-thin, shielded, and vibrating in a sawing motion at several thousand times a second. It would slice Asha's head clean off as easily as if she'd swiped it through thin air. One twitch of her wrist, and it would be over. But she didn't want that.

"Submit, Asha," Keera remembered herself saying.

But Asha had just sneered, baring bloody teeth at her. "I told them you were too weak. You won't do it. I know you, Keera. You won't last long under Admiral Korvos' command. *You* submit!"

Keera hesitated. She and Asha had been training together at the Chimeran Academy on Mars. Both of them had graduated as third lieutenants, but Keera had been assigned to a coveted position on the bridge of Admiral Korvos' ship, the *Sovath*, and Asha had not.

So Asha had challenged her for it. To say that Keera had been shocked would be an understatement. She was a *K'sar*, a telepath chosen by the gods to rule, but that was a secret she guarded well. She'd read flickers of the jealousy in Asha's mind and thought nothing of it. Everyone had dark thoughts now and again.

But Asha was one of the few people who *knew* of her gift, and she'd obviously taken care to push the vast majority of her jealous thoughts out of her mind whenever Keera was around. She'd spent all of her free time training and learning new sword-fighting techniques.

But it hadn't been enough. Keera had predicted her every move in the arena, and Asha had never stood a chance.

Tears ran hotly down Keera's cheeks. The shrieking from the stands had grown quiet, and a familiar silhouette appeared on the podium overlooking the sandy floor where they stood. A deep, grating voice boomed down to them. "Kill her! Or submit to her!" It was Overseer Damos.

Keera remembered squinting up at him, blinking tears against the glare of the dim blue spotlights shining down. "I..." Keera had been about to step back, to bow her head and drop her sword.

But in that brief moment of inattention, she read Asha's intent to grab her sword and kill her with it.

She flicked her wrist before she even realized what she was doing. A sickening *thump* sounded, and Asha's head rolled into view, her mouth and red eyes wide with shock.

Keera opened her eyes now and swallowed past a bitter knot in her throat. She focused on the sea of stars ahead.

Killing Asha had been the beginning of Keera's long, bloody ascension to finally become Admiral of the Dakkari System—otherwise known as Sol. Keera preferred the Human designation for it. Dakkas were sewer rats on Kyros, and also a pejorative Kyron name for Humans. Somehow human Chimeras had forgotten who they shared their DNA with. If Humans were Dakkas, then what did that make them? The sons and daughters of Dakkas?

Keera sneered at the thought. Supposedly the Chimeras were all equal citizens in the Kyron Federation, but the federation was rife with racism, and Human Chimeras were treated only slightly better than their human, *Dakka* forefathers.

Keera watched as the bright gray circle of the jump gate at Lagrange one grew large. Her fighter slipped into line behind a stream of ships leaving Sol. The gate flashed periodically with their departures, dazzling Keera's eyes. She felt for the boxy outlines of the data drives through her flight suit, reassuring herself that they were both there. She wished her mother had come to her before planning to defect to the resistance. Maybe she could have talked her out of it. If their cause had any hope of success, Keera would have been the first in line to join it. Even now, with their plan to develop a cure... If they succeeded, how would the Kyra react?

Keera's mind cast back to that arena, to Asha's defiant eyes, and the frenzied shrieks and hisses of the Chimeran and Kyra on-lookers...

No, there was no doubt in Keera's mind. If the resistance somehow inoculated everyone against the *Krr'd'va—the blessing of Kyroth*—it would be a bloodbath.

There had to be a way to prevent that from happening.

* * *

Clayton flew past the school, following the sound of the woman's screaming to an old, slumping warehouse girded with collapsing chain link fences. It had been shored up with old, rotting wooden boards and rusty corrugated sheet metal to make a kind of compound. Clayton pulled up and over the fence, seeing as he did so a pair of hoverbikes in a field of clumpy grass and rubble that looked like it had once been a truck loading zone. The warehouse itself was collapsed on one side, windows angled up to the sky on the other, as if a heavy boulder had fallen right in the middle of it.

The screams were silent now. Clayton flew his bike around the back and landed it behind thick bushes. Leaving the bike idling, he checked his scanners. Two purple blips inside of the warehouse marked the positions of Chimeras. Three yellow blips identified human life signs, but two of them were slowly fading. Clayton grimaced. He was too late.

He heard a noisy crash, followed by one of the Chimeras shouting something to the other in Kyro as the third yellow blip began weaving a snaking line through the warehouse. Clayton's eyes skipped up to a gaping window about ten feet above the collapsing metal side of the building.

He jumped off the bike and grabbed his rifle in both hands, stalking quickly around to where the Chimeras had left their bikes.

Another shout came from the building, followed by the shrieking report of a laser rifle. Clayton broke into a sprint, heedless of the noise he made.

Silence resonated from the warehouse. He reached the front of it, spotted the nearest opening—the rusty metal sheet of an old ground truck-loading door, jammed halfway open. Nothing but shadows beyond.

Clayton connected his left eye to the scope of his rifle and reduced the image to the top left corner to keep his vision free. The green, black, and white imagery of the night-vision scope revealed a white speck going prone under that cargo door. Clayton pulled the trigger two times fast. A bright flash of personal shields blinded the rifle's scope with the first shot, but the second bored a glowing orange hole straight through the Chimera's helmet.

Clayton ran the rest of the way to the door and crouched down in the opening, popping his rifle up like a periscope. No sign of the other Chimera.

A soft *crunch* sounded behind him.

"Hands up, dakka! Drop the weapon!"

Clayton froze and slowly turned to face the second Chimera. Its face was hidden by a full suit of glossy black armor, shining silver with the moon.

"I said drop it! I won't ask again." The Chimera hefted his rifle.

Clayton gave in, bending down to leave his weapon on the ground. His mind raced as he did so, trying to think of a way out, but his back was against the wall—literally. He could dive and roll, hope the Chimera's first shot missed or hit an extremity. The second shot would probably put him out of his misery for good, but at least he'd have a chance.

Another thought occurred to him as his hand tightened on the grip of his rifle.

He glanced up with a sneer. "I challenge you."

The Chimera tossed his head and barked a hissing laugh. "You can't challenge me. You're just a worthless Dakka. There is no honor to gain from defeating you!"

"You'd rather shoot an unarmed man while you hide behind your shields and armor?"

"It is no less than a *dakka slekess* deserves."

"Coward," Clayton sneered. If nothing else, at least he was buying time for the surviving human to escape.

"Who were you chasing in there?" Clayton asked.

"Ces dakka slekess."

"I'm sorry, my Kyro is rusty. Are you talking to me?"

"Three motherless dakka. A female, male, and their *lek slekess*—their little girl."

A sharp spike of horror shot through Clayton's heart as he remembered the woman's screams. The mother, no doubt. These Chimeras had come here hunting a family. "You killed them," Clayton said quietly.

"Two of them. I'll get the girl when I'm done with you."

It was hard to believe this soldier standing in front of him had been a human once. Somehow, the process of changing into a new species made it easier for Chimeras to brutalize the one they used to be.

"Say hello to Kyroth for me," the Chimera said.

Clayton nodded and smiled thinly at his executioner, wondering how an advanced alien species could be so primitive in their beliefs, and moreover, how they could suck formerly agnostic and atheistic humans into their polytheistic religion.

An animal cry cut Clayton's thoughts off,

and drew the Chimera's gaze away from him for a fraction of a second. A small blurry shape came running at it, screaming piteously.

Clayton didn't hesitate. He dropped to the ground and snatched up his rifle. The Chimera's head turned back to him just in time to catch two stabbing green lasers in the chest. A bright flash of shields absorbing the first shot peeled back the night, and the second shot sent the Chimera crumpling to its knees. It fired back, but missed, and then the blurry shape fell on it with hands and feet swinging, sobbing and screaming as tiny fists beat uselessly against the Chimera's armor.

"Get back!" Clayton warned the child, struggling to find a clear shot. But she gave no reply. The girl took a flailing punch from the Chimera and went sprawling. Clayton fired again, and a molten orange hole appeared in the Chimera's helmet.

The child ran back in, her fists flying once more, oblivious to the fact that the Chimera was dead.

Clayton jumped off the ground and covered the gap between them in a second. He scooped the child up in one arm and turned to run back to his bike.

"Noooo!" the girl screamed, kicking and screaming as he carried her.

"Shh, it's okay," he tried.

"No! No! No! Let go! Let go!"

He ignored her, pushing through tall grass to reach his bike. A quick look at the scanners revealed two fading purple blips, and no sign of the other yellow ones from before. The girl's parents were dead. No question.

Clayton shouldered his rifle and sat the little girl on the bike, gripping her by both of her shoulders. She struggled to break free, landing a punch on his arm and a kick to his gut that almost took the wind out of him.

"Listen to me!" he groaned. "I'm not like them. I'm good, okay? I'm like your mommy and your daddy. I won't hurt you. I promise. What's your name?"

The girl stopped struggling for a moment, tears glistening on her cheeks, her eyes silvered with the moon.

"We need to get out of here. More of them will be coming. Do you understand?"

The girl sniffed and nodded.

"I'm Clayton Cross, but you can call me Clay. Do you like dogs?"

Another nod.

"Good. You'll like Rosie then."

Clayton hopped on the bike behind the girl, pinning her between his arms as he grabbed the control bars. "Hold on tight," he added, and the girl turned and wrapped her arms around his neck. Clayton jetted back over the chainlink fence to the street. The girl squeezed his neck so tight that he could barely breathe. She was sniffling against his shoulder, her tears soaking through his sweaty shirt.

He heard her whispering something beside his ear as he slowed to pick up the ladder he'd left in front of the school, but her voice was too soft, stolen by the wind.

"What was that?" he urged, leaning back in the seat to look her in the eye. Her thumb popped into her mouth, and she looked at him with big, moonlit eyes. He gently pulled the thumb from her mouth. "What did you say?"

"Nowah."

"Noah? That's your name?" he asked, wondering why her parents would give her a boy's name.

"Nowa," she insisted.

"Nova?" he guessed.

She nodded.

"Nice to meet you, Nova. Hang on. We're going to get Rosie." He held the ladder in one hand, balancing it on the left wing of the bike as he guided it around back of the school.

Soon he was climbing up with Nova on his back. Rosie barked once when she saw them.

"Shhh," he urged, setting Nova down and hurrying over to the dog. Nova hung back, her thumb in her mouth again. She couldn't have been more than four years old. Now she was an orphan living in the Wastes.

Rosie jumped up and licked him all over when he stooped down to untie her leash from the crumbling remains of the teacher's desk. She was obviously feeling better.

"Easy, girl," Clayton whispered as he wrapped the leash around his hand.

Glancing back to the open window where the ladder was, Clayton gave up trying to figure out how he could get Rosie down it. It was leaning almost vertical against the wall, and it didn't reach all the way to the window, so she couldn't use it like a staircase. Instead, he went to the door and unlocked the deadbolt. Easing it open, he popped his rifle out to check the hall for Dregs with the scope. No sign of heat signatures.

Turning to Nova, he waved her over. "Come on. She doesn't bite. I promise."

Nova hesitated, then came crunching across the classroom. Rosie turned to watch the girl approach, her tongue lolling, a big grin on her face. Nova came right up to her and patted her once on the head. Rosie responded by giving her face a big lick, and Nova giggled.

Clayton held out his other hand, and Nova took it. Like that they left the classroom together: man, dog, and toddler, tethered to each other by circumstance and the horrors that they'd each suffered.

Clayton didn't have any hands free for his rifle; he just had to hope Dregs hadn't come crawling back in during the hours that he'd been away.

They crept down the stairs together, then down the corridor and past the open door of the storage room with the festering corpses of the Dregs that he and Rosie had killed earlier. They continued on to the front entrance and back outside.

Clayton scanned the sky in the direction of the warehouse for signs of Chimeras flying in to investigate the tracking beacons of the two he'd killed. Nothing yet.

Leading Rosie and Nova around the back of the school, he picked Rosie up and perched her in the cargo compartment, then balanced Nova on the front of the seat and himself behind her.

Soon they were racing through the Wastes, heading farther north, in the opposite direction of New Houston. He thought briefly about the task that farmer had given him, of finding his daughter, but for now it would have to wait. He needed to get somewhere far enough from the city that the sounds of a dog barking or a child crying wouldn't be heard.

Despair came swirling in as Clayton thought about the long, endless struggle that now lay before him. Surviving in the Wastes with two extra mouths to feed was not going to be easy. Life was about to get a whole lot harder, and losing his wife for the second time made that so much worse. But he had to stay positive. Sam wasn't dead this time; she was okay. His unborn daughter would be okay. And in time, he would be, too.

Nova clung to Clayton's neck, no longer crying. He felt her arms relax as she fell asleep. Sparing one hand from the control bars, he pulled himself higher up on the seat, pinning her in place between him and the dash. As he did so, he caught a glimpse of Rosie in his side-view mirror. She lay in the back, grinning broadly, her tongue out and flapping in the wind.

Clayton smiled wanly. Maybe life in the Wastes wouldn't be so bad.

CHAPTER 30

Keera strode quickly through the dark, dirty corridors of *Slek't'va* Station, which literally meant *Mother to the Stars.* She carried a heavy, grav-shielded case in her left hand, and unfortunately no weapons. Despite this being an outlaw station, there were still laws to be followed.

She'd been here only a handful of times, back when the station had been a legal trading hub in the *Vrr'ka* System. Now it was hidden away in the heart of the Mari System, five jumps and sixty-three light-years from Earth. The Mari System lay in the middle of *Frontier Space,* the vast gulf of territory between the Kyron Federation and the Chronan Empire. That made it a dangerous region to venture into. As it was, Earth was already on the front lines, hence the presence of Keera's fleet.

A motley group of three alien Chimeras strolled toward Keera, staring hard at her as they approached. For a moment, she was afraid they could tell who she was, but her facial features were hidden by the prosthetic mask she wore, and her ID implant was currently broadcasting a false identity. They were probably just staring because human Chimeras were relatively new to the Federation. Keera recognized one of the three as a Cirrk, barely two feet tall, and covered in the white fur of its species, with orange eyes and just two cranial stalks instead of four. Long canine teeth protruded down from the top of its short snout. The second had wrinkly gray skin and black-red eyes with the thick, bony head spikes of a Horval. It walked on four legs with a pair of muscular arms curled up against its chest. It had the more typical *four* cranial stalks and lumbered along with heavy *thudding* footsteps. The final Chimera was of a species that Keera had never seen before. It had four silvery pinpricks for eyes, sunken into a round, chalk-white head with a puckered black orifice for a mouth, and no sign of a nose or any cranial stalks for hearing.

A broad, echoing concourse opened up to the left as Keera reached the end of the corridor. She walked through the open doors and dove into a bustling marketplace, loud with hundreds of competing voices and crowded with Chimeras of every species imaginable. She had to block her mind to the maddening whispers of their thoughts as she wove a path across the deck.

Towering viewscreens curved up from the

walls and over the ceiling, rising at least four stories between thick reinforcing beams. The concourse looked like the converted bridge of a massive spaceship—which was exactly what the station was: an old Horval bulk carrier. Through those viewscreens, space was bright with a mix of reds, greens, and blues—gasses swirling together as they fell into the black hole that Slek't'va Station currently orbited.

Broad, squat stools filled the deck around the troughs that Horval Chimeras preferred to tables, but there were also couches for bipeds and a long, glowing blue bar counter with both high and low stools. Keera spotted a section with various types of tabletop games, and a ring for public challenges. Inside that ring, two Horvals were rearing up on hind legs and beating each other senseless while onlookers placed bets.

Appetizing smells mingled with revolting ones as Keera wove through the crowds toward the left side of the concourse. It was stacked with a ramshackle arrangement of habitat modules on three separate levels. Broad catwalks and spiraling access ramps gave access to the upper levels, while the modules on the bottom lay open with serving counters and glowing signs advertising various types of food. Above that, crowds of people meandered by the various shops. Keera reached the ramps and slowly climbed them to reach the second floor.

She shouldered through the crowds, her boots ringing on the thin metal floor grating of the catwalk. She studied the glowing signs above the doors to her left, searching for one in particular, a place she'd last been to with her mother, Lori, little over a year ago. She passed an independent dispensary that spanned three whole modules, a gun shop, a ship parts shop, and finally...

An unlabeled module with the door sealed and nothing but a glowing red number to identify it—*603*. She stabbed the call button on the door panel and waited.

The black eye of a camera glared down from just below the sign. It made an audible noise as it swiveled and focused on her.

"Yes?" a deep, gravelly voice thundered, speaking in Kyro.

Stepping closer to the door and the audio-pickups, she replied in Kyro: "Vika, it's Keera Reed."

A pause. "How did Keera Reed find Vika? Mother to the Stars is in uncharted space."

"A bounty hunter, Leeto Voth. His nav logs revealed the location of the station."

An angry hiss came through the speakers. "And Leeto shared this knowledge with Keera?"

"No, he's dead. His ship is impounded, awaiting seizure for lack of any heirs to pass it to."

"This is big unfortunate. What does Keera want from Vika?"

"I would like to hire you for another job."

"How does Vika know he can trust you?"

Keera stepped even closer to the audio pickups and whispered, "Because if I wanted to turn you in, I would have come here with my fleet, not alone. And if I *am* here to capture you, it's too late to worry about it now."

"Not if Vika slits your throat."

On that ominous warning, the door slid open, revealing a dimly lit receiving area on the other side. Keera stepped in, and the door slid shut behind her.

A small white-furred Cirrkan Chimera stepped into the foyer from an adjoining living space. Pale, pink-red eyes squinted up at her.

"Is something wrong with the clone Keera purchased?" the Cirrk asked in his paradoxically deep voice.

"No," Keera said, shaking her head.

"Good, because Vika does not do returns or exchanges," he added that with a sly smile, which briefly lifted the sides of his snout. He rubbed tiny hands together. "What job brings you to Vika?"

Keera produced the storage boxes from her flight suit. "I need you to bring someone else back."

"Big risk for big important admiral like

Keera. Thaedra would have Keera's head. Must be important for risking death."

"It is," Keera confirmed.

"Follow Vika," the creature said, waving over its shoulder.

Keera followed it from the foyer through a cramped living area. To her left a small bed lay below a dim viewscreen that gave a view to the variegated swirl of gases outside the station. A kitchen with low counters appeared to her right with a food synthesizer and appliances for cooking. Beyond that, a tiny bathroom lay open on the other side of the habitat. Behind the kitchen, she saw a Cirrk-sized VR pod sitting in a dusty corner beside a couch.

A solid metal door slid open, and they walked deeper into the habitat, heading down a narrow aisle between illuminated glass tubes. Some were empty, while others contained different species of naked aliens and Chimeras submerged in murky fluids. Umbilical cords trailed to spongy-looking organs that floated at the top of each tube. They stopped at one of the empty tubes, and Vika placed the storage boxes on a data transfer pad.

A small holographic screen appeared at Vika's eye level. The diminutive alien spent a moment swiping through displays and tapping holographic keys, nodding and muttering to himself.

"Well? Can you do it?"

"Yes, yes, Vika can. You bring payment?" The Cirrk looked up at her, and his eyes turned pale purple in the light of the holoscreen. "Cloning illegal now. Makes big expensive." The creature rubbed tiny hands together, its cranial stalks twitching and slitted black nostrils flaring at the end of its snout.

Keera nodded and hefted the heavy metal case she carried. Setting it down carefully on the deck, she placed both thumbs against the lock, and the cover hissed open to reveal a fat silver cylinder cradled by a shimmering grav field generator. "Liquid Neutronium," she explained as Vika leaned over the case with his snout gaping open. He reached for the cylinder with a twitching hand.

Keera slapped it away from the grav field. "Touch that field, and you'll lose your fingers."

"Yes, yes, Vika knows." He looked up at her with a sly grin twitching its way onto his lips. "Where did you get it?"

"Does it matter?"

"This big of hyper fuel is worth over a hundred thousand credits."

"Try two hundred," Keera said.

Vika's eyes gleamed. "Yes, this a good down payment. Vika is starting work immediately."

Keera grabbed the Cirrk by the scruff of his neck and lifted him off the floor. He squeaked and hissed, punching and kicking the air to get at her. When that didn't work, he began trying to gnaw her arm off. But she kept twisting to keep away from his teeth. "Put Vika down!"

"That's the *entire* payment," she said.

Vika stopped struggling to glare at her and cross his arms over his furry chest. "Half."

"Half," she conceded with a shrug, and set Vika back down. "But only if you bring her back in a Chimeran body like mine."

Vika's nose twitched, and he bared his teeth in a grimace. "Vika cannot do this."

"Why not? A clone is a clone."

"The Kyra ask for volunteers for big good reason. Virus fails because of mental deficiencies, not physical ones. A weak mind cannot accept the changes to the body. Would this person *want* to be coming back as Chimera?" Vika asked.

Keera thought about it. Her mother had been immune. She'd never even considered becoming a Chimera. And if her recent defection to the resistance was anything to go by, she wouldn't be happy to wake up in the body of an enemy.

"She'll get used to the idea."

Vika shook his head. "Then big likely it will fail."

"How likely?"

"Big big," Vika said, making broad, sweeping gestures with his hands.

"Fine. But can you at least make a few changes? She was immune to the virus before. Can you remove that immunity?" If Lori weren't immune, then the resistance wouldn't want her, and maybe Keera could convince her to become a Chimera voluntarily.

"No, no, not possible. All clones immune."

Keera suddenly went very still. "What do you mean they're *all* immune?"

"All! And their children, and their children's children's children!" Vika made another grand gesture with one furry hand.

That meant Clayton's wife, Samara was immune, and her kids would be, too. And their kids...

Keera's skin prickled with dread, and her cranial stalks began twitching. Someone was going to find out what she'd done. "Why didn't you tell me this before?"

"Vika thought you know. And was not so big illegal like now."

Keera thought back quickly, wondering how many people knew that she had resurrected Samara. There were the Chimeras who'd been present when she'd met with Clayton and introduced him to his late wife, but those soldiers were all dead after the last Kyron incursion into Chronan Space. And that was before Thaedra had come to power, so it was unlikely that any of them had thought to report or talk about it. Back then, cloning hadn't been illegal, just expensive, and the majority of Kyra and Chimeras viewed the process as a pointless exercise that could never really resurrect any-one.

But now... now it was a dangerous anathema to the Federation that could be used against her by someone seeking to steal her rank and status. Someone like Commander Treya.

Besides those Chimeran soldiers, who else knew about Samara? Clayton and Samara themselves, and Keera's mother and father, as well as a handful of other human witnesses from that reunion. She could hunt them all down and erase their memories of the events in question. But almost a standard year had passed—what if they'd told other people?

"I need to go," Keera said. "When will you be done?"

Vika's head tilted to one side, and he slowly stroked the fur beneath his chin, considering the question. "Come back in fifteen standard orbits. Clone being ready then."

Keera's eyes widened. Fifteen standard orbits was over *eighteen* years on Earth. "It took you half as long the last time!"

Vika shrugged. "This station orbit black hole. It big slow time for Vika's work."

Keera stifled a hiss. "Fine." What choice did she have? She turned to leave, and Vika walked with her. "When is Vika to expect other half of payment?"

Keera glared at him. "There is no other half.

I said I'd pay double only *if* you could bring her back as a Chimera, and you said that you can't."

Vika muttered something under his breath.

Keera stopped and glared at him. "Would you rather I take my business elsewhere?"

Vika's fingers fluttered nervously. "No, no, Vika do it. Keera is big hard negotiator." Vika grinned mischievously. "You impress Vika. Vika makes exception for you."

Keera nodded once, and walked the rest of the way to the door. The Cirrkan opened it, and she left the diminutive creature's habitat. The smells and sounds of the concourse came rushing back in along with the whispering thoughts of several dozen aliens standing close enough for Keera to read their minds. She was about to let their thoughts blur away into the background noise when she picked out a stray snippet that was directed at her.

What is Admiral Reed doing here? Something Illegal. But what?

Keera's head snapped around, checking for the source of those thoughts. There had to be at least thirty Chimeras up here on the cat-walk, perusing the shops. She walked to the railing and turned her back, pretending to admire the view.

Why isn't she leaving?

Keera slowly turned and walked down the catwalk, making her way toward the spiraling access ramps. She did her best to keep her mental focus on that one specific voice out of dozens. Mental voices weren't as readily iden- tifiable as audible ones, but they had a kind of tone and texture to them, and this one felt fa- miliar. It was someone she knew.

Finally, the person thought, relief coursing through them as Keera neared the stairs at the end of the catwalk. Keera kept walking, waiting until she felt the person's anticipation surge—

And then she sidestepped suddenly and glanced over her shoulder. She expected to see a Chimeran assassin standing behind her with a knife. Instead, she saw an empty stretch of catwalk, a few shoppers standing in front of a medical supply store beside her—and a bipedal Chimera with a hooded black robe standing in front of the door to Vika's cloning lab.

One final thought reached her, just a scrap of intention more than anything: a determin- ation to find out what Keera had been doing there.

Keera cut back through the crowd toward the stalker, moving fast, and wishing that she'd been allowed to keep some kind of a weapon when she'd come aboard the station.

"Hey!" she called as she drew near. "You! Who are you?"

The hood turned, red eyes wide with

shock. The face had been altered by removable prosthetics like the ones Keera herself wore, but those sunken red eyes with black circles under them were perfectly familiar. Hollow cheeks, a long face, and the person's height and frame also identified them.

"Treya?" Keera said. "You followed me."

She turned and ran, pushing through the crowds and flying down the stairs. Keera managed to stay close behind her until a group of Horval Chimeras got between them. She accidentally bumped into one and spilled a bright red drink all over it. Before Keera even had a chance to apologize, the Horval reared up, and a heavy fist slammed into the side of her head.

When Keera came to, she found two Drogan Chimeras standing over her with slitted red eyes nictating as they blinked. Their black and green facial plates moving as they spoke in rasping voices: "Are you okay?" one said. "You need to be more careful," the other added, holding out an armored hand to help her up.

Keera took the hand, the scaly armor of its palm rough and dry to the touch.

Both officers wore sidearms and the dark blue uniforms of station security. She waved away their objections. "I'm fine, thank you."

The two traded looks with slitted red eyes, their reptilian features blank and emotionless.

Keera scanned the crowds in the concourse, her eyes darting around, but she couldn't see any sign of Treya.

There was just one card left for her to play. Turning back to the officers, she said, "I was chasing someone. An officer of the Kyron Guard."

The Drogans' eyes nictated once more, and a low hiss escaped a shadowy seam between plates of facial armor. "How do you know this?"

"I recognized her. She's a Dakkari Chimera like me. We used to serve together in the Guard." That was close enough to the truth.

The two Drogans turned to each other and began whistling and hooting rapidly in their native language. One of them walked away, now speaking in Kyro and holding a hand over one short lateral cranial stalk to block out the noise of the concourse.

"You need to shut down the hangar," Keera said to the one in front of her. "Don't let her leave."

A deep thrumming sound began some-where within the bowels of the ship, and si-lence fell over the concourse as everyone looked to the viewscreens. Keera saw the swirling gases outside begin slowly scrolling away.

"What's happening?" Keera asked.

The Drogan hesitated, its head tilting as it listened to something coming over his comms. "It is too late," he explained. "A shuttle left the hangar fifteen *arcs* ago with the woman you identified on board. We must find a new place to hide."

Keera's eyes drifted out of focus as she stared at the viewscreens. If Treya had left already, it was too late for her to salvage this situation. Keera's XO would report her illicit meeting here, and the resulting investigation would lead to the discovery that Keera had stolen hyper fuel from the *Sovath*. Overseer Damos would torture her until she revealed what she'd used the fuel to pay for, and then she would die in the nearest arena as a heretic and a thief.

Keera's mind raced through a short list of options. She had her fighter and a few thousand credits to her name. She could make some kind of living here while she waited for Vika to finish growing her mother's clone. And at least now that they were leaving the black hole, the time dilation from its gravity field wouldn't slow the process. After that... Keera's thoughts trailed off, noting absently that the security guards had both left to deal with the growing tumult as people fled the concourse to get to their ships.

But Keera wasn't worried about an ambush. Treya didn't have the authority to bring the fleet, or even a squadron of Lancers. She would have come alone.

Her thoughts turned back to the problem at hand. Once her mother was resurrected, she'd have to take her to the resistance on Earth. A human couldn't breathe the air aboard Chimeran stations like this one, but besides that, natives weren't allowed to travel beyond their worlds, and the Federation offered a hefty reward for their capture. So where did that leave her? Maybe Keera's father would get his way after all. She was already an outlaw. It wouldn't make much difference if she decided to join the resistance now.

But it didn't change the fact that their cause was hopeless.

Unless...

There might be a way for her to stack the odds in their favor. The resistance had no hope of defeating the Federation, but ousting the Kyra from one star system on the edge of a war zone was another matter entirely.

DELIVERANCE

CHAPTER 31

—10 Years Later—

Samara Cross sat near the top of the stands, looking everywhere but at the patchy, blood-soaked grass in the center of the arena. Dora, her 10-year-old daughter, was on her feet with thousands of other kids and Chimeras, all of them cheering and screaming for their favorite challenger to win. Both of the men in the arena were humans, and both stood accused of serious crimes. The first, Adrian Larson, was a big burly giant of a man with hairy arms and long, sweat-matted blond hair. He was accused of rape and murder. The second man was Julio Vargas, a skinny, clean-shaven man with tanned skin, short dark hair, and light brown eyes. He was also accused of murder. Neither of them had any hope of release, but they could prolong their lives by defeating the challengers assigned to them by the Arena Master. Both men were unarmored and wearing simple, sleeveless gray shirts and matching pants.

Kyron ceremonial *Sikaths* crossed with a

booming *crack* of colliding shields that was amplified by the arena's audio system. The crowds cheered and booed. Samara forced herself to look, wincing as she noticed the rapt expression on her daughter's face. In a world without entertainment, the arena was what movie theaters had been for Samara's generation. Long ago, the ancient Romans had created their own arenas for bloody public spectacles like this one.

Ironic that it took an advanced alien race to bring us back to our barbaric roots, Samara thought.

Blades crossed with another crash. This time Adrian, the blond-haired giant got the upper hand. He slid his blade down and sliced off Julio's hand. A strangled scream escaped the smaller man's lips as he sank to his knees. The crowd roared, stomping their feet and cupping hands to their mouths to scream insults at the loser. Samara grabbed Dora's arm, trying to pull her down behind the taller kids in front of her so she wouldn't be able to see what came next, but Dora shrugged her off. Samara looked away—only to see the spectacle magnified in gory detail by the holoscreens hovering on all sides of the arena.

"Any last words before you die?" Adrian asked, holding his Sikath to Julio's throat with a thickly muscled arm.

Julio sneered, his expression conveyed

JASPER T. SCOTT

clearly by the screen, "I'll see you in Hell."

Samara jumped to her feet and covered Dora's eyes.

Her daughter struggled to pry her hands away. "Let me go!" she cried.

But Samara held fast as Adrian's blade scissored through Julio's throat and sent his head rolling down the field. The crowds went crazy. The screens followed the head as it rolled, and Dora managed to break free just in time to see it.

Dora rounded on Samara with a glare. "I missed it!"

Samara just gaped at her daughter, speechless. This was the first time Dora had been to the arena. Executions like this one were mandatory attendance for all kids ten years and older. Adults didn't have to go, but they weren't necessarily the intended audience. Public executions were just another part of the Kyra's indoctrination program, designed to desensitize children and prepare them for a life of violence.

A door opened in the far side of the arena, and a pair of Chimeras came out to escort the victor off the field. Another pair brought out a hovering garbage bin for the body.

When they were done, more Chimeras came, dragging out hovering pieces of scenery to create a more confined setting for the next pair of challengers. Jutting boulders with hanging moss, trees, and even ruined buildings glided into place. It looked like they'd transported a section of the Wastes to the arena. The Chimeras arranged the pieces of scenery, then retreated. Admiral Treya stood up and raised her hands for attention. "Please welcome our next challengers!"

The crowd cheered, clapped, and stomped their feet. Then a loud buzzer sounded, and a pair of doors opened on either side of the arena. Out came two human women this time. Neither could see the other across the scenery, and neither of them had any weapons. They would have to find them in the arena, making this challenge more complicated than the last. And more drawn out.

Samara gritted her teeth and averted her eyes, looking into the crowds instead. This time, as she did so, she saw a familiar face about ten seats down. It was Marcy Mayfield, one of the neighbors from Samara's building. Her twin sons Harrison and Liam were there, both of them wearing the black uniforms of the Guard with the red trim of 4th year cadets.

Marcy looked like she was about to lose her lunch. Samara was a nurse, so her disgust stemmed more from the principle of the matter, but she could empathize. She waved to the other woman, and Marcy replied with a fading smile.

Samara mimed a suggestion to her: covering her ears with her hands. Marcy nodded and swallowed visibly before doing just that.

Marcy didn't have to be here. Neither did Samara. They were attending to offer a dissenting opinion, to be able to tell their kids that *this* wasn't okay.

But judging by the fact that all three of their children were on their feet and cheering, their objections were falling on deaf ears.

CHAPTER 32

Rosie's ears perked up, and her tail began to wag. She sniffed around furiously, nosing up clumps of rotting leaves on the forest floor.

"Looks like she's found something," Clayton whispered. "What is it, girl?"

Rosie ignored him and began pawing at the ground, digging down deeper until a hoof print emerged in the muddy earth. Clayton's eyes widened, and he dropped to his haunches beside Rosie to examine it. Nova crowded in beside him, her hazel eyes catching a shaft of light trickling between the crowding trees. As she bent to examine the prints, her blonde hair caught the light, turning to a blazing gold. She had it tied back in a ponytail and tucked through the back of an old, faded blue baseball cap with the orange star and now-dirty white *H* of the Houston Astros stamped on the front.

"Looks like a deer," Nova concluded, and leaned back for him to get a better look.

Clayton's mind flashed back as she turned to look at him. He remembered when she was still just a toddler, too shell-shocked to say more than two words in a single breath. Even back then, he'd taken her with him on his hunting trips. He hadn't had a choice. He couldn't leave a toddler alone, and she wouldn't have let him if he'd tried, so he carried her on his hip, his shoulders, his back... pointing out the different types of tracks that Rosie found for them as they went. Nova had taken it all in, sucking her thumb and watching with curious eyes. The Sam Houston National Forest was far enough from the city that thankfully they hadn't had to worry about Dregs. Now, ten years later, she was starting to identify tracks even before he did.

Fourteen-year-old Nova frowned, her pretty face screwing up with bemusement. "Hey, Dad—hellooo..." She waved her hand in front of his face.

He smiled, snapping out of it. "Let's take a look." He leaned in, resting a hand on Rosie's back and slowly stroking her fur. She sat down and panted noisily beside them.

It was a miracle she could still come on these trips at her age. She had to be at least eleven or twelve years old, and for a dog her size, that was pretty much the limit. In spite of that, she was still just as spry as ever. That made Clayton suspect that she'd received a dose of one of the Kyra's longevity treatments. Maybe her former master had gotten her hands on a vial of *telomeric nanites*. Whatever the case, Clayton was glad not to have to watch the old girl waste away in front of their eyes.

Squinting at the mud, Clayton picked out the cloven shape of the footprint, but it was too big and wide to be a deer. "Could be a moose," he suggested, his mouth already watering at the thought of so much meat. They'd have to dry it and salt it to make jerky, and even then, they wouldn't be able to use it all.

"It can't be far," Clayton said, his gaze tracking up to scan the forest around them. It had rained last night, so these tracks couldn't be any older than that.

He patted Rosie's side—a signal. She perked up and stood, suddenly alert. "Go on, girl. Hunt," he whispered.

She knew what that meant. Rosie began trotting through the trees, her nose to the ground as she sniffed out the trail. Clayton followed close behind, and Nova stayed abreast of them both. They walked as quickly as they could, trying to keep their footsteps quiet so as not to scare off their prey. Now and then, a branch snapped underfoot, but Rosie was hot on the trail. She wouldn't lose it now even if they did scare their quarry deeper into the forest.

After about five minutes, Rosie stopped, her tail wagging and nose twitching furiously as she sniffed at a clump of mud.

Clayton went to investigate. Not mud. And not the well-formed pellets of a moose or a deer. It was a cowpie.

"Now that's interesting," he whispered.

"What is it?" Nova asked, breathing lightly as she stepped in beside him.

He pointed to the pile.

"What made *that*?" she asked, her eyebrows scrunching together.

"A cow," he said.

"How did it get all the way out here?"

Clayton just shook his head. Cows typically stuck to fields, not forests, and they tended to group up in herds. To find a loner out this far was strange.

Rosie left the pile of feces and darted ahead.

"Come on!" Clayton said.

He and Nova ran to keep up, but Rosie soon bounded out of sight. Clayton's rifle began working its way off his shoulder, so he grabbed it and ran with it in front of him, making sure to keep the barrel pointed away from Nova. She grabbed her rifle in both hands and kept it pointed at the ground in front of her as she ran.

Before long, they heard Rosie howling, calling them to her position.

They followed the sound, no longer bothering to silence their footsteps. By now, their quarry knew they were coming. That was okay. A cow wouldn't be able to move very fast through the forest.

Within seconds, the interlocking wall of trees opened up to a field of dry grass, and beyond that, a blue sheet of water sparkling in the sun. It was the northern arm of Lake Conroe. Up ahead Rosie stood on a fallen log at the edge of the trees, sniffing at the air, and beyond that, Clayton spotted the shiny black heads and shoulders of at least five Angus cattle poking above the rippling grass.

His heart skipped in his chest at the sight of so many of them in one place, and his stomach ached sharply with a fresh bout of hunger pains. Reaching Rosie's side, he snatched her collar and unhooked her rope leash from his belt. Tying Rosie to the log, he waved Nova on, and they crept into the tall grass beside one other.

Each of them went down on one knee and balanced their rifles, sighting down the scopes to the nearest of the cattle.

"You want to take the shot?" Clayton whispered.

Nova nodded and pressed her eye to the scope once more. She hesitated, taking a moment to hold her breath and steady her aim, just like he'd taught her.

Count to three and then squeeze the trigger, he remembered telling eight-year-old Nova. Clayton sighted down his own scope, watching the nearest cow's head tuck down to munch on the grass...

And then come back up.

Nova's rifle gave a shrieking report, and a brilliant flash of light stabbed through Clayton's peripheral vision.

A loud *moo!* escaped from the herd as Nova's target fell with the muted thunder of a tree. A loud mooing and bellowing erupted from the herd, and their hooves churned up a cloud of dust as they ran.

Rosie began barking repeatedly and straining at the end of her leash, desperate to get in on the action.

Clayton nodded to Nova, and they hurried across the field to reach her kill. They found it with a dime-sized scorch mark burned through the side of its head, just below the eye. No signs of life or struggle.

"A perfect shot," Clayton said as he leaned down to check the wound.

Nova beamed proudly at him. "Thanks."

Clayton kneeled in the grass with the afternoon sun beating down hard on the back of his neck and his faded black T-shirt. He laid his rifle beside him, and then unslung his pack to pick through the assorted knives and implements inside. He pulled out his skinning knives and passed one to Nova. They had a long, bloody task ahead of them. It would be dusk by the time they were done and ready to haul the meat back to their cabin.

Clayton grabbed his skinning knife and sighed, hesitating. Sometimes, he wished being a vegetarian was still an option. Gone were the days of buying neatly-cut steaks in the supermarket—or even the days of picking them out at the butcher's counter of the nearest Kyron dispensary.

Nova plunged her knife in, slitting the animal's throat to drain the blood. Clayton watched her with a frown. She'd never known anything other than this; to her it was just another day in the life.

"What?" she asked, noticing his scrutiny. She knocked her cap up and wiped her sweaty brow with the back of her arm, careful not to smear her forehead with bloody hands.

"Nothing," he said, and bent to work skinning their kill. He wished Nova could have a real childhood, like the one he'd had once upon a time, with school and other kids. He'd teach her to ride a bike, and they would have an old ranch-style house somewhere out in the suburbs. Maybe another dog to keep Rosie company. And Samara would be there. Pandora, too.

He smiled wistfully at the thought as the cow's blood ran in hot rivers over his hands.

* * *

The dying rays of the sun slanted low over the water, winking at them through the trees on the other side of the lake as they washed off their knives and hands. A dozen feet away, Rosie lapped up enough water to drown a fish, drinking her fill after a long, hot afternoon in the sun.

Clayton caught a glimpse of a stranger's reflection in the water: a bushy black beard and long black hair, sweat-matted strands draped over his face, forehead, and ears. Sunken green eyes were rimmed with deep crow's feet that had nothing to do with age and everything to do with a decade spent living in the Wilds. At least this far out from the Wastes and the city they hadn't had to deal with Dregs.

Clayton's stomach ached and growled. He glanced over his shoulder to the bright orange flames roaring at the top of the field. They had three thick steaks salted and ready to go once that fire died down to coals. And he still had some of their trail mix of dried raspberries, blueberries, and roasted pecans to go with it.

When they were done cleaning up, Nova walked further up and filled their pot with water. They couldn't cook the steaks yet, but they could at least boil water for their canteens. Clayton was tempted to drink the water raw, but the last time he'd dared to drink straight from the lake, he'd wound up with diarrhea, and that wasn't an experience he wanted to repeat with nothing but leaves for toilet paper.

Soon the three of them were sitting in the

grass by the fire, warming their hands as night fell. Rosie sat between them, her eyes dancing with firelight. It was at least five miles from here to their cabin, and walking through the forest at night was a good way to twist an ankle. Or worse. They'd spend the night by the lake instead, with their packs for pillows and the stars for a blanket.

Nova leaned back on her elbows, staring up at the night's sky, her eyes darting among those myriad points of light. "How many planets do you think are in the Federation?"

Clayton poked the fire with a long stick to turn a log. That sent a flurry of glowing embers streaking up. "I don't care to know."

"Well, I think it's fascinating. What if there are hundreds of planets like Earth, each with their own species? Or there could even be thousands! How do you think the Kyra keep an empire that size together?"

Clayton looked to his daughter with a heavy frown. "Why all the sudden interest?"

Nova shrugged, her eyes wide with wonder and curiosity as they tracked across the sky. Dangerous sentiments to have. Curiosity had sent out the *Forerunners* and brought the Kyra to Earth. And curiosity was behind the misguided dreams of every indoctrinated child on the planet.

"Keep your eyes on the ground where they belong," Clayton growled.

Nova scowled at him. "*You* went out there. You can't tell me not to think about—"

"That's exactly why I can," he snapped. "I went out there and look at what happened. You'd have a normal life right now if it weren't for that. Hell, your parents would still be alive!" Clayton's stomach clenched up with more than hunger pains as he realized that he'd just gone too far.

Nova's eyes hardened and flashed with tongues of fire. She jumped up and stalked away, heading for the gleaming silver sheet of water below.

"Nova, wait! I didn't mean..." he trailed off, struggling to come up with an excuse.

"Come on, Rosie!" she called. "Let's go for a walk!"

Rosie barked once and bounded after her.

Clayton debated chasing after them, but he knew how this went. Nova needed a minute to cool off. He'd give her some space and then she'd be fine again. So he stayed and stoked the fire, scowling into the flurrying embers. Sometimes he had a foot for a mouth.

Getting up, he removed the pot from the fire, grabbing it by the metal chain that trailed out of the fire. He made sure not to grab it too close to the pot. Carefully setting the boiled water beside him in the grass, he went to get the steaks where they'd left them by the cow carcass. They'd heavily salted as much of the meat as they could and placed it in fifteen different plastic Tupperware containers that they'd salvaged from ruined suburbs over the years. It was a pity they couldn't save more meat than that, but they didn't have enough salt to preserve the rest anyway. Hopefully some coyotes would sniff out the rest of the carcass after they left. It'd be a shame to let it all go to waste.

A working freezer or refrigerator would have solved the problem, but they had yet to salvage one. Not to mention their aging solar sheet was overtaxed as it was between charging the hoverbike and their weapons.

Clayton stalked back over to the fire with a medium-sized container full of meat. He laid a folding metal grill over the glowing logs and coals. They'd made it by tying air duct covers together with rusty wires.

He laid out the steaks, and soon the smell of grilling meat filled the air. Rosie came back over, barking excitedly. Nova's footsteps followed, whispering softly through the grass.

"You almost missed dinner," Clayton said.

She sat down on the opposite side of the fire from him, saying nothing.

He sighed and walked over. "Hey, I'm sorry, okay?"

She glared up at him, her knees tucked to her chest and arms wrapped around them to keep out the growing cold of the night. Clayton eased down beside her on creaking knees. His whole body ached from the task of tracking and slaughtering that cow.

He tried wrapping an arm around Nova's shoulders, but she pulled away, her body stiff and unyielding.

"I shouldn't have mentioned your parents," Clayton added.

"It's not fair," Nova said quietly.

"No, it's not," he agreed. "If life were fair, they'd be here now instead of me."

"No, not that," Nova said. "It's not fair that you know what's out there, and you know what it's like in the cities, and you won't tell me anything about any of it. You won't even take me with you when you go to the Wastes."

"You *know* why I don't take you."

"Because someone has to stay with Rosie in case you don't make it back."

Clayton nodded, watching stray tongues of flame licking through the grill to their steaks. Fat hissed, dripping through the rusty vents.

"What makes you think I'd want to stick around if something happened to you?"

He hesitated. "You have to keep going. Whether I'm around or not."

"Why?" Nova made a flippant gesture, as if to shoo a fly. "For more of this? It's the same thing every day. Boil water, find food, wash up, go to bed, wake up, boil water, find food, wash up, go to bed..." She looked back to the grilling steaks and stared unblinkingly to the dark wall of trees on the other side. "It's not enough. I can't live just to go on living."

Now it was Clayton's turn to be angry. "You think this is a game? Life's fucking hard. It's a damned daily struggle. If you go to bed with food in your belly, a roof over your head, and clothes on your back, then that should be good enough."

"People in the cities have all that, and they don't have to struggle for it."

Clayton snorted. "They have those things because the Kyra need them focused on raising good little soldiers for their war."

Silence fell as Nova contemplated that. He expected her to offer some other objection, but this time it was Rosie's turn. She heaved a noisy sigh and licked her lips, watching as leaping orange flames blackened the steaks on the grill and kicked up clouds of smoke.

"Damn it!" Clayton ran to get his fire-stoking stick. He used the sharpened, char-blackened end to spear the steaks and flip them, setting them down away from the fat-fueled flames now sizzling and leaping through the grill.

"I've never even seen anyone besides you," Nova whispered. She snorted and laughed. "You remember Cindy?"

Clayton stood frowning at Nova. He remembered. She'd been seven years old. He'd stopped taking Nova with him to the Wastes after a group of Dregs had almost bitten her. To make up for it, he tried to bring something back for her each time he went. He'd brought Cindy back with him one night—an old plastic doll with a torn dress, dirty yellow hair, and a faded, grayish complexion. The doll looked vaguely like Cinderella, hence the name *Cindy*.

"I used to talk to her," Nova said. "I pretended she was my sister."

Clayton remembered. She wouldn't go anywhere without that damn doll. "Not everyone has siblings," he pointed out in a gruff voice.

"No," Nova said, "but at least those kids have friends." She looked away from the fire and spent a long moment staring up at him, her face veiled in flickering shadows.

"What?" he prompted.

"What if we joined the resistance?"

Clayton flinched as if he'd been slapped. "You *know* how I feel about them. You know what they did."

"That was ten years ago. Have they ever bombed an ascension center since then?"

"That I know of?" he countered. He looked back to the steaks. "Food's ready." He speared one and handed it to Nova on the stick. Walking around the fire, he pulled another sharpened stick from his pack and speared the next piece of meat for himself. Before tucking in, he used the tip of his boot to push the grill off the fire so that Rosie's steak could cool.

"I want to go with you tomorrow," Nova said.

"No."

"If you don't let me, I won't be at the cabin when you return. I'll hike down to the Wastes myself."

"You do that and I'll—"

"What?" Nova demanded. "You'll what?"

"I'll tie you up before I go, that's what!" Clayton thundered. He tore his eyes away and took a big bite of his steak, burning his mouth in the process. Rosie slunk in and snatched hers off the grill, darting away with her prize. She gobbled the whole thing in just a few seconds and then slunk back over to sit between them, licking her lips and mesmerizing them with her big, sad brown eyes.

The next twenty minutes passed in silence as they ate with their hands and teeth. Only the sounds of their chewing and the crickets chirping stirred the thickening air between them.

"I can look after myself," Nova finally said.

Clayton looked to her, chewing endlessly on a tough chunk of meat. Nova's mouth glistened with fat and bits of gristle. "We've talked about this," he said. "It's not just the Dregs we have to worry about. Exiles are worth a lot of credits to the Chimeras."

"And yet you keep going into the Wastes," Nova countered. "If it's so dangerous, then you shouldn't leave either, so why do you?"

"Someone has to scavenge supplies." That was true, but he didn't add that he also needed to go because he'd been meeting once a month with that farmer's Chimeran wife for years to exchange information about each other's kids. It was a ritual that both he and Harold both clung to despite the risks, because the alternative was to lie awake at night worrying. Nova didn't know anything about Pandora. It was bad enough that she had lost her parents; he refused to make her feel like she was some kind of substitute for the biological daughter he'd lost.

Clayton stared at her for a long, silent minute, his heart pounding as hard as if he'd just run from a pack of Dregs.

"I'm not taking no for an answer this time," Nova said quietly.

Rosie punctuated that ultimatum with a bark, and then a growl. Clayton turned to see her standing at attention, staring up at the shadowy wall of trees at the forest's edge. She barked again, then paused and cocked her head, listening to something that only she could hear.

"Easy, girl..." Clayton whispered. He stood and walked over to her, hooking his fingers through her collar to make sure she didn't run off chasing shadows—or whatever they might be attached to.

Nova appeared beside them, checking the charge on her laser rifle. Clayton spotted the glowing number *three* on the back of the charge pack as she did so. Their aging charge packs barely held a handful of shots these days.

"What is it?" Nova whispered.

"Probably just the wind," he muttered. But the summer air was still and stagnant, and even the crickets had stopped chirping.

And then he heard it again: a low rustling sound, coming from the trees. A moment later, he spotted the snaking lines of animals creeping toward them through the tall grass. "Coyotes," he decided. "They must have smelled the meat."

Clayton reached for the loop of rope clipped to his belt, thinking he'd better tie Rosie up before she got herself into a fight.

A low, muttering hiss sounded from the direction of the approaching animals.

"Dad, I don't think those are coyotes..." Nova said.

And then bright red pairs of eyes came pricking through the shadowy grass, one after another.

"Dregs!" Clayton cried.

CHAPTER 33

Clayton looped Rosie's leash through her collar and dragged her over to his rifle just as Nova took the first shot. That burst of emerald light peeled back the night, illuminating no less than five chalk-white Dregs in the grass, naked but for clinging scraps of dirty clothing. One of them dropped, thrashing and shrieking, Nova's shot having found its mark. The other four crouched in readiness to either flee or charge, but hesitating, their eyes dazzled by the light of the laser bolt.

Clayton wrapped Rosie's leash around his waist and planted his feet against the inevitable tug-o-war. Bringing his own rifle up to his shoulder, he sighted down the scope to the next nearest Dreg. He held his breath to steady his aim, and his finger tightened on the trigger. The monster under his sights gave a piercing shriek and then darted away, vanishing in the tall grass before he could shoot it. The other three did the same thing, scattering. Clayton swept his rifle around, checking for targets. They were gone.

"Think we scared them off?" Nova asked.

He shook his head. "Stay sharp."

A loud rustling came from Clayton's right. Rosie growled, and he whirled toward the sound, staring hard into the tall grass, searching for signs of movement.

"Dad!"

Clayton spun back to his daughter in time to see her fire two quick shots. Emerald fire flashed out, but both lasers missed, setting the field ablaze. Flames leapt up, quickly multiplying. That sudden bloom of light revealed the snaking lines of four Dregs running in frenzied circles.

"Shit! I'm out!" Nova said as she fumbled to eject the charge pack and slot in another one from her belt.

Clayton stepped around the campfire to stand beside her. "Keep the fire to your back. They won't walk over hot coals to reach us."

The grass grew still once more, and an uneasy silence fell but for the crackling roar of a spreading grass fire.

"Get ready," Clayton whispered.

A piercing shriek split the night, sounding from directly behind them. They both spun toward the sound—

In time to see a ghost-white head and red eyes ducking into the grass and dashing away.

Rosie snarled and almost yanked Clayton off his feet, tugging him back the other way. He whirled to the fore just in time to see the other three Dregs creeping toward them on all fours, now barely ten feet away.

"You take left, I'll take right!" Clayton cried, bracing his feet against Rosie's tugging.

Clayton's knuckles whitened on the hand-guard and grip of his rifle, taking aim at the same time as Nova did.

And then all three Dregs lunged.

Clayton's shot hit the nearest one in the shoulder, and it fell with a *thud,* its claws scrabbling and digging up clumps of dirt and grass. A second shot ended its struggle. Nova's first bolt went straight between the eyes of the second Dreg, dropping it dead on the spot. But the third one bounded on, heading straight for her. It leapt in the air to cover the last three feet, and Nova screamed, falling over backward and narrowly missing the simmering coals of their fire.

Clayton tracked the monster as it sailed through the air—

And then Rosie jumped into his sights and knocked the Dreg off course. That movement pulled him off his feet. The Dreg and Rosie fell in a snarling, shrieking heap. Her leash broke free as the Dreg's claws slashed through it. Clayton scrambled to one knee, taking aim as Nova dropped her rifle and drew the hunting knife from her belt.

"Nova, wait!"

One slice of those claws or bite from those teeth, and she'd be infected.

Nova ignored him. Rosie and the Dreg tumbled through his scope, trading places multiple times in the span of a second. He couldn't wait for a clear shot with Nova running headlong into range of those slashing claws.

"Dad, no!"

He pulled the trigger. A bolt of emerald fire snapped out, and Rosie yelped sharply. She withdrew, limping and dragging one of her back legs. The Dreg flailed and shrieked on the ground, struggling to rise.

"Rosie!" Nova cried, running over as the dog collapsed in the grass.

Clayton fired another shot, straight through the fallen Dreg's chest, and it lay still. The rifle clicked, and the trigger grew slack, the charge depleted. Shouldering his rifle, Clayton ran to Rosie's side and fell on his knees beside his daughter.

"You shot her!" Nova sobbed, her eyes and cheeks streaming with tears.

Rosie lay panting hard in the grass with high-pitched whistling sounds periodically escaping her lips. Clayton checked her over quickly. Her fur was covered in blood, and a few shallow gashes had been torn through her back and side. Nothing too deep to treat. His gaze roved on to check the laser wound. It had gone straight through her haunches on the right side. Judging by the position of the exit wound, around the back of her leg, he'd missed her bowels and internal organs. The entry and exit wounds were both cauterized, so at least she wasn't bleeding. But the slash marks from the Dreg's claws and teeth were another matter. They had to stop the bleeding and treat her with nanobiotics to avoid an infection.

"Get the medkit," Clayton whispered.

Nova ran around the campfire while he checked the gashes in Rosie's side and back. "It's okay, girl," he whispered. They didn't have much in the way of medical supplies these days, and what they did have was ancient by now. *Hopefully nanites don't expire,* he thought.

"Shhh," he soothed again as Rosie's whimpering and panting grew louder and more urgent. She had to be in a lot of pain.

Nova dropped into the grass beside them with the medkit in her lap. "I'll never forgive you if you killed her."

Clayton grabbed the medkit, shaking his head as he sorted through the supplies. "The laser burn isn't the problem. It's the claw—"

A moonlit blur streaked into view and collided with him, knocking him flat on his back. Snapping jaws lunged for his throat and clawed hands pinned both of his arms to the ground.

Nova fell on its back, her knife flashing across its throat.

Clayton just managed to turn his head in

time to avoid the hot river of blood that gushed over him. He clamped his mouth shut and scrambled out from under the monster before he could get infected. The Dreg struggled weakly as it bled out in the grass. Drawing his own knife, he stabbed it through the back of the skull and cleaned his blade off in the grass. Clayton wiped his mouth on the back of his arm, checking to make sure none of the blood had landed close to his mouth, and his arm and sleeve came away smeared with blood.

"Are you—" Nova took a quick step toward him.

He backed away, holding up bloody hands. "Don't. I'm fine, but we need to wash off in the lake before we get infected from all this blood."

"But Rosie needs..."

"We have to wash her off, too. I'll bring her."

Clayton sheathed his knife, then heaved Rosie up and into his arms with a grunt. Nova took the medkit, and the three of them hurried down to the water. They left their rifles on the shore and grabbed homemade bars of soap from the medkit before wading in clothes and all. Rosie struggled weakly in his arms as he bent down and laid her in the shallows. He cleaned her off first, then carried her out and laid her on the pebbled beach. Then he waded back in, the water sliding over him cold and sharp as a knife. He and Nova spent the next few minutes submerged up to their necks in the icy water, scrubbing their hands and skin to get off all the blood before it dried. It was hard to catch the virus from casual contact with infected blood, but not impossible, and they couldn't afford to be sloppy.

When Clayton was done, he waded a good distance away and dunked his head to get the blood off his face. Finally, he hurried out, shivering from the cold, and joined Nova by Rosie's side. She was already spraying the dog's wounds with Regenex and synthskin. Both aerosols sputtered and died before she'd fully covered Rosie's injuries.

"We don't have enough," Nova said.

"It'll have to do," Clayton replied. "Help me get her up." They got her on her feet, and Clayton held her up while Nova wrapped her with their only roll of bandages.

"She'll make it, right?" Nova insisted as Clayton injected Rosie with their last vial of nanobiotics.

He nodded. "She's pulled through worse." That much was true. A couple of years ago, she'd tangled with a pack of coyotes that had come sniffing around the cabin to get at some venison jerky that they'd hung up to dry. Rosie had killed two of them before Clayton had run out and scared the others off with his rifle. She'd been covered in bite marks, and her skin had hung in loose, ragged folds around her neck. But she'd pulled through.

The difference was, back then they'd had more in the way of supplies to treat her.

"W-what if you hit one of her organs?" Nova asked, peering hard at the laser burn in her haunches.

"I didn't," Clayton insisted, hoping it was true.

"How are we going to get her home?"

Clayton peered up at the shadowy forest. Flames from the grass fire Nova had started licked high into the air, spreading fast and choking the air with sweet-smelling smoke. "I'll have to carry her..." He trailed off, considering the task ahead. With that fire burning they couldn't stay here for the night anymore. They had flashlights, but making a five mile hike through the forest, cold and wet, and carrying a large dog was not going to be easy.

"We should go," Nova said, shouldering her rifle, then shivering and rubbing her arms vigorously as she started up the beach toward. The grass fire was busy racing toward their packs and the meat that they'd left around their camp.

Clayton recovered his rifle from the beach and slung it over his shoulder before hoisting Rosie up and carrying her over to their things. Both he and Nova hurriedly gathered their belongings and the meat from the dead cow into their packs. Their eyes streamed with tears, and their lungs burned from all the smoke.

They retreated into the forest, coughing as they went. Nova led the way with the dim blue glow of their Kyron solar lantern. Clayton's wet clothes chafed as they walked, and he had to stop periodically to set Rosie down and catch his breath. Her ragged panting grew slower and slower with every passing minute. He didn't say anything to Nova. Couldn't. The growing knot in his throat made it impossible to speak.

After a couple of hours, Rosie stopped breathing altogether, and Clayton laid her in a bed of dry, crackling leaves. His tears pitter-pattered softly in the leaves.

It took Nova a few seconds to notice that he'd stopped, but then she came crashing over. She fell on her knees beside Rosie, stroking her fur, sobbing and hugging her and whispering that everything was going to be okay. Clayton stepped back feeling hollow and slowly shaking his head.

Nova leapt up and shoved him hard, sent him stumbling back into a tree.

"You killed her!" she screamed.

And then she began hurling her fists at him just like she'd done all those years ago with the Chimera who'd killed her parents. Blows landed all over him in a frenzied whirlwind of grief. Clayton blocked a few, but let the others through. She knocked the wind out of him and clacked his teeth together with an uppercut before he pulled her into a hug and held her still.

"It wasn't the rifle that killed her," he whispered. "She went too fast."

Nova sobbed unintelligibly against his chest, struggling only feebly now. The fight soon left her, and she went limp in his arms. They fell down together and Clayton held her as she cried.

* * *

Clayton's eyes darted around the shadowy forest, keeping watch while Nova's grief ran its course.

"She had a good life," Clayton whispered when his daughter was finally spent. "Ten years with us. God knows how many before that." He shook his head. "Twelve plus happy years."

Nova sniffed but said nothing for several minutes. At last, she spoke in a croaking whisper: "She died saving me. It's my fault that she's gone."

Clayton leaned back to look her in the eye. "It's the Dregs' fault. Period."

"Now I really am alone," Nova added.

"You still have me."

"Yeah, until the Dregs get you. If they've started roaming this far, they'll do it again. They could come sneaking into the cabin while we sleep."

"We'll set noise traps to wake us if they get close."

"We got lucky tonight," Nova insisted. "Without Rosie there, that Dreg would have gotten me."

Clayton shook his head, wondering where she was going with this. Nova eased out of his arms and stared hard at him in the dim blue light of the lantern.

"We have to join the resistance. Please."

Clayton's eyes widened. "So that we can die faster? No."

"We're going to die no matter what! At least it should mean something when we do."

"Dying for a lost cause won't give meaning to your life."

"How do you know it's a lost cause?" she snapped.

"For a start, because it's been almost a century since the Kyra came and everything is still the same. Nobody has a plan to beat them. They're just exiles giving other exiles false hope so that they have a reason to drag themselves out of bed in the morning."

Nova's eyes slid away from his, to Rosie's motionless body. "That's still better than giving up like you," she whispered.

Clayton dragged in a stale breath that smelled of wet earth, sweat, and Rosie's blood. Nova was at an age where she wouldn't be told anymore. She needed to see it for herself. Besides, if she really wanted to go find the resistance, better that she do it on the back of their hoverbike than on foot, wandering through the Wastes with Dregs dogging her every step. Clayton let out his breath, already regretting what he was about to say. "We'll go see them together tomorrow."

Nova looked back to him, her eyes widening. "Really?"

He nodded. "We'll check out their camp and listen to their recruitment pitch. I'm not promising anything more than that, but we'll look and we'll listen."

"And you'll keep an open mind?"

Clayton hesitated. "Only if they have something more than high hopes."

Nova curled up against his side. "Thank you," she whispered.

He nodded and listened as her breathing gradually slowed with sleep, his wet clothes chilling him on one side, warm on the other where their bodies trapped the heat between them. He stayed awake, periodically blinking leaden eyes to keep them open, his mind spinning with grief and fear.

Somehow their little family had worked when it had been three, but two just wasn't enough. Their grief would fade, but he'd seen Nova flirt with depression before, and he feared that this would push her over into that abyss. Hell, it might drag him down as well.

Maybe she was right. Maybe they *did* need more. But what if reaching for a higher purpose got one or both of them killed? Losing Nova would be the end of him. He couldn't lose two daughters.

Three, he amended, his gaze falling on Rosie's body.

His eyes burned and drifted out of focus as tears welled anew. An aching knot rose up and choked him. His chest hurt as though he'd been stabbed, and his stomach churned, sick with grief.

Nova let out a snorting sigh. He glanced at her with a frown. Then back to Rosie.

Something was moving in the leaves around her. Clayton's body tensed, getting ready to chase away whatever scavenger was trying to feed on her remains.

And then he saw her leg twitch.

Clayton's heart beat a fierce staccato in his chest.

Death throes? He wondered.

No, it had been too long for that. Hadn't it?

Another snorting sigh echoed out, and this time he realized that it was coming from Rosie.

Clayton jumped to his feet. Nova fell over and cried out with alarm, her hands flailing for her rifle.

Clayton landed in the leaves beside Rosie,

resting a hand on her side, waiting...

And then he felt it. Her ribs lifted gently with a feeble breath.

Nova crashed down beside them. "She's still *alive?*" Her voice cracked with hope.

"I..." Clayton trailed off in astonishment. "She stopped breathing." He'd checked. He knew she had. "The nanites in the Regenex must have sustained her."

Rosie raised her head and winked one eye at them in the dim blue light of the lantern, as if to say: *fooled ya.* Then she laid her head back down.

Clayton barked a laugh and laid his head against Rosie's side, listening to the sweetest music he'd ever heard—

Their dog's heartbeat.

CHAPTER 34

Samara sat on a stool in an examination room of the ER, watching as one of her regulars unbuttoned his shirt and peeled away the collar to reveal a big white bandage. She pulled it away and saw several scabbed-over bite marks in the side of his neck and shoulder. Others were faded white scars, but a few more recent ones were fresh and welling with blood.

"Again? You never learn, do you, Harry?" Samara frowned, her eyes tracking up to his tanned face. He looked tired, but otherwise in good spirits. It was early morning, near the end of her shift. Normally she would have tested a patient with bite marks for signs of infection, but Harold was an exception. He was unofficially married to a Chimera, and these bite marks were hers, not the work of an infectious Dreg.

Harold offered a shrug and a guilty smile that lifted the drooping corners of the bushy red mustache that connected to a matching beard. "Mona gets a little too excited sometimes. Can't really blame her for that," he said, puffing out his chest.

Samara frowned, reaching for a can of Regenex. Aiming the nozzle, she said, "Hold still," and then sprayed the wound with the nanites. When she was done, she used synthskin to seal the wound. Rolling her stool away, she regarded the farmer with narrowed eyes. "Promise me this is the last time I'm going to be doing this."

"Cross my heart," Harold said, signing over his chest.

Samara knew better. He'd be back. What he saw in that Chimeran woman, only he knew.

"How's Dora doing?" Harold asked as he buttoned his shirt back up.

Samara hesitated. "She's fine."

"You don't sound so sure about that. Something happen with her?" Harold asked, his eyes narrowing with sudden curiosity.

Samara debated keeping it to herself, but she didn't have a lot of people she could talk to. Besides, this was part of their routine: once a month, Harold would get chewed up by his girlfriend, and then he'd come to the hospital asking for Samara. She'd patch him up, and then they'd spend the next five or ten minutes making small talk about their kids.

"My girl is a third-year cadet now," Harold offered, nodding gravely with one eye twitching. "She keeps saying that she can't wait to ascend. Worries the hell outta me. Some nights I can't sleep thinkin' about it."

Samara blew out a breath. "But it's different for you. You already live with one of them. She can probably pull some strings to get Haley assigned to patrol your farm."

Harold snorted. "Yeah, and what if Haley becomes a Dreg?"

Samara hesitated. "Well, the odds of that are very low."

"Yeah, *real* low," Harold agreed. "But even a one percent failure rate is a damned scary thing for a parent."

A knowing look passed between them. The walls had ears, and they didn't know who might be listening. They couldn't afford to be caught spouting treason. Both of them knew that failures were a lot more common than the Kyra claimed. They liked to say that the Dregs' population was booming because they were breeding too fast, not because they were secretly expelling hundreds of fresh Dregs to the Wastes with every new wave of graduating cadets. Curious parents asking at the ascension centers about their missing kids were always told the same thing: the conversion was successful, but they'd already left for their postings, and unfortunately, on-going communication would only serve as a dangerous distraction.

All of those excuses were the perfect way to avoid anyone finding out that their kids had actually turned into Dregs.

"So, what happened with your girl?" Harold asked.

Samara shook her head. "Nothing."

"Come on, it's me, Sam. We're in this together. It helps to talk about it."

Samara sighed and took a moment to put the words together in her head, making sure they wouldn't get her into trouble later. "She had to go to the arena for the first time yesterday."

"Oh." Harold's mustache drooped. "I'm sorry. The first time's always rough on them. Seeing all that blood..."

Samara winced. "That's just it. Dora was riveted. She got mad at me when I tried to cover her eyes."

Harold's brow furrowed. "Well... every kid's different, I guess."

"She's only ten."

"Yeah..."

Samara leaned in and whispered, "If she's like this now, what will she be like when she's Haley's age?"

Harold said nothing to that.

"Sometimes I think it's my fault. I'm away too much, and we're always butting heads. Maybe if she'd had a father..." Samara trailed off, her eyes stinging with a sudden heat.

Harold's mustache drooped. He opened his mouth to say something, but then stopped himself. Samara watched him curiously.

"What?"

He shook his head and looked away. "It's just sad, is all." His gaze swept back to her. "But don't you blame yourself. You're doing the best you can. That's all any of us can do."

"I guess it is," Samara said. She rose from the stool, and Harold hopped down from the examination table.

"Thanks for patching me up, Sam. See you around."

She smiled wryly as she followed him out the door. "Hopefully not too soon."

He flashed a grin and a wink, and then strode off down the corridor.

Samara leaned against the wall, taking a moment to catch her breath.

"You look like you could use a coffee."

Samara jumped at the voice. Dr. Galen Rath swooped in with two steaming mugs and quickly handed one to her. "Here," he said. His fingers trailed lightly over the back of her hand as he released the mug. Samara scowled. "Don't do that."

"Do what?" he asked, raising dark eyebrows innocently above his mug.

"You know what," she replied. "It's not happening."

Galen grinned. "You keep saying that. And then it keeps happening..."

Samara turned and stalked away, absently

sipping her coffee. Galen caught up to walk beside her. "So? How about it?"

"I said *no*," she snapped.

"Okay, okay, message received!" he said, holding up his hands in surrender. "But maybe you could let me know when the next time will be when you'll say yes? I might have to clear space on my calendar."

Samara ignored him and took another sip of her coffee. Somehow it tasted like dirt now. With a grimace, she lowered the mug from her lips. She and Galen had only been together a few times, and the last time was years ago, but he still wouldn't shut up about it. She wished she'd been smarter than that, but he had a way of catching whenever she was at her lowest. Somehow, in those moments, he managed to transform himself into prince charming. When the loneliness grew unbearable, it was easier to look for a meaningless connection than it was to look for something real. Paradoxically, a real relationship felt like more of a betrayal to Clayton's memory than a fling.

"What about next Thursday?" Galen suggested. "I should be free by then."

The hospital's PA system crackled to life before Samara could slap him: "Dr. Rath to the OR. Dr. Rath to the OR."

"Whoops. That's me. Catch you later, darling."

Galen winked and hurried back the other

way, saving her from his company. Samara glared at his back as he left. The air felt lighter now that he wasn't sharing it.

Carla Morales came out of a nearby exam room pushing a medicine cart. She caught Samara's baleful look, saw the target, and flashed a knowing smile. All of the female staff were tired of Galen's advances and inappropriate behavior, even her. Lesbianism hadn't saved her from his advances, because she was still deep in the closet. If the Chimeras or the Kyra ever found out what she was, she'd be sent straight to the arena. *Can't have breeders that don't breed,* Samara thought.

"Maybe we'll get another infected patient by mistake, and he'll get bitten and turn into a Dreg," Carla suggested.

"Couldn't happen to a nicer person," Samara agreed, slamming her coffee down on Carla's cart.

* * *

Clayton and Nova went crashing through the trees to the clearing where their cabin sat. It was just 3:09 in the morning, according to Clayton's ARCs. His scheduled meeting with the resistance and then after with that farmer's wife wasn't for another nineteen hours, but he couldn't afford to wait until then. Rosie was alive, but struggling to stay that way. She needed further treatment, and they were all out of medical supplies.

Nova guided the way with the lantern across the grassy, moonlit clearing to their aging log cabin. Clayton's entire body ached, his muscles shuddering from the task of carrying Rosie over five miles of rough terrain. They stepped onto a sagging porch, and Nova lifted a simple metal latch to open the door. "Wait here," she whispered as she pushed through the rickety entrance with her rifle up and sweeping. He watched the dark blue glow of the lantern reveal the inside of the cabin as she checked for intruders. With nothing but that latch to lock the door, they relied on the cabin's remote location to keep it safe while they were away.

The door swung shut in Clayton's face with a rusty squeal of the hinges, leaving him staring at the patchwork of overlapping wooden boards and metal plates that he'd used over the years to reinforce it.

His biceps screaming under Rosie's weight, Clayton gave up waiting and kicked the door open. He stepped in to see Nova already heading back to get him.

"All clear," she said.

He nodded. "We have to be quick. Get changed out of your wet clothes."

"They're mostly dry now."

"Still. Grab fresh charge packs for your rifle and a spear."

Nova nodded and darted back the other

way, heading for her room. Clayton stomped through the kitchen and living room to his bedroom. Both their rooms lay directly off the main living area. Another rickety wooden door swung wide as he pushed through, a circular hole where the door handle used to be. He laid Rosie gently on his bed, and the ancient springs creaked. It was just a single mattress sitting on the floor, covered with dusty blankets and sheets. They'd chopped up the remains of the box springs and bed frames to patch holes in the roof. Rosie stirred and whimpered.

"It's okay, girl. We're going to get you some help," Clayton said as he slipped off his pack and rifle and placed them on the bed beside Rosie.

He stripped out of his damp clothes and sorted through the dry ones hanging from rusty wires in the open closet beside his bed. There were a handful of stained and torn uniforms that he'd scavenged from the Wastes. Black, form-hugging black Chimeran uniforms from the Guard, similar versions with faded piping of various colors for human cadets, and plain gray uniforms from Chimeran factory workers. There were also a handful of more colorful civilian clothes. Clayton took out a gray factory worker's uniform, thinking that it would work better to camouflage him among the faded urban grays of the Wastes after the sun came up.

Putting on dry socks and a spare set of boots that were half a size too big, Clayton completed his ensemble by reaching into the back of the closet and grabbing one of three different spears. This one had a hunting knife for a blade and a sturdy wooden handle that he'd carved himself from a hemlock branch. It also had a strap that he'd tied on with old electrical wires so that he could carry it over his shoulder. Slinging the spear over one shoulder, he reached back in to check over the meager collection of guns he'd stacked beside the spears, machetes, and axes. He needed something to trade to the resistance for medicine, but none of the guns in his closet would be valuable enough to trade for a dose of Regenex.

The laser rifles that he and Nova had used on their hunting trip were the most valuable items they had besides the solar sheeting and the hoverbike. They'd have to part with one of the rifles.

Clayton grimaced at the thought of losing such a valuable weapon and turned away from the closet. Grunting as he hoisted his pack onto his shoulders, he slung the sniper rifle over his right shoulder and then bent down to scoop Rosie off the mattress. His lower back spasmed painfully as he did so, and his arms and legs began shaking immediately with her weight. He pushed through the pain and hurried out of the bedroom. He found Nova already waiting in the living room. She wore a female version of the gray worker's uniform he'd chosen, and she had a spear of her own slung over her left shoulder.

"We need to roll up the solar sheeting and take it with us," he said. If they got stuck out in the Wastes longer than planned, they would need a way to charge their equipment.

Nova nodded and grabbed her lantern from the kitchen counter before turning and leading the way back outside. She latched the door shut behind them, and then walked down the creaking porch and around the side of the cabin. The gleaming silver solar sheet swept into view. Clayton followed his daughter there and then walked on to their bike. It sat on its landing struts, parked in the shadows of a simple shelter that they'd built. Four tree trunks held up a corrugated metal roof draped with plastic to seal out the rain.

Clayton laid Rosie in the grass beside the bike and then opened the cargo compartment and pulled out the musty pile of old blankets that served as her cushion. Rosie moaned softly, air whistling sharply from her nose. A reminder to hurry. The nanites had kept her alive so far, but they had to be spent by now.

Clayton put his pack in the bottom of the cargo compartment. Plastic containers of raw meat knocked together with butcher knives and the pot that they used to boil water.

"Done," Nova said, breathing hard as she ran over with a big, tightly folded bundle of solar sheeting. Clayton took it from her and placed it on top of his pack. Nova turned off the lantern and tucked it into a hollow corner of the compartment. Finally, he laid out Rosie's blankets on top, followed by Rosie herself. Moving quickly, they slotted their spears and rifles into racks that they'd fashioned on the sloping sides of the bike, and then they climbed on the seat with Clayton at the controls and Nova holding onto his waist.

"Ready?" he asked as he powered the bike on. It hummed to life and hovered up a few feet off the grass. The holographic nav display in the center of the dash flickered once, then died. That display had long-ago stopped working, along with the scanners that fed it with readings from their surroundings.

"Let's go," Nova whispered.

Clayton turned the bike toward the open end of the garage and gunned the engine. They whooshed out over the moonlit field, grass rustling loudly with the wind of their passing. Clayton pulled up gradually, flying over the trees that encircled the clearing, and soon they were speeding over the forest canopy with the wind roaring in their ears and the trees blurring into a shadowy river below.

CHAPTER 35

Clayton flew over ruined suburbs, heading east and flying parallel to the distant, glittering lights of New Houston. The lingering darkness of the night and the bike's lack of working headlights would cloak them from view, but Clayton flew down lower just in case. The glowing tips of the city's tallest buildings dropped behind the horizon, and he was forced to slow down as he wove along the labyrinthine streets, dodging rusting hulks of cars and buses and the jutting trunks of trees that had burst through the crumbling asphalt and sidewalks.

Soon they came to a solid green wall of forest, and Clayton pulled up again to fly over it to a river on the other side. He followed the river downstream, hugging the water between dense banks of trees on either side. Here and there, groups of Dregs appeared along the water's edge, having come down to the river for a drink. A few of them looked up and shrieked at their passing. Nova's arms tightened around Clayton's waist. Maybe she hadn't believed him when he'd told her that the Wastes were overrun.

"How much farther is it?" Nova asked, whispering sharply beside his ear to be heard above the wind.

"Not far," he replied. A sharp bend appeared at the end of the shimmering silver ribbon they followed. Turning his head to make sure Nova heard, he said, "Hold on to Rosie."

One of Nova's arms left his waist, and Clayton slowed as much as he could before they reached the bend. He banked hard to follow it, then straightened out and flew on for about half a mile to where the river widened and the trees cleared. On the left appeared a compound that used to be a water treatment plant. Clayton abandoned the river and flew over a flattened chain link fence, passing between open concrete troughs of stagnant water and rows of big metal pipes leading to them. Keeping an eye out for Dregs, he flew down the length of the pipes to a large concrete structure with broken windows gaping from the upper levels and a sagging roof. He landed the bike in front of a rusty metal door, but left it powered on in case they needed to make a hasty retreat.

Slinging his leg over the side, he hopped down and grabbed both his rifle and spear from the racks where he'd left them. Catching Nova's eye, he whispered, "Stay here and watch for trouble. I need to go in and send a signal to my contact. If you see Dregs coming, you take off and stay out of their reach. Go down to the river if you have to. Whatever you do, don't fire on them with your rifle. The sound will attract more of them."

"Can't I come with?" Nova asked.

He shook his head. "Rosie is in no condition to be moved, and the bike won't fit through the door."

"Well, what about you? What if there are Dregs in there?" Nova asked, her eyes darting to the rusty door of the treatment plant. It was propped open with a chunk of concrete.

"I'll be fine," he said, patting his spear for emphasis.

Nova nodded hesitantly and then slid forward on the seat to grab the control bars. "Okay..."

"I'll be back in a few minutes." Clayton went to the back of the bike and reached past Rosie for the lantern. Pulling it out, he flicked it on and walked to the entrance of the plant. He pulled on the door, and it opened with a groan of protest.

The interior of the plant was relatively intact. Rows of pumping equipment sat on the polished concrete floors with pipes leading to and fro. An upper level of rickety-looking metal catwalks gave access to pipes running higher up. Walking by it all, Clayton headed for a flaking green metal door on the far side of the building. He checked for Dregs skulking in the shadows as he went, but so far, the place was clear.

Turning the metal handle of the door, he pulled it open and stepped into what had once been a control center for the facility. Old, broken pressure gauges and control screens lined the walls. A pair of dusty chairs sat in front of an empty desk with computer screens mounted on the wall above it. Clayton walked to the desk and went down on his haunches to shine a light below. A small black box was tucked out of sight beneath a cabinet with a thick cable trailing from it to an open panel in the wall, and another thinner cable going to the charge pack of a Kyron laser rifle.

Clayton flicked a switch at the back of the device, and a single green light snapped on. Straightening, he used his ARCs to search for nearby devices he could connect to. Finding just one besides his rifle, he connected to it, and a simple command-line interface appeared before his eyes. He shrank the display and moved it over his left eye, then composed his thoughts to send a message:

Lone Wolf to Phoenix Base—urgent request for Regenex or similar. Willing to trade weapons in exchange.

Clayton was about to leave it at that, but then he remembered that he was here early, so he couldn't be sure that the resistance would send Harold's daughter to meet him. He still had an update to give to Harold's wife, Mona, at that abandoned school.

He added: *Also, need update from Pyro to give to Scarecrow.*

He sent the message, smiling wanly at the call signs the resistance had given to Harold Neem and his daughter Veronica. A line of confirmation appeared with three dots repeating endlessly behind it: *Contacting receiver...*

Clayton stood there glancing around the control center uneasily as he waited for a reply. After a few minutes of nothing, he heard a muffled skittering sound coming from the machine room behind him. That sound was followed by the echoing *scraaape* of something metallic being dragged or kicked across the floor, and then silence.

He quickly turned and crept back to the door. Turning the handle slowly, he winced as the mechanism made loud popping and pinging sounds. He cracked open the door to check for signs of Dregs.

A dark gap of shadows appeared between the door and the frame. He shone his lantern into it, casting a dim, but far-reaching blue light across the dusty concrete floor. Long shadows leapt out behind pumps and pipes, but there was no sign of anything moving around. No way to be sure without checking every inch of the place. Clayton's skin prickled with sweat, his pulse thudding loud in his ears as he strained to listen for subsequent noises.

He cracked the door open further and poked his head out to check the blind spots along the wall.

Just as he did so, a loud *bang* sounded from the metal catwalk above him, followed by a shrill cry and a dark, blurry shape dropping down.

Clayton stumbled away, dropping the lantern in his hurry to reach for his spear.

The creature darted past his legs with the familiar yowl of a cat.

Clayton smiled and shook his head. He retrieved the lantern and shut the door with a soft *click.* He tried the twist knob lock in the handle. It turned but didn't lock the door. *Figures,* he thought. Seeing that the resistance still hadn't replied, he busied himself by looking around for the cat. A flash of glowing green eyes appeared under the desk. He went down on his haunches in front of it, and it hissed sharply in response.

"It's okay," he said, and then tried to coax it out by making *pst pst pst* sounds.

The animal hissed again and ducked behind a filing cabinet.

A command prompt on the right side of Clayton's ARCs flashed with a new line of text, catching his eye:

Message received. Stay at rendezvous and await contact.

Clayton blew out an uneasy breath, hoping that they would hurry. He had told them it was urgent. Of course, he hadn't mentioned the medical supplies were for his dog, but they might not have taken him seriously if he had.

Bending down to reach for the improvised comms unit below the filing cabinet, Clayton received another hiss from the cat as he flicked the device off.

"Don't worry, I'm leaving," he whispered.

Another hiss.

Followed by a rattling sound and then the popping and pinging of metal springs. Clayton glanced sharply at the door behind him—

In time to see the handle slowly turning.

CHAPTER 36

The door swung wide, and a gulf of shadows appeared on the other side with a blurry silhouette standing there. Clayton jumped to his feet, his rifle rattling noisily. His hands flew to his spear, grabbing it in a two-handed grip even before his brain caught up and recognized the person in the doorway.

"Nova!" he whispered sharply. "I thought I told you to keep watch!"

"Shhh," she replied, and nodded sideways to indicate the way she'd come. Clayton spotted blue headlights flashing through the broken windows up near the roof of the facility. Hoverbikes.

Clayton flicked off his lantern and hurried over to the door. Nova stepped in and flattened herself to the wall beside him, breathing hard.

Chimeras, she mouthed to him, gripping her rifle in both hands.

Clayton hid behind the open door and peeked around it, checking for signs of intruders inside the facility. Nothing yet. He eased the door shut, leaving a crack that they could check for approaching threats. Those bikes might just be doing a flyover, but the fact that they were here at all suggested that they'd seen him and Nova flying in and had followed them here.

Unless the comms unit that he'd just used was somehow compromised... Clayton glanced back under the desk and caught a glint of green eyes staring back at him.

"Where's Rosie?" he asked, looking back to Nova.

She shook her head. "On the floor between two rows of machinery. She was too heavy to carry all the way here. You want me to go back for her?"

"No. She'll be fine there for now."

Nova looked like she wanted to argue, but she gave in with a nod.

Clayton didn't mention that they might need Rosie to provide a distraction if those Chimeras came nosing around inside. He peeked around the door again, staring across the shadowy gulf of pipes and machinery between them and the entrance on the far side of the facility. He didn't have clear sightlines to the door, but he knew where it was.

"What are we going to do?" Nova whispered. "Aren't there any other exits in here?"

Clayton shook his head. They were backed into a corner. There was another entrance on this side of the machine room. They could make a break for it now and try to reach their hoverbike, but that would mean leaving Rosie behind, and the Chimeras' scanners would detect them as soon as they left the building. At least in here, surrounded by thick concrete walls, they could still hide for a while. Clayton stared across the machine room, blinking sweat from his eyes and listening for the sound of a door clicking open. Maybe they wouldn't come in. Maybe their arrival was a coincidence.

"Did they see you?" he asked.

Nova hesitated. "I don't know."

"What about the bike?"

"I shut it down, but there wasn't time to move it."

"Shit," Clayton muttered.

Hoverbikes were electric, but they still generated a fair amount of heat with their grav engines. Scanners would pick up that fading heat signature from the air just as easily as they would a human's.

"How many bikes did you see?"

"Two, I think," Nova said.

"Two. Okay. Even odds, at least."

"For now. What if they called for backup?" Nova asked.

"No, they won't want to share their bounty with anyone else." Clayton's thoughts turned to strategy. At least one of them needed to get sightlines on the entrances.

"Stay here," he whispered.

"Dad, wait..."

But he ignored her, pulling the door open until it was wide enough for him to slip out. He moved as quickly and quietly as he could, crouching and running at the same time. He angled across the room, darting behind the rows of thick metal pipes and machinery until he found a fat yellow pipe with a gap of about nine inches beneath it that would allow him to see the entrances on both sides of the facility. He flattened himself to the floor, carefully slipped the rifle off his shoulder, and aimed it under the pipe. Clayton used his ARCs to line up the crosshairs of the green night-vision scope on one of the two doors, and then he visually checked the other one. Both doors were still shut. He focused on quieting his breathing. It was too loud in the ringing silence of the facility.

Another sound pricked his ears and sent adrenaline raging through his veins: Rosie's panting.

And then both doors banged open in the same instant. Clayton's finger tightened on the trigger, but both entrances remained clear.

A burst of light and a loud *bang!* blinded and deafened him. Blinking rapidly to clear his vision and straining to hear through the ringing in his ears, Clayton glanced back and forth between the two doors, checking for targets. It took precious seconds for his eyes to recover, and the first thing he heard was Rosie's muffled howling. The sound would have been much louder to her.

Clayton expected to see a pair of armored Chimeras tracking toward Rosie from one or both doors. But he still couldn't see anything come in. Had they slipped in while he'd been blinded?

Something hard and cold pressed against the back of his skull, and Clayton froze. He slowly turned to see the air shimmering beside him. A Chimera in a full suit of matte black cloaking armor appeared standing right beside him and holding a matching, long-barreled pistol to the side of his head.

His mind raced for a way to stall the inevitable, or at least to keep Nova from discovery.

So he said the only thing he could think of: "I know where the resistance is hiding." The Chimera standing over him tilted its head to one side, like a bird, but said nothing. Clayton barreled on, "I can take you to them."

It was a lie. He'd only ever been to this rendezvous point. The resistance didn't trust outsiders like him to know where their base was—especially since he'd never ingested the memory-erasing nanites that they used to keep their secrets safe.

But this hunter didn't know that.

The Chimera hesitated, obviously torn between simply shooting him in the head and collecting the reward, or testing his bluff to see if he could lead them to more exiles. But then, something unexpected happened. The Chimera spoke—

In a *human* voice.

CHAPTER 37

"**H**ello, Clayton," a female voice said. "I almost didn't recognize you under that beard."

He sat up quickly. The shaft of his spear hit the floor and knocked it off his shoulder. He recognized that voice, but muffled as it was by the helmet, he couldn't place it.

"You're with the resistance," he guessed.

A nod.

His whole body sagged with relief. "How did you get here so fast?" It had barely been a couple of minutes since he'd sent them that message.

"We were already in the area," the woman standing beside him said.

The shrieking report of a laser rifle interrupted them, and Clayton's heart seized in his chest. Had he misread things?

The woman standing beside him flinched, and her weapon snapped up, leaving the side of his head to sweep for targets.

No longer sure what he was dealing with, Clayton took the opening and leapt off the floor. He collided with the woman, and they went down together in a noisy clatter of armor.

"Drop your weapon, right now!" A quaking voice cried. It was Nova's. Had she fired that shot?

Clayton was too busy struggling with the woman on the ground to check. He tried to pry the pistol out of her armored fist, but she held on tight.

"Damn it, Clayton! Stop! It's me, Lori!"

In that instant, the voice clicked into memory, and he realized it was true. He stumbled off her, backing up quickly, and almost fell backward over the pipe that he'd been hiding behind.

"I watched you die..."

A static-filled sigh issued from the helmet as she clambered off the floor. She didn't aim her pistol at Clayton again, but rather holstered it on her hip. "Tell the girl to back off," Lori said. "We're all friends here."

Clayton twisted around to see Nova standing in the open door to the control room, her rifle aimed at someone else in a matching suit of matte black cloaking armor.

"Nova, stand down!" he said. "They're with the resistance."

"Then why did they use a stun grenade on us?"

Clayton looked back to the armored woman who claimed to be Lori just in time to see her removing her helmet. Familiar features appeared: a small nose, round face, dark hair, dark eyes. It was definitely her. "How?"

She answered Nova's question first: "We used a stun grenade because we saw the ho-verbike parked outside and thought this was a trap. Where did you get it?"

Harold's daughter, Veronica, was his usual contact with the resistance. She knew about the bike, but Lori apparently didn't. "I stole it from a bounty hunter," Clayton said. "The same one who killed you."

"Yes, I died," Lori confirmed. "But so did your wife."

"You're a clone? I thought cloning was il-legal?"

"It is," a second female voice added, this one deep and husky. Booted feet clacked on the floor as she crossed the room to join Clayton and Lori.

Nova had halfway lowered her rifle, but she still hadn't left the cover of the control center.

"Who are you?" Clayton asked as the sec-ond woman stopped on the other side of him. She reached up to remove her helmet, and he gasped as a bald, chalk-white head with sunken red eyes appeared. Four cranial stalks slowly rose from where they had been flat-tened against the bony bridge of her skull.

"It's a Chimera!" Nova cried.

"Don't shoot!" Clayton said, holding up a

hand to stop Nova. "I know her, too." This was Lori's daughter, Keera Reed. Formerly, *Admiral* Reed of the occupying fleet. Nodding to her, he went on, "You went missing a decade ago. You've been here all this time?"

"No, but I'm back now."

He'd heard about Keera's disappearance during one of his very first meetings with the resistance and again during his subsequent meeting with Harold's wife, Mona.

"You defected?" Clayton asked.

Keera nodded to Lori. "I didn't have much choice after resurrecting my mother."

Clayton frowned.

"We need to go," Lori said, looking around quickly.

Keera's cranial stalks twitched.

"Go?" Clayton asked. "I asked to trade medical supplies."

"I don't see anyone injured," Keera said.

"Rosie," Nova explained, and pointed down to the aisles of machinery on the other side of the facility.

"Show us," Keera said.

Clayton picked up his rifle and spear, and they followed Nova across the facility. Walking between two rows of dormant pumps, they found Rosie lying on the cement floor, making soft wheezing sounds as she breathed.

"A *dog?*" Lori asked, her footsteps slowing at the sight. "How did you even find one?" She looked to Clayton with eyebrows raised. The Kyra didn't approve of them keeping pets, and strays didn't last long in the Wastes with the Dregs hunting them.

"I found her out here years ago," Clayton explained. "Her master had been bitten, so I took her in. She's part of the family now."

Keera bent down beside Rosie. The dog attempted to lift her head, snarling feebly at the Chimera.

Keera hissed back, baring sharp teeth, and Rosie subsided. "We have medical supplies in our bikes," Keera said as she straightened. "But it's going to cost you. Regenex isn't easy to come by, and we have more urgent uses for it than pets."

"Please, you have to help her," Nova said.

Clayton patted his rifle. "I can trade my rifle and two spare charge packs."

Keera shook her head. "We already have weapons."

"There has to be *something* you need!" Nova protested, looking desperate.

Keera regarded her quietly. "There is." Then she looked back to Clayton. "We have weapons, but what we don't have are enough people to shoot them."

Clayton set his jaw. "You're asking us to do a job? Or to join the resistance?"

"Either. Both," Keera replied.

Clayton glanced at Nova, thinking that

saving Rosie wasn't worth risking her life. "I'll do it. You leave Nova out of it."

Keera conceded that with a shrug. "You haven't heard what the job is yet."

"Doesn't matter. I can't let Rosie die."

"I'll go get my medkit." Keera strode quietly down the rows of machinery, heading for the exit.

Nova's eyes narrowed, and she glared at Clayton. "You promised you'd listen to what they have to say."

"I did listen."

"No, you didn't. You don't even know what they want from you."

"Does it matter?"

"Yes. They need people to fight. I want to help," Nova added.

Lori looked back and forth between the two of them. "Your father said to leave you out of it."

"At least someone was listening to me," Clayton growled.

Nova shook her head. "It's not up to him. I can make my own choices."

"You're fourteen!" Clayton thundered quietly.

Nova planted hands on her hips and scowled at him. "So?"

"You're just a kid."

"Who never had a childhood. I'm not *just a kid* anymore."

"I don't want to get in the middle of this..." Lori said.

"Good, then don't," Clayton replied.

"But we could use all the help we can get," she added.

"When has that ever not been the case?" Clayton replied.

Keera came back carrying a silver case, interrupting the discussion. She dropped down beside Rosie and popped the case open. Rosie tried to growl again, but it came out sounding more like a whimper.

"Show me where she's hurt," Keera said.

Nova hurried to remove the bandages. She indicated the laser burn, which they'd been unable to treat, and then the blood-matted fur over her back and side where she'd been slashed and bitten by that Dreg. Keera quickly sprayed the wounds liberally with Regenex and then synthskin, and finally, she administered an injectable painkiller.

Nova held Rosie up while Keera wrapped her body with a fresh roll of bandages. They laid her back down, and then Keera stood and nodded to Clayton. "Ready to go?"

"Go where?" he replied.

"Phoenix base."

Clayton's eyes widened at that, then collapsed into suspicious slits. No one was allowed to know where their base was unless they agreed to join the resistance first. Either something had changed, or they were trying to trick him into joining.

"We don't have much time before the op starts," Lori put in. "Your arrival is actually great timing. We weren't expecting you here for at least another twelve hours."

"No one cares about me knowing where your base is? What if I get captured and reveal its location?"

"Like you were about to do when you thought we were with the Guard?" Lori asked.

"That was a bluff," Clayton said.

"It won't matter what you can reveal after this op," Keera explained, shaking her head.

Clayton grew even more suspicious with that statement. "What do you mean?"

"She means that one way or another, it's all going to be over after this," Lori explained. "Either for us or the occupation."

"Oh yeah, and who's the favorite to win?" Clayton asked.

"We are," Keera replied.

He peered skeptically at her ghostly face, searching those crimson eyes for some hint of doubt or deception.

Nova looked like her eyes were about to leap out of her head. "You found a way to beat them? *How?*"

A slow smile curved Keera's lips. "Come with us, and you'll see."

CHAPTER 38

Wind whipped through Clayton's long, greasy hair as he followed the hazy silhouettes of Lori's and Keera's hoverbikes farther east across the Wastes. Nova clung tight to his waist, and Rosie lay nestled in the back, covered by springy cargo webbing that Lori had supplied from her bike to make sure the dog didn't fall out.

Lori's and Keera's bikes were much newer, and the headlights still worked, but they kept them off to avoid being seen. It was just after five in the morning, and darkness still clung to the ruined landscape below. Black mounds of wreckage and the vegetation growing through them undulated like waves on a stormy sea.

The ruins soon faded to trees and overgrown farms, and then to a solid black canvas of forest. They flew low over the canopy with leaves rustling and whispering in the wind of their passing.

After about fifteen minutes, they came to a clearing where the trees became much sparser and grass grew in between. Keera dropped down to an old road, and they followed it straight to the glittering ribbon of a river. She banked sharply as she flew over the water. Clayton braked before following that maneuver to avoid throwing Rosie out.

They followed the winding river upstream, heading north. Trees quickly soared up again on both sides. Here, this far from the city, there was no sign of Dregs coming down to drink. They'd progressed from the Wastes to the Wilds, somewhere like the old national forest that Clayton and Nova called home.

Time dragged by as they flew up the river. The water trickled softly below, wind buffeted their clothes and hair, and dawn began to blush just above the trees to their right.

Within minutes, the sky was ablaze with crimson fire. Trees resolved into deep greens, and sandy shores came alive and sparkling with the sun. A lone gray wolf appeared around the next bend in the river, looking up with deadly yellow eyes as they passed.

"Look at that!" Nova said, pointing to it.

Clayton eyes widened. *A wolf. In Texas,* he thought wonderingly. With ninety-five percent of the human population gone, nature was steadily reclaiming the Earth.

The fire in the sky faded to simmering embers and cool, pastel blues. Not long after that, Keera and Lori peeled left off the river and up a sharp, grassy embankment. From there, they glided down a crumbling street. Old wooden homes flashed by between the trees. Overgrown lawns were abloom with white and purple splashes of wildflowers. Some of the homes had collapsed with age, while others were still in the process, but all of them looked abandoned.

Broken windows gaped with glittering wedges of glass and scraps of curtains fluttering in the wind. Doorways stood open, the doors either broken or fallen off their hinges. The contents of these homes had long-ago been raided for supplies.

Here and there, Clayton caught glimpses of a lake on the other side of the homes. The rotten posts of fallen fences were alive with bright green shrubs growing over and through.

This had been a community before the invasion. Clayton wondered what had happened to it when the Kyra had arrived. They obviously hadn't attacked directly. Had the residents all turned on each other, fighting over the cans of food in one another's pantries?

Clayton dragged his eyes away. They wove along the streets, dodging trees and saplings that had pushed through over the years. The place was like a maze, and Clayton quickly lost track of how many turns they'd taken.

Finally, they turned off the street and down a grassy lane that had been someone's driveway. A grassy carpet of wildflowers rolled out ahead of them. Rows of pine trees lined the path, while giant beech and cyprus trees towered above the grassy fields of the estate.

Still there was no sign of what might lie at the end of the driveway. They flew on for a few more minutes before coming to a sprawling log mansion. It was in slightly better shape than the other places they'd seen. A four-car garage was open on one side. The other three garage doors were shut, but dented and rusted through in places. Keera headed straight for the opening. Clayton thought he caught a glimpse of shadows moving around in there as they approached. He slowed and stopped the bike outside. Keera and Lori flew in one after another, their vehicles vanishing as they headed deeper into the garage.

Keera and Lori both came walking out of the garage with their helmets tucked under their arms.

"Welcome to Phoenix Base," Lori said.

"This is *it?*" Nova asked, disappointment evident in her voice.

"Appearances can be deceiving," Keera said.

But Clayton knew what Nova meant. They'd both expected a more established compound, maybe a bunker or a prison—not an abandoned mansion that probably leaked like a sieve when it rained.

"Park your bike inside," Keera said. "We don't want anyone to see it from the air."

"Is that a real concern out here?" Clayton asked, eyes scanning the big, clear dome of blue sky overhead. Patrols didn't usually come out this far. That was how he and Nova had stayed safe for all these years at their cabin.

"We don't like to take chances. Especially now that we're so close to victory."

"Who's we?" Clayton added.

"You'll see," Lori said. "Park the bike, and we'll introduce you to the others."

Clayton twisted the throttle and coasted into the shadowy garage. It took a moment for his eyes to adjust to the darkness. Once they did, he spotted six hoverbikes already parked in two rows of three, all facing the far side of the space. Clayton parked his bike behind one row, as far from the open door as possible. He heard footsteps coming in behind them and turned to see Lori and Keera standing there. Clayton dismounted with Nova, and they grabbed their rifles and spears from the racks on the sloping sides of the bike. Lori unfastened the crash webbing that held Rosie down, and she lifted her head sleepily.

Nova patted her on the head. "Good girl."

She winked at them, and Clayton hoisted her out. "Where to?" he asked, looking to Keera.

"Follow me."

She led them past the bikes to a side door. It clicked open, the hinges squealing, and they emerged in a wide hallway with dusty, buckling wooden floors. Fresh planks had been laid down in two separate places to bridge holes with rotting black edges. Clayton glimpsed a shadowy lower level between those sagging boards.

The hallway led to a brightly-lit great room and adjoining kitchen with two stories of broken picture windows stacked atop each other and overlooking the lake.

A group of four people rose from faded couches and chairs that were bleeding white and yellow stuffing. They all wore the black uniforms of the Guard, stripped of the insignia and the bird of prey emblem of the Federation. All four were humans.

Clayton recognized two of the four. One of them, a tall man with dark skin and a shiny patch of scar tissue on his right cheek, was Sergeant Sutton. The other was *Pyro,* or Veronica Neem, Harold's daughter. Her curly red hair and green eyes reminded him of her father. The other two were an Asian man and a young, possibly-Latin woman that he didn't recognize. The Latin woman had a cute, almost girlish face and a perfect complexion. Long dark hair fell in a wave past her shoulders. If he had to guess, he'd say she'd stopped aging at just eighteen years of age. That, or she was actually eighteen.

"Well, well, look who's finally decided to

join the good fight," Sutton said in his thick southern drawl.

"This is all of you?" Clayton asked, glancing back to Keera and Lori, his eyes wide with astonishment.

"Of course not," Sutton replied. "The others are asleep downstairs, so kindly lower your voice. This is Diaz," Sutton said, pointing to the Latin woman. "But we call her Widow. Squinty-eyes standing beside her is Doc. He's our medic."

The Asian man glared at Sutton for the racial comment. The sergeant smiled and held up his hands in surrender. "You know I'm just playin'. We all love you, brother."

"How many of you are there?" Nova asked as Clayton shuffled into the living room and lowered Rosie into the armchair that Sutton had vacated.

Clayton shot his daughter a frown. "Asking a resistance cell about their numbers is like asking a woman her age. Or her weight."

Nova looked confused. "Why would anyone care about their age?"

Clayton smiled. "Never mind."

"Who's the mutt?" Sutton asked, changing the topic with a lopsided frown that he owed to his burn-scarred cheek.

"Rosie, and she's not a mutt," Nova replied.

"Well, she sure as shit ain't a thoroughbred," Sutton replied.

"I found her in the Wastes," Clayton explained. "Her owner was infected and asked me to take care of her."

"After you took care of the owner?" Sutton asked with one eyebrow raised.

"She did it herself, but yeah, it was with my gun."

Sutton nodded and looked to Nova. "Sixteen, to answer your question," he said. "We used to have several dozen more, but we've lost a lot of good people over the years. I suppose now we have two new recruits, though. Ain't that right, Captain?"

"I'm not a captain, and keep my daughter out of it," Clayton said with a warning glance in her direction. He received a scowl from Nova for a reply, but at least this time she didn't push it. Maybe she was beginning to realize just what he'd meant when he'd told her that the resistance was a lost cause.

Pyro looked confused. "She's your daughter?"

Clayton ignored the question and looked to Keera and Lori, then to Sutton, wondering who was in charge. He decided on Sutton. "Whatever you're planning, seventeen people aren't enough to pull it off."

Sutton looked to Keera. "You haven't told him yet, Admiral?"

She shook her head. "No."

Admiral, Clayton thought. For Sutton to

call her that, she had to be one of their leaders, too. "Told me what?"

She stepped forward. "We don't have to pull anything off. We could sit on our hands, and we'd still win. Victory is already a given, and..." she trailed off with a grin. "We have a cure."

Clayton traded looks with Nova, her expression blank with shock.

"It works?" she asked for both of them.

"You tested it?" Clayton added.

Keera nodded. "Yes."

"It even works on people who've been recently bitten," Lori said. "It won't turn a Dreg back or make them sane, but it will stop a human from turning into one."

"How long have you had it?" Clayton asked. If true, this was a game-changer for exiles like them.

"Not long," Keera said. "We've only been with the resistance for a few months now, and work on the cure could only be finished once they got access to Lori."

Clayton nodded slowly. "Okay, fair enough. You said victory's a given. Care to explain that?"

Keera turned to look at a bulky black tower standing in a hallway to one side of the kitchen. *A generator or power supply of some kind?* Clayton wondered.

"Specter, would you come out here,

please?" Keera said.

Not seeing anyone there, Clayton assumed she must be speaking to someone in a room further down the hallway. He noticed wires trailing from the power supply to a rusty refrigerator and snaking along the floor in the hall.

At least they fixed up a fridge, he thought. That was one better than he and Nova had managed so far.

Silence thickened the air as everyone stared into the hall, waiting for *Specter* to show his or herself. A warm breeze whistled in through the broken windows. Birds chirped outside, flitting between the trees. Crickets sang.

Rosie's head popped up from the chair, and she barked once, staring into the hallway along with everyone else.

Clayton was about to ask what they were waiting for when he heard a sudden *creak* from the sagging floors a few feet away.

Rosie growled softly and tilted her head, staring at the spot.

Whatever had caused the noise was invisible. *Cloaked,* Clayton decided. His gaze darted around the room for some sign of where *Specter* might be. He wasn't the only one. Everyone else was busy looking around with him.

"It's okay, you can show yourself," Keera said. "They're friends."

"To *you*, perhaps," a deep, sing-song voice grated out directly beside Clayton's ear. That voice. It wasn't Chimeran, or human. It was Kyron.

He recoiled from the sound, his heart slamming against his sternum. "Show yourself!" he demanded, backing up a few steps and reaching for his rifle. Rosie sat up, barking and snarling.

"Easy," Keera warned, stepping in front of Clayton and grabbing one of his wrists to stop him from raising the rifle. "You don't want to do that."

Clayton scowled and wrenched his arm free.

"He seems hostile," the sing-song voice added.

"He's just wary like you," Keera replied. "Deactivate your cloak, please."

The air shimmered, and the tallest Kyra Clayton had ever seen appeared standing in front of him. It wore a full suit of matte black cloaking armor with massive, translucent, rainbow-shimmering wings spread out behind its back. The Kyra stood almost six feet tall on skinny legs, bent at the knee with slender arms curled up against its chest. The Kyra's wings retracted with an audible *clicking* sound, and a pair of red eyes appeared, glowing deep within the alien's otherwise inscrutable helmet.

"You can't trust it," Clayton said, shaking

his head.

"Likewise," the Kyra added. "In my experience, those who are the most suspicious are also the least trustworthy."

Clayton snorted and shook his head. "Said the Kyra who won't even show his face."

Specter cocked his head in a distinctly bird-like fashion, and then gave a hissing laugh. "Very well."

The smooth black faceplate of its helmet became perfectly transparent, revealing a male Kyra's features with sunken red eyes and bony, chalk-white skin. A fish-scale pattern of black veins ran underneath. It was all too familiar, but something was wrong with this Kyra's appearance. Its features were glowing —*luminous*—and its eyes were strangely dead looking.

Nova stepped over to him, her jaw slack and hazel eyes wide. She grabbed his arm, long nails biting through his uniform. "What is that?" she whispered. Even Rosie seemed scared. She'd stopped barking and had ducked behind the back of her chair.

"This is my face," Specter said. "But I am not a Kyra. I am a Chrona."

CHAPTER 39

"**A** Chrona?" Clayton echoed, looking to Keera for confirmation. She nodded and smiled tightly at him.

"The enemy of my enemy is my friend," Sergeant Sutton added.

"Or just another enemy," Clayton replied, his eyes narrowing on the holographic face of a Kyra projected within the Chrona's helmet. "You're a machine."

"Congratulations," Specter said. "You are smarter than the average biological."

Pyro snorted at that and shook her head, sending curly red hair flipping over her shoulders. The other two, the Asian man and the Latin woman took their leave, heading for the hallway running by the kitchen.

"What is your real name?" Clayton asked, his eyes fixed on the machine in front of him.

"My real name is expressed in quinary and communicated soundlessly. The nearest translation that you would understand is a number with sixteen digits that expresses how many other beings chose to shed their biological roots before me."

"Now you know why we call him Specter," Lori said.

Clayton looked to Keera. "Where did you find him?"

"In Chronan space," she replied.

"And he didn't kill you? You're a Chimera. An *enemy* soldier."

"*Was* an enemy soldier. After I became an exile, I sought them out to enlist their help. They didn't know about Earth because it's a relatively new addition to the Federation, and they agreed to help us liberate it."

Clayton's eyes narrowed on the glowing Kyra face in front of him. "In exchange for what?"

"We are not the evil monsters that the Kyra have made us out to be," Specter said, extending its skinny arms and spreading small, three-fingered hands palms-up, as if to indicate his surroundings. Maybe Specter meant that his being here at a resistance base should be proof enough that he was on their side.

What did any of them even know about the Chrona? He'd only ever heard of them, never seen them for himself, or heard them described. And he certainly hadn't known that they were essentially larger, robotic versions of the Kyra themselves.

Clayton wasn't ready to trust him—*it,* he amended. *Machines don't have a gender.* "You didn't answer my question. In exchange for what? What do your people get out of liberating mine?"

"Simple," Specter said. "The Kyra are determined to destroy us. They won't stop until they have won and every last Chrona is destroyed. There have been countless atrocities on both sides, and this war has been raging for nearly a thousand standard orbits. Now, finally, we are driving them back. We have managed to do this by targeting the source of their strength—worlds like this one where the native populations are being bred for war. By setting these peoples free and making it impossible, or at least difficult, for the Kyra to return, we are reducing their numbers and turning the tide for ourselves."

"So you're doing this for you, not for us," Clayton concluded.

"All sentient beings act in the interests of their own continued survival. It is merely fortunate that ensuring our survival also favors yours."

"A win-win scenario," Sergeant Sutton said.

"But that means you're not the good guys," Nova said.

Pryo arched thin red eyebrows at that, looking as though she wanted to say something.

But the Chrona beat her to it. "Good and evil are subjective designations that change according to the benefit and detriment of the individual that you ask," Specter replied.

"No, there are absolutes," Clayton argued. "The greater good, for example."

"By that definition, the Kyra and their Chimeras are the most numerous homologous group in the galaxy, and therefore it would be evil to defeat them. Is that your contention?"

Clayton frowned. "Aren't you basically a digitized Kyra yourself?"

"Your point?"

"Just ironic, that's all. Maybe we should skip to the part where you tell me how we're going to kick the Kyra's collective butts off Earth and make sure that they don't come back."

"Simple. A Chronan fleet will be here in less than twenty-four of your Earth hours. It will defeat the Kyron fleet in orbit, and we will land soldiers to eliminate any Chimeras who refuse to surrender."

"Sounds good to me," Clayton said. "Then what?"

"Then, we will distribute the cure that the resistance has developed and inoculate the entire human population against the Chimeran virus."

"Just like that?"

"They've been mass-producing it," Keera explained. "They'll use drones to distribute it to the cities through their water supplies after the Kyra are defeated."

"So what are *we* doing here?" He looked to Keera and Lori. "You mentioned an op, but it sounds like there's nothing left for us to do other than wait."

Nova nodded along with that, her brow deeply furrowed.

"There is one thing we still need to do before the fleet arrives," Specter said. "The Kyra are a vengeful species. When they realize that they're about to lose Earth, they'll kill you all before they leave just to make sure that none of you can volunteer to join *our* side of the war."

"So if they can't have us, no one else can," Clayton mused. "Sounds like a woman I used to date."

Lori smiled wryly at that. "Samara?"

"No, before her." An icy chill shot through his veins with the reminder of his wife and daughter. "How will the Kyra kill everyone?"

Sergeant Sutton answered by raising his arm to reveal the scar on the underside of his wrist, where his ID implant had been dug out. "There are toxins in the implants, remember? They'll initiate a global kill sequence, and everyone living in occupied cities around the planet will drop dead in a matter of seconds."

"Including your wife and daughter," Pyro said.

"I don't have an implant," Nova replied, shaking her head.

"His other daughter," Pyro explained.

Nova's eyes widened and darted to Clayton. "Your what?"

"You never told her?" Pyro asked. "Shit. Sorry, Clay."

"Yeah. Thanks."

"What is she talking about?" Nova demanded.

He took a deep breath. "I have another daughter. In New Houston."

Nova began backing away from him, shaking her head.

"It doesn't matter. She wasn't even born by the time I became an exile. I've never even met her."

"But she's *yours.*"

"So are you," he said, taking a quick step to close the growing distance between them.

But Nova wasn't listening. Her eyes were bright and starry with tears. She turned and ran down the hallway.

"Nova, wait!" He started running after her, but Keera pulled him back. "I'll go after her."

"She doesn't even know you."

The door to the garage banged open as Nova left.

"No, but I know what it's like to feel like an orphan."

"Yeah, except she *is* one. You at least had two biological parents."

"Only one of whom raised me. My father

408

wanted to kill me. Perhaps Nova will be able to appreciate that a Father is the one who raises you, not the one who shares your DNA. I'll be back."

Keera dashed down the hallway after Nova, and Clayton turned back to the others with a scowl.

The Chrona caught his eye, tilting its head back and forth in a gesture that he didn't recognize and making a low hissing sound. "And biologicals wonder why we chose to digitize."

"Shut up," Clayton said.

CHAPTER 40

Clayton sat on one of two couches in the living room and listened while Lori and Pyro sat on the opposite couch to explain their plan. Sergeant Sutton excused himself, saying that he had preparations to make.

"We'll use a cloaked shuttle to fly to a sewer entrance just outside the walls," Lori explained.

"You managed to steal a shuttle with a cloaking shield?" Clayton asked, astonished by that revelation.

"The shuttle is mine," Specter clarified.

"Aha." That made more sense. "All right. Go on."

Lori nodded. "The entrance to the sewers will be guarded, but Keera, Specter, and I will use our cloaking armor to sneak up and incapacitate the guards with a paralytic agent.

"Their implants won't register them as falling asleep or being killed, so it won't sound any alarms, and they won't be able to call for help. Once we're inside the sewers, we'll follow them into the city where an operative will

410

be waiting for us with a Ryde. We'll take it to a point one block from the ascension center, and then cover the rest of the distance on foot."

Lori waved to a glossy black holo-projector sitting on a chipped marble-topped coffee table between them. A glowing, shaded-blue schematic of the ascension center sprang to life, hovering a foot above the table. Clayton recognized the dome-shaped base of the structure. Four pillars came together from the corners to a flat landing platform some thirty stories above the top of the dome.

Lori made a pinching gesture to zoom in on the front entrance of the center. "Keera, Specter, and I will sneak up with our cloaks engaged. We'll inject the guards with the paralytic agent, and then Specter will scan their minds for door codes and any other pertinent security codes that we might need. Meanwhile, Keera and I will scan their ID implants and duplicate their tracking signals with spoofers to allow us to walk in through the front entrance without triggering the alarms. We'll leave the guards outside with Specter and then head straight for the security room over here —" Lori pointed to a room on the second floor. "Once there, we'll insert a virus that Specter has prepared for us to hack the security system, and then we'll cloak ourselves and tell Specter to join us inside."

"Why bother doing all that if you're already spoofing the guards' tracking IDs?" Clayton asked.

"Because the signal spoofers won't fool them for long, and our cloaking shields won't hide us from the facility's security system. Once it's been hacked, they'll have to send down special scanning teams from the *Sovath* just to see us. We'll also have complete control over the facility, and the virus will block the Guard's access to the comms transmitters on the roof, which means that they'll have to leave the facility to call for reinforcements. That's where you and the rest of our team comes in. You'll be waiting outside, ready to pick off any Chimeras who try to leave."

Clayton nodded, squinting at the schematic as the sun caught his eye. Specter took a step toward them and spread his wings to shade the table, dimming the light as effectively as a pair of sunglasses.

"Thanks..." Clayton muttered, glancing up at Specter.

The Chrona just looked at him, its glowing red eyes dimming and then brightening again.

"You can actually fly with those?" Clayton asked, noticing the robot's strange anatomy. Even if Specter were made of the lightest alloys and mostly hollow, he still had to weigh a few hundred pounds.

"My body is equipped with grav engines," Specter explained. "With their assistance, the wings are enough to allow me to glide and fly the way I once did as a Kyra."

"I guess if a hoverbike can fly, so can you," Clayton reasoned.

"Not to mention a destroyer like the *Sovath*," Pyro added.

Lori cleared her throat.

"Sorry," Clayton said, nodding for her to go on.

"Once we've hacked the security system, we'll proceed down the corridor and up the stairs to the tracking center over here." Lori traced a line with her finger to another room, this one on the third floor.

"What if they already have the scanners they need to see you at the center?" Clayton asked.

"They won't," Lori replied. "The Guard keeps them locked in the armory aboard the *Sovath*. They don't want the technology falling into the hands of the resistance."

"Let's hope you're right," Clayton replied.

Lori continued, "Once we get to the tracking center, Specter will hack into the tracking system and use another virus to disable every tracking implant on the planet."

"He can do that?" Clayton asked.

"I can," Specter confirmed.

"What if they realize what you're doing and stop you or lock you out of the system before you can disable the implants?"

"Unlikely," Specter said. "We will be quick, and they will assume that the attack is designed to destroy the center, not hack its systems. The comms lockout will make it hard for them to alert anyone to the contrary until we have already accomplished our objective."

"They don't know we have a Chrona helping us," Lori added. "We would never be able to hack their systems like this on our own, and they know it, so they won't be prepared for that possibility."

Clayton leaned back against the couch, stroking his ragged beard. "It's a good plan."

Lori smiled. "Yes."

"If it works," he added.

"It has to," she replied.

Clayton heard a door creaking open and glanced down the hall to see Nova and Keera emerging from the garage. Clayton rose to his feet as they drew near. He was about to go apologize to Nova, but Keera warned him off with a shake of her head. Nova walked right by him without a word, crunching over broken glass and stepping through the empty frame of a sliding glass door to a deck outside.

"She'll be okay," Keera said. "I spoke to her. She just needs some time."

Clayton frowned, staring at Nova's back as she leaned against a rusty railing and stared quietly over the lake. Rosie lifted her head from the armchair where she sat and began panting. She was also watching Nova.

"I'll go get her some water," Pyro said, rising from the couch.

"Did you tell him the plan?" Keera asked.

Lori nodded and Clayton tore his eyes away from his daughter. "It sounds good on paper, but we're going to attract a lot of attention to ourselves in a short amount of time. If anything goes wrong, we won't get a second chance. We're going to be surrounded and outnumbered with no way to reinforce our position. The garrison is only four blocks away. There are a few hundred Chimeras stationed there at any given hour of the day or night, not to mention thousands more who will be asleep in apartments around the city."

"Which is why it's critical that you take out anyone caught trying to leave the center before they can call for help," Lori said.

"What about the landing platform on the roof?"

"Specter will use the security system to block access to both the roof and the exits. They'll have to blow the doors to leave, and that will buy us time," Keera said.

Pyro came over with a plastic dish full of water for Rosie. She lapped greedily from it. Clayton watched her, his eyes drifting out of focus as his stomach churned uneasily.

"What's our exit strategy?" he asked.

Pyro left Rosie's side with an empty dish

and handed him a scuffed and beaten plastic water bottle full of *cold* water. His eyes widened in surprise at the unexpected luxury. He flipped up a dirty spout and drank greedily while Pyro went crunching through broken glass to give another bottle to Nova.

Clayton took a break for air and wiped his beard and mustache on his sleeve. "So?" he prompted.

Keera shook her head, and Lori winced.

"You don't have an exit strategy," he realized.

"We've timed it so that the Chronan fleet will arrive within half an hour of the tracking system going down. Once Chimeran reinforcements start arriving from the garrison, everyone will fall back to the center. With Specter in control of the facility, it should be easy enough for him to hold off the Guard until the Chrona arrive and start landing their troops. At that point, the tide will turn in our favor, and we'll go out and join them in clearing the streets."

Clayton glanced at Specter, still standing with his wings spread to shade them from the glare of the rising sun. He looked just like a life-sized version of the bird of prey emblem of the Kyron Federation.

"When do we leave?" Clayton asked.

"Midnight," Lori replied.

Clayton glanced at the clock in the top left corner of his ARCs. It was just after seven in the morning. "I guess we should get some sleep before then. We've been up all night."

Lori smiled. "Does that mean you've decided to join us?"

He nodded but said nothing.

"Nova is insisting that she be allowed to join the fight," Keera said. "But I understand if you still don't want her involved."

Nova and Pyro stood together on the deck, their backs turned as they leaned against the railings. "I'll talk to her," he said.

"Of course," Keera replied.

"I'll show you and Nova to one of our spare rooms," Lori added. She started across the great room to the deck, and Clayton followed her.

Specter folded his wings against his back and watched them with glowing red eyes as they walked by. Clayton's stomach churned uneasily once more. Maybe it was just hunger pains. He'd been up all night without anything to eat.

Or maybe it's the robotic wild card who's the linchpin of this entire operation, Clayton thought. His and Lori's boots ground pebbles of broken glass against the floor as they stepped through empty door frames to the deck.

Something about that Chrona was setting him off. Maybe it was the fact that Specter used to be a Kyra. Just because he'd digitized his consciousness untold centuries ago didn't mean that he or the other Chrona were better than the Kyra they were fighting.

CHAPTER 41

A warm breeze brought the fresh, sharp-scented smell of pine trees to Clayton's nose. He and Lori joined Nova and Pyro by the rusting metal railings to admire the shimmering lake through a shadowy curtain of branches, leaves, and needles.

Nova's body stiffened when Clayton appeared beside her, but she said nothing. He resolved to fix things with her once they were alone. Right now, he had a more pressing matter to address. Turning to Lori, he whispered, "Are you sure that we can trust Specter?"

"He helped us develop the cure," she said.

"Your entire plan hinges on his involvement."

"What are you worried about?" Lori asked. "If he were going to betray us to the Kyra, he would have done it already."

Clayton shook his head and glanced back into the darkened interior of the mansion. He couldn't see either Keera or Specter in there anymore. "The problem is that we're trading the devil we know for one that we don't."

"Keera knows them," Lori replied. "So do I. I was on the *Sovath* during several battles with them."

"And? What did you learn?"

"That the Chrona and the Kyra hate each other. They both think they're the superior race."

Clayton snorted. "At least that makes sense. Did you ever see what the Chrona do after taking an occupied world?"

Lori hesitated.

"Does *anyone* know?" he pressed.

"The Kyra claim that they are evil, and the Chrona say the same thing about the Kyra. But I was there when Keera's predecessor ordered his fleet to bombard an occupied planet before the Chrona could force them to retreat. Specter isn't lying about that."

"So what's stopping the Kyra from bombarding Earth?" Clayton asked, his eyes widening with that revelation. It wasn't just the toxins in people's ID implants that they had to worry about. The Kyra could set fire to Earth's cities in the blink of an eye.

Lori grimaced and looked away. "Specter says they'll draw the Kyron fleet away with a smaller one, and then jump a second fleet in behind them to keep them surrounded. They've promised to protect us."

"They could fail. Or that could be a lie." Clayton noticed Nova leaning farther over the railing to stare at Lori with big, horrified eyes.

Lori met both of their gazes at once. "Then why would Specter bother helping us to infiltrate the ascension center? They should just jump their fleet in now and get it all over with."

"Maybe, but I'm still struggling to see what they gain from saving us. Kicking the Kyra off Earth, sure, that makes sense, but why do they care whether or not we die?"

"They've been arming native populations to join their side of the war. Others have chosen to digitize. Keera got to see their rebel fleet—nine different liberated species, each of them manning their own ships and fighting with the Chrona to defeat the Kyra."

"So they want soldiers, too," Clayton concluded. "It's just more of the same."

"These were volunteers," Lori explained.

"The Chimeras are volunteers, too," Clayton said.

"Yeah, indoctrinated kids," Pyro snorted and shook her head. "Not the same thing."

Clayton sighed and shook his head, rubbing tired eyes.

"You should get some sleep," Lori reminded him. "Nova? Are you coming?"

She nodded and turned away from the view, waiting for Lori to lead the way.

Keera and Sergeant Sutton watched them from the kitchen as they came in. Keera was eating a bloody chunk of raw meat over the sink with her hands. Blood dripped steadily from her chin like a leaky faucet. Sergeant Sutton was speaking with her in low tones, his voice indistinct, but he stopped as soon as they came in.

Clayton frowned at that, but decided not to press for details. Catching Pyro's eye, he said, "I have a meeting with your father's wife a few hours before this all goes down. Is there a message you'd like me to pass along to him in case things don't go our way?"

"No meetings," Sergeant Sutton said, making a cutting gesture with his hand.

Clayton scowled at him. It had been a month since he'd last received an update about his family. He needed to know that they were okay before the shit hit the fan.

"What if we go with him?" Pyro suggested. "We might be able to get Mona to join us. Having a Chimeran Sergeant on our side could make a big difference."

"We've tried to recruit her and your father before," Sutton replied. "They both refused."

"That was years ago, before we had a real chance of defeating the Kyra. Now we do."

"Telling her anything about what we're planning is a big risk," Lori said. "She could blow the whole op."

"Not if we're careful," Pyro insisted. "You could sneak up on her at the rendezvous and steal her comms unit, make sure she can't report us. Then we explain the op to her and see if she's willing to help. Her squad patrols my dad's farm and the entrance to the sewers. She could give us a chance to slip into the city without having to incapacitate anyone."

"No," Sutton insisted.

Keera looked up from her food and wiped the blood from her chin on the back of her hand. "Pyro's right. Getting into the city is the riskiest part of this entire operation. If someone discovers that we paralyzed the guards before we can reach the ascension center, the op will be over before it's even begun."

Sutton shook his head. "What if she just pretends to be on our side and then betrays us? She could have a whole platoon waiting for us at the entrance of the sewers."

"I will know if she is lying," a familiar singsong voice said. The air shimmered as he decloaked and materialized beside the towering black power supply in the hall beside the kitchen.

"It's worth the risk," Keera added.

"I disagree," Sutton said.

"Your concerns have been noted," she replied.

He looked away and stalked out of the kitchen, muttering something under his breath as he walked by Specter and down the hall. Keera watched him go, her crimson eyes narrowing to slits.

So she's the one in charge, Clayton realized. *But Sutton doesn't like it.* He wondered who the other resistance members would listen to if push came to shove, and hoped that wrinkle in the chain of command wouldn't become a problem in the heat of battle.

"We'll go see your stepmother together," Keera decided.

"She's not my stepmother."

Keera waved Pyro's objection away and nodded to Clayton. "What time and where is the meeting?"

"Twenty-two hundred hours at an abandoned school in the Wastes."

"That's just a few hours before the op," Keera said. "We'll have to stage it from there."

"Do you have anything... else to eat?" Nova asked with a wrinkled nose as Keera tore off another bite of raw steak.

"I'll have something sent to your room," Lori replied. "Let's get you two settled in first."

* * *

After leading Clayton and Nova to one of the bedrooms in the old log mansion, they left their things on a pair of bare mattresses on the dusty floor. Clayton went to fetch Rosie and found her sprawled out on the armchair, her eyelids slowly sinking shut.

"Come on, girl," he said as he picked her up carefully. She whimpered as the movement disturbed her injuries, but she didn't struggle.

Clayton carried her back to the bedroom, noticing as he did so that Lori and Pyro were busy serving food from the refrigerator onto two chipped ceramic plates. They came in behind him, just as he was laying Rosie down at the foot of Nova's mattress.

Lori passed one of the two plates to him, and his plastic water bottle from before, now freshly filled. The plates each contained a blackened ear of corn still in the husk and several chunks of roasted venison. Clayton had two pieces of meat while Nova only had one, but Pyro explained that the extra piece was for Rosie.

He smiled and nodded his thanks.

Nova added hers in a quiet voice, and they immediately began peeling and eating the corn, a rare delicacy for them. This was one better than their usual meals: it had both a vegetable *and* meat.

"Let me know if either of you need anything else," Lori said as she and Pyro left. Lori lingered with her hand on the doorknob. "I'm just two doors down on the right."

"Thank you," Clayton said again between bites of corn. It was cold, but still juicy and delicious.

The door clicked shut. He and Nova quietly ate on their respective mattresses. A curtain of tattered bedsheets ballooned between them as wind gusted past a broken window. The curtain was pegged to the floor and the windowsill with rocks, making the room at least reasonably dark.

Clayton finished with his corn and took a break before dealing with the tough-looking hunk of venison. He looked up from his plate to find Nova's back turned to him, facing the wall as she ate.

"Nova," he said, setting his plate aside.

She went on chewing without reply.

Rosie eyed Clayton's plate from the foot of her bed and licked her lips. He smiled and grabbed the larger of the two pieces of venison, tossing it to her.

She caught it in the air and held it between her front paws as she gnawed off a big bite.

"You must be feeling better," he said, smiling as he watched her eat and taking the moment to compose a proper apology to Nova.

"You could have told me about her," she said, half-turning from the wall to look at him.

Clayton shook his head. "I didn't want you to feel jealous or like you were some kind of substitute for what I lost."

"But I was. I am."

"Maybe," he conceded. "But that doesn't make you any less of a daughter to me. If anything, the fact that I raised you and not her makes *her* less than you."

"Blood is blood," Nova said, shaking her

head. "She is, and I'm not."

"I don't look at it that way. Even if she were here with me, I'd never treat her any better than you."

"You don't know that."

"And you don't know otherwise," he replied. "So you're just going to have to take my word for it."

Nova conceded that with a nod as she took a small bite of her venison. "All this time," she began. "You've been coming to the Wastes because of her?"

What were she and Pyro talking about out there on the deck? he wondered. "Yes," he said, deciding to go with the truth.

"So you've been risking your life just to hear that they're okay."

"Not just for that. I was also scavenging supplies for us. People throw out the damnedest things. Things we need. Like the uniform you're wearing right now."

Nova appeared to consider that as she chewed, and he took the opportunity to bite off a chunk of his own roast. It was just as tough as he'd guessed. Maybe tougher. Even fresh venison wasn't particularly tender.

"I'm going with you tonight," Nova said.

Clayton felt an objection rising in his chest, making his whole body tense. He swallowed and started to give her an ultimatum—but then he stopped at the determined look on

Nova's face. She might be able to forgive him for keeping his other daughter a secret, but she'd never forgive him for forcing her to sit this battle out.

"You could die," he said.

"I know," she replied.

"You could get other people killed," he added.

"How?"

He gestured helplessly. "By forcing them to cover you, or getting yourself into trouble."

"I can take care of myself."

Clayton hunted for another argument, something, anything that might convince her to stay out of it. "If I lose you..."

"You won't."

"You can't promise that." His voice shook along with his hands.

Nova smiled sympathetically and left her mattress to come sit beside him on his. She grabbed his hand to stop it from shaking. He blinked to clear a blurry heat from his eyes.

"We need to do something more than just survive," she said. "This is our chance to make our lives count for something. You can't take that from me. I won't let you."

Clayton stared at her, taking in the soft, girlish contours of her dirty face. But those hazel eyes held a hardness and a wisdom that went far beyond her fourteen years. Long, stringy, sweat-matted blonde hair hung in front of her eyes. He pushed it out of the way.

"You need a haircut, kiddo," he said.

Nova cracked a crooked smile and pushed the hair out of his eyes. "You, too."

They both laughed at that and went back to eating their food. When they were done, Nova got up and kissed him on the top of the head. "I love you, Dad."

He nodded back, the words getting stuck in his throat. She returned to her mattress and lay down, using her pack for a pillow. He did the same, and soon they were both drifting off to sleep.

Clayton dreamed of a horde of Dregs chasing him and Nova through the Wastes. They fired and fired at them, but never managed to make a dent. At some point, the Dregs vanished into the swirling darkness, and it was just the two of them, sitting on a bare mattress in a dusty bedroom. Nova looked to him, her face ghost-white and her head bald, black veins whorling underneath. Crimson eyes blazed, and she smiled, revealing sharply-pointed teeth. "I love you, Dad," she said in the husky voice of a Chimera.

And then she lunged for his throat. A sharp pain tore through him, and he woke up with a start, his heart pounding and his throat still stinging with the pain of her teeth ripping through it. Was his sleep paralysis back? He tried curling his fingers, then his toes. No. He was fully awake.

Clayton took a moment to calm down and get his bearings. It was dark now. He swallowed past the pain of a dry throat and rolled over to see Nova lying asleep on the mattress beside his. The sheet-curtains billowed between them, and a narrow slice of starlight fell over her, turning Nova's face a ghostly color. He shivered and sat up, blinking to clear his bleary eyes and staring hard at Nova to make sure that she was still fully human. Maybe she'd been bitten down at the lake and hadn't told him.

But there were no signs of hair loss, no sheen of sweat to indicate a fever, and no trickles of blood leaking from her eyes or ears.

Clayton blew out a shaky breath and lay back down, staring up at the naked wooden beams of the ceiling.

He checked the time on his ARCs. The displays flickered a few times before coming back from their power-saving sleep mode. The time appeared in the top left corner.

8:19 PM

Not long now.

As if to punctuate that thought, he heard footsteps thumping softly in the hall. They stopped at his door, and it creaked open. Lori stood there in her suit of cloaking armor with the helmet tucked under one arm.

"It's time," she whispered.

CHAPTER 42

Clayton and Nova followed Lori down a rickety wooden staircase to the basement. They emerged in a room with the windows and sliding doors all curtained by old sheets.

The only light came from the dim blue glow of Kyron solar lanterns. The stylized floor tiles looked like stone, and the walls were rough with peeling paint. A line of tables ran along the wall opposite the curtained, lake-facing windows.

More than a dozen operatives were lined up at those tables, picking over an assortment of weapons. All of them wore matching black Chimeran uniforms and some kind of black grease on their faces and in their hair.

Clayton plucked at his gray cadet's uniform as Lori led them over to the tables. "You have any spare uniforms for us?" he asked, realizing now that they should have chosen the black ones at their cabin.

"Let's get you two kitted out first," Lori said as she led the way to the tables.

"Our rifles still work just fine," Clayton

pointed out as he studied the remaining weapons that everyone else had passed over. He didn't recognize more than a few of them. "All we need are new charge packs if you have some."

Lori ignored him as she walked down the line of tables, hunting for something in particular. Having apparently found it, she stopped and set her helmet down. Lori plucked a short-barreled black rifle off the table and handed it to him. The weapon was much smaller and lighter than the SWMD-issue laser rifle that he already had slung over his shoulder.

"The EKR-7, used by Chimeran Commandos. It's fully automatic with a stealth, semi-auto mode that's silenced and spectrum-shifted to make it both quiet and invisible when it fires. It'll give you fifty shots per pack when set to kill and thirty on stealth," Lori said. "The scopes have both night-vision and scanning modes, but without the armor that goes with them, you won't be able to use the scanning mode. We've adapted them so that you can connect your ARCs and fire safely around corners."

"Nova doesn't have ARCs," he pointed out.

"No?" Lori asked, looking to her.

Nova shook her head.

"Well, you can still use the scope the usual way."

Clayton handed her his old rifle. Lori took the aging weapon and laid it on the table before handing a second EKR to Nova. She gave up her sniper rifle, the same one he'd stolen from the bounty hunter who'd killed Lori. It was probably the very weapon that had shot her. The irony was, Leeto Voth had stayed dead, but Lori was alive and well.

Lori passed a pair of spare charge packs to each of them, which they tucked into the slots on their belts, replacing the deteriorating ones from the older rifles. Walking on down the line of tables, she picked over a scattering of other weapons until she found a pair of long-barreled, matte-black sidearms like the one she herself wore.

"These are Stingers. They're the Kyra's own weapon of choice. Smaller and lighter than a rifle, and much more powerful per shot. Like the EKR's, they have a stealth setting for covert operations, but you'll only get six shots per pack versus ten on the regular kill setting." Lori turned the weapon on its side to reveal a selector switch above the trigger marked by familiar symbols from the Kyron alphabet. Their rifles had similar switches, but they only had three settings: safety-on, kill, and overload.

"Between *kill* and *overload* are two settings you likely haven't seen before," Lori said as she tapped them with her finger. "After *kill* comes *stealth.* It's a semi-automatic mode on the rifles, so don't expect it to spray the room with lasers. Finally, right before overload, is a stun setting, but it won't work on armored targets, so keep that in mind."

Clayton nodded.

"With the Stinger pistols you can spare some of the charge to engage the weapon's cloaking shield for concealed carry." Lori indicated a sliding switch on the side of the barrel. She slid it forward, and the weapon shimmered brightly before disappearing in her hands. Lori flicked it back, and the weapon reappeared. "The shield will slowly drain the charge, so be careful how you use it. You could wind up drawing the weapon only for it to let you down when you need to fire."

Clayton grabbed the EKR rifle by its strap and slung it over his shoulder so he could take one of the Stingers from Lori.

"I could give you holsters for these," she said as she handed Nova the second pistol, "but that might defeat the point of having a concealable sidearm."

Clayton nodded his agreement and looked to Nova. "Tuck it into your belt," he suggested, even as he did so himself. He wedged the grip at an angle and then tightened his belt to make sure it wouldn't fall out.

"Anything else?" he asked.

Lori nodded. "Time to trade those worker

grays for Kyron blacks."

They followed her to a full-length wardrobe, and Lori handed each of them a relatively clean black uniform.

"You can go change in the bathroom if you like," she said to Nova.

But she was already getting undressed. Clayton turned to shield her from view as best he could as they both stripped down to their threadbare underwear and pulled on the new uniforms. By the time they were done putting their utility belts and weapons back on, everyone else had already left the basement.

"One last thing," Lori said. She handed a small, circular metal container to each of them. "Kyron shoe polish. Smear it all over your faces and hair, but watch your eyes."

They did as they were told. The smell of it filled Clayton's nostrils with a noxious stench that made him dizzy.

"You'll get used to it," Lori said as she grabbed her helmet and put it on, hiding her face without the need to wear any shoe polish herself. "Now we're ready."

* * *

After arming themselves, he and Nova went to say goodbye to Rosie. She was still asleep, but she woke up as they scratched her belly and patted her head. Nova poured her bottle of water into a dish from her pack, and Clayton left out some of the raw, salted meat from the cow they'd slaughtered. Someone stepped into the open doorway behind them and leaned against the jamb in a full suit of armor.

"It's time to leave," Lori said quietly.

"Is anyone going to stay back and look after Rosie?" he asked, while scratching her behind the ear.

"No. We're short-handed as it is. But this area is clear of Dregs, so she should be safe until we return. Just shut the door to make sure she doesn't run off."

Clayton grimaced and looked to Nova. "You could still stay."

"We'll be back for her," Nova replied, but suddenly she didn't sound so sure.

Clayton blew out a breath. "Yeah. Let's hope so." They grabbed their packs and made for the door.

"You won't need those," Lori said.

"You don't know that," Clayton replied. "I'd rather be prepared." The truth was that neither he nor Nova had much to their names, but if they ended up fleeing back through the Wastes for some reason, he didn't want to be doing it without his survival gear.

Lori hesitated, looking ready to argue, but she gave in with a shrug. "I guess you can leave them on the shuttle."

They shut the door behind them and followed Lori down the hall to the great room where everyone else was already gathered. Sergeant Sutton, Keera, and Specter stood at the head of the group, barring the hall to the barricaded front door and the side door of the garage. Pyro walked over and handed him and Nova each a comms piece. "Put them in your ears," she said.

"Nova doesn't have a neural implant or ARCs to interface with comms," he said.

"She won't need them," Pyro replied. "They're already set to the right channel. You just have to activate them by touching the button on the side." She showed Nova how, and then helped her fit the device into her right ear. "Don't use it unless you have something important to say."

"Copy that," Nova replied.

Keera cleared her throat for attention and addressed the group, reminding them to stay alert and watch each other's backs. She mentioned sticking close to their team leaders, and Clayton raised a hand.

"You didn't assign us a team."

"You, Nova, and Pyro are all with Richard. Team Charlie. You'll meet up with him once we're inside the city. He'll be waiting for us with the Ryde."

"Your father, Richard Morgan?" Clayton asked, his eyebrows flitting up with surprise.

"Yes. Team Alpha is led by Sergeant Sutton, also known as *Scar,* and Bravo is headed up by Diaz—call sign, *Widow*." Keera pointed to the Latin woman that Clayton had seen when they'd first arrived, and she raised her hand to indicate herself. Her dark hair was tucked into a ponytail, her perfect complexion now hidden by ugly smears of shoe polish.

Clayton nodded and Keera went on, "Once we've got as close as we can with the Ryde, Lori, Specter, and myself will make our way on foot to the ascension center and infiltrate as planned.

"As soon as we've taken out the guards, we'll double click the comms to let you know. You'll follow your team leaders to your pre-arranged sniper points. Remember to keep those entrances clear as long as you can. If anyone comes out, they'll alert the garrison. With any luck, we'll have the center's comms down before anyone can sound the alarm, but if you hear the alarm go off, you make a run for the center. We'll fortify ourselves as best we can until the mission is complete."

While Keera spoke, Clayton spent the time studying their group of operatives. There was an equal mix of men and women, but Nova was the only one underage. Almost all of them were faceless strangers to him, and the shoe polish didn't help. He counted eighteen in all, including Specter.

"Any questions?" Keera asked.

No one raised their voice. Keera's gaze

found Clayton once more, and she nodded to him. "Where's the school?"

"About thirty klicks north of the city, a few blocks west of East Fork River," he said. "If you follow the old I45 south toward the city, it'll get you close."

"You'll have to guide us in," Keera decided. "Sergeant?" She nodded to him.

He clapped his hands together and said, "Move out!"

Everyone followed him down the hall and through the garage. They walked around the side of the mansion to a grassy, starlit field at the edge of the lake. A large patch of grass was strangely flattened over there and sheltered from a breeze that played lightly through the rest of the field. It looked as if that patch of grass had been recently trampled by a herd of cattle.

Sutton stopped before reaching it, but Specter continued on. He raised a three-fingered mechanical hand as if to hail someone, and then the air shimmered brightly and a large, gunmetal gray ship appeared sitting in front of them. It was big and triangular with sloping sides and a vague suggestion of wings at the back. The side of the shuttle opened up, and a boarding ramp dropped down. Specter led the way, and Sutton waved over his shoulder as he followed the Chrona inside.

Bright white lights snapped on, revealing

an interior that was all metallic grays. Clayton trailed behind the rest of the group with Lori and Nova. When he reached the top of the ramp, he found that it was standing room only in the broad aisle between the two rows of bench seats on either side of the shuttle. It was like the inside of a Ryde, but without the windows.

Hearing metal ringing on metal, Clayton turned to see Specter and Keera disappearing up a ladder at the far end of the troop bay where he stood. They were probably headed for the cockpit.

Looking away, he found himself staring into the opaque black visor of Lori's helmet. She inclined her head to him, saying nothing. The landing ramp groaned shut and sealed with a hiss of pressurizing air. Clayton noted the lack of a proper airlock in the shuttle, but he supposed that made sense for a race of machines. They didn't need air to breathe, so there would be no difference to them whether the cabin stayed pressurized or not. Silence rang loud inside the ship but for the rattle of weapons and the rustling of fabric and clomping of boots as people shifted in their seats and shuffled their feet in the aisle.

Standing beside Lori, Sergeant Sutton was the first to break that silence.

"Y'all sittin' around here actin' like this is a funeral! Straighten out those backbones.

We've got a war to win! Hooah!"

A scattered muttering of *hooah's* answered back.

Sutton cupped a hand to his ear. "What was that? Sounded like a mouse just farted through its teeth! Try again!"

"Hooah!" they all yelled.

Clayton stayed silent and Nova looked to him with eyebrows raised. "It's an army thing," he explained.

Sutton caught his eye next. "What about you, Captain? You ready to give 'em hell?"

Clayton was about to remind Sutton that he wasn't a captain anymore, but he stopped himself. For the first time in more than a decade, he was actually starting to feel some claim to his old rank. He nodded back. "Hooah, Sergeant."

Sutton grinned with a flash of yellow-white teeth that contrasted sharply with the shoe polish on his face and bald head. "Damn straight," he said.

And then the shuttle came to life around them, humming and shivering underfoot. Clayton cast about for something to grab onto, but the inertial dampeners must have been dialed all the way up, because the take-off was so gentle that he barely felt it.

Lori spent a moment tapping commands into a control panel in the ceiling, and then the inside of the shuttle vanished, leaving nothing but a pale suggestion of the bulkheads and floor that made it seem like they were racing over the moonlit fields and trees in a glass box. Nova gripped Clayton's arm in a tight fist.

"Don't look down," he said, even as he did so himself, his head spinning with vertigo. Flying was one thing, but the illusion of standing on thin air while he did so was something that only an avian race like the Kyra or the post-biological Chrona could appreciate.

"Helluva thrill, ain't it?" Sutton said, laughing.

Someone threw up with a loud splattering sound, and a revolting smell swirled up Clayton's nostrils.

"Ah hell!" someone else said. "Every damned time! Keep that shit to yourself, Hurl!"

Laughter rippled through the cabin, and Clayton smiled despite the fact that he was holding onto his venison and corn by a thread.

The landscape whipped by close below them: trees, grass, and undulating ruins all blurring together with the sheer speed of their flight. Within just a few minutes, they reached the crumbling remains of the I45 and slowed down as they followed it south toward New Houston.

The comms piece in Clayton's ear crackled to life with Keera's voice: "Lone Wolf, let us know where to turn off."

"Copy that," Clayton said, pressing a finger

to the manual transmit button on his comms piece. He moved to the front end of the aisle to get a clear view of where they were headed, but nothing was recognizable from the air. He shook his head, searching for familiar landmarks.

For a moment, he was afraid that they'd missed the school already, but then he spotted the gleaming ribbon of the river, followed by the warehouse where he'd found Nova.

"Up ahead, about five hundred meters. Bank left and head for the river."

They turned off the highway and flew toward the river.

"There!" Clayton said as he spotted a familiar rectangular, flat-topped building.

"Where?" Keera asked.

He described the building to her, and a moment later the shuttle began heading straight for it. They hovered down into the grassy field that used to be a parking lot. Before they even landed, Clayton spotted Mona's hoverbike parked at the bottom of the front steps. He checked the time on his ARCs. 9:31 PM. She was early. Now all they had to do was convince her to join them.

CHAPTER 43

Two hours earlier...

Samara and Dora sat eating a quiet meal of mashed potatoes and grilled fish. They sat at opposite ends of a small, four-seater table beside the windows of their apartment. Samara looked up from her plate, at the glittering towers of the city, monochromatic with blue and white lights for Chimeran and Human buildings respectively. The ascension center lay cloaked in shadows just four blocks away. It was the tallest building in that part of the city, with four pillars coming together from the windowless, dome-shaped base to support a flat, square landing platform about forty stories above the streets. The landing platform was rimmed with red and blue spotlights, and the tall, skinny spires of comms transmitters rose from each of the platform's corners with blinking blue and red lights to warn inbound pilots of their presence.

Samara looked away, trying to catch her daughter's eye. The tension between them was thick. They'd had an argument while Samara was cooking dinner. Dora had been studying the enemy's language on the living room couch, practicing it out loud. She'd asked Dora to keep it down, saying she had a headache, and Dora had walked off in a huff, saying that her mother would be happy if she failed. Dora took her studies so seriously, always scoring at the top of her class. She was hoping to be chosen for early ascension.

Samara swallowed a mouthful of fish and shook her head, deciding to address the matter head-on. "Why don't you want to stay on Earth? Stay human? You could get married and have kids and support the war like that."

Dora's nose wrinkled with that suggestion, her green eyes squinting just like Clayton's used to. She reminded Samara of him in so many ways.

"Because if I stay here, then I'll be *stuck* here," Dora replied. "And it's *boring* on Earth. Don't you want to see other worlds? You could sign up, too. We could ascend together."

Samara smiling thinly at the suggestion. "I haven't been trained like you. They won't assign me to active duty, and even if they did, I'd probably get picked to join a patrol on Earth. Maybe you should ask for that after you ascend. Fighting wars is dangerous. You could get killed before you ever see any of the Federation. If you serve your enlistment here, you'll still have a chance to see the galaxy later, but on your own terms."

Dora scooped up a forkful of mashed potatoes and fish and shook her head as she chewed. "I need to help them fight. The Federation could lose the war."

Would that be such a bad thing? Samara wondered, but didn't say. "What do you know about the Chrona?" she asked instead.

"Just that they're not going to stop until we're all dead. They don't take prisoners. They're evil."

"But you've never seen or talked to any of them. You don't even know what they are."

"Some of the instructors at my school say they've seen them."

"But they won't describe the Chrona to you?"

"They're not allowed to talk about it."

"I heard a rumor that they're all machines," Samara said.

Dora shrugged. "So?"

"So, they might be hard to kill."

"The Kyra are just as advanced as they are."

"What if I asked you to stay on Earth for me?" Samara asked.

Dora looked up from her plate with flinty green eyes. "You can stay if you want. I don't care. But I'm leaving as soon as I graduate."

"Your father would be so disappointed in you."

Dora's eyes flashed. "You're a Dakka. I don't

expect you to understand."

"Excuse me?" Samara demanded. "I'm your mother, and you will treat me with respect!"

Dora pushed out her chair, rising from the table.

"Where are you going?"

"I have a test to study for." And with that, Dora stormed to her room and slammed the door. A few moments later, Samara heard the sound of Dora's muffled voice practicing alien words so that she could communicate better with Kyra overseers when the time came.

It was enough to put Samara off her food. Frowning, she pushed out from the table and took both plates to the kitchen, where she scraped them off into a plastic container and placed the leftovers in the refrigerator. She'd take them with her to the hospital. She refused to help feed the Dregs by throwing food away.

Checking the time on her ARCs, Samara saw that she only had a couple of hours left before her shift started. She needed to get ready.

An hour later, she was brushing her teeth and staring at her reflection in the foggy mirror above her bathroom sink and thinking back over her argument with Dora. She was only ten, and she was already desperate to leave. Samara couldn't help thinking that if Clayton had been around, Dora wouldn't be so eager to pledge her life to the Kyra's war. But then again, Dora *was* only ten. Maybe when the time for ascension actually came, she would change her mind.

Until then, fighting with her about it was just going to push her daughter farther away. Samara decided she needed to change tactics. On her way out, she went to check in on Dora and say goodbye, but her daughter's room was empty. She went out to check the apartment's other bathroom. Also empty. Dora was gone.

Samara's heart began pounding in her chest. A lot of bad things could happen to a ten-year-old girl walking around the city in the middle of the night. She tried calling Dora's comms.

No answer.

Then she thought to check Dora's tracking signal. A yellow dot appeared, overlaid on a map of the city on the right side of Samara's ARCs. Dora's signal was coming from the middle of the arena.

Her eyes widened at that. The arena was supposed to be closed. What was she doing *there?* And how had she gotten there so fast? She must have snuck out as soon as Samara had gone to shower and get ready for work.

A bad feeling seeped into the pit of Samara's stomach. There was only one reason that people went to the arena. Private challenges weren't unheard of among Chimeras. Maybe one of her teachers had invited her to witness one. Yet another part of an educational system that was designed to brutalize Samara's little girl.

Her whole body shook with adrenaline and rage as she headed for the door. She called ahead to the hospital as she left, telling Carla that she was going to be late for her shift, and why.

"Do you think one of her classmates challenged her?" Carla asked.

Samara froze as she waited for the elevators in the hall outside her apartment. The thought that Dora might be more than just an innocent bystander hadn't occurred to her.

"She's just a kid. Who would challenge her?"

"We've had plenty of kids come in here with broken bones and lacerations from illegal challenges. A couple of years back one of them even died."

"Send an ambulance," Samara said as the elevator dinged open and she rushed inside. "I'll meet them there."

CHAPTER 44

Clayton left the transport to meet Mona with Specter, Lori, and Keera. All three were cloaked and trailing quietly behind him. He used a Kyron flashlight mounted below the barrel of his new rifle to light the way, sweeping for Dregs as he went. Dim blue light peeled back the shadows inside the school as he walked down the hall to the classroom on the second floor where he and Mona usually met.

The occasional footstep crunched in the corridor behind him, making him flinch and spin around to check for Dregs. But each time it happened, he saw nothing there. It was just his cloaked escort.

Clayton knocked three times on the door of the classroom. The door clicked open almost instantly, and he saw a familiar Chimera standing there in a black uniform just like his, but with the three blue bars of a sergeant over her right breast and the gleaming metallic bird of prey emblem of the Federation clipped to her upper right sleeve.

Mona hissed quietly as the beam of his tactical light made her squint. "You're early."

"So are you," Clayton replied.

"Good. Come in. We don't have much time."

Clayton hesitated, and half-turned to indicate the empty hallway behind him. The air shimmered, and one of either Keera or Lori appeared in the doorway.

Mona hissed again, louder this time, and she took a quick step back. A plasma pistol flew out of the holster on her hip, and she aimed it over Clayton's shoulder.

"Who is this?" Mona demanded.

"A friend," Keera said. "We need to talk."

Mona's brow furrowed at the sound of another Chimera's voice. Her cranial stalks twitched, and she shook her head. "You're a traitor."

"So are you," Keera replied. "You're here to meet with an exile. May I come in? There's a lot to discuss and not much time to discuss it."

"Who's there?" a second voice croaked. A human man's voice. Clayton peered around the door jamb with his rifle to see Harold sitting on the floor with his back propped against the wall, a sheen of sweat glistening on his face.

"Hey there, Clay," he said.

"What's he doing here?" Clayton demanded, pushing through the entrance. "His tracking ID is going to get us caught!"

"I gave him a spoofer and signal blocker before we left," Mona said.

Keera stepped in behind them. "He doesn't look very well."

"He's infected," Mona explained.

Harold's head sagged to his chest, then came back up. "I was hoping you might be able to arrange a way for me to see my daughter before I turned. Can't be sure that I won't become a Dreg, and if I do, then this is goodbye."

"We have a cure," Keera said, striding across the room to reach him.

"You have a what?" Mona exclaimed.

Keera went down on her haunches to examine Harold. "How long ago was he bitten?"

"Early this morning, five AM," she said. "Dregs broke through the fence. One of them sliced him open with its claws before the patrols got there."

Harold pulled up his shirt to reveal a blood-soaked bandage wrapped around his torso.

"Then there's still time," Keera said. She straightened and turned to Mona, who was staring at her with a mixture of hope and suspicion. "We'll cure him, but we need something in exchange."

Mona shook her head. "How do I know that the cure works?"

"If it doesn't, you don't keep your end of the deal, and we gain nothing. But the cure is fast-acting. He should start feeling better within the hour. You'll get to see him improve."

"What do you need?" Mona asked.

Keera twisted off her helmet and tucked it under one arm.

Mona sucked in a sharp breath, recognizing who she was. "Admiral!"

"Not anymore," Keera replied.

She went on to explain about the resistance's plan to defeat the occupation. Near the end of that explanation, Specter revealed himself, and Mona stiffened.

"You can't trust the Chrona," she said.

"But you *can* trust the Kyra?" Specter countered. "Your world is enslaved. Your children are indoctrinated to fight in their war. If you were so content with their rule, why are you here on Earth, mated with a human male, instead of fighting on the front lines alongside the Kyra?"

Mona gave no reply.

"We need to get into the city," Keera said. "There's an entrance via the sewers that your squad patrols. If you can pull your men away so that we can get in, we'll cure your husband and call it even."

Clayton frowned at that, wondering if ransoming the cure was the best way to enlist her help.

"You're not giving me much choice."

Mona's eyes slid back to Specter. "You do realize, even if this plan works perfectly and the Chrona are as trustworthy as you say, a lot of people will die in the fighting."

"This is war. People die," Keera replied. "Just think about how many we'll be saving when the Kyra are no longer turning children into Dregs and soldiers."

"I'll need you to create a distraction. Some excuse to pull the patrols away."

Keera appeared to consider that, her red eyes narrowing in thought.

"I might have an idea," Clayton said.

CHAPTER 45

"**I** told you we needed our things," Clayton whispered to Lori as he stood in the shadows of a stand of trees beside Harold's farm. He unslung the pack from his shoulders and pulled out half of the containers of raw meat, passing them around. Together, the three of them hurried through the trees to the one Clayton had used over a decade ago to get across the fence. It was still there, a towering shadow silhouetted against the bright red glow of the razorbeam fence. The nearest patrol was walking down the inside of the fence a few hundred meters away with their backs turned and the blue beams of their lanterns bobbing as they went. By now Mona would be back on patrol with the rest of her squad. At least, she'd better be, or this might not go the way they planned.

The three of them crept down to the base of the tree. Clayton and Lori quickly placed a few chunks of raw meat around the trunk of the tree, while Keera produced a long black sword from a scabbard on her back. It was a ceremonial Sikath, used in Kyron and Chimeran challenges. She turned it on with an audible *hum* as the blade began rapidly sawing back and forth. It would make short work of the tree. Keera used it to cut a big wedge out of the side facing the fence, while Lori and Clayton crept back into the cover of the trees, leaving a trail to the one they were about to fell. They almost ran out of meat before they finished seeding the small stand of trees with bait.

Lori nodded to him as she hefted a big, bloody steak that she'd held back in reserve. Blood dripped audibly to the dry leaves between her feet. "I'll go get the Dregs," she said.

"I'll go with you," he replied.

She shook her head. "I'm armored, and I can cloak myself to get away. You can't. Get back to the shuttle and wait with the others. We're done here."

Clayton gave in with a sigh and watched as Lori ran up a short, grassy hill to reach the Dreg-infested ruins above the trees. The air shimmered faintly as she vanished, leaving nothing but a floating piece of meat for Chimeran Patrols to see.

Clayton followed the tree line down to a strangely-flattened patch of grass. He felt around against an invisible barrier for the entrance of the shuttle and knocked lightly on it. Machinery hissed and groaned as the landing ramp dropped down. He winced at all the noise the mechanisms made, but the trees between them and the fence would hopefully keep the patrols from hearing anything. The darkened interior of the shuttle appeared, marking a shadowy entrance to the otherwise invisible transport. Sergeant Sutton waved to him from inside, half of his body missing behind the cloaked side of the shuttle.

Clayton ran lightly up the ramp to find everyone else crowded inside and waiting. Specter wasn't there, but he was probably up in the cockpit.

"So?" Sutton asked in a whisper. He leaned out the door to search the moonlit field for Lori and Keera. "Where are they? Did it work?"

"We'll know soon," Clayton replied. He noticed Harold and Pyro sitting together on the floor beside the ladder to the cockpit. Nova stood beside them, sticking close to Pyro.

Harold was looking even better now than he had after they'd all left the school. The cure was real. Clayton still couldn't believe it. Harold stood up. His daughter tried to help him, but he waved her away. "I'm fine," he said. To Clayton, he added, "I want to come with you. You're going to need all the help you can get."

He looked to Sutton, deferring the question.

The sergeant's lower jaw zagged back and forth as he considered it. The shiny patch of scar tissue on his cheek twitched. "Get him a weapon, Pyro."

"But he's—"

"I'm fine," Harold said again.

"The man's got a right to fight for his freedom, the same as any of us."

Pyro turned and walked past the ladder to a locker and pulled it open, revealing more Sikaths like the one Keera had taken, and a few assorted pistols and rifles. She handed an EKR rifle to her father just as a muted crash came rumbling through the open door in the side of the shuttle. That was immediately followed by the shrieking wail of an alarm as a section of the fence went down. Clayton hurried to the entrance of the shuttle and watched from the top of the ramp with Sutton as a dark line of Dregs came bounding down from the ruins, the long grass rustling around them as they went.

"Where's the bait?" Sutton asked.

Clayton pointed to a tiny floating black speck as it disappeared between the trees.

Sutton chuckled lightly at that. "Well, I'll be damned. Never seen food running for its life before."

Clayton smiled tightly at that, but the expression vanished as one of the Dregs peeled off from the rest and stood up straight, peering toward them with its cranial stalks twitching to hear through the blaring sirens coming from the farm.

They both ducked out of sight and flattened themselves against the inside of the shuttle. "Shit," Sutton muttered as he reached for the control panel to close the hatch.

Clayton peeked around the opening just in time to see that Dreg's head go flying off. "Wait," he said. "It's dead."

A moment later, they heard footsteps ringing softly on the ramp, and both Keera and Lori de-cloaked inside the shuttle.

"It's time to go," Lori said, sounding out of breath.

Clayton stared out the door, watching as the last two Dregs disappeared between the trees.

Heavy footsteps rang on the rungs of the ladder, and Clayton saw Nova and Pyro making way for Specter as he came down.

Taking that as their cue, everyone got up from their seats, their weapons rattling and boots shuffling, and soon they were all rushing quietly down the ramp. Specter closed the ship behind them, making it completely invisible once more, and then they dashed through the fields, following Keera and Lori to the entrance of the sewers on the other side of the trees.

* * *

Samara found her daughter lying alone in the middle of the arena, the sand around her darkened with blood. She fell on her knees beside her little girl, her worst fears realized.

"Dora!" she cried. A deep laceration ran crosswise from her chest to her navel. It glistened darkly with blood in the ambient glow of the city lights.

"Mom?" Dora moaned, coming to briefly. Her eyes fluttered to slits. Then she mumbled something, and they rolled up in her head as she passed out again.

"What have you *done?*" Samara cried as she shrugged out of her coat and used it to staunch and put pressure on the wound.

A few seconds later, she heard sirens come warbling in. She turned to the street access she'd come through a moment ago and saw the flashing red and blue lights of an armored black *Ryde* that the hospital had re-purposed as an ambulance. A pair of paramedics came rushing into the arena with a hovering stretcher and a medkit.

"Over here!" she called, sparing a hand from pressing on Dora's chest to wave them over.

The paramedics worked fast, spraying the wound with Regenex and synthskin. Then they moved Dora to a floating stretcher and guided it into the back of the ambulance, where they hooked up a bag of blood to replace what Dora had lost. Her vitals beeped along weakly as they cruised soundlessly down the streets to the hospital.

"Is she going to be okay?" Samara asked.

"We'll do everything we can," the nearest paramedic said, while injecting Dora's arm with something. It was Don Alger. She recognized him from his dark hair and goatee, his blue eyes and tanned, golden skin. The other paramedic was Lisa Colebert, a fifty-something woman with gray streaking through her short brown hair and deep crows feet around her brown eyes. She'd survived the invasion and had received her longevity treatments too late to keep her looking young forever.

Samara sat on a bench beside Dora's stretcher, holding her daughter's hand and quietly sobbing.

Why? Was all she could think, over and over again. What could possibly possess a ten-year-old girl to engage in a duel to the death with one of her peers?

But the answer was obvious, and she sat seething with rage, quietly hating the Kyra all the more for it. *There's no evil so pure as that which corrupts an innocent heart,* she thought.

Her thoughts were interrupted by a shrill, whooping siren that wasn't coming from the ambulance.

"What's going on?" Samara asked, sitting up straighter in her seat. "What is that?"

Both paramedics froze, and Don's eyes widened as he listened. "That sounds like the air raid siren from the garrison. The city's under attack."

CHAPTER 46

Fifteen Minutes Earlier...

The sewers turned out to be a drainage duct from the city streets that emptied out into a nearby river. The entrance was blocked with a heavy iron grate, but Keera made short work of it with her nano-edged sword. They had to wade through the river up to their waists and help each other up to reach the entrance, but thankfully the inside of the pipe was relatively dry, and it didn't smell nearly as bad as Clayton had been imagining.

Keera and Specter hoisted the piece of grate they'd cut back into place once all of them were inside, and then Specter welded it back into place with two quiet zaps from invisible lasers that leapt out of integrated weapons in his shoulders.

Clayton, Nova, Pyro, and Harold brought up the rear as everyone followed Keera, Lori, and Specter through the sewers. After rounding the first bend, they flicked on their tactical lights to keep from stumbling in the dark. Keera, Lori, and Specter kept a gap of a few dozen paces, not using flashlights, but rather the night-vision optics in their helmets. Specter soon cloaked himself, but Clayton saw him re-appear now and again as falling trickles of water from adjoining pipes and ceiling grates washed over his invisible silhouette.

They moved quickly, single-file, with their feet splashing noisily in the few inches of water at the bottom of the pipe. Everyone kept their rifles up and sweeping, checking adjoining sewer lines for signs of trouble, but they saw neither Chimeras nor Dregs.

Finally, Keera and Lori stopped beside a ladder leading to a manhole cover. One of them climbed the ladder and popped the manhole open, then the other started after her and waved for the rest of them to follow.

Sutton's voice whispered through Clayton's earpiece. "Tac lights off."

And one by one, their under-barrel lights flicked off, plunging the sewers into darkness. A pale shaft of light still shone down the open manhole from the city above, lighting the way like a beacon. Clayton shuffled toward the bottom of the ladder. He glanced back to see Nova, Pyro, and Harold right behind him.

The four of them emerged from the manhole one after another in a darkened alley, not far from the arena. A big black Ryde hovered at a pickup point just a few feet away, shielding them from view of the stores and upper-level apartments visible at the open end of the alley. It was long after curfew, so most of those apartment windows and all of the stores were dark. The group hurried to the waiting Ryde and clambered through a narrow door in the middle of the armored transport. As Clayton did so, he heard an ambulance's siren screaming somewhere in the distance. That made him hesitate, and his thoughts turned to Samara. She would be starting her shift at the hospital right about now.

"Hurry up," Pyro whispered, pushing through from behind. Clayton stepped out of the way, and Nova and Harold pushed in behind them. He crossed gazes with a familiar face at the far end of the aisle. A tall, trim figure with piercing blue eyes. It was Richard Morgan, Keera's father, and Clayton's old contact with the resistance. He wore a matching black uniform from the Guard, and like everyone else, shoe polish darkened his face and blond hair.

Richard's cheeks dimpled with a smile as the door slid shut, and the Ryde leapt forward, cruising down the street. "It's good to see you again, Clayton," he said.

And for once, Clayton had to agree.

* * *

They cruised to a halt at an alley just before the ascension center.

"Everybody out," Keera said, pushing her way down the crowded aisle to the entrance.

"Make it quick and stick to the shadows."

The door slid open for Keera as she touched the panel beside it, and everyone followed her out. The alley was flanked by two rows of low-rise, ten-floor apartments with a couple of dim blue lights radiating from upper-level windows to indicate that they were Chimeran buildings. No patrols watched the lower levels or entrances, however, and sticking to the shadows was easy enough in the alleyway.

Richard joined them, and the Ryde rolled on, empty and searching for its next group of passengers.

Keera's voice came crackling over the comms as she turned to address the group. "Everyone, you know the plan. Stick close to your team leaders and wait for our signal."

The air shimmered as both she and Lori cloaked themselves. Specter was already cloaked and likely waiting somewhere nearby.

Richard sidled up to Clayton with the rest of their team. "We're the last to go," he explained, nodding to the open end of the alley where two distinct groups had formed, one behind Sergeant Sutton, the other around the Latin woman known as Widow.

They all waited quietly in the shadows, pressing their backs against the wall of the nearest building. Clayton listened for the double-click of the all-clear signal that Keera had mentioned, but long minutes passed, and still no signal came.

But then they got a different kind of signal. The shrill, whooping cry of a Kyron air raid siren screamed to life. Seconds later, the windows in the apartments above them began radiating cold blue light into the alley, the lights snapping on as Chimeras woke up.

The teams traded horrified looks with one another. They weren't even in position yet.

"Scar to Phoenix leader, what's your status? Over," Sutton said.

Nothing but static hissed in Clayton's ear.

CHAPTER 47

The whooping cry of sirens from the garrison droned on.

"What's happening?" Nova asked.

"We need to abort," Richard said. "Something went wrong."

"*Can we* abort?" Clayton replied. "Won't the Chronan fleet come anyway?"

Richard met his gaze, his jaw clenching.

"Yes," Pyro said. "They'll come whether we've disabled the tracking IDs or not. There's no way to call them off now."

Clayton shook his head. "Then according to Keera, the Kyra will execute everyone before they go. That means there's no going back. We have to see this through." He pressed a finger to his earpiece. "Sergeant, if we're going to move, now is the time."

"Copy that," Sutton replied. "You heard the Captain, let's push up. All teams on me. Go go go!"

Sergeant Sutton led the charge from the alley, his team sticking close behind him. Widow went next with hers, but Richard hesitated when it was his turn to go. His eyes were wide, his head slowly shaking. "This is suicide," he said, backing a few steps deeper into the alley.

"Maybe," Clayton agreed, "but it's our chance to make our lives count for something. Let's not waste it." He took a long step toward the end of the alley and waved the others on behind him. "Everybody stay close. Harold, Pyro, keep eyes on our six."

"Copy that," Pyro whispered, answering for both of them.

Clayton grabbed his rifle in both hands and ran lightly from the alley, following the two teams ahead of him. Nova and Harold stuck close, while Pyro hung back a few steps to cover their six. They clung to the shadows beneath the eaves of storefronts and apartment lobbies as they went. One block away, he saw one corner of the featureless black dome of the ascension center. A massive elevator shaft rose from there like a leaning skyscraper to the landing platform above. The dome flashed with the reflected green light of lasers. The muted reports of weapons fire came echoing down the street.

Then the comms crackled as someone tried to say something. Clayton pressed the transmit button and got an earful of a shrill, screeching noise.

"Shit," he muttered. "They're jamming our

comms."

"Maybe that explains why we haven't heard from Keera," Harold said.

Clayton nodded, but said nothing. He glanced behind them, searching for Richard, but there was no sign of him. He'd stayed in the alley. Clayton blew out a frustrated breath. After all these years, he was still the coward who'd suggested they execute his Chimeran daughter rather than risk keeping her alive.

Up ahead, Sutton's team darted left, crashing noisily through a window on the ground floor of a building across from the ascension center. The muted sounds of weapons fire sounded from within. Widow followed with Bravo team, and Clayton jumped through the broken windows after them.

He emerged with his team inside of a Kyron dispensary packed with aisle after aisle of plainly packaged food and household goods.

Flickering green lasers lashed the front of the building from the direction of the ascension center, burning neat, glowing holes through the windows rather than breaking them. Clayton saw everyone pinned down behind pillars between the windows and the front doors. Operatives aimed their rifles without looking, using their ARCs to line up their shots. Their rifles fired quiet and invisible spectrum-shifted lasers.

To one side of the front doors, behind a

shelf of packet breads and boxed milk, he spotted Lori, Keera, and Specter. Sergeant Sutton was there with them. All four were de-cloaked and crouching around a holo-projector on the floor. A shaded blue schematic map glowed in the air above it. Clayton crept down the aisle to reach them, the footsteps of his team padding softly behind him.

"What happened?" he whispered.

"They saw us coming," Lori explained. "Where's Richard?"

"He decided to stay at the drop point."

Keera hissed and Lori just shook her head. He noticed that she was favoring one arm, and saw the dark, glistening sheen of blood running down her armor.

"You're hit," Clayton said.

"I'll be fine," Lori replied, waving away his concern.

"How did they see you?" Pyro asked, crowding in. "Weren't you cloaked?"

"The centers must have upgraded their scanners since I was in command," Keera said. "They saw right through our cloaking shields."

"Shit," Clayton muttered. "Now what?" He glanced up as a flurry of green lasers came strobing through the dispensary. "Soldiers from the garrison must already be on their way."

"Correction," Specter said. "They already have us surrounded. I detect one hundred and ten life signs covering this building from the outside, and that's just what's in range of my scanners."

"It's only a fraction of what will still be coming," Keera said. "We're lucky they want to take us alive, or we'd be dead already. They're trying to run us out of ammo."

Clayton looked over to where operatives were still firing around corners with invisible lasers to keep Chimeras from advancing on the dispensary.

"We can't let them do that," Clayton said.

"We could storm the front entrance," Sergeant Sutton suggested. "Your armor is shielded conventionally, not just cloaked," he added, nodding to Keera and Lori. "We should be able to get you through to the front entrance."

"And then what?" Keera countered. "You'll all be dead, and we'll be left to deal with countless soldiers inside the center."

Clayton couldn't believe it, but he was starting to agree with Richard. This *was* suicide. "There has to be another option."

Nova pressed in beside him, looking frightened. Pyro and Harold were both at the other end of the aisle, covering the broken windows they'd come in by.

"There is one alternative," Specter said.

But before he could explain, Pyro's voice called to them from the other end of the aisle.

"They're coming!"

"You two! Reinforce her position!" Sutton snapped, pointing to Clayton and Nova.

They turned and ran down the aisle to join Pyro and Harold on the other side of the broken window they'd come in by.

Clayton connected his ARCs to the scope of his rifle and aimed it around the side of the pillar where he and Nova had taken cover. He saw several squads running up the street toward their position in full suits of glossy black armor. Thankfully, none of them were cloaked —at least none that he could see. He set the scope to night-vision mode and flicked the rifle's fire-mode selector to *kill*.

No point trying to be stealthy now.

"Ready?" he whispered to Pyro. She nodded, and he glanced over his shoulder to find Nova getting ready to fire around the other side of the pillar.

"Let's give 'em hell," Clayton said.

He aimed one-handed through the broken window, keeping himself behind cover. The enemy soldiers began fanning out to cover positions as they drew near. Several of them darted into Restoration Park, where Clayton had met with Richard a decade ago. The enemy soldiers hid in the playground and behind trees.

Clayton tracked one who was too slow to get behind cover. Bright green lasers snapped out from their position, raking him with fire. His shields flared brightly, absorbing the first shot, and then he crumpled to the street as the others punched through his armor.

Bright green lasers came snapping back at them from a dozen different locations at once. Clayton heard Nova cursing sharply, and spun around to see her ducking back into cover with her shoulder smoking.

"Are you okay?"

She nodded. "Just grazed me."

For now. She wasn't equipped for this. Not the least of which because she didn't have ARCs to connect to her scope, so she couldn't stay behind cover while she fired like everybody else.

"Just stay behind the pillar," he said to her. "We don't need you getting shot."

"You can't hold them all off on your own."

"Give her one of yours," Pyro suggested as she squeezed off another shot.

She made a good point. Clayton grabbed Nova's rifle and stared at it for a moment before the prompt to connect his ARCs appeared. He connected the left lens to the scope of her rifle, leaving his right contact connected to his own. Holding his eye open, he plucked out the lens. "Tilt your head back."

Nova did so, and he put it in her right eye.

"Ow," she said as he grazed her eyeball with his fingertip, and then—"Woah... that's *stellar*."

473

"See that window in the top right?"

Nova nodded. "That's your scope. Aim with that and keep your butt behind cover."

"Copy that," Nova replied.

Clayton popped his rifle out and aimed around the side of the broken window once more. He spotted a pair of soldiers running single file toward them from the alley, having taken advantage of his inattention and the fact that neither Pyro nor Harold had a clear line of sight on them. Clayton popped off a shot, over-loading the leader's shield with a bright flash of light. They flattened themselves against the wall.

Then came a *crunch* of broken glass on the floor between him and Pyro, but there was nothing there.

Clayton's skin prickled with warning, and his rifle snapped up, tracking an invisible target.

Then a pair of blazing blue lasers tore through the air between them, and a commando in matte black armor appeared, de-cloaking between him and Pyro. The soldier crumpled to his knees and fell over face-first in the broken glass. Clayton glanced in the direction of that shot and found Specter's glowing red eyes looking his way, the barrels of the integrated lasers in his shoulders deployed. He nodded to the robot, and it nodded back.

Pyro leaned down and grabbed the commando's Stinger pistol, tucking the spare weapon into her belt.

"We're not going to last long like this," Harold said. "They're getting closer."

Clayton fired another shot to keep the two he'd pinned down from advancing.

"Specter said he had an idea," Nova pointed out as her own rifle gave a stuttering report of three shots in quick succession.

Sutton's voice roared through the dispensary. "All teams, ready up! We're going to push on to the main entrance of the center! On my mark!"

Clayton's guts clenched with apprehension.

"So much for Specter's plan," Pyro muttered.

He looked to Nova and saw her firing another two shots, sending an advancing Chimera scurrying behind a Ryde stop.

"Mark!" Sutton cried. "Hooah!"

A dozen other voices echoed that battle cry. Pyro and Harold fell back, their rifles stitching the broken window with emerald fire to cover their retreat. Clayton waited for Nova to go first, keeping her back covered with a few parting shots of his own as they left their cover position.

The sound of shattering glass and shrieking lasers filled the night as resistance operatives broke through windows to avoid bunching up in the front entrance of the dispensary.

Clayton reached the front of the store and hesitated. Acrid smoke and the sharp tang of ozone from lasers ionizing the air filled his nostrils as he took a deep breath. He couldn't lead his daughter in a suicidal charge.

But that was when he noticed that no one was actually firing on their people as they ran to the center. There was a line of three armored troop transports blocking the street. Two were on fire, and Chimeran soldiers lay in tangled heaps around them.

The air above the street shimmered, and a familiar, wedge-shaped shuttle appeared hovering twenty feet up.

Clayton blinked in shock.

"We've got air support!" Pyro crowed, and then she leaped through the window with her father. "Let's go!"

"Hooah!" Nova cried, vaulting over the gleaming wedges of glass in the window sill.

Clayton dashed through after them, bringing up the rear. He hadn't even heard Specter's shuttle opening fire on the enemy's lines. His ship must have the equivalent of a *stealth* setting for its guns.

Maybe we can trust Specter, after all, he thought.

By the time he was halfway across the street, a series of deafening *booms* rolled through the sky, followed by dazzling flashes of light. Clayton's gaze snapped up to look, and he saw the drifting black shadow of the *Sovath* silhouetted against the night with explosions rippling along the top side of its hull.

A cheer went up from the resistance fighters. Keera and Lori stood by the front doors, waving them into the relative cover of the entrance, while Specter fired solid blue beams from the lasers in his shoulders to trace a molten line around the doors, cutting a hole. Clayton sprinted across the street, running faster than he'd ever run in his life. Just as he reached the walkway to the entrance of the center, flickers of emerald fire leapt out from the flaming blockade of troop transports. More soldiers had arrived. Those lasers struck down two soldiers in Bravo Team, one of whom lay still, dead where she lay. The other, a man with curly black hair and a shaggy beard like Clayton's immediately began screaming for help.

Clayton angled toward the man, and someone else turned back to help. It was Widow. Pyro and Harold stopped to lay down covering fire along with Specter's shuttle while Clayton and Widow grabbed the wounded man by his arms.

"Leave me," he rasped between ragged gasps for air.

"Not a chance," Widow replied. "You're not dead yet."

Clayton grunted in agreement as they

dragged the injured man to cover in the entrance of the center. There was a charred, glistening black hole in the right side of his chest. He was clutching it with a bloody hand and gritting his teeth, tears slicing clean lines through the smears of shoe polish on his face.

"Doc! They got Preacher!" Widow said as they crouched to one side of the doors, sheltered by the wall beside them.

The Asian man Clayton had seen at Phoenix Base ran over and shrugged out of a heavy-looking pack. "Looks like a tension pneumothorax," he said. "His lips are blue." Doc produced a medkit and quickly cut away Preacher's uniform. He used a hollow tool with a sharp blade to punch a hole in Preacher's chest, right above the collapsed lung. He cried out as blood and air shot out of the puncture. Then he sucked in a whistling breath, and some of the color returned to his lips.

Nova crowded in, one eye glowing with displays on the contact Clayton had given her. She helped cover them with her rifle, but Clayton could see that the Chimeras who'd shot Preacher were falling back under the heavier guns of Specter's shuttle. The street was exploding with each burst of sapphire lasers.

Doc quickly taped the tube into place, then sprayed both sides of Preacher's laser burn with Regenex, followed by synthskin. He finished by injecting a painkiller. "Good to go,"

Doc said.

"Thanks," Preacher managed.

Just before Doc shut the medkit, Clayton noticed a row of silver canisters inside of it that looked like the one they'd used to inoculate Harold against the Chimeran virus. He counted five canisters, and a blank space where one was missing. Good to know they had spares. If they wound up fleeing back through the Wastes on foot, the Dregs would be a very real concern.

Clayton looked away, checking Specter's progress with the doors. Another series of explosions rumbled through the air, reminding him of the *Sovath*, embattled and succumbing to enemy fire. "Your fleet is here early," Clayton said.

"Yes," Specter replied. "I mentioned an alternative to the Sergeant's suicidal charge. That was it."

"Good call," Clayton said.

"It was the only call," Specter replied. "Brace for enemy fire," he added as the bright blue glow of his lasers vanished, plunging the entrance of the center into shadows. The molten orange line he'd drawn around the inside of the doors was now a perfect oval. "My sensors indicate five enemy targets waiting behind the doors. Take cover."

"Cover!" Keera added, and everyone flattened themselves to the walls beside the doors.

Specter kicked them, and the cut sections fell inward with a tandem *boom.* Blue lasers stuttered out from his shoulders in a rapid-fire sequence, the barrels tracking independently across the corridor behind the doors. Only one emerald laser beam answered back, splashing harmlessly off his armor.

"Enemies neutralized. All teams, on me," Specter said as he stalked through the doors.

CHAPTER 48

Samara watched Dora sleep from where she sat in the corner of a private room on the tenth floor of the hospital. Dora was still recovering from surgery to repair the damage that a stolen Sikath had done to her internal organs. She hadn't woken up yet, but her surgeon, none other than the misogynistic Dr. Galen Rath, had assured Samara that Dora had a good chance of pulling through.

For once, Samara was happy he was around. Galen was the best surgeon the hospital had. She didn't want to know what might have happened to Dora if he hadn't been there to patch her up.

Galen had said that they'd managed to stop the bleeding in time. Now all they had to do was wait for her to rest and recover while the nanites they'd injected repaired the remainder of the damage.

Thunder rolled, shivering through the window beside Samara. She dragged her eyes away —

And saw explosions pocking the sky with

JASPER T. SCOTT

fire above the drifting hulk of the *Sovath.* Belated shock waves hammered the window, each one like a slap to Samara's face, demanding that she wake up.

But this wasn't a dream. She slowly stood up from the chair and walked to the window for a better look. The *Sovath* was returning fire with massive starbursts of emerald lasers leaping into space, followed by the streaking orange tails of missiles. Samara gaped at the sight, unable to believe what she was seeing.

Someone was attacking the Kyra.

The door to Dora's room burst open, and Galen rushed in, his usually blithe, charming expression now blank and stricken.

"We're under—"

"Attack. I know," Samara said.

Galen leaned hard on the door frame to catch his breath.

"The *Sovath* is going down," he added, pointing to it through the window.

Samara spun around to look, and watched as the big, teardrop-shaped destroyer listed sharply toward the ground. It began falling slowly, going down nose-first. Thick, sapphire-blue laser beams stabbed from orbit, raking the top and sides of the destroyer with fiery orange lines of explosions. Escape pods sputtered out in a glittering wave, followed by the dark, needles of Lancer fighters and the boxy rectangles of assault shuttles.

"They're abandoning ship," Samara whispered as Galen appeared standing at the window beside her.

He nodded slowly, saying nothing.

"Who's attacking them?" she asked.

"The Kyra only have one enemy that we know of," Galen replied.

"The Chrona," Samara whispered. She sent a quick glance over her shoulder to where Dora lay, safely oblivious to the chaos going on outside.

"It's not going to clear the city," Galen whispered.

"What?" Samara's gaze snapped back to the window, and she saw the tail end of the Sovath vanishing behind the Northern walls of the city. A few seconds later, there came a blinding burst of light as it exploded.

Samara blinked flash-blinded eyes. The floor began rumbling with the tremors of that impact even before she heard the explosion.

"Get down!" Galen cried, pulling her to the floor beside him. The window exploded with a *boom*, and a wave of hot air rushed into the room.

Samara rolled over, shattered glass falling off her back. Her ears were ringing and stuffed with cotton as Galen helped her to her feet. She ran over to Dora before doing anything else. Her daughter was still asleep, with no obvious signs of new injuries. No—wait. That wasn't true. A small gash in her forehead was welling with blood. Samara spun around, looking for gauze or a can of synthskin to stop the bleeding. Dora's IV bag sprayed a thin stream of water to the floor. And beyond that, the broken window gaped at the flaming ruins of the *Sovath* in the Wastes at the northern end of the city. Several skyscrapers had been flattened, one of which was on fire, and telescoping down before their eyes. A mushrooming cloud of smoke and debris shot up where it had stood just a second ago.

Galen leaned against the wall for support, his jaw slack. He turned to her and said something that didn't make it through the cotton in her ears. She shook her head and cupped a hand to her ear.

A text prompt to chat appeared from him on her ARCs. She accepted it.

The Sovath took out the northern wall.

Samara blinked in shock, realizing that he was right. She shouldn't have been able to see the remains of the *Sovath* from here. The wall must have been knocked down along with those skyscrapers when it crashed.

We're just five blocks away, Galen added. *We need to secure the entrances before Dregs start flooding the city.*

Samara nodded slowly, her eyes dazzled and mesmerized by the leaping orange flames of the biggest fire she'd ever seen in her life. The heat and light of that blaze was going to start attracting Dregs like moths to a flame. They were just dumb brutes, but long years of hunting human exiles across the Wastes had taught them to look for smoke and fires. And this fire would be visible for miles in every direction.

CHAPTER 49

Clayton and Widow helped Preacher to his feet. He winced as the movement disturbed the laser burn in his chest. Everyone ran through the front entrance after Specter, sticking close to the deadly robot.

Preacher pulled away from them, breathing hard. "You go. Someone has to stay here and watch our six." There were already four soldiers standing there, including Sergeant Sutton, but Preacher didn't look like he had it in him to keep up, so Widow nodded. "Make 'em pay for that lung," she said as she hurried through the doors with Doc.

"That we will, ma'am," Sutton said.

Clayton and Nova ran close behind Widow with Pyro and Harold. Up ahead, Specter's lasers added to the dim blue light already pouring from the center's light fixtures. Green lasers stabbed belatedly out from Keera and Lori's Stinger pistols, and the sound of armored Chimerans clattering to the floor echoed through the air—their enemies falling one after another.

They followed the twists and turns of the corridor, heading deeper into the center. Lasers periodically leapt out from the head of the group as Lori, Keera, and Specter cleared out the stragglers. It seemed like most of the Chimeras guarding the center had come out to support the ones from the garrison, so the guard in here was light.

Clayton's heart soared as he realized that they might actually pull this off. They reached an intersecting corridor, and both he and Widow stopped. She held up a closed fist, indicating they should freeze, but Nova didn't recognize it. Clayton stopped her from barreling on by holding out an arm to catch her across the chest.

She shot a curious look at him, but she got the message and fell back.

Both he and Widow swept the intersecting corridor with their rifles, checking for targets before blundering across. The corridors were all lined with doors, so they couldn't assume that this one had been cleared just because someone else had already walked through ahead of them.

When no enemy soldiers jumped out, Widow swept her left hand past her hip, indicating they should move up. She led the way again. Clayton lingered in the corridor to cover Nova as she darted by.

And then he saw it. Something that both he

and Widow had missed: a rifle peeking around the jamb of an open door near the far left end.

"Cover!" Clayton cried as he dropped to the floor where he stood. A laser chased him down, blazing through the tip of his left shoulder. He held the trigger down, raking the corridor with return fire that would at least blind the enemy if nothing else. Harold and Pyro joined in, but it was Nova who landed a lucky shot, actually hitting the enemy soldier's weapon.

The charge pack overloaded with a *bang,* and a fiery burst of light that leaped out of the open doorway. They heard the enemy soldier clattering to the floor a split second later.

"Clear," Pyro said, and they darted through the corridor to the other side to follow the vanishing black forms of the rest of their group.

"That was a hell of a shot, kid," Harold added as they ran.

"Thanks," Nova replied, beaming up at him.

"Don't get cocky," Clayton warned.

They caught the rest of the group at the bottom of a staircase and ran all the way up to the third floor, skipping their plan to neutralize the security system. There was no point disabling it now that their cover had been so thoroughly blown.

They ran down the corridor to the tracking room, reaching the door without incident, but it was locked.

"Stand back," Specter said, and bright blue lasers snapped out of his shoulders once more to cut a hole. Everyone else fanned out to watch his back, their rifles aiming back the way they'd come.

Suddenly, one of Specter's lasers flipped up and over his shoulder, tracing a fiery line through the ceiling before vanishing against something invisible at the far end of the corridor. A Chimeran commando appeared decloaking there with half of its helmet sinking into a molten ruin against its skull. The commando had been aiming a Stinger pistol directly at Specter's back.

It fell in a clattering heap. Clayton wondered where it had come from, and hoped that Sergeant Sutton and his team hadn't just been executed by an invisible soldier. He tried activating his comms to check, and received another earful of jamming noise for his trouble.

"We're through," Specter declared a moment later. "Two targets on the other side. Stand by."

He kicked in the door again and shot both Chimeras in the head before either of them could react.

"I'm glad he's on our side," Nova whispered.

"Me, too," Clayton replied as they surged after the Chrona with ten other operatives.

Keera turned to them on her way through.

"Everybody watch the entrance."

Soldiers nodded with an echoing series of grunted *hooahs* as they fanned out through the entrance, taking up positions inside the room and to either side of the ruined door.

Clayton followed Keera to a desk beneath a wall of viewscreens on one side of the room where Specter was already busy executing their plan.

They crowded around and watched as he opened a compartment in his thigh and pulled out a gleaming silver cable with a strange, fork-like plug on the end.

The plug shimmered and molded itself to the shape of a data port in a glowing blue cube below the desk. Clayton recognized it as a Kyron quantum computer. It didn't look like much, but that one machine could have stored and run the mind maps of a billion people living in a simulated version of Earth.

"I'm in," Specter said after a moment, his crimson eyes brightening and darkening several times per second. Soon after that, he added, "I've just disabled every implant in the city."

"Can they turn them back on?" Nova asked.

Clayton turned to see her standing behind him.

"No. They require manual re-activation, one at a time."

"So we did it?" Clayton asked, not sure he

believed it.

"Not entirely."

Keera looked to them, then back to Specter, her expression inscrutable inside her helmet.

Clayton caught on as Specter's words echoed back through his head. "Wait, you said you disabled every implant in the *city?*"

"That's correct."

"What about the rest of them?" Keera asked.

"I thought you said you could disable them all from here," Clayton added, his suspicions mounting by the second. Maybe Specter had over-promised.

"This node has been isolated from the sat-net. I was unable to access the rest of the tracking network."

"That means the Kyra can still execute everyone else on the planet?" Nova ventured.

"Saving one city is better than saving no cities," Specter pointed out.

"That's not good enough!" Clayton thundered.

Specter glared at him with the cold, unblinking eyes of a machine.

"He's right," Keera said. "There are fifty-seven occupied cities on Earth besides New Houston. If we don't do something, millions will die. There has to be a way you can get access to the rest of the implants."

"We've got incoming!" Lori cried from the entrance of the room.

And then a flurry of emerald lasers shrieked in and out of the room, flashing to and fro and filling the air with the sharp, coppery smell of melting metals and ozone.

Lasers splashed across the viewscreens above the desk. Specter returned fire with strobing blue lasers while Clayton and Nova dashed into cover with Keera.

Then a violent tremor shivered through the floor, followed by the booming roar of a distant explosion. The laser fire quieted on both sides as everyone stopped to wonder what had just happened.

Nova looked to Clayton in the smoky gloom of the tracking center. They were crouched behind an island counter lined with holo-projectors on top and storage cabinets below. One of Nova's hazel eyes glowed bright with the light of the ARC he'd given her; the other was dark and gleaming. "What was that?" she asked, coughing into her sleeve.

"Something big," Clayton replied.

"The *Sovath*," Keera said. "It just blew up."

"What? How do you know that?" Clayton asked.

"Because the comms jamming just went down."

And then Sutton's voice crowded into his ear with a rush of static: "...to fall back! Lost

Mac, Reaper, and Hurl. You've got incoming! Sixty or seventy—"

Static garbled whatever else he'd just said.

"Say again, Scar," Keera replied.

"Sixty or seventy Elites."

"Copy that, we're on our way out," she said.

"Elites?" Clayton asked.

"Veteran Chimeras," Keera explained. "Not like the dumb grunts we get down here at the garrison. They all wear cloaking exoskeletons and carry advanced tracking weapons like what Specter's been using. They're mobile weapons platforms piloted by Chimeras—and they can fly, not that they'll need to in here. We need to get out of here *now*," Keera said.

Clayton peeked over the top of the island, his eyes darting around the smoky interior of the tracking room, searching for some way out besides the one currently flashing with lasers.

But there wasn't one.

"This is a dead-end!" Nova cried.

CHAPTER 50

Specter came stalking over to where Clayton was hiding with Keera and Nova.

"I can get us out," the Chrona said. "There is a corridor that branches directly off this one. It leads to an outer wall. I can cut a hole and fly us out while the others lay down covering fire from here."

Keera gave a low hiss. "What's the point of that? You can't fly all of us out."

"What about his shuttle?" Clayton asked. Maybe it could be waiting to extract them.

"It was destroyed by enemy fighters," Specter replied.

"Then what are we talking about?" Keera demanded. "I'm not going to save myself and leave everyone else here to die."

"We could still deactivate the rest of the tracking network. If we could somehow reach one of the satellites, I can access the network directly from there and disable the remainder of the ID implants."

Keera's eyes widened. "He's right." She looked to Clayton, then back to Specter.

"There might still be ships landed on the roof."

"Go," Clayton said. "We'll cover you."

Keera hesitated, then gave in with a nod. Clayton stood up and activated his comms. "Everyone get ready to lay down covering fire! We've got a mission to accomplish!"

* * *

"On my mark," Clayton said.

There came a lull in the stream of lasers pulsing through the open door. Keera looked at her mother from where she crouched on the opposite side of the entrance to the tracking room. Both of their faces were hidden behind their helmets. This could be the last time that either of them saw each other.

"Go," Lori whispered over a private comms channel in lieu of a more emotional goodbye.

Keera nodded back. She couldn't read her mother's thoughts the way she could with other Chimeras or Kyra, but after spending almost a century together, neither of them needed words to express their feelings.

"Ready?" Clayton whispered from where he crouched beside her.

"Let's do it," Keera replied.

"Mark!" Clayton cried, and everyone jumped out of their cover positions and laid down a solid wall of laser fire.

Keera crouched under their lines of fire and darted down the adjoining corridor. Specter was taller than she was, but he went down on all fours and bounded out like a dog.

He ran right by her, still on all fours, heading for the end of the corridor. Keera sprinted after him with two of her cranial stalks turned back the way she'd come to listen for sounds of pursuit. Yet all she heard was the echoing roar of laser fire assaulting her sensitive ears.

They reached the end of the corridor. It wasn't a dead end. A pair of armored security doors blocked the right side, while the left was lined with offices or classrooms.

"Watch the doors," Specter said as the lasers in his shoulders began stitching molten orange lines across the wall.

Keera kept the doors on both sides covered with her Stinger pistol, blinking sweat from her eyes despite the temperature-regulating mesh built into her armor. She listened to the deafening reports of laser fire still roaring behind her and glanced back that way, hoping no one had died to cover her escape, and hoping even more fervently that this plan would work.

The doors burst open beside her, and she dropped to a crouch. Two identical fourth-year cadets appeared in simple black uniforms with red trim and Stinger pistols in their hands. Twin boys.

"Halt!" one of them said, raising his weapon in both hands.

"It's a Chrona!" the other said.

They both fired, one narrowly missing Keera, the other hitting Specter in the shoulder. One of the robot's lasers sputtered and died with a stream of black smoke.

Keera fired back instinctively, pulling the trigger over and over until the weapon *clicked,* and the trigger grew slack. Both boys fell over with glowing orange holes in their chests and lay still. The room on the other side was a holo-training lab. They'd been in here, practicing through the night for their ascension tests. Probably hoping to score high enough that they'd be assigned to the front lines rather than menial patrols on Earth. And now they were dead.

Keera grimaced, wishing she'd thought to set her pistol to stun, but there hadn't been time.

Specter interrupted her thoughts with a booming *thud* as he kicked the wall. The cut section pushed out a few inches. He kicked it again, and it broke free, crashing and tumbling down the sloping sides of the dome. Keera stepped up to the edge and watched the debris break apart as they fell. She wondered if the others could safely slide down the sides of the dome to the ground. It had to be at least 25 feet to the street, and the sides of the dome were steep. With the augmented strength of her armor, Keera and Lori could probably do it, but everyone else would break their legs on impact.

Specter turned to her. "Are you ready?"

She nodded.

"Engage your cloak."

She did so, and the air shimmered around Specter as he did the same. The next thing she knew, invisible arms folded her into a crushing hug, and she went flying through the hole in the side of the ascension center, diving head-first toward the street below. Keera's stomach plunged, and she screamed.

But then Specter's grav engines hummed to life, and he spread his wings. They went soaring back up and rose swiftly through the air. Keera gasped at the sensation of flying. No wonder the Chrona hadn't wanted to give this up.

Looking down, she saw the smoking ruins of the Garrison's troop transports— and hordes of Chimeran Elites in their bulky black exosuits storming between to reach the entrance of the center. They hadn't even bothered to cloak themselves, preferring to use their personal shields instead. Looking up, Keera saw the big, flat black shadow of the landing platform at the top of the center. It grew steadily larger and closer as Specter flew, his wings whooshing loudly in her ears.

A river of stars and sky lay between the landing platform and the adjacent row of buildings. A trio of starfighters went roaring through that gap: a dark, needle-shaped Kyron Lancer in front, and two arrowhead-shaped Chronan Blades in pursuit. They fired a steady stream of blue lasers at the Lancer, lighting up its shields with repeated impacts.

Specter flew out above the landing platform and landed right on the edge of it, releasing her. Keera cast about quickly and saw two flaming wrecks on the platform where Lancer fighters had recently crashed. A third, intact Lancer was just now hovering down for a more controlled landing. It was the only starship left. Keera heard Specter's voice booming out of thin air beside her. "Over there!"

They ran for the fighter together, their footsteps hammering the deck in tandem. The cockpit canopy slid open, revealing a pilot but no co-pilot. The pilot leaped over the side of the fighter, falling on hands and knees on the platform. Keera saw the ghost-white head of a female Chimera as the pilot ripped off her helmet.

"I will eliminate the target," Specter said over the private comms channel that Keera shared with him and Lori.

The pilot looked up at the sound of their approach. She was female, familiar-looking. That was when Keera noticed the excessive number of blue and red bars that made up the rank insignia on her uniform. She was an admiral. *The* admiral.

"Wait!" Keera told Specter. "Don't shoot her." She flicked her Stinger pistol over to stun just as a matching weapon flew out of a holster on the pilot's hip.

"Who's there!" the admiral cried. She clambered to her feet and swept the pistol around blindly, unable to see through Keera's and Specter's cloaking shields without the aid of sophisticated scanners.

Keera took aim and fired. Blue fire rippled over the Chimeran woman and sent her crumpling to the platform. She and Specter both stopped beside her.

"It's Admiral Treya," Keera explained. "Do a brain scan. She might have intel we can use. I'll get the fighter ready."

"Understood," Specter said. He de-cloaked himself, preferring active shields to the kind that wouldn't hide him from aerial attacks, and then he crouched beside Treya to place a palm against her head and scan her mind.

Keera ran for the open cockpit of the fighter, grabbed the edge of it, and pulled herself inside. Drawing the Sikath from her back, she laid the sword in a special rack along the inner right side of the cockpit and then settled into the seat to run through a quick preflight check. She had to make sure that the fighter was still in good condition.

The results flashed up on her main display a second later. No damage, but the shields were low. Treya had landed to flee the battle, not because she'd been forced down. Keera wasn't surprised. She had been too much of a coward to openly challenge her for her position, and this was just more of the same.

A *thunking* roar of metallic footfalls came to Keera's ears. She turned to see Specter vaulting over the side of the fighter to land in the co-pilot's seat behind her.

"Scan complete," he said.

"What did you learn?"

"The admiral had several useful pieces of intel. Her access codes will help me to hack into their tracking network much faster than I otherwise might have."

"Good," Keera said as she shut the cockpit canopy. She set the shields and engines to a hundred and fifty percent power, and completely killed power to weapons.

"I also obtained recent data on the movements of the Kyron fleet," Specter said. "The 42nd Fleet is just twenty light-years away. Admiral Treya called them for support as soon as my fleet arrived."

Keera activated the grav engines, and the Lancer leapt off the landing platform. Pulling up, she pushed the throttle to the max, and they rocketed into the sky, the sudden acceleration buffered by inertial dampeners.

Keera processed what Specter had just said as clouds swept past the cockpit in gauzy gray streaks. Flashes of light lit up the clouds from within as the darting black specks of Lancers and Blades chased each other through the night.

"And? What's the situation?" Keera asked.

"When the 42nd Fleet arrives, they will overwhelm us and force us to retreat."

Keera felt the blood draining from her face as the clouds fell away. Black sky surrounded them, the stars washed away by the flickering light of Chronan blue and Kyron green lasers. Scores of flaming, crashing starfighters rained down like meteors, punching holes in the rippled canvas of clouds below. The fighter's heads-up display highlighted those crashing fighters with purple, friendly target boxes, identifying them as Kyron Lancers, while a much larger number of red enemy target boxes darted around them. The Chrona were winning. Earth was about to be liberated. But that victory wasn't going to last for more than a few hours.

"How would you like to proceed?" Specter asked.

"We stick to the mission," Keera said, setting her jaw. "With the tracking system offline, at least people will have a chance to flee the cities and escape before the Kyra take back the planet.

"Understood," Specter replied.

"Will you still be able to release the cure?"

Specter was quiet for several seconds, perhaps consulting with his superiors over his integrated comms system. "Yes," he replied. "We will begin distributing it immediately. We expect it to reach 95% of the population before the Kyra's reinforcements arrive."

"Good." Keera nodded to herself. Maybe the Kyra would decide to cut their losses and abandon Earth rather than stick around and re-engineer their virus to defeat the vaccine.

If not, at least Phoenix would have given people a fighting chance to survive in the Wastes and Wilds beyond the cities.

CHAPTER 51

"**H**ere they come!" Lori cried.

A blinding wave of heavy laser fire shot out from the advancing wall of Chimeran Elites approaching from the stairs. Enemy fire bit out chunks of the ruined doors, and even the walls began to glow with the heat of repeated impacts.

Two soldiers fell with gaping, fire-rimmed holes in their chests before they could scramble out of the way. Clayton, Nova, Pyro, and Lori crowded around the melting edges of the doors, aiming their weapons via their ARCs and trying to push the Elites back, but their shots flashed harmlessly off the heavy shields and thick armor.

"We need to surrender!" Lori said, ducking back into cover as a chunk of the wall beside her exploded in a rain of concrete pebbles. "If they wanted us dead, they would have used a grenade or a rocket to take us out!"

"No one's surrendering!" Widow replied.

Clayton had to agree: capture, interrogation, and torture didn't sound any better than death to him.

"We just need to buy a little more time!" Clayton said, slotting a fresh charge pack into his rifle and setting it to *overload*. He aimed around the side of the doors with Nova and Pyro, and clicked off three super-charged shots at one of the incoming Elites. Those shots punched a hole through both shields and armor, dropping his target where it stood. Harold took his place while he fell back to reload. The barrel of his rifle was glowing bright red with the heat of those overloaded shots. He ejected a smoking charge pack that would never take another charge, and slotted in another one from his belt.

A suspicious lull in the firing came, and Clayton aimed his rifle around the corner to see the Elites dragging heavy, deployable fortifications into the corridor. They dropped down behind that wall, and weapon barrels poked out of small circular holes in the shield.

"Great," Clayton muttered, sinking deeper into cover with Nova and Harold as a dazzling emerald stream of lasers came flashing toward them once more.

"They're going to wait us out!" Lori said.

"Gutless bastards!" Harold cried.

"They've got us pinned," Pyro added. "They can wait all day."

"Not if they're losing the battle in space," Clayton pointed out.

Lori just looked at him as if she knew something that he didn't.

"Did they make it?" he asked, nodding to her.

"Yes!" Lori shouted back.

"Then ask if Specter can send reinforcements to our location!"

"I already did. They're not landing troops until the skies are clear."

"Then we have to hold out until then!" he said.

"Easier said than done!" Pyro said as another enemy barrage sent her scrambling away from the wall. It was actually glowing from repeated impacts.

Harold reached into a pocket and handed something to Clayton. "Here!"

He stared at the comms piece in his hand. "I already have a—"

"It's my personal comms," Harold replied. "Samara knows the number. She'll answer it. Give her a call!"

Clayton warred with himself briefly before fitting it into his other ear and connecting the device to his ARCs. He backed away from the entrance to place the call. Doc took his place by the doors just as a familiar voice answered, sounding out of breath. "Harold?"

Clayton's eyes stung with tears, and a trembling smile quirked onto his lips. "Hi, Sam. It's me. Clayton."

* * *

Samara worked with Carla, the charge nurse, Dr. Galen Rath, and several others to blockade the sliding glass doors of the ER on the ground floor. They dragged and stacked chairs from the waiting room in front of the doors. Other staff members and patients were busy barricading the remaining entrances on the ground floor of the hospital.

The comms rang endlessly from the reception desk as people called emergency services. Between Dregs pouring into the city and the battle raging outside, the number of injured and dead was rising with every passing minute.

"We're out of chairs," Carla said, stacking the last one.

"It'll have to hold," Samara replied.

Don Alger, one of the paramedics who'd helped Dora, came rushing down the hall from the direction of the medical dispensary and maternity wing. "We've disabled all of the other entrances," he said, his chest rising and falling quickly as he tried to catch his breath. "But we didn't have time to block them. We saw a few Dregs sniffing around the main entrance and had to fall back before they could see us."

Worried mutterings filled the waiting room as patients, nurses, and doctors traded glances with one another.

"Does anyone have a gun?" Samara asked, looking around quickly.

No one spoke.

"I do." Galen raised a hand.

"You'd better get it," Samara said.

He nodded and took off at a run, heading for his office in the surgical wing. His doctor's coat flared out behind him like a cape as he went.

Samara took in the rest of them with a sweeping look. "Everyone else, find whatever you can that you could use to kill a Dreg. Scalpels, bone saws, crutches—anything!"

A loud, banging sound started up behind her, rattling the doors of the ER and making her flinch.

"What was that?" one of the female patients from the waiting room cried.

"Someone's at the door!" a man said.

Samara crept toward the doors with Carla, peering through a forest of chair legs to see human faces pressing against the glass. A woman and two small kids. Their muffled screams shivered through the barrier.

"Help me get the doors open!" Samara cried. Carla shot her a panicky look as she began pulling at the wall of interlocking chairs that they'd just finished building. "We can't leave them out there!" Samara insisted.

And then the woman on the other side screamed and ran as a chalk-white monster went bounding after them on all fours. It shrieked, and the woman's screams cut off suddenly.

Samara stood staring through the doors in shock, straining to hear some sign that those three had survived. But all she heard was the muffled thunder of explosions above the city.

Carla pulled her away just as two pairs of glowing red eyes turned her way, spotting her through the glass. They came running, and soon both Dregs were hammering on the doors to get in, shrieking and hissing in frustration. The people in the waiting room collectively screamed and retreated in a stampede of departing footsteps.

More Dregs joined the first two, and soon glowing red eyes and pale, pressing bodies were all Samara could see.

"We need to go," Carla said in a shaky voice.

Samara couldn't tear her eyes away.

"It's not much, but..." Galen trailed off as he saw the Dregs at the doors. He had an ancient-looking revolver in one hand.

Samara's pocket began vibrating and trilling softly with an incoming call. Her ARCs identified the caller as Harold Neem. She fished the comms out of her pocket and put it to her ear. "Harold?" she asked, breathing hard, her system flooded with adrenaline.

"Hi, Sam. It's me, Clayton."

A thousand different thoughts and emotions coursed through her in the span of just a few seconds. The first was that this was a dream. Maybe she'd fallen asleep in that chair in her daughter's room, and everything that had happened since then was just a dream.

"Sam?"

"You died," she said, blinking rapidly and shaking her head.

"Who did?" Galen asked with a knitted brow.

"I didn't die," Clayton replied. "I've been living in the Wastes."

Samara heard a roar of weapons fire crackling through from his end of the comms. "Where are you?" she asked in a flat monotone, still numb with shock.

"The ascension center. I'm here with the resistance. Listen, I don't have much time. Are you safe? Where are you?"

"At the hospital."

"And Pandora?"

"She's here, too."

"Is she *okay?*" Clayton asked, his voice rising sharply.

"Yes. She'll be okay."

"Good."

"How dare you," Samara finally managed, realizing what it meant that Clayton was using *Harold's* comms to contact her. "You're the reason he's always asking about Dora!"

"Yes."

"You could have let me know you were alive!" Samara cried.

The sound of glass shattering drew her eyes to the corridor that led to the maternity wing.

"We need to go!" Carla cried.

"Come on!" Galen added, dragging her toward the examination rooms and the OR.

"What was that?" Clayton asked through a roar of weapons fire and static on his end.

"Dregs!" Samara replied, running after Galen and Carla. The sound of sharp claws skittering on the tiled floors drew their eyes to the other side of the waiting room. A pair of Dregs came skidding into view, running on four legs, their red eyes wide and feverish with hunger. They bared sharp teeth at the sight of fresh meat and came bounding toward them.

"Come on!" Galen planted his feet in the swinging doors, and took aim with the revolver, firing twice. Both bullets ricocheted off the floor, missing completely.

"Sam!" Clayton cried.

Samara's comms piece fell out as she and Carla burst through the doors beside Galen. He fired another shot, and this time it hit, drawing an agonized shriek from one of the Dregs.

"Let's go!" Galen cried.

All three of them ran down the corridor together, heading for the stairs and the elevators. Both Dregs skittered after them still shrieking and hissing behind them.

"I just called the elevators!" Carla said, angling toward a trio of gleaming silver doors rather than the stairs.

All we have to do is get inside and shut the doors, Samara thought. The Dregs wouldn't be able to follow them in.

The nearest elevator dinged open.

And then the lights went out, plunging the corridor into darkness. The elevators were no longer an option.

"The stairs! Go!" Galen cried. "I'll cover you."

The sound of gunshots rang out behind them as she and Carla hit the bottom of the stairs and began vaulting up them two at a time.

Then the gunshots stopped, and the shrieking roars of the Dregs and Galen's screams took their place. Then the sounds of their feeding was all they could hear. Samara ran after Carla with everything she had, her whole body shivering with adrenaline and shock. The stairwell was utterly dark, but Carla produced a pocket light to illuminate the way. She hit the third floor landing and grabbed the gleaming handle of a metal door to leave the stairwell, but Samara stopped her with a sharp whisper: "Dora's on level ten!"

Carla nodded and they ran on together.

CHAPTER 52

"**I** have to get out!" Clayton said, looking around desperately. "I have to help them!"

"You can't!" Pyro said, pointing at the stream of lasers still pouring through the entrance.

"I could give you my armor," Lori suggested, her voice reaching him over the comms in his ear. "You could make a run for the hole Specter cut in the side of the building and slide down the dome to the ground."

"That could work," Widow added. "The armor and shields will absorb a few shots. You should be able to make it."

Clayton glanced at his daughter. Nova nodded back and smiled. "Go. They need your help."

But he couldn't leave her here alone to die or be captured.

Just then, the lights in the ascension center flickered and died, leaving nothing but the sporadic green glow of lasers flashing back and forth in the entrance.

The resistance was keeping up a steady

stream of fire despite the impenetrable wall of fortifications the Elites were hiding behind. It was the only way to make sure none of the Elites tried sneaking in with their cloaking shields engaged, but their weapons were running dangerously low on charge. At this rate, they only had a few minutes left before they were all out and the Elites stormed in, capturing them all anyway.

"It's now or never," Lori said.

"Give the armor to Nova," Clayton decided. "She can go."

"What?" Nova asked, shaking her head.

Lori nodded and stood up, removing the helmet. The armor splayed open with a flurry of clicking metal joints, and she stepped out.

"I don't even know where the hospital is!" Nova said.

"I'll tell you how to get there," Clayton replied.

Lori waved her over to the open suit. Clayton grabbed Nova's arm and waited for a lull in the shooting before he darted across the entrance to the other side of the room. He and Lori helped her line up her limbs inside the suit, while Lori went through a quick explanation of its functions.

"It reads your thoughts through the helmet," she said. "To cloak, just think *engage cloak.* To use the shields, think *activate shields* or something similar. The suit has its own AI, so you don't need to get the words exactly right."

"It's that easy?" Nova asked.

"Yes," Lori confirmed. "Try sealing your-self up."

The suit clicked and clattered as armor plates swung back into place, sealing Nova inside.

"You can do this," Clayton said.

She nodded back with big eyes as Lori placed the helmet over her head.

"Now activate the shields," Lori said.

"How do I know if it worked?" Nova asked, her voice now coming from speakers in the chin of the helmet.

"The HUD should tell you."

"The what?" Nova asked.

Lori slapped her chest, and the armor flared brightly.

"They're on. Time to go. Are you ready? You'll have to be quick."

Nova shook her head, and Clayton pulled her into a hug. "You can do it," he said again. "The hospital is straight down the street we came in on," he added as he pulled away. "It's a fifteen-story building, all gray on the out-side with lots of windows. There's a U-shaped driveway running past a covered entrance. That's the emergency room, where the ambu-lances park. They look just like the *Ryde* we came in on."

"Did you get all that?" Lori asked.

Nova nodded.

"Watch out for Dregs," Clayton said. "They won't smell you through the armor, but they might still give you trouble."

"Here," Lori added, and handed Nova her Stinger pistol. "It's got a fresh charge, but it's the only one I've got, so make it count."

"What if I miss the hospital and go to the wrong building?" Nova asked, her voice all but drowned out by sporadic bursts of laser fire trading places in the entrance.

"Look for Dregs," Clayton suggested. "Sam said they were breaking in."

"Time to go," Lori added. "Are you ready?"

"I think so..."

Lori crouched with Nova beside the chipped and shattered entryway, waiting for another lull in the firing. That break came just a few seconds later as the Elites took a break to reload.

"Go!" Clayton said, slapping her armor.

Nova darted out, and everyone laid down covering fire for her. Clayton leaned around the entrance and sprayed the Chimeran fortification with laser fire. His rifle clicked dry as he emptied his last charge pack.

Clayton fell back into cover, touching a hand to his comms. "Nova, did you make it?"

"I'm through," she replied in a ragged whisper. "They didn't get me."

Clayton slumped against the wall, relief coursing through him. If nothing else, at least she had a chance to get out of this.

Lori caught his eye in the flickering light of dwindling laser fire and leaned in close to whisper something that only he could hear. "You made the right choice. The Kyra have re-inforcements coming. We're not going to get out of this."

Clayton stared at her in horror as she pulled away.

"I'm out!" Widow cried.

"Dry as a bone," Pyro added two seconds later.

"Anyone else still have charge?" Lori asked over the comms.

"Not me," Doc replied.

The others just shook their heads.

"This is a long drop!" Nova put in.

"Use friction to slow your fall," Clayton answered, imagining the sloping sides of the dome-shaped ascension center.

"The armor is augmented with a powered exoskeleton," Lori added. "You can take it even if you don't think you can."

"Okay..." Nova replied. "Here goes..."

Clayton held his breath through several tense seconds before asking again, "Did you make it?"

But Nova didn't reply. Clayton traded glances with Lori. She offered a tight smile while his mind raced with all the things that could have happened to her.

A rush of static hissed in his ear, followed by Nova's voice. "I'm out. They didn't see me." It sounded like she was running.

Relief coursed through him.

"I think I see the street we came in on," she added. "Where do I look for Sam inside the hospital?"

Clayton's whole body went cold. He'd been so focused on getting help to his wife and daughter that he hadn't stopped to think about just how big the hospital was. Nova could make it there and still never find Samara or Dora.

CHAPTER 53

Keera docked to the satellite with a soft jolt of contact. "Now what?" she said to Specter.

"Now you need to open the cockpit so that I can get out."

Keera reached for the emergency air hose under the pilot's seat. She pulled it out and attached it to a port in the chin of her helmet. The Lancer's sensors reported swirling clouds of friendly and enemy fighters all around them, including the larger blips of Kyron destroyers and Chronan cruisers trading broadsides in higher orbits. She hoped none of them realized what she was doing docked to this satellite.

Reaching for the lever beside her right arm, she opened the cockpit with a blast of escaping air. Specter clambered out immediately, crawling over the top of the fighter to the satellite.

Keera sat listening to the sounds of her breathing, watching the clouds over the dark side of Earth flashing with the muted blue and green flickers of lasers. Fiery orange explosions rippled above the clouds as dozens of star-fighters exploded with every passing second.

She couldn't believe it had all been for nothing.

No, not nothing, she decided. *Taking out everyone's ID implants is something—assuming this works.*

Glancing away from the battle, back to the Lancer's sensor display, Keera saw a pair of purple blips headed straight for her. Two Kyron Lancers breaking for orbit, fleeing the battle raging in Earth's atmosphere. But this fighter would look like a friendly to them, so she wasn't worried.

Except that they weren't angling away from her.

She was just about to hail them over the comms when she realized that her ID implant was disabled. As soon as she opened the comms, they'd realize that she wasn't authorized to fly this fighter. In fact, for all she knew, Treya had already woken up and reported it as stolen.

Keera cursed her stupidity for not killing Treya when she'd had the chance. "Specter, we've got incoming," she said over their private comms channel.

"Just a few more seconds..."

The warning squawk of an enemy weapons lock alert sounded inside her helmet.

"We don't have a few seconds!" she

screamed.

And then the simulated visuals of six fire-linked pairs of green lasers flashed up from the planet, slicing her fighter to pieces around her.

Keera's armor shielded her from the radiant flashes of energy, but the Lancer disintegrated, and she went drifting free of the satellite in a severed piece of the cockpit, spinning end over end. Stars and the dark side of Earth traded places over and over as she careened toward the planet below. Keera gritted her teeth against the G-forces, no longer shielded from them by the fighter's inertial dampeners. Reaching for the ejection lever, she pulled it. Something thumped through the bottom of her seat, but the locking bolts failed to release, and an error flashed up on the HUD inside her helmet: *Ejection failure.* That meant she couldn't float down with grav engines to cushion her fall.

Keera smirked at the bitter irony of surviving that attack only to burn up as she made atmospheric entry at terminal velocity.

"Specter?" she tried. "Please tell me you did it."

No answer came back over the comms.

The fighters must have gotten him, too.

She tried to pick out the remains of the satellite they'd been docked to, but the aspiring meteor she was pinned to was spinning too fast for her to see anything but a blur.

Then the back of her seat jolted as something collided with it. She craned her head around to see Specter holding on. He placed a finger to the smooth black surface where a mouth should have been.

She got the message. They shouldn't draw attention to themselves by sending messages over the comms. That was why he hadn't replied.

Keera turned back around to watch as Earth grew steadily closer and larger below them. She could only hope that Specter had had enough time to complete the mission.

Soon, the dark side of Earth was all she could see. Dark, tufted clouds, and sporadic flashes of lasers lit up the night. Here and there, an explosion bloomed. The battle was winding down. For now.

And then Keera felt something besides the bottomless plunge of weightlessness. They were slowing down dramatically.

She remembered Specter's integrated grav engines and marveled that they were strong enough to slow their fall.

Maybe I'll survive this, after all, she thought.

CHAPTER 54

Samara and Carla cowered in Dora's room, watching as the wooden door shivered and thumped with the repeated impacts of Dregs' fists and claws. Dora was sitting up in her bed, staring at the door with huge, terrified eyes.

Samara and Carla each held a scalpel in one hand as their only form of defense.

"Are you ready?" Carla asked.

Samara shook her head.

And the Carla's pocket began vibrating. She pulled out a comms unit and fitted it to her ear. "Hello?" she whispered. Carla's eyes widened, and she removed the comms unit to offer it to Samara. "It's your husband."

Samara put the device in her ear.

"Clay?"

"Where are you?" he asked.

"What?"

"Where are you! Someone's coming to help."

"Tenth floor. Room 1057. I'm with Dora. They're coming through, Clay!"

"Hang on. Help will be there soon." The call

ended in a click as Clayton hung up.

Samara slowly removed the comms unit.

"What did he say?" Carla asked.

"That help is on the way."

A louder, more insistent thud issued from the door and claws began poking through, splintering the wood.

"Not fast enough!" Carla replied.

Furiously scratching claws splintered through the door, breaking a bigger and bigger gap until they could see glowing red eyes and chalk-white skin. Samara ran to the door, and stabbed her scalpel through, slicing one of the Dregs' arms open.

It retreated with an agonized shriek, but another one quickly crowded in, taking its place. A bone-white arm shot through the door and long black claws raked across Samara's chest before she could get away.

"Sam!" Carla cried.

"Mom!" a weak voice croaked.

Samara shook her head, stumbling away, her whole body on fire from the pain. Carla stared at her in horror, her eyes wide with shock. They both knew what this meant, but at this rate, it wouldn't matter. They were going to be eaten alive long before she could turn.

* * *

Clayton told Nova where to find Samara and Pandora, but he still wasn't sure that she would even be able to find the hospital. He had to try something else.

"Scar, this is Lone Wolf, do you read?" Clayton tried for the second time in as many minutes.

Lori just shook her head. Sergeant Sutton was either dead or out of comms range. One of the two.

"Nova is on the way. She'll make it," Lori insisted.

Clayton grimaced and shook his head. Activating his comms once more, he tried again. "Scar, this is Lone Wolf, do you read?"

But rather than Sutton's voice, he heard Keera's come crackling back through a wave of static. "Lone Wolf, this is Phoenix Leader. What's your status?"

"We're overrun!" Lori replied. "Did you do it?"

"Mission accomplished," Specter said. "The enemy is routed, and the cure is being distributed. It's over."

"Not for us," Pyro put in. "We're still pinned down."

The lasers flashing through the entrance had stopped at least five minutes ago, but those Chimeran Elites were still waiting behind their fortifications. Maybe they thought the lull was some kind of trap.

"Get to the hospital," Clayton added. "Tenth floor. Room 1057. My family is there. They need help."

525

"Go there yourself," Keera added.

"Didn't you hear what Pyro said? We're pinned down."

A shrill flurry of laser fire came echoing down the corridor, but this time it didn't flash through the entrance. The sound of armor and weapons clattering followed as soldiers fell, followed by a sharp, ringing silence.

"You're clear," Specter said.

Clayton risked leaning around the ruined entrance to see what had just happened. It was pitch black inside the ascension center. They couldn't see their hands in front of their faces, let alone decide whether or not the Chimeras were still out there.

But he did manage to see *something*.

A dozen sets of glowing red eyes were visible at the far end of the corridor, down by the stairs.

The Chrona had arrived.

"We're clear," Clayton repeated, slowly rising to his feet.

One pair of eyes broke off from the rest and came bobbing toward them. Specter's voice boomed out. "It's safe to come out!" he said.

Blue beams of light flicked on one after another as the surviving members of the resistance risked turning on their tactical lights and shining them down the corridor.

Those lights bounced back to them, reflecting off the black armor of the Chrona and a heap of fallen Elites that lay between them and the stairs.

"Where is Keera?" Lori asked.

"Right here," she said over the comms, stepping out from behind the ranks of the Chrona.

"I have to go," Clayton said, looking to Lori.

"Let's go together," she said. "We can re-group at the hospital."

He nodded back and sprinted out of the tracking room on cramping legs.

Hang on, Samara, he thought. *I'm coming.*

* * *

"Here they come!" Carla cried, backing away quickly as the door exploded in a wave of splintered wood. Two Dregs squeezed into the gap at the same time, each of them fighting to be the first one through. They got stuck in the opening and began slashing at each other with their claws and teeth. Black blood gushed from ragged wounds, and then one of them ended it by slicing the other's throat open.

Samara jumped on the survivor with her scalpel, cutting its throat too. The creature subsided, its body spasming as it fell on top of the one it had killed.

More Dregs appeared behind them, shriek-ing and struggling to claw their way over the dead ones. One of them gave up and began eat-ing its own kind instead. Samara fell back to Dora's bedside with Carla.

The remains of the door shivered and shook as Dregs fought over the carcasses in the gap.

"That won't hold them for long," Carla whispered. "We should take the chance to patch you up."

"I'm fine," Samara replied.

"No, you're not. You're losing a lot of blood."

"We don't have time," she replied. "And I'm dead anyway."

"But—"

The corpses in the broken door broke free as the Dregs on the other side dragged them out. Another two took their place, walking through sideways on two legs. They advanced slowly, maybe thinking that the other pair's mistake had been their impatience.

"Get ready," Samara whispered, refusing to even blink. The Dregs crept toward them on two feet, both of them covered in the black blood of their own kind. One of them hissed as it advanced, revealing sharp, blood-stained teeth. Red blood. It had fed recently. On a patient or a doctor, or maybe a nurse like Samara and Carla.

"Mom..." Dora whimpered as the Dregs drew near.

Carla shot a panicked look over her shoulder, to the broken window behind them. "I'm sorry!" she said in a cracking voice. "I can't..."

And then she made a break for the window. One of the Dregs shrieked, running after her.

But Carla made it to the window and vaulted straight through, screaming as she fell ten floors to the street below. The Dreg that had been chasing her leaned out the window, peering down after Carla with a look of dismay on its face.

The other one hissed as it came within reach of Samara. She gripped her scalpel in a shaking fist and swiped it wildly in front of her. "Get back!" she screamed, barring the way between the Dreg and Dora.

The other one turned away from the window and began advancing on them from the other side, its bare feet crunching through broken glass without even blinking.

The one in front of Samara noticed and decided to stop hesitating. It lunged. She stuck her arm straight out, and the scalpel tore through its chest. A river of infected black blood poured out. Samara twisted, angling for the heart. The Dreg thrashed as it died, slashing her arms with its claws. She shoved it away and rounded on the other one just as it leapt on top of Dora.

She stuck the scalpel in the side of its neck, and black blood gushed all over Dora's face and mouth. She didn't even try to avoid it. The Dreg fell on top of her in a heap of twitching limbs, and Dora actually smiled.

Samara rolled it off of her with a horrified cry.

"I'm going to become a Chimera now," Dora said.

"Not if you become a Dreg!" Samara screamed.

A low hiss issued from outside the door, reminding them of darker possibilities. The ones out there busy feasting on their own kind were watching them from the darkness of the corridor, their mouths dark and dripping with blood. They slowly stood up and started toward them.

Samara took a step toward the door, and her head swam with a wave of dizziness. She'd lost too much blood. There was no way she would be able to kill these two as well.

She swayed unsteadily on her feet, struggling to keep her eyes open.

"Come on!" she screamed as much to wake herself up as to goad the approaching monsters to come faster.

A new sound roared into hearing along with the strobing green flashes of laser fire, and then a figure in matte black armor stepped into the open doorway, holding a long-barreled pistol.

"I'm too late," it said in a small, girlish voice.

Samara shook her head. "Who are you?"

The armored figure glanced over its shoulder, then back to her and removed its helmet. A pretty young girl with blonde hair appeared standing there.

"You must be Samara."

She just nodded.

"I'm Nova. Clayton's daughter."

And with that, Samara passed out.

CHAPTER 55

Clayton ran down the street outside the ascension center with the surviving members of the resistance and an entire squad of Chrona leading the way. They used the tac lights of their rifles to illuminate the darkened streets. Bright blue lasers snapped out from the machines, cutting down Chimeran stragglers and Dregs alike. The night air was cool as it ran through Clayton's sweaty hair and beard. His whole body ached—feet, legs, back, and shoulders, all protesting against yet another mad dash through the middle of the night. But all the while, his heart pounded out a furious cadence in his chest, pure adrenaline driving him on. He couldn't reach Carla on the comms anymore. It just rang and rang with no reply. Either they were trying to be quiet to avoid attracting Dregs to her location, or...

He tried not to think about what else might have happened. Instead, he called ahead over the squad's comms. "Nova, did you make it?" he asked.

This time not even she replied. Clayton ran

all the faster, pulling ahead to the front of the group. He glanced up as the distant, muted roar of an explosion echoed somewhere above. The sounds of battle were growing sporadic now. It was over, just as Specter had said.

But only for now. The Kyra still had reinforcements coming, and according to Specter, they were at most nine hours away. The resistance needed to flee the city and get back into the Wastes before then.

This time Clayton would be taking Sam and Dora with him.

Acrid smoke darkened the air as they drew near to the north end of the city. The hospital building came swirling through the haze...

Dregs were everywhere, but the Chrona cut them down in a matter of seconds. They reached the entrance of the ER, to find the doors shattered and a makeshift blockade of chairs on the other side. Finally, Nova's voice crackled into Clayton's ear.

"I found them," she said, her voice thick with tears. "I didn't make it in time. You need to hurry! She won't... she won't wake up..." Nova broke off sobbing.

Clayton burst through the entrance of the ER ahead of the Chrona.

"Clayton, wait!" Lori called after him.

He drew the hunting knife on his utility belt and used his rifle to light the way to the stairs. He found a half-eaten human corpse at the bottom, with a Dreg hunching over it, still feeding. It looked up at the sound of his approach with a blood-smeared mouth and hissed, baring bright crimson teeth. Clayton jumped over a swipe of its claws and slashed his knife through the back of the Dreg's neck, severing its spinal cord.

Entrails were coiled all over the floor like purple snakes. Jumping over them, too, Clayton reached the stairs and took them two at a time, pulling himself up with the help of the banister.

By the time he reached the tenth floor, his head felt light, dizzy with exhaustion, but he pushed through and down the hall. He scanned the darkened numbers on the doors as he went, running past the 1020s, 1030s... and finally reaching 1057. The door was splintered open. The bloody corpses of four Dregs lay heaped in the corridor. He stepped over them and into the room—

And found both of his daughters on the floor with Samara in their laps. Dora was covered in black, infected blood, her face a nightmare to behold. Nova looked fine, her armor intact, her helmet off, but her suit was slick with red blood from where she cradled his wife in her arms.

Samara's clothes were drenched with blood, and her eyes were shut.

Clayton fell on his knees beside them and

began checking Samara's injuries.

"I'm so sorry," Nova sobbed, catching his eye with a tear-streaked face. "I tried…"

Dora watched them both with big, staring eyes, mute with shock.

Samara's chest was torn open in four deep parallel gashes. A Dreg's claws.

Clayton fell back on his haunches, blinking sweat from his eyes, despair clutching his heart. He cast about helplessly, looking for something to staunch the flow of blood from Samara's wounds.

A stampede of footfalls arrived, metallic Chronan feet and rubberized boots alike. Members of the resistance crowded in. First Keera, then Lori. Doc came in behind them with Widow, Pyro, and Harold. No one else would fit.

"Is she…" Lori trailed off as she drew near.

Doc pulled out his medkit and got to work right away. "She's alive," he said, checking Samara's pulse the old fashioned way with a pair of fingers over her carotid artery.

"She's infected," Clayton replied in a numb voice, his eyes drifting out of focus as Doc worked. "They're both infected," he added with a glance at Dora. "They need the cure."

Doc nodded and reached for the silver cylinders.

"Belay that. They don't need the cure," Keera replied.

"Those are claw marks!" Clayton cried, pointing to them as Doc sprayed the wounds with Regenex and synthskin.

"She's a clone," Keera added. "Clones all have a natural germline immunity to the virus."

"They *what?* When were you planning to tell me *that?*"

"Even your daughter is immune," Keera added, nodding to her.

At that, Dora finally snapped out of it. "I'm immune?"

"Yes," Keera confirmed.

"No..." She sounded crestfallen.

Clayton wondered what he was missing. Harold's wife had always said that Dora was a good little rebel with no interest in becoming a Chimera.

"I've done the best that I can," Doc interrupted. "But we need to replace the blood she lost before she goes into hemorrhagic shock."

"There should be plenty of blood around here," Lori said, looking back to the broken entrance. "This is a hospital."

"I'll go find the blood bank," Widow offered.

"I'll go with you," Pyro added. "What type is she?"

"A-positive," Clayton said.

"Help me get her up onto the bed," Doc added.

Clayton lifted her up with Doc's help. Harold helped, and they eased her down onto the bed. It was covered in the black blood of a Dreg. Two of them lay dead on either side. A half-empty bag of saline already hung on a pole beside the bed.

"Serendipity at work," Doc said, noticing the bag. "This will hold her for now." He cleaned the IV needle off with gauze and sterigel from his kit and bent over Samara to insert the needle.

"Is she going to be okay?" Dora asked with big, glassy eyes.

Clayton glanced at her.

"Yeah," Nova answered for him, walking over and wrapping an arm around her sister's shoulders. "Don't worry. She'll be just fine."

Doc glanced up from taping the needle to Samara's wrist, but said nothing. Clayton would have felt better if he'd been the one saying that Samara would be fine.

Keera waved Clayton over to where she stood in the entrance with Specter and Lori.

"We need to leave the city before the 42nd Fleet arrives," Keera whispered.

Clayton looked back to Samara. "She can't be moved right now."

"I know," Keera replied. "That's why I'm mentioning it. We can't afford to stay here past dawn. If she hasn't recovered by then..." she trailed off, shaking her head.

"What's the Chrona's position?" Lori asked. "Will your people stay to defend us? Have you sent for reinforcements of your own?"

Specter regarded them with unblinking red eyes. "No. We will retreat within a few standard hours."

"Can't you take us with you when you leave?" Lori asked.

"Our vessels are not pressurized," Specter replied. "You would not survive."

Keera hissed softly between her teeth. "At least that much of what the Kyra say about your people is true. You don't take prisoners because you don't have anywhere to put them."

Specter inclined his head to that, but said nothing.

"So we're on our own," Clayton concluded. "That's great. Nice to know."

"They set us free, and they're busy inoculating the entire planet," Keera said. "They have done a lot. We can do the rest."

"The Kyra could still sterilize us all out of spite once they realize we're immune," Clayton pointed out.

"They could," Specter admitted. "Your people need to flee the cities before they return."

"Can you send a message to warn people?" Lori asked.

"I can try," Specter replied.

"Please," Keera said. "They need a fighting chance."

"Let them know about the cure while you're at it," Lori added. "Everyone should start drinking the water."

Specter nodded and left the room.

The reminder of water made Clayton's throat ache. His tongue felt like sandpaper against the roof of his mouth. He reached for the canteen on his belt, unscrewed the cap and took a deep gulp. Everyone else did the same.

Pyro and Widow came running back in carrying five bags of blood between them, both of them breathing hard. "We didn't know how much we'd need."

"That's perfect," Doc said, grabbing one of the bags. He got to work replacing the saline with blood, reusing the same IV line.

When he was done, he stepped back and nodded at his handiwork.

"How long does she need?" Keera asked.

"Maybe a couple of hours. Maybe five. We won't know until she wakes up."

"Great," Keera muttered. "All right, everyone find a room and lock yourselves in for the night. We're holing up here for the next few hours."

"Who's keeping watch?" Harold asked. "There's still Dregs out there. They could slip in while we're asleep."

"And we're flat out of charge on all of our

weapons," Pyro added.

"The Chrona have already secured the stairs," Keera replied. "We'll consolidate any remaining survivors on this level and assign watches of our own just to be sure."

"And then?" Widow asked, her brow furrowing as she shook her head.

"Then we secure transport back to Phoenix base."

A shuffling of feet sounded in the entrance of the room, drawing their eyes to new arrivals.

Familiar ones.

"Looks like I'm late to the party," Sergeant Sutton said as he and Preacher crowded in.

"It's good to see you alive," Keera said.

Clayton smiled tightly at him.

No one else said anything.

"Well, hell, can't a man come back from the dead to a little fanfare?"

Keera explained about the Kyra's reinforcing fleet, and Doc walked over to finally check and treat the laser burn in Lori's arm. She protested at his prodding, but gave into it after he injected a painkiller.

"Well, shit..." Sutton muttered once Keera finished explaining the situation.

On that note, everyone dispersed from the room to look for more survivors. That left Clayton alone with his family. Harold and Pyro stayed with them, with Harold saying he

needed a chance to catch his breath and recover.

They all crowded around Samara's bed,
watching the slow rise and fall of her bloody
chest. Dora went to sit in an armchair by the
broken window. She pulled her knees up to her
chest, her eyes wide and staring with shock.
Clayton found a blanket and dragged it over
Samara for modesty's sake. Harold looked on
with a wan smile, his eyes wet with tears. He
wiped one away as it fell. "She'll pull through,"
he said.

"How's Mona?" Clayton asked, remembering that Harold had a family of his own to
worry about. "And Haley," he added.

Harold slowly shook his head, and Clayton's guts clenched up in anticipation of the
worst.

"I lost contact with them just before I gave
you my comms. They were at the farm when
the *Sovath* was coming down. I told them to
head for the sewer entrance, but..." Fresh tears
trickled down, and Harold shook his head
again.

The odds of them getting far enough away
to avoid that crashing destroyer were slim at
best. Even if they'd made it to the sewers, the
explosion had almost certainly buried them
alive.

Pyro pulled her father into a hug, and he
sobbed quietly against her shoulder.

Clayton looked away, back to Samara, then to Nova. She'd walked over to Dora, trying to coax her out of the chair so she could get cleaned up, but the younger girl wasn't listening.

Clayton went to join them. "Do you know who I am?" he asked, his boots crunching as he stood on glittering wedges of glass from the window. A cool breeze gusted in, carrying with it an acrid haze of smoke. The *Sovath* was still burning.

Dora looked up at him, blinking once.

"I'm Clayton. Your father."

She blinked again.

He rested a hand on Dora's shoulder.

Nova shook her head. "She's in shock."

Clayton crouched to get to eye level with her. She was still covered in black blood. "Get me something to clean her up," Clayton said. Nova nodded and hurried off.

"Pandora?" he prompted. "Can you hear me?"

"It's my fault," she whispered, almost too soft to hear.

"What?"

"It's my fault. Mom was just trying to protect me."

Nova returned with a wet towel from an adjoining bathroom. Clayton used it to wipe his youngest daughter's face, cleaning away the blood. A set of vaguely familiar features appeared.

She looked like him. Green eyes the same shade as his own shone in the faint blue glow of the tac light on his rifle.

Dora began to cry as he finished cleaning her face. Then her shoulders shook with heavy sobs, and he pulled her into a hug. Nova joined in, and the three of them held each other, a united front against the horrors that they'd witnessed and all of those yet to come.

CHAPTER 56

Clayton awoke to a roaring sound and people shouting. He jumped to his feet, eyes darting in the darkness, searching for Dregs or Chimeran soldiers. But there was nothing.

"What's going on?" Nova moaned sleepily.

"I don't know. Stay here. Watch your sister."

Clayton snatched up his rifle, flicked on the tac light, and drew the hunting knife from his belt. He followed the sound of panicky voices to the room next door. There, he found Lori, Keera, Harold, Pyro, Doc, and half a dozen others all crowding around a broken window.

"What is it?" Clayton asked, shouldering in to look. The glowing blue engines of dozens of starships were streaking up from New Houston, clawing for space.

"The Chrona betrayed us," Lori whispered. "It was all a lie."

"What?" Clayton shook his head quickly, confused. "But Specter said they were going to leave." This wasn't a betrayal, it was just them getting the hell out before the Kyra could return to drop a hammer on their heads.

"That's not what she means," Keera said quietly. "Follow me."

Clayton turned and followed her across the hall and down past at least a dozen doors. They walked by the entrance of the stairwell. A chair was propped under that door, and Sutton and Widow stood guarding it with knives.

Keera led him to a room at the end of the hall with another chair propped under the door handle. A prickle of dread shivered down Clayton's spine, and he gripped his knife more tightly. Keera removed the chair and opened the door. A rotten smell gusted out, rocking Clayton back on his heels.

The room was a full-sized suite with a bed, a couch, and a living room. It was crowded with at least twenty survivors from the hospital, all of them slumping on the furniture and the floor. Some were obviously patients by the gowns they wore; others were members of staff—nurses and doctors. Clayton passed his tac light over them, his unease mounting steadily.

These survivors had bloody clothes torn away in places to reveal bandages where their injuries had been patched up. They were sweating and moaning, their faces pale and waxy. Veins stood out darkly beneath almost translucent skin. One of them threw up into a bucket. Another into a bedpan. And then his light passed over the ghost-white face of a female Chimera. She looked up with dark trickles of blood leaking from the corners of her eyes. A rank insignia with eight different red and blue bars gleamed over the right breast of her black uniform, marking her as having a particularly high rank.

"You saved one of *them?*" Clayton asked.

"The Chrona found her and brought her here before they left," Keera said. "I asked Specter to track her down for me."

"Keera," the woman croaked, reaching up with a bloody hand. "You can't leave me in here..." she said, trailing off weakly. Her chin sagged to her chest, and then her whole body spasmed, and she vomited up dark blood into her lap. She looked up again, but this time her eyes were wild and feral. She shrieked and hissed at them like a Dreg, and began dragging herself across the floor to reach them. She wasn't moving fast, but she was determined.

"You know her?" Clayton asked, his nose wrinkling up with disgust.

"I do," Keera confirmed. "That's Admiral Treya. She used to be my second."

"What's wrong with her? It looks like she's turning into a Dreg."

Treya shrieked weakly and gave up trying to reach them, collapsing at the feet of a doctor with a bandaged arm. He cursed under his breath and reached for the Chimera with a scalpel. Keera didn't try to stop him. He stabbed it through the side of the Chimera's head and then collapsed from the effort that took and lay gasping on the floor beside her.

"What the hell happened to these people?" Clayton asked, glancing around and taking in pale, waxy faces.

"We only had five shots of the cure with us," Keera explained. "It wasn't enough for everyone that the Dregs had infected, so we told them to drink the water instead."

Clayton's stomach dropped. He spun around in the entrance, back to where he'd left Nova and Dora. "I have to warn—"

Keera stopped him with a hand on his arm. "We've already shut the water off."

Clayton looked back to her. "So, the cure that the Chrona released was actually the virus?"

"A new version of it," Keera confirmed. "It even infected Treya, and Chimeras are supposed to be immune. I've never seen people develop symptoms this fast. We could be looking at something much more virulent." Keera pulled him out of the room and shut the door, propping the chair under it for safety, even though nobody in there looked like they had the strength to leave.

"They knew that the Kyra would take the planet back..." Clayton said slowly, realization dawning. "Scorched Earth."

Keera nodded. "There won't be any point to the Kyra re-occupying the planet if everyone's already dead or turned into a Dreg by the time they get here."

"But that doesn't make any sense," Clayton said. "You cured Harold."

"We tested the cure multiple times and inoculated all of ourselves. It does work. But we only tested the first batch. Whatever the Chrona mass-produced and then spread through the water supply must have been something else."

"Then they never planned to cure us," Clayton realized.

Keera shook her head. "It doesn't look like it, no."

"Then what was the point of all this?" Clayton asked. "If they just wanted was to deprive the Kyra of a supply of soldiers, they could have let the Kyra execute everyone through their ID implants, or used the tracking network to do it themselves."

"They could have," Keera confirmed.

"So why didn't they?"

"This virus infected a Chimera," Keera said quietly. "If you're asking me to guess, the Chrona just tested a bio-weapon on us. One that will wipe out Kyra, Chimeras, and humans..." she trailed off, shaking her head. "Maybe all forms of biological life in the galaxy."

"We never should have trusted them," Clayton growled.

"Hindsight's twenty-twenty," Sergeant Sutton said, striding over to them from the stairwell.

Clayton turned to see him approaching with Nova.

"Sam's awake!" Nova called out to him.

"We need to bug out while we can," Sutton added. "Before all of those people in there turn into Dregs and start attacking us."

"He's right," Keera added.

Clayton ran toward Nova, and she turned and followed him back to their room. They burst through the broken door one after another to find Samara sitting up and cradling Dora like a baby in her lap.

"You're awake," Clayton breathed as he arrived by her side, his face searching hers for signs of distress. Harold and Pyro looked on from the other side of the bed.

Samara looked tired, but there was a familiar fire in her blue eyes as they found his. And then they widened with astonishment.

"I don't believe it," she whispered.

He pulled her and Dora both into a hug, and then withdrew, kissing Samara on the lips.

Samara started crying, her tears running between them in salty rivers.

"This can't be real," she mumbled between gasps for air.

"It's real," he mumbled back, and then he kissed her again.

"Ewww..." Nova muttered as they pulled apart. But she was smiling.

Sergeant Sutton and Keera arrived and crowded into the room with the remainder of their squad. "Is everyone ready to go?" Keera asked.

Clayton turned from his wife and two daughters to take in the greasy black faces of his comrades in arms. There were fewer of them than before, but somehow, miraculously, most of them had survived: Widow, Doc, Keera, Lori, Sutton, Preacher, Harold, Pyro, Nova, and Clayton himself. They'd been eighteen when they'd left Phoenix Base; they'd lost eight in the fighting and gained three more with Harold, Samara, and Pandora.

"None of you drank the water?" Clayton asked.

"No," Doc replied, answering for all of them.

"Keera ordered us to hold off on that," Widow explained. "Just in case."

"You suspected that Specter would betray us?" Clayton asked, his eyes narrowing on Keera.

"I only knew the stories that the Kyra tell about them, about how violent and brutal they are. How little regard they have for organic life."

"And yet you struck an alliance with them anyway," Clayton accused.

"The Kyra lie about everything," Samara whispered, grabbing Clayton's arm to still his rising anger. "She couldn't have known they were telling the truth for once."

"We didn't have a choice," Keera added. "Getting their help was the only way we were ever going to set Earth free. We had to risk it."

"And look where that got us!" Clayton replied. "Everyone we were trying to save is infected! They might as well be dead. You killed us all."

"Said the man who led the Kyra back to Earth in the first place," Keera replied. She tilted her head suddenly to one side. "I wonder who has more blood on their hands."

"This isn't the time for accusations," Lori said, stepping between them.

Clayton's anger left him in a rush. They were right. "Did you try the cure on any of the people in that room?" he asked.

"We used all five canisters," Doc said. "It didn't work. This is a new strain. Something the Chrona cooked up themselves. The cure they helped us to develop only works on the original virus, which means none of us are immune," Doc said.

"Probably not even the clones," Keera pointed out.

Clayton turned around to look at Samara

and Dora. His wife's lips quirked up in a shaky smile. "We'll be okay," she said.

"You don't know that," he replied. "The city's overrun with Dregs, and we have to leave. We don't even have any weapons to fight our way out."

"None of that matters," she replied. "The only thing that matters is that we're alive and we're together." Her gaze drifted to Nova, and she smiled. "All of us."

Samara's hand slipped into Clayton's, her fingers lacing through his. Dora's eyes flicked up to his, sharp and curious.

"Are you really my dad?"

He nodded.

"We need to go," Keera prompted.

"You heard the Admiral! Double time! Let's move!" Sutton added, clapping his hands for attention.

Dora climbed out of her mother's lap, and Clayton and Harold helped Samara get off the bed. "I can do it," she said, swinging her feet over the side and stepping down gingerly. "I'm okay."

"Are you sure?" Clayton asked.

She nodded.

"What about the survivors in the other room?" Clayton asked as they all filed out into the hall.

"The *infected* survivors?" Keera countered.

"We don't know that none of them are

going to survive."

"And we can't afford to stick around to find out. We left them with a few knives. The doctors have their scalpels. They know what to do."

"At least remove the chair from the door so they can get out," Clayton suggested.

Keera looked at him, her red eyes hard in the gloomy darkness of the hallway. "Sergeant?" she prompted.

"Copy that," he said, and tore down the hall ahead of everyone else.

The group carried on, their knives out, and tac lights sweeping. They met up with Sutton at the entrance of the stairwell. He held the door for them as they walked through single-file.

Clayton kept his family close, making sure not to let any of them out of his sight for even a second. The resistance's victory might have turned to a defeat thanks to the Chrona's betrayal, but Samara was right: at least they were alive and they were together.

Now we just have to stay that way, he thought.

"I wonder if Rosie's started to miss us yet," Nova asked.

"Who?" Samara replied.

"Our dog."

"You have a dog?" Dora put in, her voice full of wonder.

"Oh yeah," Nova said. "She's the best."

"I've never even *seen* a dog," Dora said, finally coming out of her shell. "Do you think she'll like me? Does she bite?"

"She'll love you, sis," Nova replied. "She only bites Dregs."

Clayton just smiled at their exchange. Maybe the end of the world wouldn't be so bad after all.

GET THE SEQUEL FOR FREE

The story continues with...

Fractured Earth (Ascension Wars Book 3)

(Coming June 2020)

OR

Get a FREE digital copy if you post an honest review of this book (https:// geni.us/occupiedearthreview) on Amazon and send it to me here. (http:// files.jaspertscott.com/freefractured.htm)

Thank you in advance for your feedback! I read every review and use your comments to improve my work.

KEEP IN TOUCH

SUBSCRIBE to my Mailing List
and get two FREE Books!

http://files.jaspertscott.com/
mailinglist.html

Follow me on Bookbub:

https://www.bookbub.com/
authors/jasper-t-scott

Follow me on Amazon:

https://www.amazon.com/
Jasper-T-Scott/e/B00B7A2CT4

Look me up on Facebook:

Jasper T. Scott

Check out my Website:

www.JasperTscott.com

Follow me on Twitter:

@JasperTscott

Or send me an e-mail:

JasperTscott@gmail.com

OTHER BOOKS BY JASPER SCOTT

Suggested reading order

<u>Ascension Wars</u>

First Encounter (Book 1)
Occupied Earth (Book 2)
Fractured Earth (Book 3)
(Coming June 2020)

<u>Scott Standalones</u>
No sequels, no cliffhangers

Under Darkness
Into the Unknown
In Time for Revenge

<u>Rogue Star</u>

Rogue Star: Frozen Earth
Rogue Star (Book 2): New Worlds

<u>Broken Worlds</u>

Broken Worlds: The Awakening (Book 1)
Broken Worlds: The Revenants (Book 2)
Broken Worlds: Civil War (Book 3)

New Frontiers Series (Loosely-tied, Stand-alone Prequels to Dark Space)

Excelsior (Book 1)
Mindscape (Book 2)
Exodus (Book 3)

Dark Space Series

Dark Space
Dark Space 2: The Invisible War
Dark Space 3: Origin
Dark Space 4: Revenge
Dark Space 5: Avilon
Dark Space 6: Armageddon

Dark Space Universe Series (Standalone Follow-up Trilogy to Dark Space)

Dark Space Universe (Book 1)
Dark Space Universe: The Enemy Within (Book 2)
Dark Space Universe: The Last Stand (Book 3)

ABOUT THE AUTHOR

Jasper Scott is a USA Today bestselling author of more than 20 sci-fi novels. With over a million books sold, Jasper's work has been translated into various languages and published around the world. Join the author's mailing list to get two FREE books: https://files.jaspertscott.com/mailinglist.html

Jasper writes fast-paced books with unexpected twists and flawed characters. He was born and raised in Canada by South African parents, with a British heritage on his mother's side and German on his father's. He now lives in an exotic locale with his wife, their two kids, and two Chihuahuas.

Made in the USA
San Bernardino, CA
20 May 2020

72063437R00344